Praise for *USA TODAY* bestselling author Jennifer Snow's Wild River series

"Heartwarming, romantic, and utterly enjoyable."
—*New York Times* bestselling author Melissa Foster
on *An Alaskan Christmas*

"This first title in the Wild River series is passionate, sensual, and very sexy. The freezing, winter-cold portrayal of the Alaskan ski slopes is not the only thing sending chills through one's body."
—*New York Journal of Books*

"Set in the wilds of Alaska, the beauty of winter and the cold shine through."
—*Fresh Fiction* on *An Alaskan Christmas*

"Jennifer Snow's Alaska setting and search-and-rescue element are interesting twists, and the romance is smart and sexy... An exciting contemporary series debut with a wildly unique Alaskan setting."
—*Kirkus Reviews*

"Prepare to have your heartstrings tugged! Pure Christmas delight."
—*New York Times* bestselling author Lori Wilde
on *An Alaskan Christmas*

"*Alaska Reunion* has a little bit of everything—drama, humor, friendship, and love. It's a well-written story that will draw readers in."
—*Harlequin Junkie*

JENNIFER SNOW

Sweet Home Alaska

ISBN-13: 978-1-335-44861-3

Sweet Home Alaska
Copyright © 2022 by Jennifer Snow

Love on the Coast
Copyright © 2022 by Jennifer Snow

Recycling programs for this product may not exist in your area.

For questions and comments about the quality of this book, please contact us at CustomerService@Harlequin.com.

HQN
22 Adelaide St. West, 41st Floor
Toronto, Ontario M5H 4E3, Canada
www.Harlequin.com

Printed and bound in Barcelona, Spain by CPI Black Print

CONTENTS

To Wendy—
your everyday strength and courage continue to inspire!

Sweet Home
Alaska

PROLOGUE

SKYLAR TOOK ONE last desperate gulp of air before she hit the tumultuous waves of the North Pacific Ocean. Pain radiated through her from the ten-foot fall from the boat, but within seconds she felt numb in the frigid water. Sinking lower and lower beneath the dark surface, bubbles rose all around her as gasps of panic and shock allowed precious air to escape. Ice pans bobbing above her prevented a clear path to the surface. They got farther away the deeper she plunged.

Just how far would the tow take her under?

Water churned around her as the unforgiving waves tossed her about. Her lungs ached from holding her remaining breath and her limbs struggled to tread through the current. Eyes wide, she scanned the water around her... seeing nothing except a narrow path illuminated by the light on her helmet.

A dark shadow crossed the murky beam and her heart raced as her free fall slowed then stopped, and she began the unmerciful trek back to the surface. Moving her arms and legs as quickly as she could with the freezing water paralyzing her, she looked above as she struggled to make her way up.

Survival...that was all that mattered. She had to stay calm and focused.

Something brushed against her, forceful and strong, but instead of hindering her ascent, it accelerated it. She looked around, but saw nothing at first. Then another shadow…and another force as though she were being propelled upward.

Sealena.

Instead of fear, an eerie sense of calm enveloped her as she moved faster, following her light to the surface. She could see the boat now, and with a few more desperate strokes through the waves, her head crested the top of the water. She inhaled deeply and battled to stay above the merciless waves threatening to take her under again. Her limbs ached as hypothermia threatened to set in. Wind and blowing snow made it difficult to see as she frantically scanned the water around her for any sign of help. But with the poor visibility, no one could see her.

Skylar was left bobbing alone in the frigid North Pacific Ocean.

CHAPTER ONE

Three Days Earlier...

THEY SAY YOU can't go home again. If only that were true.

As Skylar Beaumont drove past the town limit sign with its featured serpent queen, Sealena, welcoming visitors to Port Serenity, the weight of expectation immediately settled on her shoulders.

Could she really do this?

Her heart had been pounding since she'd deboarded the plane in Alaska, her insecurities barely contained during the two-hundred-mile drive to her hometown.

Her reflection in her coast guard uniform in the rearview was one she'd never doubted she'd achieve. A third generation coastie, Skylar had been around the sea her entire life, fascinated by its mysteries, astonished by its paradoxical sense of danger and calm. She'd always known she'd follow in her father's and grandfather's footsteps. She just hadn't exactly wanted to follow those legendary footsteps back to the jagged shores along her hometown.

Being stationed here meant that everyone would naturally assume she'd gotten this far this fast because of her family name...that her father or grandfather had had some influence over her unusually speedy career advancement. Nothing could be further from the truth. She'd busted her ass at the academy for four years, working harder than everyone else, putting in extra time and excelling in her courses. Then she'd worked alongside the experienced crew of the *North Star* cutter on the East Coast for two years, gaining her on-sea requirements to write the captain's exam. And she'd aced it.

But maybe her last name had helped a little in securing the competitive spot at the academy in the first place...

Nope. She squared her shoulders and gripped the steering wheel tighter as she fought against the self-doubt. She'd been accepted into the highly competitive program based on her transcripts, her letters of recommendation (not from anyone with her last name) and her own application letter. She'd earned her spot.

Still, expectations were high and she had a lot to prove.

She was there now and until she could request a transfer or apply for a new position, she'd have to make the best of it.

Pulling off the highway, she drove along Main Street, which cut through the center of town. It was just after nine, and the shops were flipping their Closed signs to Open. Tourist season hadn't officially launched yet, but in the coming weeks, as the late spring weather turned milder, the town's population would explode, nearly tripling with visitors. By summer, all the local inns would be full and the outdoor restaurant patios would be a constant flutter of laughter and loud music. The marina and beach would be hotspots for families, fishermen and water sport enthusiasts.

Skylar scanned the familiar surroundings as she drove. She'd lived in Port Serenity her entire life. She'd loved it there as a child, especially during tourist season. She craved the bustle and all the strange, exciting faces of visitors flocking there for the chance to see Sealena for themselves.

A glimpse of the serpent sea witch was a rare occurrence indeed, but not an impossibility according to the old fishermen who were happy to recount their tall tales to anyone willing to listen, encouraging tourists to pay an outrageous price to get out on the water for the search themselves. It had been fun to see the renewed excitement on people's faces as tourists arrived in Port Serenity for the first time.

Unfortunately, that excitement seemed to dull over the years as Skylar had learned what this popularity had cost the town. As she'd realized that Port Serenity really only belonged to one family: the Wakefields. Their name adorned almost every awning on the main street. Wakefields' Pharmacy, Wakefields' Convenience and Grocery, Wakefields' Outpost and Fishing Supply... The wealthy Wakefields had reinvented the town and in doing so, they basically owned it. It was no secret that the mayor consulted the family patriarch, Brian Wakefield, on every major decision.

And no one opposed. Everyone appreciated the security the Wakefields' businesses had provided when the fishing industry had struggled to support families. The influx of tourists meant every local had a way to make a living. Like her cousin Carly, who ran the bookstore and local museum. Restaurants, inns, cafes and gift shops capitalized on the sea witch's popularity and likeness, making enough during tourist season to keep afloat all year. It was hard to fault the Wakefields.

Unless of course you were a Beaumont.

Skylar's own family had been generations of civil servants, protecting the community they loved. Her great-great-grandfather, Castor Beaumont, had been a state trooper. It was rumored that he'd been responsible for arresting Earl Wakefield, his former childhood friend, on smuggling charges. The man had done time for bringing contraband into Alaska through Port Serenity; the town had been divided and the family feud between the Wakefields and Beaumonts had begun.

Small towns held long grudges.

As she turned the corner at the end of Main Street and the ocean came into view, her chest tightened. It felt as though things had frozen in time the day she left. The scene unfolding was eerily familiar. A father and his daughter stood on the water's edge skipping rocks along the surface. An older woman sat on a graffiti-tagged concrete bench wearing a pensive expression as she stared at the waves and the sun rising over the horizon. A young couple strolled along the wooden pier, hand in hand, a young puppy excitedly walking ahead with a stick in its mouth. Farther down, a seniors' group did sunrise yoga on the sandy area of the small beach and several fishermen enjoyed a morning beer on the docks with their fishing poles doing the work along the shore.

On the other side of Marina Way, there were boarded-up beach huts that would open in the hotter summer months, selling ice cream, refreshments, swim gear and overpriced Sealena-themed souvenirs. Among them was a small hut that advertised adventure whale watching tours, bird island excursions and trips to the ice fields in winter.

In the distance, there was a small research cabin that housed the Marine Life Sanctuary and beyond that, a lighthouse stood high on the hill above. Sailboats and power boats lined the coastline below.

Everything looked exactly the same as the day she'd left.

Though her pulse raced as she approached the marina and the nondescript coast guard station, her heart swelled with pride at the sight of the *Starlight* docked there. With its deep V, double chine hull and all-aluminum construction, the forty-five-foot response boat was designed for speed and stability in various weather conditions. Twin diesel engines with waterjet propulsion eliminated the need for propellers under the boat, making it safer in missions where they needed to rescue a person overboard. Combined with its self-righting capability to help with capsizing in rough seas, it had greater speed and maneuverability than the older vessels. The boat was the one thing she had total confidence in. And she would be in charge of it and a crew of five.

The crew was the tougher part. She was determined to gain their trust and respect. She was eager to show that she was one of them but also maintain a professional distance. Her father and grandfather made it look so easy, but she knew this would be her hardest challenge, to command a crew of familiar faces. People she'd grown up with, people who remembered her as the little girl who'd wear her father's too-big captain hat as she sat in the captain's chair in the pilothouse.

Did that hat finally fit now?

Weaving the rental car along the winding road, and seeing the familiar Wakefield family yacht docked in the marina, her heart pounded. The fifty-footer had always been the most impressive boat in the marina, even now that it was over thirty years old. Its owner, Kurt Wakefield, had lived on the yacht for twenty-five years.

Kurt had died the year before. Skylar peered through the windshield to look at it. Had someone else bought the boat? Large bumpers had been added to the exterior, and pull lines could be seen on deck. She frowned. Had it been turned into some sort of rescue boat?

It wasn't unusual for civilians to aid in searches along the coast when requested, but the yacht was definitely an odd addition. There had never been a Wakefield who had shown interest in civil service to the community...except one.

The man standing on the upper deck now, pulling the lines. Wearing a pair of faded jeans and just a T-shirt, the muscles in his shoulders and back strained as he worked and Skylar's mouth went dry. She slowed the vehicle, unable to look away. Almost as if in slow motion, the man turned and their eyes met. Her breath caught as familiarity registered in his expression.

And unfortunately, the untimely unexpected sight of her ex-boyfriend—Dex Wakefield—had Skylar forgetting to hit the brakes as she reached the edge of the gravel lot next to the dock. Too late, her rental car drove straight off the edge and into the frigid North Pacific Ocean.

HOLY SHIT.

Dex Wakefield dropped the lines he was securing and hopped over the side of his boat onto the pier, risking a sprained ankle at the ten-foot drop. He hurried at a breakneck pace toward where the small Fiat bobbed among several small ice pans, the hood sinking below the water.

Skylar Beaumont had made quite the unexpected entrance.

Ignoring the chill in the late April air, Dex kicked off his shoes and jumped into the water.

Goose bumps covered his exposed flesh and his breath came in small pants as he tried to adapt to the shock. Ice bobbed next to him as he took a deep breath and dove below the surface in time to see Skylar open the driver's side door and escape from the sinking vehicle.

Swimming toward her, he reached for her and wrapped an arm around her waist as they moved toward the dock. "What are you doing?" she asked.

"Saving your life."

She removed his arm from around her waist before gripping the wooden planks of the pier overhead. Her breath came in quick gasps and her teeth chattered. "I'm fine. I don't need your help."

His ex hadn't changed, not one little bit. Still as independent and stubborn as ever.

He moved back an inch and treaded water as she climbed out onto the wooden dock. Her coast guard uniform dripped with water, and her tight blond bun was slicked to her head.

The sight might stir a reaction from him, if his limbs weren't about to freeze off. He was actually grateful for the chilled water. It numbed the myriad of emotions he knew he'd be struggling with soon enough.

Skylar was back. She was standing right there. On the dock. In Port Serenity.

He'd think he was dreaming if the cold ocean didn't reassure him he was definitely awake. And about to get hypothermia.

He climbed onto the dock next to her as the car continued to sink and cleared his throat. "What happened?" From his vantage point on the yacht's deck, she'd been staring at *him* and not paying attention to how close she was to the edge.

She shook her head as she wiped water from her cheeks and forehead. "Miscalculated the edge of the dock, that's all." She avoided his gaze, which confirmed his suspicion that she'd been momentarily distracted by him. "Why did you jump in?"

"To help you."

Her scoff wasn't exactly the "thanks" he'd been expecting.

"You're welcome," he mumbled anyway, running a hand through his soaking dark hair. The tips felt like they might snap off like icicles.

"The water level here is like seven feet deep. Now we're both soaking wet and feeling awkward." She glanced around, her cheeks blushing a deeper shade of red as people noticed them.

Several fishermen approached. One pointed to the car and shouted, "I'll call the fire department!"

Skylar gave a weak smile and quick wave. "Appreciate it!" Wasn't the first time a car needed rescuing. She sighed as the back end of the car disappeared below the surface.

Say something. Don't just stand here like a moron.

Unfortunately, he had no idea what to say. Casual chit-chat seemed inappropriate, but a confession of never-ending love seemed a little over-the-top for the first conversation since their breakup.

"So...you're home." Most obvious statement ever, but he wasn't sure. Maybe she was just visiting her family or something, though she hadn't in over six years. He knew through the grapevine that she met her dad once a year in Wild River at the popular ski resort for the Christmas holidays, continuing a Beaumont holiday family tradition they'd started when Skylar's mother was still alive. Other than that, Skylar had avoided Alaska while away at the academy, or at least Port Serenity.

Plus, no one in town had mentioned her impending return now.

"Yep. I'm home," she said tightly, still avoiding his gaze. She shifted awkwardly from one foot to the other, rubbing her arms in the cold. Obviously, this wasn't the way she'd been hoping to reunite.

He was grateful that their first meeting was awkward for other reasons besides the fact that she'd broken his heart when she'd left town and *she* no doubt remembered that series of events as quite the opposite.

Though he was sympathetic about the car. The water damage to the engine and electronics could be costly, and the car might always hold a faint smell of seawater in the fabric.

No amount of pine scented air fresheners could erase that persistent odor.

"You're stationed here?" His pulse raced at the thought. She'd always said she wanted to travel the world. Be stationed anywhere but their sleepy hometown. Why the change of heart?

She nodded. "Yep."

She didn't sound thrilled about it. So, it wasn't by choice then.

That made his stomach drop. For the briefest of moments, he'd allowed the slightest bit of hope that maybe...

Man, he had to stop dreaming. Of course she hadn't come back for him. They hadn't even spoken since that last conversation over six years ago. The one that had destroyed him.

But that was a long time ago.

He cleared his throat. "How've you been? How was the academy?"

She shot him a look as she shivered in a blast of cold Alaskan wind. "You want to catch up? Now?"

Right. Probably best to keep the reunion short before they both froze to death. "Did you want to come on board my boat?" he asked awkwardly. "Get some dry clothes… A towel?" Obviously, anything she'd brought with her was submerged with the vehicle.

She shook her head quickly. "I'll just walk to Carly's. It's only a block away."

Carly, the cousin who ran the local bookstore and museum in town. Made sense she'd be staying there. The two had always been really close. But it meant that Carly must have known Skylar was coming back. Who else knew and why hadn't anyone thought to give *him* a heads-up?

"Yeah…right…of course," he mumbled then cleared his throat as she turned to leave. "You look amazing in that uniform," he said—because it was true and because he couldn't not say it. The words had come from the intense feeling of pride surfacing in his chest. She'd done it. She'd followed her dreams and had succeeded, just like he always knew she would.

Resisting the urge to hug her was difficult. Seeing her again had immediately caused all of his repressed feelings to return. All the memories, all the plans for the future… He'd missed the hell out of her these past six years and here she was. Back in town.

He'd never allowed himself that hope.

"Thanks…" she said awkwardly, her gaze questioning, less guarded for a fraction of a second. Then she turned away and pointed down the street. "I should go. I have to figure out what to do about the car."

Obviously the priority and the only thing she was concerned about. This run-in with him wasn't having the same impact on her emotionally. What had he expected?

"Hope you didn't pay a lot for it," he said.

"It was a rental."

Ouch. "Hope you had insuran..." He stopped, seeing her lower lip suck in. "Well, let's just hope you can drive a boat better than you can drive a car."

She looked far from impressed by his attempted joke. "Bye, Dex." And with a wave tossed over her shoulder, the love of his life walked away from him.

Again.

CHAPTER TWO

"HEARD YOU MADE quite a splash arriving in town," Carly said from the doorway of the spare room that Skylar was occupying indefinitely.

Skylar cringed as she sat on the edge of the bed and tied her running shoes. News about her mishap had spread through town already. So much for making a quiet entrance. Those fishermen sure liked to talk.

At least the rental company had been a lot more understanding about it than she'd expected. Of course, they might not be so accommodating on her wallet once the estimate came in from Tom's Auto Repair, where the car had been towed once the fire department pulled it out of the marina.

The whole thing had been mortifying. Made a million times worse by Dex's involvement. It had been the sight of him, moreover the sight of the old yacht transformed into a rescue boat, that had thrown her. She'd thought he'd abandoned the dream they'd once shared, so why turn the boat into a volunteer response unit? Unfortunately, she'd have to talk to him to find out and she was hoping to avoid him as much as possible. Standing there face-to-face with him after no contact in six long years, her head and heart had been all kinds of messed up. He'd looked gorgeous even soaking wet, with pieces of seaweed clinging to his T-shirt. The eighteen-year-old boy she'd left behind was older and definitely more mature, but those same piercing blue eyes and light stubble along his jawline had brought her back in time to when she could lie in his arms and stare at that face all day.

Today, she'd struggled to meet his gaze.

Just seeing him made it difficult to breathe, with the embarrassment, uncertainty and a lot of unsaid words. If she reexamined the past, let him close for even a second, she knew she'd be in trouble. He'd always held her heart, which meant he also had the ability to break it. And this day had made it painfully obvious that nothing had changed.

She forced a smile, turning to Carly. "I may need to borrow your car for a week or so…"

"No problem," Carly said, coming all the way into the room.

"And thanks again for letting me stay with you." Though depending on how long she stayed, she might have to do some redecorating of the spare room.

Unlike Skylar, Carly was obsessed with the small town's mythology, the stuff Skylar viewed as a tourist trap. Her cousin's apartment had almost as many figurines and collectibles about Sealena as the museum and bookstore she ran, one floor below. Carly's mother had run the store, which was owned by John Wakefield before she'd remarried and moved to Anchorage. Being from the maternal side and not an official Beaumont made it easy for Carly to overlook family loyalty and work in the tourism industry in Port Serenity.

Skylar understood why her cousin worked at a job that perpetuated the Wakefields' influence over the town. Everyone needed to work. What she couldn't overlook was the large artwork hanging above the bed—Sealena holding two ships high in the air, saving them from a raging storm. *That* would be a source of nightmares. She hoped her cousin wouldn't be too offended if she suggested relocating the art temporarily.

Of course, Skylar could have moved back into her family home across town. Her old bedroom was still the same way she'd left it. But she was desperately trying to be as independent as possible.

Working with her dad was going to be challenging enough.

"I love having you here," Carly said with a warm smile reflecting in her dark brown eyes. "Even if it's because you don't want to sign a year lease on a place and commit to staying in Port Serenity a second longer than necessary."

Skylar didn't deny it. She'd never been successful in hiding anything from Carly. Not even her feelings about being stationed back home for her first captain assignment. Her cousin was more like an older sister. Growing up, they'd been inseparable. If there was one good thing about being back home after years away, it was reconnecting with Carly.

Carly sat on the edge of the bed with a mischievous gleam in her eye. The kind only good gossip could inspire. "Hey, you know who else recently moved back to Port Serenity?"

Growing up, Skylar had longed for the anonymity of a big city, away from the gossip that could set the small town abuzz. But she *was* curious, despite herself. With a population of four thousand people, there were hardly enough people to leave, let alone boomerang. "Who?"

"Isla Wakefield."

Skylar's heart raced for a dozen different reasons. "I thought she was working as an adventure tour guide off the coast of Mexico?" Isla Wakefield, Dex's sister, was two years younger than Skylar and the two of them had never gotten along. If Carly wasn't Facebook friends with the other woman, Skylar wouldn't have known what had become of the spirited, energetic terror.

"It was actually Belize, and then she worked on some cruise ship for a while," Carly said. "She moved back unexpectedly late last year after her grandfather died." She shrugged. "We all assumed she was back for the funeral, but then she stayed."

Maybe she'd gotten tired of working for a living. It wasn't as though anyone with the last name Wakefield ever had to. Four generations ago, the Wakefields had taken the sleepy fishing town and turned it into a thriving tourist destination by claiming the Sealena mythology. In fact, the serpent queen had been rumored to exist in Alaskan waters for centuries, but the town chose to believe it was the brainchild of Isla's great-great-grandfather. The man was credited with "saving" the community when the local fishing industry had been going through hard times, and there was a bronze statue of him erected at the marina. As a child, he'd always looked like a pirate to Skylar…

Probably because he *had* been. The Wakefields might make their fortune honestly now, owning almost every business in town, but rumor had it that that hadn't always been the case.

"Anyway, I just wanted you to know…in case you ran into her," Carly said, a note of worry entering her tone as she began to tie her dark, thick hair into a long braid.

Skylar waved a hand as she stood and reached for her Apple Watch. "Water under the bridge. That was all years ago," she said, hoping her time away made it harder for Carly to detect bullshit when she heard it.

"Well, that's a relief. Wouldn't want another scene at the Serpent Queen Pub." Her cousin raised an eyebrow over the pale pink rims of her glasses.

Skylar's cheeks flushed at the mention of her not-so-finest-moment. She'd desperately tried to erase the memory of graduation night from her mind over the years. Maybe it wasn't such a distant recollection for others... Small towns had long memories.

"No fear of that. I will be flying completely under the radar...*after* today's incident of course." She put on her watch. "I have to go for a run, burn off some of today's excitement, but I'll see you tonight?"

Carly looked thrilled at the prospect of a long overdue girls' night. "Boxed wine, Doritos and trashy reality TV?"

Skylar laughed. Their old high school ritual when they'd had the metabolism for such a dinner, even when they were underage. She'd missed those girls' nights with her cousin. One was definitely overdue, but... "I'd love to, but *someone* committed us to dinner with my dad, remember?"

Carly's braid swished around her shoulders as she shook her head. "Damn it," she said. "Why didn't you stop me?"

Skylar hugged her cousin quickly as she passed into the hall. "I seem to remember suggesting we tell my father that I wouldn't be back until tomorrow, but you ve-toed the idea." She'd been more than willing to postpone the family reunion for an extra day, giving herself time to adjust to being home, wrap her mind around the idea that in a few days she'd be working alongside and technically under her father's command. But Carly couldn't lie if her life depended on it.

"I guess I'll see you at your dad's place then!" she called as Skylar descended the stairs.

A moment later, Skylar shivered as she stepped out into the late April Alaska wind. In Connecticut, spring had been well under way, so the chill here would take some getting used to. The weather was just another reason she was less than thrilled to be back. She'd been desperate for a posting in a warmer climate, protecting a warmer ocean...preferably one without a sea creature lurking beneath the surface.

A place where long-repressed feelings couldn't resurface either.

THE SERPENT QUEEN PUB was bustling even despite the early hour. As the only watering hole in town, it was the hot spot for after-work drinks, all-night benders, celebrations and drowning ones' sorrows. The pub boasted small-town charm, with rustic furnishings and modern technology. Its decor included dark-stained wood, large windows that looked out over the marina and local family crests painted on tin panels on the ceiling. Old oil lamps had been refashioned into hanging light fixtures above the bar, wooden barrels had been repurposed as bar stools and framed photos of generations of sailors made everyone feel welcome and at home. The room's focal point was a large statue of Sealena, and a framed photo of the bar's founder hung behind the bar. Dex's great-great-grandfather, who everyone said was the spitting image of Dex himself.

Loud music from a local folk band blasted from the speakers and groups of friends laughed and chatted above the noise. Dishes clanged in the kitchen and the bartender, Zac, sang horribly off-key as he filled a row of shot glasses with whiskey.

But nothing could drown out the whirlwind of thoughts in Dex's mind. Skylar was home. The love of his life was back in the small hometown that she'd been desperate to leave forever.

He hadn't expected to see her, so he hadn't exactly rehearsed what to say, how to act... He hadn't had time to put up a shield, so his heart had picked up where they'd left off, right back to loving her.

Zac placed the pint of beer on the bar in front of him and grinned, the expression making it impossible to believe the man had stood behind the bar serving drinks since Dex was a boy. No one in town could correctly guess his age. Never married, no kids, no family—no one could even remember where Zac had even come from. He'd always just been there behind the bar. A landmark in his own right. "Heard there was some excitement down at the dock this morning," he said, pouring some peanuts into a tiny bowl in front of Dex.

"We really should discuss putting a barricade along the dock at the next town meeting," he mumbled.

"Or you could try not distracting the ladies with those bulging biceps while you work on that impressive boathouse of yours," Zac said.

If only he believed that was what had happened. If Skylar had felt an ounce of interest, she hid it well. "Thanks for the tip."

He picked up his beer and carried it to the corner table where the off-duty members of the Port Serenity Coast Guard sat drinking and eating wings. They were celebrating a successful rescue of a small fishing vessel stuck in the ice about thirty miles off the coast the night before. Dex had assisted on the call with his converted family yacht.

He pulled out a chair and sat, scanning the table. Yep,

everyone was avoiding his gaze. "Did you all forget to tell me something?"

The men exchanged looks. No one looked like they wanted to comment.

"Surprise?" his friend, Doug Fields, said, hiding a guilty-as-shit look behind his beer bottle.

Dex scoffed. It had been a surprise all right. The sight of his ex had knocked the air from his lungs faster than the plunge into the marina. She'd looked breathtaking and so far out of his league dressed in her captain's uniform... Even soaking wet. He'd never doubted she'd excel at the academy. She came from a long line of strong, passionate law enforcement officers, but he knew it was her own dedication and hard work that got her where she was. Skylar Beaumont was a force, with a spirit so intense, she would have completely intimidated him if it wasn't for the insane attraction that had once existed between them.

Still existed, at least for him.

"No one thought to tell me she was being stationed here?" He wasn't officially part of the crew, but a heads-up about something like this would have been appreciated. It wasn't as though she'd be his boss, but he suspected she'd have something to say about his volunteer position. Her father never hid his own disdain about it.

He also felt a little inferior. Skylar was a commanding officer of a response boat and he was an unemployed trust fund volunteer.

"We weren't really sure how to tell you," Doug said. The cutter crew member offered a sympathetic look that Dex was desperate to brush off.

"Why? The thing between Skylar and me..." He shook his head. "It was nothing—a teenage forbidden love thing…" Their relationship had been a secret because of their families' generations-old feud. Only a few close friends, Carly and Dex's sister, Isla, had known.

"So, having her back in town has zero effect on you?" Doug asked, running a hand over his wavy, sandy blond hair and leaning back in his chair.

"Zero." Thank God Dex had a poker face.

Doug glanced beyond him out the window and nodded, slightly unconvinced. "Okay, so, seeing her is no problem?"

"None." Dex turned to follow the other man's line of sight, and his poker face started to slide.

Damn, if Skylar had looked amazing in her uniform, she looked like a dream in the leggings and tight, long-sleeved tee she wore now as she passed the pub window. The familiar sight had his throat tightening.

How many times had they run the pier together? Pretending not to be running together.

Keeping their relationship a secret from their families and almost everyone in the small town had been nearly impossible…fun in the beginning, but then he'd wanted to get serious. He'd wanted to tell everyone.

She'd been worried about the feud, but he'd wanted to show the Beaumonts that he wasn't his great-great-grandfather. That while he wasn't proud of the questionable business habits from previous generations, they also weren't something he could change. He wanted them to see him for who he was, that he was good enough for Skylar. He'd tried to be good enough for her.

Then he'd messed everything up.

There were a lot of things he wanted to tell her. So much he wanted to explain.

Standing, he took a swig of liquid courage…then decided

to take the beer glass with him as he strode out of the pub. He took a deep breath as he started to jog after her, steady handed so as not to spill the liquid.

He swallowed hard at the sight of her shapely curves ahead of him as her feet bounced off the pier's weathered wooden planks. She'd always had an amazing, athletically built body. His seventeen-year-old self had barely been able to keep his hands off her. Apparently, that desire hadn't faded.

He should turn back. This wasn't a good idea.

Unfortunately, hearing footsteps behind her, she glanced behind herself and saw him.

No turning back now.

The look of pleasant surprise in her bright blue eyes gave him a moment of hope as he reached her, before her gaze settled on his beer stein. She frowned and picked up her pace.

He sped up and passed her. Then jogging backward to face her, he asked, "Wanna race?" Maybe things didn't have to be so serious. Maybe just being friendly and leaving the past in the past was the way to go.

But she scoffed. "It wouldn't be a fair challenge." She paused. "For you."

Clarification hadn't been needed. She'd always been the faster runner. He'd pretended to have his ego hurt by her athleticism, but secretly he'd admired her for the achievements. He'd loved that she could kick his ass at anything... at everything, all day long. "I wouldn't be so cocky if I were you. You've been away for six years."

She didn't even glance at him as she continued down the pier, barely breaking a sweat. "When have you ever beaten me?"

"That one race in senior year…the Wild Coast nationals… My time was better than yours," he said, slightly out of breath from the pace they were keeping. Man, was he really this out of shape? He worked out with the crew at the station's gym, but maybe he needed to add some cardio. He'd definitely let himself slide a little since his high school football days.

Skylar raised an eyebrow, finally looking right at him. "You mean, the one where it turned out I was competing on a broken ankle?"

He laughed. "A win is a win." He took a swig of beer, draining the glass, then set it on a wooden post without slowing his pace. "What do you say—rematch?"

She looked conflicted, which made him feel a little less like he was stranded in uncharted waters at sea, in a dinghy all alone. If she agreed, maybe it would mean they really could move on.

But then she checked her watch and cleared her throat. "I'm actually late for dinner with my dad." She turned and headed back in the opposite direction. "See you around."

He sighed as he stopped running and watched her go. "Absolutely. Rain check," he called after her, knowing there wouldn't be another opportunity. Skylar might be back in their small hometown, but he had a sinking suspicion that she would avoid him as much as possible.

A COMFORTING FAMILIARITY mixed with an inexplicable anxiety wrapped around her as Skylar walked into her family home later that evening. After her second run-in with Dex, Skylar felt like she was on an emotional roller coaster already. She'd known this homecoming would have its challenges, but she'd failed to estimate the significance of them.

This was the first time she'd been home since leaving for the academy and the first time being there without her mother. Her mom had cancer twice, beating breast cancer when Skylar was twelve. Unfortunately the second bout had been fast and there had been no time for treatment. Diagnosed with stage four pancreatic cancer, she'd been gone less than a month later. They'd spent those final few weeks together at her mother's favorite inn in Wild River before her mom had insisted Skylar leave as planned for the academy. She'd wanted Skylar to be free of memories of her final days.

It had felt like an impossible request to grant, but Skylar's father had insisted they follow her mother's wishes, allowing her that peace. Focusing on her studies had been hard in those first few months, but Skylar had been grateful for the chance to say goodbye and then the distraction of her course load. She knew her mother was proud of where she was and the life she was building for herself. That had been a blessing.

Walking into the house now, she unexpectedly felt like that teenage girl hiding things from her family again. Seeing Dex had felt like no time had passed since the day he'd broken her heart by telling her he wouldn't go to the coast guard academy after all. That he'd changed his mind, was no longer planning the future they'd talked about for months… That he was ending things instead of fighting for a relationship with her.

That maybe their families were right.

She'd hoped that now with a new maturity, she could see him and not feel the dull ache of longing, the sting of disappointment and betrayal…the pain of not having had him by her side during one of the toughest storms of her life,

starting adulthood with all its uncertainty after just having lost her mom. But there it was, even stronger than ever.

Of course, he'd seemed unaffected. Laid-back, charming
Dex without a care in the world had been able to jokingly
challenge her to a race without a blink of remorse in those
dark, seductive eyes that had always pulled her in with their
hint of what couldn't be, what shouldn't be.

Passing the collage of family photos in the hallway, she
paused to glance at a picture of her before her high school
winter formal. In a red Cinderella-style dress that she'd
taken weeks of searching to find to wear to the holiday
event, her hair and makeup done by Carly, her heart ached
seeing her younger self's mischievous smile.

Her date looked less happy, since he was part of her
ploy to get out of the house so she could meet up secretly
with Dex. Brad's date had been posing for a similar photo
with Dex across town in the Wakefields' mansion. It had
only taken a signed trading card of Brad's favorite baseball
player and a charm bracelet for Tiffany to secure their help.

Back then, the hidden relationship had been fun, exciting… Sneaking around had added an element of adrenaline that only fueled their already overactive hormones.
But they'd both eventually wanted to tell everyone about
their relationship. With Dex joining her at the academy,
they could have put an end to the secret. They'd tell their
parents after they'd both been accepted and then they'd
leave together…

Then Dex had bailed.

"There she is!" her father's voice boomed behind her
and made her square her shoulders as she turned with a
respectful smile.

"Sir."

"At ease," he said with a grin. "Hi darlin'." He opened his arms wide and Skylar immediately felt the uneasiness in her stomach subside.

"Hi, Dad." She'd always thought of her father as two separate people. As her mentor, admired and respected with a slight reservedness whenever he was in uniform. And as the soft, kind-hearted amazing dad when he spent time with her and her mother.

"So good to have you home."

She knew he'd been lost at first without her and her mom. He'd thrown himself into work to help fill the void and escape the loneliness at home. Before her mom's death, he'd been talking about an early retirement. But here he was, still working.

He pulled back and studied her closely, his perceptive gaze holding a hint of suspicion. "Though I'm also a little surprised." He paused. "And not just because you drove off a dock."

She sighed. Of course he'd heard she wasn't exactly off to a great start.

Should she confess that Port Serenity hadn't been her choice? She was here now. No sense hurting her father's feelings. He'd always wanted her to be stationed here like he'd been and his father before him. But, he'd also understood her desire to step out from under his shadow and travel the world.

"It's temporary," she said carefully, "but what better place to start my new posting?" She forced an optimistic tone, hiding her dread of working alongside him.

It wasn't that she didn't want to continue to learn from him, she just knew everyone would struggle to take her seriously, see her as anything more that Captain Beaumont's daughter. With his experience and being the most senior crew member, he outranked her, but they were both commanding officers of the ships. Could they maintain a strictly professional relationship at work? Would she be able to command a crew her way without his interference? Interference he'd never think to engage in with someone who wasn't family.

But if her father sensed her turmoil, he didn't show it. "Drink?" he asked her and then Carly as she entered the room.

"I brought wine," Carly said, carrying the bottle into the kitchen.

Skylar followed her dad into the other room, where the smell of lasagna hit her and her stomach rumbled. She hadn't eaten yet that day. After the incident at the dock, the meetings with Dex and getting settled into her new accommodations, she hadn't had much appetite, but apparently the scent of cheese and Bolognese sauce was enough for her taste buds to temporarily forget her stress. "Smells so good in here. Garlic bread?"

Her father opened the freezer and took out the loaf. "What's Beaumont lasagna without garlic bread?" he asked.

Skylar laughed, but it died on her lips as she looked past him to the fridge. A familiar piece of paper was stuck there with a picture frame magnet of the three of them in Wild River. "Is that a copy of my final transcript? How...? Why...?"

Her dad looked sheepish. "Okay, so I pulled a few strings to get an official copy."

Her gut dropped. How many other strings had he pulled along the way? Nope, she wouldn't lose confidence. She'd earned her spot at the academy and this transcript was proof that she deserved to be there. Her grades were fantastic. But her father's actions were inexcusable. Had he had something to do with this posting?

"Dad..." Keeping her voice calm was a struggle.

"I'm sorry. I'm just so proud of you. Top of your class." He lifted his arms in a "raise the roof" motion, his excitement preventing him from seeing her annoyance.

Behind him, Carly was shooting her a look that begged her to let it go. Carly's mom had raised her alone, and Carly had longed for a father. She always said she envied the relationship that Skylar had with hers. And truth was, Skylar knew how lucky she was. She and her dad had always gotten along. With their shared interests and passion for the ocean, they'd been so close.

So, again she forced a smile and let it go. She couldn't be upset with him when he was beaming with pride. As much as she wanted to stand on her own, she *was* a Beaumont and she couldn't change that.

Despite the number of times as a teen she'd wished she could so that the relationship with Dex wouldn't be so forbidden.

She shook her head as she reached for the wineglasses. Silly teenage love. That was all it was back then. Broken promises had a way of hardening the heart. At twenty-five, she could see things for what they were.

What they still are apparently...

Dex hadn't changed a bit. Still gorgeous, still charming, still rich and still unmotivated... Still a Wakefield.

There was obviously no escaping genetics.

IN HINDSIGHT, APPROACHING Skylar on the pier may not have been the best way to play things. Not if he planned to show her that he was a better man than she thought. Not just someone who was happy to coast through life, living on his family's money without goals or ambitions of his own. Unfortunately, it was hard to change someone's perception when he wasn't sure he could really prove that he was anything but.

Past regrets weighed heavy on him as Dex climbed aboard his home on the water that night. Those regrets had been easier to ignore before Skylar's return.

Twenty-four hours ago, he'd been perfectly content with his simple small-town life. Or at least making the best of the cards he'd been dealt. Suddenly, things were different.

Hanging his keys on the hook near the door, he flicked on the interior lights in the main cabin, which served as his main living space. He'd lived on the boat with his grandfather since he'd graduated from high school, until the older man passed away last year. Truthfully, *The Mariana*, affectionately named for his grandmother, had always been more "home" to Dex than anywhere else. As a child, he'd spent entire summers on the boat with his grandad, sailing all along the Alaskan coast, fishing and exploring or just camping out on deck when the boat was docked, staring at the millions of stars overhead.

Turning it into a volunteer rescue boat in recent months had helped to make his inheritance feel less privileged. Refurbishing the boat and giving back to his community gave him a sense of purpose, a focus as he'd mourned the loss of the family member he'd been the closest to. The new steel hull, aluminum pilothouse and rubber bumpers at the tip of the bow had changed the esthetic but increased functionality. Fat racing tires added to the side for protection when the boat neared tankers and freighters may have reduced the sale value of the vessel, but he had zero intentions of ever selling it anyway.

In the bow, he'd installed two FM radios, two CB radios, a ship to shore AM radio, top-quality radar and huge searchlights, making him that much more useful on rescue missions. The local coast guard crew knew they could depend on him.

If only Skylar knew it...

Sitting at his desk with his laptop open, he clicked on a website he frequented far too often lately. Leaning back in his chair, he waited for the beautiful images to load. Golden hair, dark hair, black eyes, blue eyes... So many to choose from. Where did he even start? As he surveyed the selection of adoptable animals, he once again couldn't decide which dog he liked most.

German shepherds had always been his favorite breed, but the expressive golden retriever faces just melted his heart. He scrolled through the listings, but reading their individual journey stories only made the decision even harder...

The yacht door opened and Dex quickly closed the laptop as his sister entered.

"You will not believe who is back in town," Isla said with her usual overdramatic flair.

"Skylar Beaumont." Normally, he'd play the game, but he wasn't in the mood. Twice that day he'd had an opportunity to talk to her and make amends, and he'd chickened out both times, relying on surface level banter and humor as a shield.

"You've seen her?" His sister's protective instincts seemed to float around her as she pushed her pink-blond hair behind her ear. Hadn't it been a pale blue, maybe purple, yesterday?

She was always fashionable, but her look changed faster than her love interests. Dex couldn't keep up with his high-strung, passionate, adventure-seeking sibling. He'd long ago stopped trying.

Unlike Isla, he preferred routine and comfort. Same old, same old. There were no surprises in his wardrobe. Jeans, T-shirts and hoodies. He'd had the same hairstyle since he was five years old and the only thing about his appearance that ever changed was the length of his facial hair...mostly during sports playoff seasons when he let it grow to avoid bad luck for his favorite teams.

"Only briefly," he said. Both times, he'd crashed and burned. If she was staying in Port Serenity, they'd need to figure out a way to co-exist. Dex couldn't handle another tension-filled exchange. Either it would get easier, or it would grow harder and harder on his aching heart.

"I drove past her on Main Street earlier, standing outside Wakefields' Wine and Spirits, looking like she'd rather have her arm chopped off than go in. As though entering one of our businesses would be betraying her dear old dad." His sister removed her sweater and tossed it onto a chair, still raging.

"Can't fault her for being loyal to her family," he muttered.

Isla didn't seem to hear him. "The nerve of her to even come back here. I mean, didn't she vow never to step foot in Port Serenity ever again?"

He rolled his eyes. His sister's memory of that graduation night before Skylar left town was obviously clouded.

"Not exactly, and that was almost six years ago. Let's drop it and move on."

Her green eyes narrowed as she studied him. "Drop it and move on? You can do that? You can live here in the same small town with the woman you've been pining over—"

"I haven't been pining."

"You haven't dated anyone since her." Hands on her hips, his baby sister was ready to argue her case.

"That's because of other reasons," he mumbled.

She nodded slowly. "Okay. I'll pretend to buy that." The conversation had moved into territory that neither of them wanted to talk about. "Were you looking at dogs again?" she asked, collapsing into a chair and setting her bag by her feet.

"No," he lied.

She shot him a look, one microbladed eyebrow raised almost to her hairline. "Bullshit. You closed the laptop faster than if you'd been looking at porn. We're not getting a dog," she said.

"*You're* not getting a dog. *I* might."

"I'm deathly allergic."

"More reason to get one so you'll move out," he said with a grin.

"No dog," she said as though the issue was closed as she leaned over to unlace her hiking boots. She knocked a foot into her bag and a brochure fell out of the flap. He bent to pick it up.

"What's this?"

"Nothing," she said standing quickly and reaching for it. "Just a tour through the mountains—a spring camping thing..."

He held it high above his head, where her five-foot-nothing frame couldn't reach it even if she jumped. "You going?"

"No."

"Why not? You love this stuff." Hiking, rock climbing, parasailing, cliff diving...the more dangerous the better for Isla. She'd always been a daredevil. As a kid, she'd climb anything she could find. Terrified the life out of his parents, but they'd quickly learned that she was steady on her feet. They learned to give her the space she needed to fly, knowing she was capable enough not to fall too often and strong enough to bounce back when she did.

"It's a week long," she said casually.

Right, and she was back in Port Serenity, living with him on the yacht to be his babysitter. He knew she tried to make it sound as though she'd gotten tired of adventuring around the world...but he knew why she'd come back when their grandfather died. With their parents now retired and wintering in Florida, she had taken on the responsibility of looking out for him.

And he hated it. He was the older brother. He was the one who was supposed to take care of her. It used to be that way. His parents had adopted Isla at age three and had brought her to Port Serenity, and Dex had instantly assumed the role of protector. He was only two years older, but he'd taken the job seriously. No one messed with his baby sister. This recent role reversal didn't sit well with him.

"I'll be fine," he said.

Isla scoffed as she snatched the brochure out of his hand. "Really? With Skylar Beaumont back in town, I seriously doubt that." Her tone softened just a little as she cautioned. "Try to remember—once a Beaumont, always a Beaumont."

CHAPTER THREE

THE COAST GUARD vessels lined the marina as the sun crested the horizon. Their majestic sight evoked pride in her, as always. The Port Serenity station and fleet of five rescue boats and twenty crew members might be small, but they were responsible for protecting a large area of US waterways. With a special ops division that went out for three months at a time in search of drug traffickers and one of the best rescue swimmers in the world, the station had a lot to be proud of.

Two days after falling into the marina, Skylar boarded the *Starlight* in her freshly laundered uniform. It was just after seven and her first meeting with her crew was scheduled for eight. She wanted some time on the boat alone first. Get familiar with her, summon some confidence before she had to take command of a crew of familiar faces. An hour to reacquaint herself with her career goals.

"Gooooood morning!"

Her father's voice approaching from behind her made her stop and shut her eyes tight. Of course, he was there. She counted to three before turning to face him. He was also in uniform, looking polished, clean-shaven and oozing authority. "Hello, Captain Beaumont."

Take the hint. We're at work. Keep it professional.

The flash of his cell phone camera sent her frustration immediately to a ten.

"Dad!" she hissed, forgetting her own rule. "What are you doing?"

"Capturing your first day at work," Keith said, looking at the photo. He frowned. "Your eyes were closed. Let's try again." He raised the phone but she moved quickly, forcing him to lower it.

"You're not on shift today." She'd made sure her first day was one he had off so she could ease in without pressure.

"I only came in for the staff meeting...in case you needed backup. Then I'll head out."

Backup?

"I think we need some ground rules."

Keith nodded and attempted to look serious, but the grin forcing its way onto his face belied the effort. "Ground rules, okay."

She sighed. He wasn't going to take this seriously no matter what she said. "At work, we're not father and daughter."

He waved a hand. "We're always father and daughter."

"Right, but I need the crew to see me as their commanding officer and I need you to respect my position as well."

"Of course. Absolutely." He nodded. "One photo?"

Oh my God.

She glanced around quickly then posed. "Take it fast."

"Smile."

If only she could without it looking like a grimace.

"Perfect," he said, reviewing the shot. "Want to grab coffee?"

She gritted her teeth and forced patience into her tone. "No. I was going to take a tour of the boat. Alone," she added when he started to nod.

"Oh. Right. I'll get out of your hair," he said, looking disappointed.

She wouldn't give in to the pout. "I'll see you at the meeting," she said.

"Okay. If you need anything…"

"You'll be the first to know," she said waving him on. She watched as he headed toward the break room then she turned and kept going.

Shake it off. First day. It has to get better. He's just proud and excited, he'll relax in time.

Starting below the pilothouse, Skylar moved slowly through the engine room, the survivors' compartment, the forepeak and the head, ensuring everything was in order. She'd grown up around these vessels and her sharp eye and attention to detail missed nothing in her inspection.

Heading toward the pilothouse, her pulse raced seeing the coast guard's motto painted on the wall—*Semper Paratus*. Always ready. Was Skylar ready? Accepting the responsibility months ago in the safety of an office was a whole lot easier than facing the immense pressure of commanding this boat now that she stood on board.

She glanced down at her chair and sighed. An inflated life donut sat in her place with a sticky note that read: "Just in case." A fun joke…but Skylar had known gaining the respect of the old-school crew who still saw her as the young girl who used to play on the boat's deck with her Little Mermaid dolls would be challenging enough. Crashing her rental into the marina had just given them all more fodder to tease her with.

It wouldn't be easy to gain their respect, based on some of the unimpressed faces staring back at her in the stations' meeting room shortly after.

"What's wrong with the equipment we have?" Lieutenant Miller asked from the back.

Other than the fact that it was a million years old? "It's dated," she said carefully, not wanting to offend on her first day.

She'd thought introducing the new equipment she'd ordered to the station the week before would be met with agreement. This crew was all about safety first, and the heavy-duty float coat and helmets with reflective tape and lights were state-of-the-art. She had to wonder if the crew would be more receptive if someone else was presenting the equipment. Someone older...someone male...and a different surname?

Her gaze shifted to her father standing in the back of the room. His expression was unreadable.

Was she doing okay?

This was a lot more intimidating with him standing there.

"Our stuff still works. We're not about wasting funds on unnecessary purchases," Lieutenant Miller said.

Skylar repressed a sigh. So the new foosball table they'd replaced the lunch table with was necessary?

Her father stepped forward.

Oh hell no.

She waved a hand at him to stand down. She had this. He reluctantly did.

"This equipment meets the new coast guard regulation standards," she said firmly. Currently, the upgraded gear was optional and at the discretion of each station, but Skylar wanted to start her career with the best chances of survival for herself and her crew. "Consider the old equipment retired," she said.

Miller must have heard the implied "no arguments"

in her tone as he crossed his arms and sank in the chair wordlessly.

Small battle won. She'd take it.

Unfortunately, it was the only silver lining of the day. Hours later, Skylar sat staring out the window in the pilot-house at an unexpected snowstorm. The weather had come on fast. That day had been overcast and humid, but the forecast hadn't called for the blowing wind and thick snow covering the partly frozen marina.

Weather in this part of Alaska was always unpredictable.

Static sounded on the radio before a mayday call sounded on Channel 16:

"Mayday Mayday Mayday. This is sailing vessel *Alaska Swift*. Tour boat vessel *Alaska Swift*. I'm in trouble. My vessel has lost power and we are adrift in the storm. We are requesting immediate assistance. Unsure of our position. I have ten people on board. Mayday."

Grabbing the radio, Skylar responded. "*Alaska Swift*, this is coast guard station Port Serenity, responding unit, *Starlight*. We have received your mayday distress call and assistance is on the way."

Lieutenant Miller and Captain Fields had entered upon hearing the call and she turned to them. "*Alaska Swift*. That's still Mr. Jensen's tour boat, right?" The older man had been operating out of the marina in his twenty-foot charter for over forty years. From what Skylar remembered, he took small groups just outside the inlet for whale watching, bird sighting excursions and ice tours in winter when the water in that area permitted passage.

"Yes. That's him."

"He's adrift and unsure of position. Do you know his

usual route?" They needed to establish a search pattern as quickly as possible and get out on the water.

"I'll call the tour office, get the route from Alice," Captain Fields said, reaching for his cell phone.

Skylar nodded and forced a calming breath as she prepared for her first rescue on board this response boat. *Her* response boat.

Within minutes they had the info from the tour boat's office manager and they launched into action. Skylar and the crew created their search pattern, covering about twenty miles in every direction around the boat's usual cruise pattern. Unfortunately, wind direction suggested the boat was drifting west, toward the jagged cliffs... Not ideal.

Helicopter blades sounded in the distance as the rescue chopper started and then lifted off the pad. It would fly ahead and locate the exact position of the vessel, giving the crew on board *Starlight* a visible marker in the sky.

At her post, Skylar maneuvered the boat out of the dock and took a deep breath to steady her thundering heart rate. She'd trained for this. She'd prepared for this. She'd gone on countless rescues. But a small part of her felt caught off guard. She hadn't expected this on the first day on the job.

Ten minutes later, they exited the inlet and Skylar held tight to the wheel as she navigated the cutter through the twelve-foot seas and forty-miles-per-hour winds toward the helicopter's position. Thick snow blowing across the ship's helm made visibility nearly impossible and she was grateful for the new gear with the stronger lights.

The *Alaska Swift* had drifted far off course in a short period of time. It was already dangerously close to the mountainside and being tossed about on the waves like a toy sailboat caught in the spiral of a draining bathtub.

Lieutenant Miller approached as she slowed the vessel. "Dex Wakefield is asking if we require assistance."

"Not necessary," Skylar said. *That* added pressure wasn't what she needed right now. She had this, and she didn't need her ex-boyfriend adding to her tension.

"Are you sure? He says he's left dock already."

"Tell him to stand down," she said a little more harshly than she'd intended. Dex might be a great volunteer asset to the team, but he wasn't professionally trained and she didn't need to be adding another rescue to the day's schedule.

"Copy that," Lieutenant Miller said, heading back to the radio.

"What's the plan?" Captain Fields asked. "Tow them into the harbor?"

Skylar quickly scanned the tiny tour boat's distance from the dangerously rocky shore. "I don't think there's enough time to throw them the tow rope. That boat is headed toward the rocks. We need to get everyone off."

Captain Fields frowned, but nodded. "Copy."

It took all her strength not to question whether the other captain would have called things differently if he was at the helm that day. Doug was deferring to her as this was her mission to command.

The helicopter flew back toward the shore as the cutter crew launched the life rafts into the water and assisted the passengers from the *Alaska Swift* onto the boats. The task was far from easy considering most of them were elderly and terrified, and the treacherous North Pacific Ocean waves were tossing the response boat about. Skylar's crew acted with speed and efficiency as they brought the shaken but grateful group aboard and Lieutenant Miller led the way below to the survivors' compartment, where they'd be warm and safe, out of danger and out of the storm.

But Mr. Jensen looked panicked as he turned to Skylar. A blanket draped over his sagging shoulders and water dripping from his hair onto his wrinkled forehead, his eyes widened as he noticed her change in direction. "What about the boat?"

"I'm sorry, Mr. Jensen. We can't tow it. There's no time…"

"That's my livelihood headed straight toward those rocks." He looked distressed as tears rimmed his crinkled eyes.

The tug at her chest was intense. Mr. Jensen and his tour boat were such a big part of the community and the business was all the man had. His family no longer lived in Port Serenity and she knew the tour groups were a source of companionship in his lonely days. Skylar hesitated, re-evaluating the situation.

What was the right thing to do? What was her gut telling her? And was that advice aligned with her heart?

What would her father do?

She shook that last thought away. Her father wasn't here. This was her mission.

Everyone was safely on board. They'd done their job in less than ideal conditions. Her first rescue mission would be a success if she returned the response boat and all the endangered passengers back to safety…but Mr. Jensen wouldn't see it that way.

He'd always been kind to her. She thought of how he'd untangle her fishing line when it would get stuck on the pier or give free tours to her and her friends on his slow days. She sighed. Damn it.

She turned to Lieutenant Miller. "Do you think you could get a tow line to the anchor?"

He hesitated, but she saw him take in the look on Mr. Jensen's face. "If you can get close enough without hitting, I could jump across and attach," he said.

Confidence from her crew gave her the courage to try. "Okay, let's do it."

She motioned for Captain Fields to take command of the boat. "What are you doing?" he asked as he took the wheel.

"I'm going on deck to throw the tow line." It was a dangerous task, and she wouldn't put the crew in this position without actively joining them. With his height and build, Lieutenant Miller was the best crew member to make that leap between the vessels, but she wouldn't leave him on deck in this storm alone.

"You sure?" Captain Fields asked.

"Yes," she said without an ounce of hesitation in her tone despite the sweat pooling on her lower back.

A moment later, on deck, Skylar and Lieutenant Miller pushed through the biting cold and blowing snow and yelled to communicate over the howling winds. Holding the side of the hull, they made their way to the lines as Captain Fields maneuvered the boat alongside the *Alaska Swift*. The waves tossed both boats around and water covered the smaller vessel's bow. It was just twenty feet away from the shoreline.

Maybe this wasn't such a great idea.

"Waiting for a clear jump," Lieutenant Miller yelled, getting into position.

Skylar nodded, knowing he'd never hear a response.

The boats bumped together slightly and she swallowed hard, her heart in her throat. He had one shot to jump across. If he fell or slipped, he could get crushed between the vessels. She eyed the tour boat, drifting farther away...

It was too close to the rocks. They were too late.

"Miller!" She reached out to call it off, but she was too late. Seeing his opportunity, her crew mate leaped across, landing safely on the other side.

Thank God.

"In position!" he yelled.

They needed to act fast.

Skylar tossed him the tow line and stood watching as he secured it to the anchor line. He nodded when it was complete.

She gave the signal to Captain Fields where he watched from the pilothouse, and he turned the boat back toward the harbor. Lieutenant Miller stood on the deck of *Alaska Swift*, watching the lines and Skylar's heart pounded as she kept an eye on her crewmate.

This would be dangerous in any type of weather, but these conditions were treacherous. They'd attached themselves to a small boat being pummeled by the waves. If it capsized, it could cause *Starlight* to get dragged under as well. Everyone's safety was at risk.

On high alert, Skylar scanned the deck, holding tight while the wind blew snow across her face. She kept watch of the lines as they motored away from the ragged shoreline to the west, bringing the tour boat back into the harbor. It was working...they'd almost reached the inlet and she felt herself relax.

Unfortunately, she relaxed just a second too soon. There was no escaping the unexpected large wave that crashed over the boat, sending Skylar falling overboard into the dark, depths of the water.

STAND DOWN, SHE'D SAID.

Dex had to respect Skylar's wishes as the new commanding officer of the crew, but watching through his binoculars from his own deck, he saw he couldn't sit by. The *Alaska Swift* was in danger and he knew they were evacuating the boat instead of trying to tow it.

May not have been his choice of action, removing the passengers from a sturdy boat onto life rafts, but it been Skylar's call to make.

Now it was Dex's turn to make a call.

He was a volunteer. Therefore, he wasn't subject to her commands. He set off in the direction of the distress call. Darkness made it more difficult to navigate as he approached the coordinates. Along the way, he saw a small aluminum fishing boat abandoned and overturned, crashed against some rocks along the coastline. Its occupant looked safe on the shore, a blazing fire going and a tent set up to ride out the storm.

Resilient and resourceful. The best words to describe Alaskan residents. People who lived in this rugged, beautiful part of the world knew to always be prepared for the unexpected. Nature held many surprises, many of them challenging.

Like this freak snowstorm.

Dex checked his watch. Damn, he should have left dock immediately instead of questioning it. The initial call for assistance had come in forty minutes ago. He expected to see *Starlight* on its way back by now.

He radioed the boat as he drew closer. "My coordinates are three miles southwest... Everyone accounted for? Over."

Static.

His equipment wasn't as high tech as the response boat's. He drove faster through the storm, taking the impact as the boat hit hard on the waves. He approached the cutter being tossed around the violent water. *Alaska Swift* was being hauled behind it.

Wow. She'd actually been able to save Old Man Jensen's boat. Impressive. But where was she? He couldn't see Skylar inside the pilothouse...or on the deck...

He radioed again. "This is volunteer vessel *The Mariana* at your assistance. Everyone accounted for? Over."

Static...then Captain Fields slightly high-pitched voice. "Commanding officer Beaumont is overboard. Repeat— man overboard."

Dex's heart raced. What the hell had Skylar been doing on deck? He peered through the window and saw Lieutenant Miller on the deck of the *Alaska Swift*. Of course. She wouldn't have sent a crew member out there and stayed in the pilothouse...even though it was her damn job to drive the boat!

"Any sign of her?" he asked, desperate to keep his tone calm. His hands sweat on his wheel and his mouth had gone desert dry. What if she was hurt? What if she'd gone under? The new response boats didn't use propellers, but the old tour boat did.

"Negative," Captain Fields sounded worried as it came over the radio.

Dex was on a new mission to find Skylar. Using his night vision, he scanned the dark water, straining to see through the storm.

Come on, Skylar... Where are you?

A flash of bright white light and a figure floating in the water caught his attention as adrenaline pumped blood through his veins. Skylar. She was wearing new float gear and a reflective helmet, otherwise he might not have seen her.

He radioed the cutter. "Survivor located. Will assist."

"Copy," Captain Fields said sounding relieved. "Assistance required?"

"Negative. Bring those boats back to safety." If they stopped, the tow line could get tangled. "I'll bring your commanding officer on board *The Mariana*." Skylar wasn't going to like it, but then she shouldn't have found herself needing rescue.

Moving at lightning speed, he turned his boat toward her and approached, riding out the crashing waves. Idling, he fought through the bitter wind and blowing storm to the front deck. Grabbing the life preserver, he tossed it down to her in the water.

"Grab hold!" he yelled over the howling wind.

Her momentary look of panic faded to relief as she saw him. She reached for the preserver and wrapped her arms tightly around it.

Dex pulled it toward the boat.

Their gazes were locked and he didn't dare take his attention off her. How long had she been overboard? Hypothermia took very little time to set in in these temperatures. He pulled harder and faster toward the ladder at the back of the boat.

Reaching it, she climbed, looking unsteady. He carefully helped her on board and inside the warmth of the cabin, taking her immediately into his arms. He had no intention of releasing her until she told him too. For six years, he'd fantasized about having her in his arms again. This wasn't the way he'd envisioned it, but his heart pounded at the closeness. Her wet, shivering body plastered against his, dripping hair and an expression of adrenaline-filled gratitude had him falling for her all over again for the millionth time.

She was there. On his boat. With him.

"Can we not make a habit of this?" he asked, his voice hoarse with emotion as adrenaline coursed through his veins.

Skylar peeled slowly away from him, her eyes holding a look of challenge as she said, "I told you to...to...st...stand down," she said through chattering teeth, weakening the strength of her disapproval.

He grinned as he retrieved a heated blanket from the emergency supply kit and wrapped it around her shoulders. "Then it's a good thing I don't work for you," he said.

CHAPTER FOUR

THIS HAD TO be the worst outcome ever. Of all the things Skylar had prepared for that could go wrong on a mission, getting rescued by her ex-boyfriend and being brought on board his yacht-turned-volunteer rescue unit would never had made the list.

Not even the far-fetched but stranger things could happen list.

She shrugged off the blanket and approached Dex's communication systems. He'd really decked the place out with some high-end equipment. It would be impressive if this whole situation wasn't confusing as hell.

Hadn't Dex claimed not to want to do this for a living? Or was it really that he hadn't wanted to do it with *her*?

"I have to radio my crew. Try to get back on board." A mild panic was setting in the longer she was away from her boat. She needed to get back to her rescue, to the crew and the survivors, make sure Mr. Jensen's boat made it back into the marina safely. There was debriefing and securing to be done. Her job wasn't over yet.

Dex avoided her eyes as he cleared his throat. "I…uh… told Fields to focus on getting the boats back into harbor, out of the storm."

Her eyes widened and she felt her nostrils flare. "You what?"

"I told them I had you safe and sound and they should

stay the course." His tone held a hint of apology, but it was mostly unwavering—he obviously didn't regret the decision he'd no right to make.

"That was hardly your call." Though she begrudgingly knew it was the right one. She couldn't expect the crew to rescue her from the ghost of relationships past, putting everyone's safety at risk out of ego or a deathly fear of being alone with Dex. If only there was a way to ensure her heart wasn't at risk that evening.

She squared her shoulders. *Pull it together.*

The thing with Dex had ended a long time ago. And it hadn't been as serious as she'd thought. He was just an old acquaintance at this point. A high school sweetheart, an adolescent crush. Everyone knew those weren't meant to last.

So why was her pulse racing and why was she wishing she was still wrapped in his arms?

His sweater and jeans had a Skylar-shaped wet spot on the front where he'd held her moments before. He didn't seem to mind. In fact, he'd held her like he hadn't wanted to let go and for a brief instant, she'd have been happy if he hadn't.

That wouldn't be happening again.

She cleared her throat. "So, what's your plan?"

His eyebrow raised as though he was surprised she was deferring to him.

She shrugged. "Your boat, your plan," she explained. At that moment, she was still shaken from the turn of events and she didn't completely trust herself to be the one calling the shots.

"Right. Okay…" He gestured for her to follow him up the impressive staircase to the living quarters. "Weather's getting worse. I think our best bet is to hunker down on Fishermen's Peak, a few miles west. Wait it out."

The idea made her chest tighten. Stranded on the small island offshore all night with Dex while they waited out a storm seemed like a bad idea...and Fishermen's Peak of all places?

Just the thought of the secluded island brought back a memory she'd long repressed, one that had been far too painful to take with her when she'd left Port Serenity. One that was resurfacing now like a letter in a bottle tossed at sea...

That summer day six years ago had been warm and bright. Not a cloud in the sky, no chance of rain in the forecast. The ocean waves were few and the water looked calm—a perfect day for a kayaking trip.

Loading up their swim gear, towels and a picnic lunch, she and Dex had set out early in the morning, headed for Fishermen's Peak. It would take several hours round trip... plus time on the island for lunch and a hike, some swimming off the pebbly shores.

Skylar's seventeen-year-old heart was pounding in her chest as she told her parents she was going for the day with a friend from school. It wasn't technically a lie. She just hadn't specified which friend from school. She hated not being completely honest with them, but they'd never have agreed if they'd known she was going with Dex.

Alone.

But this was the day they'd been waiting for. Neither had voiced it of course. But she knew he knew she was ready. She was excited about the trip to the secluded island, away from the small-town and couldn't wait until they were completely alone, without having to hide the relationship, hide their feelings from neighbors, friends and family. For one day, they could be together.

Truly be together.

Meeting him near his kayak on a quieter end of the beach, her heart was bursting out of her chest with anticipation. He'd been so patient with her. He'd been willing to wait as long as she wanted to.

Now, the sight of him in a pair of board shorts and sandals, bare chest and wet hair, made her pulse race and her body spring to life. Their make out sessions were always full of desire and passion but they'd always stopped before crossing the line. He'd always gone at her pace, respecting her boundaries.

That day she had no intentions of asking him to stop.

He'd smiled as she met him at the edge of the water, then scooped her into his arms and placed her inside the boat. He'd secured their gear below the seats and turned to face her.

"Ready?" he'd asked.

"So ready," she'd said as they'd set off for an experience that had changed everything.

At least for her it had.

Maybe Fishermen's Peak didn't hold the same meaning for him anymore. Maybe, like their relationship, like her, he'd left that incredible day in his rearview.

He stopped in front of a room now and opened a door. "Help yourself to any clothes in here."

Her stomach dropped, glancing inside. Was there a woman living on the boat with him? She'd kept tabs on the pulse of things in Port Serenity through her family and Carly, but she'd never been able to bring up Dex's relationship status and no one had offered the information.

This was not good. Putting on clothes that belonged to Dex's new significant other might make her physically ill. She'd rather die from the cold wet uniform she wore.

"It's Isla's room," he said awkwardly, as though reading her thoughts.

Isla's room. She hesitated. That was only slightly better. "You sure she won't mind?"

"Of course not. Make yourself comfortable, I just need to text her to let her know that her house won't be where she left it..." Dex said, reaching for his cell phone as he left her to get changed.

Maybe don't mention that the woman she loathes is borrowing her clothes.

Skylar sighed as she entered the room and looked it over. How on earth did the woman live this way? Clothes were strewn everywhere, over the unmade bed, over her chaise lounge, over the floor... The small antique wooden vanity and matching dresser, which Skylar knew once belonged to her grandmother, were full of makeup and hair care products. At least a million pairs of shoes were the only thing organized, lined up neatly by color on a shoe rack under a porthole window.

Priorities.

Skylar could never live in such disarray. Her father had run the house like a military training camp. Every morning, they were up at 07:00 hours to make beds, run, eat a healthy breakfast, wash dishes and then set out for the day having accomplished more than most people did in twenty-four hours. Weekends were no exception. More daily chores were added and studying was to be completed before Skylar was allowed to hang out with friends.

Most teenagers would have resented it, but she appreciated her upbringing because it kept her focused and it had definitely helped when she'd gone to the academy. She already knew the proper way to make a bed, iron a uniform, shine shoes…the early morning routine had been a part of her everyday life for so long, it had made the strict policies and expectations at school seem natural.

Opening the closet, she scanned for something loose that looked like it might fit. Isla was a size smaller than she was and they definitely did not have similar styles. Pink, purple, pale blue fabrics hung on the hangers… Skylar's closet consisted of black, navy, white and occasionally a dark red. Isla's choices were casual, fun, stylish where Skylar had a preference for polished, professional and modest. Digging through, she found an oversized Harvard sweatshirt and matching track suit pants—gray with dark blue lettering. She removed her wet uniform, folded it neatly, then quickly put on the soft sweats.

Going to the mirror, she removed her hair from her bun, picked up a brush and combed through, letting wet tendrils frame her face. She rummaged through the makeup supplies, found a package of disposable makeup removal cloths, and took care of the raccoon eyes and remnants of lipstick. She was desperate for a shower, feeling and tasting the salt water still on her skin, but she was already uncomfortable enough on Dex's boat…in Isla's clothing. Getting naked would feel far too intimate.

But it didn't have to be awkward. Not unless she made it awkward.

She stared at her reflection in the mirror and squared her shoulders. "Just two old friends forced together by circumstances beyond our control."

By fate?

Nope, she wasn't going to follow that disappointing narrative.

What would her father think about all this? By now, he'd know she was out on a rescue. He'd probably have gone down to the station... She swallowed hard the irrational sense of betrayal. That was ridiculous. It wasn't like she'd planned this. He couldn't possibly be upset or hold her responsible for ending up on a Wakefield boat.

Like her, he'd focus on the facts. She was lucky to be safe. The crew coming back for her would have put everyone on board at risk. She was lucky Dex had been there.

Otherwise...

A shiver ran through her at the memory of being in the water. Sinking. The darker depths closing in all around. Then something propelling her upward. She'd heard far too many similar stories over the years. Tall tales. Exaggerations. Fishermen looking for a captive audience. There were many explanations for the things that happened at sea that seemed unexplainable, and many ways to dispel the myth that it could be a sea serpent queen offering her protection.

Skylar had stopped believing the fairy tale a long time ago, but tonight...

She shook her head. No more foolishness. She couldn't hide out in here forever. She had to rejoin Dex.

She turned away from the mirror but not before noticing the words *Stay. Safe. Side. Stay.* Written in what looked like Liquid Paper on the corner of the vanity mirror.

Huh, must be some sort of wilderness survival code. Isla was always out searching for her next adventure. A wild child, daring, reckless and impulsive. She'd been that way as long as Skylar could remember. The only thing the two of them had ever had in common was their desire to see the world.

Skylar knew why *she* was back in Port Serenity. But why was Isla?

"WHAT DO YOU mean you got stranded?"

Dex pulled the phone away from his ear at his sister's shriek. "Look, the snowstorm's getting worse." A glance outside from where he'd docked safely revealed the flakes had gotten thicker and the wind had picked up even more. Under other circumstances, when he was docked safely at the marina, Dex loved nights like this. "I can't risk the journey back," he told Isla. And he also really wanted this time with Skylar. He wasn't sure when he'd get another chance to be alone with her one on one.

Now that he'd rescued her from the North Pacific Ocean, maybe she might have enough gratitude to…have a real conversation at least. He was dying to know how she'd been these last six years, what the academy was like, how she was finding the new position. If it was everything she'd dreamed it would be. If being home was really upsetting her or whether she thought she might eventually like being stationed in Port Serenity. If she'd thought of him at all while she was away…

There was so much he wanted to know, even if he didn't have the guts to ask that last one.

"Where am I going to stay?" Isla asked, annoyed.

"Go to the Sealena Hotel. I'm sure they have a room available." It wasn't tourist season yet and even during the busier months, the local hotel always kept several rooms available for locals finding themselves in need of a place to stay. Their family owning the property meant Isla could enjoy a free stay and hot prepared meals for the evening, which helped to ease Dex's guilt about leaving her stranded.

"Fine," she huffed. "But you shouldn't be alone," she said, a slight note of worry entering her voice.

"Who said I was alone?" he whispered, hearing her bedroom door open upstairs. "Gotta go."

"What do you mean?" Isla asked.

"I'll talk to you tomorrow," he said quickly and disconnected. He would not be telling Isla the identity of his overnight guest. Though, she was bound to find out. The whole town would hear about it soon enough.

Skylar descending the stairs in his sister's old sweats had *him* sweating. Her hair was down, hanging in damp, loose waves around her shoulders. Makeup free and casual, she looked exactly like the girl he'd fallen in love with.

Was still in love with.

Heading to Fishermen's Peak might not have been the best idea... Especially if she remembered the last time they'd been there as vividly as he did...

His seventeen-year-old hormones had been on overdrive the morning of their long-ago kayak trip. The sneaking around had only amplified the adrenaline coursing through him as they'd paddled out of the inlet, hidden by the early morning fog, and out into open water.

That day was the day they'd talked about—in code—for weeks. Dating six months in secret, they'd fallen hard and fast for each other and now they were both ready to take their relationship to the next level. He'd been ready for months, but he'd wanted to wait until Skylar was a hundred percent sure. She was now.

And Dex was terrified. Terrified of doing something

wrong. Terrified she'd change her mind. Terrified that she was feeling pressured.

But her smile when she'd met him on the beach and the way she'd kissed him with so much passion before he'd lifted her into the kayak, had stolen his breath away, and he knew in his gut that she wanted to be with him as much as he wanted to be with her.

The two-hour journey by boat had felt excruciatingly long and yet far too quick and as they'd pulled the kayak to the shore, hiding it out of sight of any boats that might pass the island, Dex's teenage heart had nearly exploded in his chest.

This was the day they'd been anticipating and he was desperate to make it a day Skylar would never forget.

He certainly hadn't.

"Hey," he said as she reached him at the base of the stairs now. "You look…" *sexy as hell* "…dry," he said awkwardly. Reading the room prevented him for saying anything about her sexiness out loud.

"Thanks. Hope Isla won't mind staying somewhere else tonight," she said.

They both knew his sister was going to freak out when she discovered who Dex was spending the night with, but Isla wasn't there right now and Dex wasn't even going to check the text message from her that had just chimed in his pocket. Or the million others that would no doubt arrive.

"It's not a problem at all. She'll stay at the inn."

A silence fell between them and Skylar avoided his gaze as she surveyed her surroundings.

"So, why the…upgrades?" she asked and he heard the note of confusion in her voice.

He understood. Years before he'd been as eager to pursue a career in the coast guard as much as she was, then he hadn't gone through with applying...and he'd never told her why.

How did he explain the boat without revealing the entire truth? This was the first time they'd had an opportunity to talk in so long, and hitting her with the real reason he'd backed out seemed a little too much too soon. So, he was chickening out. "When Grandpa died last year, I thought it might be a good thing to do. Give back to the community in a small way."

She nodded, looking around. "You've installed some impressive equipment," she said tightly.

"Would you like a tour?" he asked.

She hesitated, like she might. But then she cleared her throat. "Maybe later."

"Okay." He shoved his hands into his pockets and rocked on his heels. He wouldn't take it personally. This had to be confusing for her. "I think you've seen most of it anyway." He motioned to the living room. "Want to relax in here?" And not retreat to Isla's room.

She nodded, looking as apprehensive as he felt. "Sure."

"Drink?"

"Sure," she said again, as though she didn't want to fully commit to any decision in case things went sideways.

He was desperate to keep the conversation casual...two old friends catching up. Stranded on the island where they'd made love for the first time.

Who the hell was he kidding? They were in a pressure chamber with a ticking clock.

At the bar in the corner, he poured two glasses of red wine and carried them back to the sofa, where she sat with one leg curled under her. It was a relaxed position, though she seemed anything but as she took the glass from him. "Thanks."

He contemplated where to sit. On the sofa? Next to her or one cushion away? Or the leather armchair across from her. She was staring at him while he stood there overthinking the decision.

Screw it. The armchair was too far away.

He sat half a cushion away, ignoring the uncomfortable gap beneath his butt, as he turned to face her. He held out his wineglass in a toast. "To a successful mission."

She hesitated. "If it was successful, I'd still be on my boat."

He sighed. "Everyone is safe, so that's a win in my books."

"Yeah," she said quickly clinking her glass against his and taking a sip.

He heard the note in her voice that suggested half a win had always been good enough for him.

Half-assing Dex, who never took anything serious enough.

Not Skylar. She was a perfectionist. This mission was far from how she'd wanted it to turn out.

He wished he could change her perception of him, but that wouldn't happen overnight.

He cleared his throat. "Have you seen your dad since you've been home? Besides at work, I mean."

She nodded.

"How is he?" He'd never been close to the Beaumonts. They'd made it very clear that he wasn't good enough for Skylar. Plus, to them, anyone with the Wakefield last name had been tarnished with the same historical brush. Things hadn't changed in the time that she'd been away either.

He wouldn't tell her that her father had tried to get the coast guard to ban him from using his rescue boat. But in a town like Port Serenity, in an emergency situation, every sailor with anything from a dinghy to a cruise ship was appreciated for their assistance.

"Dad's good," she said, taking another sip of wine.

"How many sips are we going to need before we get past two-word answers?" he asked, unable to bite back the ever-increasing annoyance bubbling within him.

Three minutes. That was all it took for Skylar to be infuriating. She'd always had this effect on him. Before they'd gotten together, her cool, distant resolve, yet obvious attraction to him had made her irresistible. Their family's feud had made them perfect enemies, but that tension simmering just below the surface whenever they were around one another had only fueled their chemistry.

She sighed. "Look, this wasn't exactly the way I'd planned on spending the evening."

"Me neither," he said, releasing a deep breath. Though this was better than anything he could have planned. "But we're here now. Safe. With food and wine. A pretty storm outside. A fireplace. Can't we try to move past the obligatory awkwardness we're supposed to feel based on our history and just try to enjoy catching up? A temporary truce at least for tonight?"

She stared at him, those mesmerizing blue eyes searching his expression. As though she wasn't sure how he could do that. Put their past aside and just be cordial, polite…as though his heart wasn't pounding in his chest, old feelings weren't trying to kill him, that resisting the urge to kiss her was easy for him.

No, this wasn't easy. But they needed to start somewhere. He couldn't ignore her the way she was intent on ignoring him and go on living his life as though a tornado hadn't just blown through.

She nodded. "Okay. You're right. Six years should be long enough for this not to be complicated."

It was far more than complicated, but she'd relaxed her shoulders and settled back against the sofa cushion.

"You asked about my dad," she said. "Well…he's obviously thrilled that I'm back."

"I'm sure everyone is," he said.

She shook her head, a wry laugh on her lips as she stared into her glass.

"What?"

"I'm pretty sure he had something to do with this placement."

"You'd think he'd really interfere like that?" he asked.

She cocked her head to the side. "He had a copy of my transcript stuck to the fridge. One that I didn't give him."

Dex couldn't help but laugh. Captain Beaumont had never made it a secret that he wanted his daughter to be the next generation of captains in Port Serenity, upholding the family's legacy. But he'd always encouraged Skylar to follow her own path. Dex had envied her that. His own father being laser focused on Dex having a football career—one Dex had never really wanted—had created a wedge between him and his dad. He'd been great at the game, but it hadn't been his passion. Ultimately, that choice hadn't been his to make either. "Okay, so maybe it's not too far-fetched."

Skylar smiled. A small one. But he'd take it. Little victories.

"I'm sure he just wanted you home. I'm sure it has to be

tough on him with your mom gone." He paused. "I was so sorry to hear that she'd gotten sick again," he said gently.

Skylar tensed and simply nodded.

He could understand how hard that must have been for her, especially having to leave for the academy so soon after. His heart had broken for her back then and he'd desperately wished he could have been there for her. One of many regrets. Something he hoped to be able to explain to her in time.

She stared into her wine glass, seemingly lost in thought and he felt as though she might call it a night. He didn't want it to end just yet, so he cleared his throat.

"Where did you want to get stationed?" he asked, turning more on the couch toward her and bridging the gap between them a little more in the process. Their knees were just inches apart.

"I don't know." She shrugged. "Somewhere warm. Preferably without freak snowstorms."

He nodded. She'd always talked about Florida or California. Winters in Alaska were no joke and he understood the appeal, even though the idea of leaving Port Serenity to follow her to her warmer destination had always been the harder part of their plan. "You already checking the job posting board?" he asked and held his breath. He didn't doubt it for a second.

Her eyes met his and she seemed to struggle with the answer he already knew. "Yes," she said and it was almost a whisper.

Their gazes held for an excruciatingly long time. The thumping in his chest grew faster. His body was on high alert, sensing the close proximity. She looked so beautiful and all he wanted was to touch her, kiss her, hold her.

Especially now that she'd confirmed that he might not have long to do it.

She searched his face as though looking for answers to questions that had long plagued her.

He couldn't give her any. Not tonight anyway. So instead he leaned toward her. Inches from her, he slowly reached out and tucked a strand of damp blond hair behind her ear.

"I missed you," he said. And he'd miss her again once she left.

But right now she was here. And he'd kick himself if he didn't at least take this unexpected second chance.

Was she really going to kiss him?

Seriously big mistake. Then again, she could always blame it on the near-death experience. The fireplace, the wine, the close proximity...the fact that they were on "their" special island.

Dex's gaze was burning into hers. Questioning. Wanting.

He was just inches away. The next move was up to her.

Just kiss me already! Don't make me make this decision!

"Skylar?" he said gently, reaching out to touch her cheek.

Damn it, she was going for it. She leaned in and closed her eyes as her lips touched his. Soft, inviting lips. Exactly how she remembered them. Dex hadn't been her first kiss, but he was definitely the most memorable. Unlike other teenage boys she'd casually dated throughout high school, he'd always had a self-control that was sexy and infuriating. He had never been demanding or awkward or selfish. His kiss had always seemed to be meant for her pleasure, her enjoyment. As though he were on a mission to make her teenage fantasies come to life. He hadn't had to try very hard.

73

That moment though, there was definitely a level of desperation in his kiss as he pulled her toward him and she sank into his body.

She wrapped her arms around his neck and deepened the kiss, her tongue slipping inside his mouth to tangle and explore. It had been too long since she'd kissed anyone, kissed *him*, and it didn't feel wrong.

It felt too right.

His hands slid the length of her body, up over her arms, shoulders and neck and cupped her face. Her fingers tangled in the back of his hair as her mouth crushed his even harder, almost daring him to pull away, challenging him to be the one to end the connection. Retreat. Realize what they were doing and put on the brakes.

He didn't. It was as though he didn't need air as he continued to steal her breath.

A long moment later, she gave in first and reluctantly pulled away. Another second longer and she might not stop at just an impulsive kiss.

And worse, she might not regret it.

Dex opened his eyes and he stared into hers, his gaze intense. She swallowed hard as she removed her fingers from his hair and let her arms fall to her sides. He released her and moved back, inhaling deeply.

The urge to dive back into his arms was overwhelming. Being this close to him, her body on fire from the passionate kiss combined with the intensity of the events that day… It took all her strength to resist reaching out for him again.

He cleared his throat. "I guess we should call it a night." He sounded like it was the last thing he wanted to do, but as usual, Dex was a gentleman.

Damn him!

She nodded. "I think that's probably for the best."

A fleeting look of disappointment crossed his handsome, flushed face as he gently, quickly touched her cheek before letting his hand fall away. "For the record, I don't want to."

For the record, she didn't either.

STARING AT THE ceiling in Isla's room ten minutes later, Skylar strained to listen to the sounds of Dex getting ready for bed. Just ten short steps down the hall. Her heart raced and she knew there was no way she could sleep.

She groaned, putting a pillow over her face to stifle the noise. What the hell had she let happen that evening? Opening her heart up to her ex-boyfriend had to be the worst idea ever. In less than a week, she'd gone from avoiding Dex at all costs to falling straight back into his arms.

If only the kiss hadn't been so incredible. If it had been awkward or unpassionate, she could have some hope of preserving her heart, keeping the bubbling emotions trapped below the surface. But instead, that damn kiss had been everything, tempting her to leave the safety of Isla's room and dive headfirst into impending heartache on the other side of Dex's door.

No. Do not leave this room. Nothing good would come from getting out of this bed.

She sighed, reaching into her uniform pocket for her cell phone, which had miraculously dried out and seemed to be working. In the chaos, she'd forgotten to text Carly and her cousin would obviously be worried sick by now. She'd missed three calls and texts from her.

Where are you?!?

It was after midnight, but her cousin would still be awake. Skylar felt terrible for leaving her hanging like this. Her father would have gotten an update from the crew and she really didn't want to think about his reaction right now.

She typed quickly...

Rescue went a little sideways, but I'm okay...

Okay might be an overstatement.

I'm on Dex's boat.

That was all she'd tell her cousin right now. No sense in having her worry about the near drowning incident or the odd sensation she'd experienced in the water. She was safe. At least physically. Though aching with a desire for her ex that was causing her major conflict.

Holy sh*t!

Holy shit exactly.

It's nothing. No big deal. He was in the right place at the right time.

She refused to think about the outcome if he hadn't been.

Stay safe.

I'll be home in the morning once the storm clears. xx

Skylar released a deep breath as she tucked her phone

under the pillow and rolled to her side, watching the snow fall outside the bedroom window.

The storm outside might clear by the morning, but would the storm within her heart?

SKYLAR BEAUMONT WAS on his boat, just down the hall and there was absolutely nothing Dex was going to do about it. The kiss had already crossed a line that he wasn't sure he could retreat from. For his own self-preservation, that was as far as he'd let things go that evening.

This wasn't just some woman he was insanely attracted to. This was Skylar. His high school sweetheart and the woman he'd never stopped loving. A woman who believed he'd selfishly broken her heart years before. He had to be careful not to hurt her again. He needed to come clean with her soon.

Opening his bedside table drawer, he retrieved a pill bottle containing his epilepsy medication. He stared at the label for a long moment, then opened it, popped two pills into his mouth and swallowed hard. Being diagnosed with the disease his senior year had changed everything. His entire world had been derailed, his life plans put on hold. It had been the hardest time of his life. Eventually, he had to tell Skylar. Maybe then she might be able to forgive him for the past. Maybe the knowledge that in breaking her heart, he'd shattered his own might lead to forgiveness.

He undressed and climbed into bed. Light from the moon illuminated the space in a cozy glow as the snowstorm calmed to just softly falling flakes outside.

Dex lay on his side, staring out the window, knowing down the hall, his ex-girlfriend and the love of his life, unable to sleep, was doing the exact same thing.

CHAPTER FIVE

TWELVE HOURS AGO, they'd been in the middle of a raging snowstorm and now the skies had cleared and a warm breeze rustled the trees on Main Street outside the Sealena Bookstore and Museum. Hard to believe the weather could change so quickly and dramatically.

Equally hard to believe that just twelve hours ago, she'd been making out with her ex.

Skylar repressed a groan as she poured coffee into a mug with the serpent queen's face on it, gripping a handle shaped like the creature's tail. There was no escaping Sealena, living with Carly above the museum in honor of her.

Maybe she should look at getting her own place while she was in town. Someone had to be willing to go month to month on a furnished space.

"Remind me to buy you a real set of mugs," Skylar said, sipping the coffee as her cousin prepared to open the store the next day.

Surprisingly, despite the circumstances, once she'd finally drifted off, she'd had the best night's sleep that she'd had in years. The gentle rocking of the boat had lured her into a deep sleep.

And her dreams had been filled with everything she hadn't allowed to transpire in reality the evening before. Over the years she'd had non-PG dreams about Dex, but her psyche must have sensed his close proximity, as the dreams had definitely chartered NSFW territory.

Waking up, she discovered they were docked back in the harbor already. And she'd been a little disappointed. Dex had obviously not wanted to delay the return and he'd seemed more reserved when they'd parted ways. Almost as though their connection the night before hadn't happened. Or that he was regretting it.

She sighed. The whole event had been surreal, anyway. What had she expected? That the ex who had dumped her was interested in reigniting the spark? Was *she*? That seemed like a fast track to renewed heartache.

Carly struggled to reposition the large Sealena statue in the corner of the store to make room for several smaller ones that had just been delivered by a local sculptor. The carving was breathtaking and Skylar would have been tempted to buy the art piece herself, if it had been any other figure. "You used to love this stuff as much as I did when we were kids," Carly said. "In secret, of course." She winked.

Sure. Until Skylar had stopped believing in magic and fairy tales. Myths. Things that were simply not possible...

She stared at the sea serpent queen on her mug. It *was* just a fairy tale, right? Should she mention to her cousin what had happened in the water? That feeling of another presence around her...helping her.

She cleared her throat, but the words refused to come, especially when she realized how silly they would sound. No need to feed into Carly's obsession even more when it must have been a current or something. Skylar wouldn't allow all the hype surrounding her in the small town to cloud her mind. Sealena was a story. Nothing more. This place had a way of messing with the most logical minds.

"So...anything happen last night?" Carly asked, opening the blinds in the front window and switching the closed sign to open as the clock hit 10:00 a.m.

"Other than almost drowning?" Skylar shook her head, but stared into the dark liquid in her cup, avoiding her cousin's gaze. She also wouldn't feed into Carly's hopeless romantic side by recounting the passionate kiss. It had been nothing.

If Dex's hurry to get them back to Port Serenity that morning was any indication, it was less than nothing. Just an impulsive move brought on by the tense situation they'd found themselves in.

Her cousin's expression changed to one of relief. "Thank God you're okay. That must have been terrifying."

"No, the terrifying part is having to go back to the station today and face the crew." She rubbed her forehead and checked her watch. "Which I can't put off much longer." She was expected at the station anytime now. Everyone must have seen *The Mariana* back in the harbor, so she needed to make an appearance soon.

"I'm just glad Dex was there to help."

Yep, real hero. One who had somehow managed to weasel his way back into her heart...and arms the night before.

"I mean, who knows how long you could have been out there without assistance." Carly shuddered.

He had definitely been rewarded for the effort.

"I should get going," she said, scanning the shop for a to-go mug. "Do you have any travel mugs without Sealena on it?"

Carly frowned as she thought for a moment. Then she

snapped her fingers. "Actually, I do." She reached under the counter for a box and rummaged through it. "Here it is." She extended a travel mug to Skylar.

Skylar's mouth dropped. "What the hell is this?"

Carly laughed and shrugged. "A lot of companies like to send me these samples. The whole mythology thing and all…"

Skylar took the cup and sighed. "Bigfoot?"

"I believe the correct term for that guy is Sasquatch," she said with a grin.

"Sure you can spare it?" she asked sarcastically, as she rinsed it. This wasn't exactly what she'd had in mind.

"It's all yours," her cousin said, putting the box back under the counter.

Skylar sighed as she poured her coffee into it and secured the lid. Right now, anything was better than Sealena.

Behind her, the door opened and a woman Skylar didn't recognize entered. "I can't believe this is April weather. Please tell me it gets warmer. Fast," she said with a laugh, stomping snow from her boots on the mat.

Carly grinned as she greeted her. "Nope."

The other woman's gaze landed on Skylar and she walked toward her, hand outstretched. "Hi! You must be Carly's cousin, Skylar."

"Yes," she said, accepting the handshake.

"This is Rachel Hempshaw," Carly said, coming around the counter to join them. "She just moved here from Seattle."

"Oh, wow… For work?" It was hard to imagine this chic woman would move to a small Alaskan town for any other reason. Based on her faux leather leggings, low heeled suede boots and a trendy coat that she definitely hadn't bought in Port Serenity, Skylar would have pegged the woman as a tourist.

"For love, actually," she said with a slight blush.

"She's dating Callan Parks," Carly said.

Ahh...so this was the mystery woman who'd made the former marine reconsider long stretches at sea. "Right! I heard he'd given his resignation last month. He'll definitely be missed." Callan had worked in the special operations division of the coast guard, apprehending drug smugglers on the waterways. He'd retired from service the month before as he'd wanted a more stable career to raise his niece, whom he was appointed guardianship of after his sister died.

The special division team had recently gone out for another three-month mission, so Skylar hadn't seen any of them since she'd been back.

"They have the most incredible meet-cute story," Carly said, jumping up onto the counter. Skylar checked her watch. She really had to go, but Carly said, "You have to hear this. Tell her," she told Rachel before settling in to listen to a story she'd obviously heard before.

Rachel laughed at Carly's persistence. "Well, I was on a Sealena-themed cruise out of Seattle on a work assignment..." she started. "I worked for a magazine called *Dispelling the Myth*..."

"And the boat was seized by the coast guard!" Carly said excitedly.

Rachel shot her a look. "Am I telling this story or are you?"

Carly laughed. "Sorry, you were taking too long to get to the best part."

Skylar was surprised by a pang of irrational jealousy.

Her cousin and this new-to-town woman seemed really close already.

"Anyway, long story short, I fell hard and fast and moved here within two weeks."

"That's incredible," Skylar said. This woman had actually given up a career in the city for love? For life here in the small-town? "So, *Dispelling the Myth*?"

"I came to prove that Sealena wasn't real. Not worth the hype," Rachel said sheepishly.

"And we converted her!" Carly said, smiling proudly.

Rachel shook her head and pointed a finger at Carly. "I'm still evaluating."

"Skylar's somewhat of a skeptic too. You two will get along great," Carly said and Skylar heard the note of remorseful uncertainty in Carly's voice, the unvoiced words, "if she stays in Port Serenity."

Rachel sent her an intrigued look. "Actually, I'd love to chat with you sometime about this whole Beaumont versus Wakefield family feud." Her eyes widened as she leaned closer. "I'm writing a new blog about the history of this place and, well, you're sort of a big part of that history."

"That's a great idea," Carly said.

Skylar nodded uneasily. This woman wanted to blog about their families? Documenting the decades-long feud?

That could get tricky seeing as how not all Beaumonts had successfully managed to escape a Wakefield's charm.

She cleared her throat and her nod was non-committal. "Of course. Happy to help," she mumbled as she checked the time. "But right now, I have to get to work."

Rachel beamed. "No worries! I'm not going anywhere."

Great. Now, Skylar had to somehow avoid her cousin's new friend.

Entering A Helpful Paw, Dex took a deep breath. Being inside the dog training facility felt significant. He wasn't just adopting a stray dog. The seizure alert dog would be a companion to him and assist in his care. It wasn't a decision to be made lightly. It was a huge, lifelong commitment. Choosing the right partner was important.

Getting the dog meant fully accepting his condition, but he couldn't change the fact that he had seizures. Running from his epilepsy wouldn't make the condition go away.

Isla needed to feel confident leaving him alone. With the dog there, she just might. *He* just might too.

"Dex?" A woman he assumed was Kendal Riley, the coordinator of the facility asked, approaching him. They'd spoken on the phone several times and emailed to set up the appointment.

"Yes. Kendal?"

"Welcome to A Helpful Paw. So glad you could make it." *This time.*

This hadn't been the first appointment he'd made to visit the facility over the years. This time he hadn't been able to cancel. He was ready now and he refused to question the reasoning too deeply.

But a certain blonde tornado crashing her way back into his life might have been the extra push he'd needed. Being with Skylar the night before had him all kinds of messed up. Rescuing her from the water had been exhilarating, and the tension that had simmered between them was undeniable. The kiss had been everything he'd been longing for.

And then that morning, he'd panicked. Waking up with her in his home, with the memory of the passionate kiss, he'd set the boat on course to get back to the harbor as quickly as possible. When they'd parted ways, it had felt awkward. It was like the morning after of something that hadn't occurred, which was almost worse, because now he was left wondering what the hell could happen between them.

He knew that one kiss wasn't all he wanted. But before he could consider another shot with Skylar, he needed to set the right course for his own life, his own future.

Being here was the first step.

"The place is amazing," he said, scanning the massive area where they exercised and trained dogs. Trainers and volunteers interacted with the canines in separate bordered pens. Both humans and dogs looked to be having a blast, playing with balls and practicing rescue exercises.

Along the walls behind the desks were shelves boasting awards and pictures of dogs with their owners.

"We're very proud of it. We've been here for over thirty years. We currently have over twenty dogs being trained. Most are former police- or military-trained dogs, but we also have some younger pups that we are grooming to be seizure response dogs."

"That's incredible," he said watching a German shepherd pup who couldn't be more than a few months old sitting next to a potential owner, following the trainer's commands.

"As a private facility, we aren't government controlled or sponsored under any health or charity organizations."

Meaning the dogs came at a hefty price tag, not covered by insurance or government assistance. He'd looked into the other options which provided dogs to people who needed them with minimal or no cost, but there was a very long waitlist and they paired dogs based on need. Dex could afford to pay for one and therefore didn't feel right adding his name to the list when there were others who needed one more than he did.

"I understand," he said. "I appreciate the way your company operates and the speed of the process."

"Great." Kendal smiled. "Do you have a preference of species or age?" she asked.

"Not really. Maybe a younger dog?" An older dog might have the experience, which would put Isla's mind at ease, but Dex liked the idea of being the pup's sole owner and developing that special bond. They'd both be new to this, learning together and that somehow took the pressure off them both.

"Wonderful. We have two almost ready. What would you like the dog to do? We can work out a plan."

"I'm not really sure." He'd read their website, but being there, it felt like all his preplanning had gone out the window.

"Okay, no problem. There's two main types of therapy dogs. Seizure alert dogs are trained to find help during or after a seizure, but seizure predicting dogs are a lot harder to achieve. There's no guarantee of success and it usually happens in cases where strong bonds have been formed."

Dex nodded his understanding.

"I've reviewed your application and your needs assessment profile you filled out on the website last year. Has anything changed with your condition?" she asked.

"No, I'm still considered altered awareness." He could understand what was happening around him during the seizure, but couldn't do anything about it. He needed care and comfort first aid only. He was taking the medicine prescribed by his doctor and he could drive during the daytime only.

"Okay, the seizure alert dog will bark to alert caregivers that a seizure is occurring and stay close to provide safety and comfort until help arrives. They will attempt to remove any harmful substances or articles from the area as well."

"Ultimately, I'm hoping with the dog, I could feel more confident living on my own."

She nodded. "Okay, then maybe we should train them to activate an alarm to alert people nearby?"

He'd rather not have everyone at the marina know about his condition, but it was better than having his sister spend her life as his babysitter. He nodded. "That would be great, yeah."

"The dogs are trained to lie next to you to prevent injury and even put their bodies between you and the floor to break your fall at the start of a seizure."

"Seems very altruistic," he said watching the training.

She laughed. "Don't kid yourself. They love their jobs." She motioned for him to follow her as they approached the pen with the German shepherd pup.

"There is a lot to consider when pairing a client with a new support companion, but I have a good sense about these things and I think Shaylah might be the right fit for you."

Dex watched as the pup followed her trainer's commands and his chest tightened with a sense of knowing. "She's fantastic."

"She was the smallest of the litter, with the most heart. She has a lot to prove," Kendal said, smiling at the dog affectionately.

Dex cleared his throat. "So, next steps?" He wouldn't allow himself to second-guess the situation. He'd made his decision and now he was eager to move forward.

Kendal looked pleased as she turned to him. "Well, we start your training."

"*My* training?"

"Didn't think you were getting off that easy, did you?" she asked with a wink, leading the way to her office.

CHAPTER SIX

AFTER WORK, SKYLAR reluctantly headed down the board-walk toward the Serpent Queen Pub. She'd only been inside the Wakefield-owned watering hole once and that was one time too many. But the crew was meeting for drinks and she needed to do some damage control after her accident, regain their respect and trust. They'd all been understanding, reassuring her that she'd made all the right calls, but still she felt uneasy...

She'd let her heart dictate her actions. She shouldn't have decided to tow Mr. Jensen's boat. It had worked out, but it had been risky and the outcome could have been a lot worse.

Unprofessionalism, questionable judgment, poor decision-making will not happen again... From now on, course of action will be determined by the rule book, not instinct or compassion...

Her rehearsed spiel evaporated from her mind as she pushed through the Serpent Queen Pub's doors and saw the balloons and banner congratulating her on the rescue hung on the wall. Her crew were all standing with raised beer mugs to greet her.

An unexpected lump rose in the back of her throat.

Here in Port Serenity what mattered most was community—they'd all survived and so had Mr. Jensen's business.

"There she is—our fearless leader!" Doug called out as she approached.

She smiled as a small sense of pride washed over her. Maybe following her gut sometimes *was* the right call. It had gained her points with her crew, after all.

Her gaze settled on Dex, smiling wide among the group and her heart pounded. So much for blaming the kiss on special circumstances. If they were completely alone right now, she knew she'd find a way to his lips immediately. The rush of heat coursing through her couldn't be denied. How long could she resist temptation?

Looking away, she approached the table and accepted a beer from Doug.

"To a successful rescue," she said and they all drank.

By the time her mug was empty, the stress of the last few days had almost completely subsided and Skylar was enjoying catching up with her former friends—now colleagues.

"I can't believe you did that!" she exclaimed as Doug recounted a prank they'd pulled on her father involving a toilet seat and some cellophane wrap.

"He was a good sport about it," Doug said with a grin.

Skylar's shoulders relaxed as she sank into the booth. Her father knew when to be serious, when it was important to take command and when to relax and have fun. He had that delicate balance with the crew figured out. Everyone adored and respected him.

She hoped she could eventually fill those shoes she hadn't wanted to wear.

She scanned the pub for Dex but didn't see him anywhere. He'd greeted her with a smile when she'd first arrived, but then had headed toward the pool tables with Dwayne.

She didn't see him anywhere now as she headed toward the restrooms.

Had he left? There was a sinking in her gut that she couldn't ignore. First, that morning's hasty goodbye and now he seemed to be avoiding her. He hadn't joined in on the celebration. She sighed. She needed to pull it together. It was just a kiss. An impulsive kiss with an ex who'd made it clear years ago that he wasn't interested in a future with her.

She wouldn't read anything more into the kiss or start thinking "what if." It would only lead to more heartache.

In the restroom, she stared her reflection in the mirror above the sink, forcing several deep breaths.

She couldn't change what happened but she could keep a clear head moving forward. She and Dex were in the past. She wouldn't reopen old wounds or allow new feelings to cloud her judgment. She was in Port Serenity to do a job, one that required focus. She wouldn't allow anything to distract her.

A stall door opened behind her and she was yanked inside. Eyes wide, heart racing, she quickly turned to see Dex as the stall door closed.

She raised an eyebrow and forced her tone to be light, despite the thumping in her chest. "Um, this is the ladies' room."

"Would you have preferred the men's room?" he asked, wrapping his arms around her waist and drawing her closer in the confined space.

Honestly, she wouldn't have cared, but she wouldn't let him know that. She'd just spent the last two minutes pep talking herself out of this exact situation. And yet here she was wanting to sink into him and abandon all common sense.

But one of them should at least acknowledge that this was a recipe for disaster, before they went ahead and did it anyway.

"Dex, this is probably not a good idea," she said, the words sticking in her throat.

"You're right," he said.

"I am?"

"Yes. But ask me if I care," he murmured against her lips.

She sighed, wrapping her arms around his neck. She was doomed. She had zero willpower when it came to Dex Wakefield. Who had she been trying to kid?

"Do you care?" she whispered, her lips dangerously close to his.

"Nope," he said kissing her gently. He backed them toward the closed door and pressed his body into hers. She could feel just how much he didn't care pressed against her thigh. So, the passion from the night before hadn't completely sizzled out. Heat coursed through her as he kissed her again. Deep, passionate kisses that had her craving so much more.

"I." Kiss. "Want." Kiss. "To." Kiss.

"Yeah?" she asked, eyes closed, mouth slightly open. Right now, she'd probably agree to anything. Her body certainly wouldn't object to whatever he had in mind.

"Take you to dinner," he said, kissing her neck.

Not what she'd been expecting. Making out in secret was one thing. She could explain that away as hormones and attraction. He was hot as hell, and they were just two single people acting on raw impulse. But dinner was something else entirely. That was a date. That was a step toward something serious. As much as she wanted to say yes, her stomach twisted at the idea.

They hadn't been able to make it work before. They'd been fooling themselves to think that they could now. She wasn't going to stay here, and as history had demonstrated, he wouldn't leave with her.

A long-distance thing would never work…and there was still the issue of their families. Sure, they were adults now, but that changed nothing. A family feud was a family feud.

And now she also had her profession and her crew to think about. She was in town starting her career, and she couldn't complicate things with a messy relationship with Dex. She'd never want the crew to feel uncomfortable or as though they'd need to take sides, if—or more likely *when*—this relationship went sideways. Again.

She couldn't deny her desire to be with Dex, spend more time with him, spend more time *kissing* him…but, she had to think with her head this time, not her heart. And her mind was already reeling a million miles an hour and getting way ahead of just one simple dinner date.

"I don't know, Dex."

"There's a new restaurant outside of town," he said, sensing part of her reasoning for hesitation.

That made her feel a bit better, though the idea of sneaking around to be together once again didn't fill her with much pleasure.

Years of hearing about the family feud made it challenging… But, what her family didn't know couldn't hurt them, right?

Same rationalization as always. It worked.

"Okay," she said. "Tomorrow at seven?"

He hesitated, looking slightly anxious. "How about five?"

"You eat dinner at five? Are you fifty years old?" she teased.

"Just can't wait to see you, that's all," he said kissing her again as they heard the bathroom door open.

Her eyes widened and her heart nearly stopped.

A woman hummed to herself in the next stall… Dollie. Dex's aunt, who ran the bar.

Dex suppressed a laugh as he pressed his forehead to hers and they stilled as they waited for Dollie to finish up at the sink.

"Dex, next time I catch you in the ladies' room, you better be cleaning it," Dollie said.

"Yes, ma'am," Dex said sheepishly as they heard her open the door.

"And it's nice to have you home Skylar," the woman said as she left.

Skylar released a deep breath as a sense of déjà vu washed over her.

Sneaking around was definitely going to be a problem.

As HE RAN his razor over the stubble along his jawline, his hand shook slightly. Dex felt better than he had in a long time now that he was committing to a dog. It would still be weeks until Shaylah was his, after they started working together with the guidance of their trainer, but he was ready.

Or at least he would be in a few weeks.

Isla wouldn't be impressed at first, but this was good for her too. His sister needed to live her life, *her* way and not have to make decisions based on him. With her inheritance and the earnings she'd saved from working on the cruise

ship, she could easily afford her own place in Port Serenity. Or not, if she decided to travel again, which he knew
made her happiest of all.

Isla loved their family and she loved the security of having Port Serenity to call home, but Dex knew a part of his
sister would always be a wandering soul, never fully at-
taching herself to any one place or person. Isla's past before
joining their family had been full of uncertainty and insta-
bility. She'd had no one to depend on so she'd learned to
depend on herself, even at such a young age. She'd opened
herself up to family and close friends over the years and
Dex hoped someday she'd fully connect with a special
someone and learn to trust.

So far, his sister's relationship record revealed she preferred casual fun to lasting, meaningful love.

Dex sometimes wished he could adopt his sister's phi-
losophy, but unfortunately he was a hopeless romantic to
the core, still pining for his first true love.

He shook his head and laughed. He was as nervous now
as he'd been the first time he and Skylar had gone out.
This date wasn't so different. The first one had been at an
ice cream shop in a neighboring town fifteen miles away.
They'd ridden their bikes and met there after school so that
no one would see them together. Skylar had been nervous,
but he'd been excited to finally get a chance with her. He'd
been into her for years and their family's feud, which had
always made things tense between them, hadn't been a de-
terrent to him finally going after what he'd wanted.

Watching her devour a triple scoop waffle cone, chocolate on the tip of her nose, Dex had fallen immediately
as he'd leaned forward and surprised them both by licking it off.

Not exactly as smooth as a romantic kiss, but it had broken the first date awkwardness and had helped break the physical touch barrier too. After that initial connection, the two of them had barely been able to keep their hands and lips off one another.

He grinned at the memory.

The restaurant better have ice cream.

THIS WAS A bad idea. Why on earth had she agreed to an actual date with Dex?

Because his kisses had caused her to experience brain freeze, like a gulp of a slushie on a hot day, that's why. It was the only reason for agreeing to spend more time alone with him. If she wanted to survive this placement and leave Port Serenity unscathed, she had to stay away from him. Opening her heart to him again was the least sensible decision she'd made since being back home...and there'd been a few less than stellar judgment calls.

She should cancel.

She removed her uniform and hung it in the closet, before reaching for a pair of leather leggings and a loose-fitting sheer red sweater. A little sexier than her usual wardrobe...

Best thing to do was call him right now and tell him that she'd changed her mind. About dinner. About them. Better yet, she could text. That way his smooth talking couldn't change her mind.

She dressed and searched through the closet for her low-heeled, black leather boots.

He'd probably be relieved. His invite had been as impulsive as her acceptance. In the light of day when his lips weren't devouring hers, he too, must be coming to the real-

ization that this—them together—was never going to work.
It hadn't in the past and absolutely nothing had changed.
She was still career driven and determined to see the world.
He was still...Dex.

She went into the bathroom and yanked her hair out of
her tight bun. The loose blond waves that fell to her shoulders were the best hair day she'd had in forever... Could she
really waste a great hair day sitting at home all evening?

She sighed.

As she applied fresh makeup, she knew she was really
going to do this. No amount of common sense had ever derailed her before in her relationship with Dex.

And it looked like it wouldn't now either.

HE'D TOTALLY EXPECTED her to cancel.

So, the sight of Skylar walking down the sidewalk had
his heart pounding even louder. As per her insistence, he
was parked several blocks from Carly's house, on the cul-
de-sac. And a sense of déjà vu continued to plague him.
How many times had he parked his bike blocks away from
her home when all he'd really wanted was to pull up in front
of her house, walk up to her door, shake her father's hand
and tell him he'd have Skylar home by curfew? But she
hadn't been ready back then...and she was obviously not
ready for people to see her with him now either.

Still, she was going through with their date. That was
what mattered. She'd had plenty of time to reconsider, come
up with countless excuses and bail. She hadn't.

That meant a lot.

And she was a knockout. Wearing black leather pants
that hugged all her fantastic curves and a loose fitting,
nearly see-through sweater with a black bandeau bra un-

derneath, heeled boots and more makeup than she wore to work, she'd definitely made an effort.

That had to mean something as well.

He got out of the car as she approached and she quickly waved him back inside the vehicle. "What are you doing? Get back in before someone sees you."

He laughed, walking to the passenger side door. "There's no one around." He wouldn't have a problem with everyone knowing about their date that evening. The only reason he'd suggested a secret outing was for her benefit.

Like before. He'd have always screamed their relationship from the rooftops if it wouldn't have made her uncomfortable, put her in a bad position with her family.

He opened the door and leaned closer as she moved past him. "You look and smell amazing," he said, breathing in her familiar scent. He loved that she never wore perfume, just a soft-scented lotion. That smell had lingered on his pillow and on his favorite sweatshirt she always borrowed long after she'd left town and it had nearly killed him, but he hadn't wanted it to fade.

Eventually it had. And now he wanted the scent everywhere, all the time.

She climbed in and he shut the door. "Be cool, play it cool," he muttered to himself as he walked around the front of the vehicle.

Getting back behind the wheel, he started the car. "Hungry?" he asked. *Keep the conversation light. Don't spook her with a full on confession of love.*

"A little." Obviously, she was still uneasy about this. She glanced out the window and folded her hands on her lap.

He reached across and touched them. Quickly, gently. "You sure you're okay with this?" he asked. He wanted this date more than anything else in the world but if she was uncomfortable…

She took a deep breath, but then nodded. "Yes. I want to have dinner with you."

Relief flowed through him as he headed down the street. "Good."

Silence filled the vehicle for a long beat before she spoke. "Nothing changed at all around here while I was away."

Nope. Nothing. Things had remained completely the same.

"Nothing has changed in Port Serenity in over fifty years." Same stores, same people, same life. While it gave him a sense of comfort, he knew the slow, predictable pace didn't appeal to Skylar. And he couldn't resist the urge to try to convince her of its unique charm. "But I think there's something appealing about that—the way the town has endured. No big corporations have come through capitalizing on the town's charm."

She shot him a sideways look. "Maybe not big corporations, but let's be honest, there's a level of exploitation here."

He sighed. Same old source of contention between them. She would never be completely on board with the way his family had transformed the town generations ago and made their wealth from it.

"Are we going to have this fight again?" he asked with a grin.

"They weren't fights, they were…heated disagreements," she said with a reluctant grin of her own.

"Well, as long as it ends the same way."

Her cheeks blushed and he knew she was instantly brought back to those intense make out sessions that always followed their…heated discussions about his family enterprises and the lack of respect for the Beaumont heroes in Port Serenity.

She cleared her throat and looked away. "I suppose things will start to get busy around here soon with tourist season."

"Huge influx of visitors should be arriving anytime now," he agreed. Admittedly, tourist season wasn't his favorite time of year, but it helped to keep the community alive.

"Do you ever take tourists out on your yacht?" she asked casually, but he caught the hint of curiosity in her voice.

"I told you, you were the first non-family woman guest I've had on the boat," he said glancing at her.

She blushed slightly again. "I just meant for tours and stuff."

He laughed. "Nope. Not even for tours…and stuff."

She looked pleased and he was suddenly glad his heart's policy of no hookups was working in his favor. He'd considered dating over the last six years and there had been a tourist or two who'd caught his eye, but every time he thought about starting a new relationship, something always held him back. He used his illness as an excuse to justify his reluctance to himself and his sister when she drove him crazy with attempted setups, but he knew it was because he'd given his heart away before and Skylar had taken it away with her.

"So, where are we going?" she asked, tucking one leg under her and turning to face him on the seat.

"You'll see," he said.

Twenty minutes later, he took the exit toward Sirens Bay. The community was a single street along the coast that stretched about ten miles. It was home to about three hundred people, but was known for its amazing steak house owned by a starred Michelin chef from Las Vegas who'd retired in the area a few years before.

"Sirens Bay?" Skylar frowned.

"Unlike Port Serenity, some places *have* changed," he said as he drove slowly along the coast toward the restaurant. In this part of Alaska, the current in the North Pacific was stronger and the waves crashing along the shore made it impossible to swim or surf, but the view was incredible. Cars were parked all along the view turnout to admire it and he suspected at night it made the perfect make out spot. Too bad he needed to be home before dark.

A moment later, Skylar's expression was one of surprise when he pulled into the lot of the impressive upscale dining facility.

"Wow. Where did this come from?"

Dex explained as he parked the car in the crowded lot. Admittedly, he'd been hoping the place wouldn't be this busy this time of day. Didn't most people go out to eat at fancy places later in the evening? Skylar was right. Only his grandparents ate this early.

Worried, he glanced at her, but she didn't seem fazed.

He reached for her hand as they walked toward the Sirens Bay Steakhouse, relieved when she didn't pull away.

"This place is really impressive," she said.

Dex admired the dark wood two-story restaurant nestled among the tree line with its floor-to-ceiling windows. He'd only eaten there once before with his father when it had first opened. Hid dad had needed to check out their "competition" fearful that Mr. Gregson was planning to turn Sirens Bay into another tourist destination, but he'd been satisfied when the chef confirmed his only interest was the restaurant. There would be no mermaid statues erected or siren-themed museums opened anytime soon.

Dex opened the door and held it for Skylar to go in first. She smiled as she stepped inside and took in the intimate atmosphere, but her eyes widened as they approached the hostess stand.

"Oh my God. That's the mayor," she said, glancing into the main dining room.

Dex swung around quickly to look. Of all the places. Of all the nights. The mayor of Port Serenity was indeed dining with his wife near the front window.

He shrugged casually but even he suddenly felt on edge. "It doesn't matter."

Only apparently it did as Skylar was backing away, out the door.

The pretty young hostess looked confused. "Do you have a reservation?"

Dex nodded as Skylar shook her head no.

"We do," Dex told the hostess. "Just give us a sec."

Skylar had disappeared outside.

Dex hurried after her and jogged to catch up to her sprint toward the car. "Wait. I have an idea." They could leave now, but if this date didn't happen, there wouldn't be another one. She'd use it as an excuse to retreat, push him away.

"We can't actually go in there," Skylar said, stopping at the car and folding her arms across her chest. At least she looked disappointed. That gave him hope.

"Maybe we can," he said carefully.

"How? Mayor Crinly is your mom's cousin. You can't not talk to him if he sees us. And his wife runs the *Gossip Mill* in town."

Mary Crinly ran a newspaper in Port Serenity *actually* called the *Gossip Mill* where no secret or topic was off-limits. And this—Dex and Skylar together—would be fodder for weeks. Not much happened in the small town and this would be big news. He could already see the headline: *Is generations of feuding over for the Beaumont and Wakefield clans with this love connection?*

"We can go in separately," he said.

She frowned. "That doesn't make any sense."

"Hear me out." He took a deep breath and thought fast. "We go in five minutes apart. Sit alone at separate tables… and…and text one another."

Her expression showed she thought he'd lost his mind.

"Come on. It will be fun." Not as fun as holding her hand across the table, toasting this opportunity to reconnect, having an intimate conversation that he hoped could move past superficial subjects and into real territory… But it was better than nothing.

Would she agree?

"Maybe we should go somewhere else…"

They could, but with Port Serenity not an option, they'd have to drive at least another hour outside of town, and his driver's license had restrictions he wasn't ready to reveal to her. "This place is worth it, I promise."

She bit her lip. "What if they see us?"

"It's a simple coincidence. I'm doing recon for the pub. You've just arrived back in Alaska, heard about the restaurant and wanted to check the place out."

She raised an eyebrow.

He shrugged. "Look, worst-case scenario is that Mary writes a story about two 'enemies' coincidentally dining at the same place at the same time. It will just throw everyone off the scent." He didn't love it.

She hesitated. "Didn't you make reservations?"

"Yeah, but at this time of day I'm sure they're unnecessary. I'll call and change mine to a table for one as soon as I know you've been seated."

Skylar sighed. "Fine."

He heard the warning in her tone. If this went sideways, he'd blow any opportunity to have this date again. "Great. This will be fun," he said with forced enthusiasm.

Skylar shot him a look over her shoulder as she headed back inside.

Two minutes later after a confirmation text from Skylar that she'd been seated, Dex called the restaurant, changed his reservation and waited three and a half minutes before heading in himself. Inside the hostess looked suspicious as he approached. "Dex Wakefield, table for one."

"You just called, right?"

He nodded. "Got stood up, I'm afraid."

She glanced toward the dining room where Skylar was nervously sipping her water and avoiding his gaze. "By the woman who just came in alone?"

So, they weren't fooling the hostess. He leaned closer. "Okay, so truth is, we're a couple...but sometimes you need to spice things up."

The young woman's expression changed to one of interest as she nodded. "Ah, I get it. Right this way."

She led him to the table directly across from Skylar's and he saw Skylar's expression take on a look of panic. He cleared his throat. "Could I have the one in the corner?" he asked.

The hostess shrugged and led him to that table instead.

"Have fun." He saw her offer a conspiratorial grin to Skylar on her way past.

Skylar took a deep breath as she picked up her menu. At least she'd agreed to stay. It might not be the evening Dex had planned, but now he just needed to make sure it was even more memorable.

THIS WAS RIDICULOUS. Why had she agreed to this?

The way her stomach dropped seeing the mayor and his wife should have told her that this was never going to work. She and Dex couldn't even have a meal together without her worrying what would happen if her family found out. If her *dad* found out. Her father and Brian Wakefield were the current generation to keep the feud going and they expected their children to take up the helm. It was silly, but deep-seated enough to cause Skylar major guilt just being there. Her dad had always been the biggest reason she'd hidden their relationship. She wanted to stay on the pedestal he'd put her on. Get the grades, go to the academy and don't date a Wakefield.

The waiter approached and she tried to focus on the menu. It was just a dinner date. She and Dex weren't getting married or anything...

The waiter stopped at her table and set down a bucket of ice with a champagne bottle inside. "Good evening, miss," he said.

"Oh, I didn't order this..."

"The gentleman did." He nodded discreetly toward Dex, and Skylar's cheeks flushed. Great, now they'd dragged the restaurant staff into their ploy. Admittedly, it was a little fun.

"Thank you," she said, as he opened the bottle and poured some of the champagne into a delicate flute.

"More time with the menu?"

"Yes, please."

As he walked away, her cell phone buzzed. Reaching for it, she read the text from Dex:

To reconnecting...

She glanced his way and saw him holding his own glass of champagne in the air. She shot a glance toward Mayor Crinly and his wife, who were so wrapped up in one another they didn't seem to notice anyone else around them before quickly holding hers up in his direction than taking a sip.

Her phone buzzed again:

What are you having?

Everything on the menu looked good. And the omission of prices on the single page suggested that the bill would reflect the five-star quality. She knew she'd never even see the bill. Dex would ensure that.

She set the menu aside before she could second-guess her choice and replied.

Chicken and seasonal vegetables.

Boring.

She laughed.

What are you having?

Steak and ribs...but I'd rather be devouring something else.

She swallowed hard as another text appeared:

You look incredible, btw.

She didn't have to glance his way to know his gaze was locked on her. She could feel the intensity from across the room. She dared a glance his way, taking in the way he sat back in the chair casually confident admiring her from afar.

Thank you. You clean up nicely as well.

She'd been too nervous to really notice how fantastic he looked when he'd picked her up, but now she fully appreciated the dark blue dress shirt he wore, the sleeves rolled and the collar undone. He'd always looked incredible in dressy clothes. She always thought he'd look amazing in a uniform... Her phone buzzed.

So...any broken hearts at the academy?

Only hers...

Is that your way of asking if there's someone special out there?

Only him. There had ever only been him for her. She'd tried with other men but there had never been the same connection, the same spark she had with Dex. All others paled in comparison to the relationship she'd had with him, even at such a young age. Being back with him now only confirmed it.

No one.

That's a relief.

Is it?

Skylar waited an excruciatingly long moment before his text popped up.

I missed you. A lot.

Skylar's chest tightened. She'd thought about him more than she'd ever admit. Wondered what he was doing with his life, if he'd found someone to settle down with. Had kids… Wondered if he thought about her even half as much.

She started to text her reply, but the waiter reappeared and she placed her order. Then she lost her nerve as she watched as Dex placed his. He obviously sensed her hesitation, as his next text changed subject.

How is working with your dad?

A simple, easy reply would be to say good, but Skylar hesitated. How was it working with her father? She admired him and respected him, but he was inadvertently making things a little harder for her. Just that day she'd walked into the break room in time to catch him telling Doug stories of how she used to play with toy boats in the bathtub, pretending they were rescue vessels saving her Barbie doll. It was difficult to expect her co-workers to respect her when her father still thought of her as his little girl.

Complicated and slightly frustrating at times.

Understandable. Have you set any boundaries with him?

She thought she had, but maybe they could use a good heart-to-heart, straightforward conversation about the best way to make the workplace relationship work. No more personal and embarrassing family stories for starters.

I will.

Do you think we should set some?

Her heart raced and she swallowed hard.

Now, who's boring?

Dots as he typed… Skylar waited.

Remember you said that once I get you alone again in the car.

Her cheeks flushed as the waiter reappeared with a basket of bread rolls and placed them on the table. Skylar hid her phone screen as she thanked him, then she grinned as she resumed typing:

Why? What are you going to do?

DAMN. SKYLAR WAS calling his bluff. And not that he didn't have a million ideas of what to do with her and that incredible body once they were alone, but was she really ready to hear them? They'd shared two amazing kisses so far and it was obvious they both wanted more. He swallowed hard as he glanced across the restaurant at her.

Sitting patiently. Waiting for his reply. The smug look on her beautiful face had his competitive side rearing its head. She asked for this and there was no way he'd back away from any challenge she put forth.

First, I'm going to kiss that smug look right off your beautiful face. Then I'm going to slide my hands up under that ridiculously teasing sweater and...

He hit Send and watched as she read the message. He saw her reach for her water glass instead of the champagne and he grinned. Mission accomplished. She was warming up.

She typed and then his cell buzzed.

Not sure what to do with them once they are under there?

His grin widened as he read. He took a sip of his champagne before responding:

I'm going to massage those fantastic breasts until you're begging me to touch you absolutely everywhere.

Sent before he could filter the words. Before he could bring things back into a more PG territory. He waited to see her reaction as she read. Would she put on the brakes? Or would she want more?

He took another sip of his drink but nearly choked on it as he read her quick reply:

Once I beg, then what?

His gaze locked with hers across the room and his

body sprang to life. This teasing her was torturing him. He shifted on the seat under her piercing, challenging gaze. No turning back now.

Then I'll remove every piece of clothing between us and press my body to yours.

He watched her cross and uncross her legs and take a bigger gulp of water.

His waiter appeared with his meal, but Dex's appetite for food had vanished. The tightening in the front of his pants made it difficult to think about eating.

Across the restaurant, Skylar's waiter delivered her dinner and she too looked ready to ask for a to-go bag. He waited. If she wanted to leave, he'd happily reheat his food at home later. But she reached for her fork and knife and cut into her chicken. He watched as she lifted the fork to her lips and closed her eyes to savor the taste. She licked the corner of her lips and he felt his own lips part.

Ah, so she was playing her own game. He sat back in his chair as she continued to enjoy her food in the most tantalizing manner possible. He glanced around the restaurant, suddenly feeling protective. No one else better be checking her out.

Skylar's eyes locked with his and her gaze burned through him. Fire in her expression said she was up for anything and everything he was suggesting. She sipped her champagne and ran her tongue along the rim of the glass, and Dex couldn't take anymore. They'd be no enjoying his food until he'd had the pleasure of tasting her.

He flagged for the waiter and sent Skylar a questioning gaze to confirm the dinner portion of this date was over.

She nodded quickly and his mouth went dry as his palms started to sweat.

"Something wrong with the food, sir?" his waiter asked, a knowing look in his expression.

"No, thank you, but something else…came up. Can I get this to go?"

"Absolutely, sir." He reached for Dex's plate and leaned closer, lowering his voice. "And I assume we'll pack up the lady's as well?"

"And bring both bills to me please."

WAITING FIVE MINUTES before joining Dex in the parking lot had taken every ounce of restraint. Skylar's body was on fire and she pressed her legs together once she was in his car. A block away, they parked in the road turnout so the mayor and his wife wouldn't see them when they left the restaurant.

Dex immediately reached for her and it was like they were seventeen again.

Hands groping, mouths crushing, clothes flying off at record speed. His shirt and her sweater tossed into the back seat. Unbuckling his dress pants as he slipped a hand into her leggings. Only Dex had ever had this effect on her. This wild desire to have someone.

Right. Now.

She wrapped her arms around his neck, her breasts confined by the lacy bandeau bra pressed against his bare chest. Her lips against his, she deepened the kiss and moaned. She bit his lower lip, an intense craving for him running through her. Why the hell couldn't she get enough of him?

She'd thought she'd moved on. But if her body's reaction was any indication, she'd only been denying herself.

And now she was bingeing on everything she hadn't allowed herself to have.

She wanted Dex. Bad. Wanted to feel his hands all over her body. Wanted to feel his lips roam every inch of her skin. Wanted to feel him inside her.

This had to be just physical. Once she'd satisfied this urge, that would be it.

Yeah, and Alaska didn't get snow. Who was she kidding? There'd be no closing this Pandora's box.

"Your body feels even more incredible than I remember," Dex said, holding her tight with one arm as his other hand slid the length of her to slip under the bra and massage her breast.

Her breathing was labored as she pulled back to look at him. "Have you thought about..." she wouldn't say "me." That would sound far too desperate. "...this?"

"Only every day for the last six years," he said.

His honesty made her pulse race.

"I thought about this," he said gently. "And I thought about you."

His expression went way beyond lust, and her body stilled. Was it possible that he hadn't let go either? But he'd been the one to end things.

Her heart was pounding so loud, he had to hear it. "Dex..."

He kissed her quickly to cut off her words. "Let's not go back. Let's keep moving forward with the now... What's happening now," he murmured against her lips.

Skylar swallowed hard. Could they do that? Just let go of their shared history? She wasn't sure, but all she wanted was to act on these impulses that were drawing her to him.

She nodded as she pressed her body closer. She dipped

her hand inside his open pants, finding the opening in his briefs and sliding her fingers inside to grip his erection. She stroked slowly and he released a deep growl as he tightened his hold on her. His breathing was labored, the effect she was having on him obvious.

It would be so easy to keep going... Go all the way with him.

But...

"If we're pretending we don't have a history, this would technically be a first date." Her hand stroked the length of him again as she licked his bottom lip suggestively. His Adam's apple bobbed. "And you know I'm not the type to put out on the first date," she said with a sly smile.

He groaned as his grip tightened on her waist and he pressed his forehead against hers. "My own words coming back to cockblock me," he said as he reluctantly released his hold on her.

She laughed as she climbed back onto her own seat. Her pulse still raced and her body demanded a better reason not to be satisfied right this minute, but as much as she wanted him, Skylar knew she had to be careful.

History or not, Dex Wakefield still had her heart. And the ability to break it.

CHAPTER SEVEN

DEX COULDN'T ERASE his smile as he got back to the yacht, carrying the meal he hadn't even touched.

This had been the best night he'd had since Skylar left, and he hummed to himself as he unlocked the cabin door.

The date hadn't exactly gone as planned; it had turned out better than he ever could have imagined. They'd said things in those text messages they might not have had the courage to say sitting across from one another. They'd been honest.

And when things had taken a sexy turn, he hadn't fought it.

Knowing she'd been just as desperate for him only so-lidified his feelings. She could claim to have gotten over him while she was away, but that was bullshit. Holding her, kissing her, touching her had felt like no time at all had passed. And surprisingly, like no heartache or regret lay between the past and now. At least not for him. They were starting off fresh. They didn't need to go back and rehash the past. They'd shared a great night and Dex was desper-ate to keep this momentum.

He flicked on the living room lights.

"Who's Shaylah and why is she excited to come live with you?"

His sister's voice made him jump and nearly drop the takeout container. "What the hell are you doing lurking in the dark like a weirdo?" he asked, fighting to keep his tone free of guilt.

"Don't avoid the question," she said, sending him a look that dared him to lie to her.

He sighed. "Shaylah is a German shepherd pup. A seizure response dog from A Helpful Paw."

Her mouth dropped and her eyes widened. "You bought a dog?"

He headed toward the kitchen and she followed. He set the food on the counter, taking a moment to avoid her gaze. "I told you I was looking into it."

"Looking into it. Not doing it," she said as though the idea was absurd.

He crossed his arms across his chest. "How do you know anything about it anyway?"

Now it was her turn to look guilty. "Your laptop was open on the table and the message popped up on the bottom of the screen. I wasn't snooping," she said defensively.

He hadn't really been trying to hide it from her. Just putting off the argument. His sister's disapproval was a consideration in all of this, but not enough of one to change his mind. He walked toward her and placed his hands on her shoulders. "Can we argue in the morning? I'm beat." And he was trying to maintain the high of being with Skylar. His baby sister's interrogation was destroying his mood.

She looked ready to keep going, but then she paused, sniffing the air around him, sniffing his shirt.

Uh-oh.

Her eyes widened. "You were with Skylar Beaumont."

What the hell? "I don't know what you're…"

"La Vie Est Belle."

"La Vie what?"

She huffed. "It's Skylar's signature scent. I used to like that body lotion too, but now it just makes me break out in hives." She moved away from him and started scratching.

Dramatic as ever.

Dex rolled his eyes. "I'm going to bed." He headed toward the stairs, but she hurried after him.

"Hey! Not so fast! The dog or Skylar—pick one argument to save for tomorrow. The other happens now."

He owed her something after she'd given up living her own life to be there with him. He appreciated her and her sacrifices, and she did deserve to be included in at least one of his recent decisions.

"Isla, the dog make sense," he said, choosing the much easier topic. "You need to be able to live your life and I know you don't want to stay here. I love you, but I don't want a twenty-four-hour—*human*—babysitter." He and the dog would take care of one another. He'd feed, shelter and train Shaylah and give her all the love and affection a dog could ever hope for and Dex wouldn't feel like a burden.

"A dog can only do so much," Isla said, unconvinced.

"*You* can only do so much," he said gently. He walked back toward her.

She plugged her nose and said stuffily, "I can dial 9-1-1 at least. Have you ever seen a dog use a cell phone?"

"Look, I really appreciate you taking time out of your own life to come back here and help. But a year's enough." He paused. "And the dog is really fantastic. Next time I go to the training facility, why don't you come with me? See for yourself."

She folded her arms and narrowed her eyes at him. "You know I won't because I'm allergic."

Kinda what he'd been counting on.

She released a deep breath. "I just think that this might have something to do with Skylar. Maybe her being back in town is making you fast-track the decision without thinking things through."

She might be right that his need for more independence…and his own space…could be because of the appearance of his ex in town and once again in his life, but something had to give him that final push.

He shrugged. "Either way, *that* argument is for tomorrow." He winked at her and kissed her forehead. "Night, sis."

She looked annoyed at not getting her own way, but she grumbled a good night.

"Take a shower at least!" she called up the stairs after him.

And erase the scent of the woman he couldn't get nearly enough of? Not a chance in hell.

SKYLAR WASN'T REGRETTING the date.

It was more a back-and-forth conflict that had plagued her all night as she'd tossed and turned. Conflict about whether she'd been smart to open up to him, about whether putting on the brakes had been the right thing to do.

They'd needed to clear the air to ease the tension since she'd been back. And the make out session had done that… or maybe it had just made the sexual frustration worse. Either way they'd started something that Skylar wasn't ready for.

Forgetting their shared history, moving on from the pain of their past and starting fresh as adults sounded great in theory, but it was difficult to pretend they were just two

people attracted to one another. Things were more complicated than that.

Sitting on a stool behind the counter of the museum, she
clung to her coffee cup like a life preserver.

Carly had been at her book club when Skylar had arrived
home the evening before, and she'd been glad of the opportunity to be alone with her thoughts. She wasn't sure how
her cousin would feel about Dex, and Skylar hadn't wanted
to hear a voice of reason or caution while riding the high
of going to second base with her high school sweetheart.
But in the light of day, she knew she'd want Carly's advice.

"You got home late," she said to Carly as her cousin
placed new Sealena-themed picture books by a local author on the shelf near the window. "Didn't realize book
club was an all-nighter."

Carly laughed. "There was a lively debate about vam-
pires versus werewolves as the hotter shapeshifters in romance that got a little rowdy. As a werewolf supporter, I
had to stay for the final verdict."

"And?"

"Werewolves won hands down," she said as though it
should have been obvious. She positioned the "new release" sign behind the table, then eyed her. "Did you go
out with the crew?"

Her cousin's tone was casual, but Skylar sensed something was up. Should she tell her cousin or keep things to
herself a bit longer?

"Just a friend…"

Carly's grin was wide. "You mean an old flame?"

Skylar groaned at her cousin's perceptiveness. "That
obvious, huh?"

"Let's just say, I recognize this guilty, lovelorn look on

your face." She hurried over, poured herself a fresh cup of coffee and pulled up a stool next to Skylar. "Tell me everything."

Skylar sighed, weighing just how much to reveal. What was less incriminating—the make out session or the vulnerability they'd both displayed? "Honestly, it feels like we picked up right where we left off, sneaking around. Feels like high school senior year all over again."

Carly's gaze was wistful. "It's kinda romantic."

Maybe when they were kids, but now it was just a bad idea. "But mostly complicated, headed straight for disaster, right?"

"I'm not exactly the best one to give you advice about practicality when it comes to matters of the heart." Her gaze shifted across the store just as Oliver Klein and his daughter, Tess, entered. Immediately her cousin's cheeks flushed and she ran a hand through her hair before waving at the father and daughter.

"Hey, guys!"

Oliver's face lit up, and the two seemed to share a moment of connection that would go unnoticed by anyone other than Skylar.

Was there something going on between her cousin and the town's lighthouse keeper? Oliver was a widower now. Carly had been best friends with his wife, Alison, until she and their older daughter, Catherine went missing at sea on one of the calmest days of the year two summers ago.

A tragic mystery that had stunned the entire town. Alison was a competent sailor who practically lived on the water. She was a nurse and a strong swimmer. She and Catherine knew the safety precautions on the ocean... Yet, the boat had been discovered empty miles off shore and their bodies had never been found.

Oliver hadn't been the same since, but he was valiantly raising his younger daughter alone.

"Hey, guys. Nice to see you both again," Skylar said with a smile.

"Great to have you home," Oliver said. "Congratulations on the posting."

"Thank you," she said. She appreciated it, but she imagined Oliver's low opinion of the coast guard hadn't changed. He didn't blame them for never finding his wife and daughter, but they had never been able to give the widower closure.

"What brings you two in?" Carly said, a mischievous gleam in her eye.

Tess hurried to hug her. "Are they here yet?" The little girl was practically buzzing with excitement.

Carly's expression was almost as bright. "They just came in," she said, taking the little girl's hand and leading her to the stack of books she'd just finished displaying.

"A Sealena fan?" Skylar asked Oliver.

"She insisted she needed this book immediately," Oliver said, eyeing the Sealena cover with a little disdain. Skylar suspected the Serpent Queen rightly had some explaining to do in the lighthouse keeper's opinion too.

But Tess reached for a copy and hugged it to her chest. "Mine!"

Carly laughed, then shook her head. "I think I actually have something better behind the counter."

Tess's big green eyes widened then she looked dubious. "Better? Good luck, Carly," she said but she followed, taking the book with her.

Skylar suspected it would take the jaws of life to extract the book from the little girl's arms.

Carly winked at Oliver as she retrieved another copy of the same book from behind the counter and handed it to the little girl.

Tess frowned. "It's the same book."

"Is it?" Carly asked. "Look inside."

Tess opened the cover flap and Skylar hadn't thought it was possible, but her eyes lit up even more as she read. "To Tess, the Sealena expert I someday hope to be." Her little mouth dropped. "It's signed by the author!" She excitedly told her dad.

"Wow, that's wonderful." Oliver sent Carly an appreciative look.

"Isn't Carly the best?" Tess said, flipping through the book.

"She's quite something," Oliver said, his gaze lingering on Carly for a beat.

Her cousin's attention was focused on the little girl and she obviously didn't catch the way he looked at her.

"Quite something. What the hell does that even mean?" she asked Skylar the moment Oliver and Tess left the store. She tore open another box of books and started rage-stacking them on the shelf.

Skylar laughed. "You two definitely have something going on. When did this happen?"

"It's not happening," Carly said, sounding distraught. "I mean, we do this annoying little dance around it but nothing actually happens."

"Maybe he's not ready?" It had been two years, but Skylar wasn't sure time could really erase a loss like that. She'd carried a lot of hurt around for a long time and she and Dex had only ended a relationship…nothing like the grief Oliver had suffered.

"He's definitely not ready. Thing is, I don't think he ever will be."

"Have you told him how you feel?" Skylar asked gently. "Maybe he needs you to make the first move."

Carly shook her head. "No. I've been close a few times, but I can't bring myself to do it. Alison was my best friend and these feelings for Oliver came out of nowhere. It doesn't feel right to move forward. There's Tess to think about…" She sighed. "I think we're destined to just be friends. Best thing for all of us."

Skylar nodded slowly. She sympathized with Carly's situation. She and Dex were complicated, but Carly's dilemma seemed impossible.

DEX WAITED UNTIL he heard Isla leave before getting out of bed. He couldn't avoid the discussion about Skylar forever, but he was still feeling good about their date and he didn't need his sister ruining it. He knew he could be setting himself up for new heartache, but he was willing to risk it.

Pulling on a pair of old sweats and a T-shirt, he jogged down the stairs to the kitchen. Fresh-brewed coffee and the unmistakable scent of cinnamon rolls hit him and he sighed seeing the sticky note next to his coffee mug:

Can a dog bake your favorite breakfast?

Pouring coffee into the mug, he took a sip and then bit into a still-warm roll, closing his eyes to savor the taste of cinnamon and sugar on his tongue.

His sister did have a point.

He carried the breakfast to the table and sat at his open laptop. Clicking on the Epilepsy Foundation's website, he noticed new messages in his support chat inbox. He opened it and saw a new one from Marcus.

Long time, just checking in...

Marcus was the person the organization had paired him with after his diagnosis. The other man had been living with the same condition for ten years and at first Dex had been reluctant to talk about his experiences and fears with a stranger...with anyone. But he'd quickly appreciated the gentle encouragement and support he'd received from Marcus. He always remembered the first thing the man had told him when he'd talked about his future and how his illness might derail his plans.

You can still have everything you want, Dex. You just need to know it won't always be easy, and then do it anyway.

Marcus's words had helped him when he was lost, in those first few months following his diagnosis. When his world had been turned upside down and his life had completely changed...

He remembered thinking that it had to be unsafe how red his father's face was when he entered the house an hour late.

A wise seventeen-year-old would have been worried he was about to be grounded all summer, but Dex was flying so high from his afternoon with Skylar on Fishermen's Peak that nothing—not even his father's wrath—could bring him down. It was a struggle to keep the smile off his face while his dad reamed him out.

"You're going to miss warmup," Brian Wakefield said, pacing the foyer with Dex's football gear already packed, the big duffel bag slung over his shoulder as he checked his expensive watch.

Dex kicked off his sandals and grabbed his running shoes from the closet. "Not if you let me drive."

Okay, maybe that was the wrong thing to say.

Who could have known his father could look even more furious?

How upset would he be when Dex told him he wasn't planning on going to university on the football scholarship he'd been awarded?

"That's a good idea," his mother said appearing in the door frame of the living room. She tossed him a pair of socks and he shot her a doubly grateful look. She always had his back. While he and his dad had shared interests in sports and cars, he was definitely closer to his mom. They had the same sense of humor and she was less intense than his father. Easier on him with fewer expectations.

"He doesn't have his license yet," his father said.

"He has a permit."

And next week was his driver's test. Only another seven days until he could drive his father's Jeep alone with his friends. With Skylar...

He blushed and avoided his father's gaze thinking about the things he wanted to do to her in that back seat. That summer was going to be epic. He had so much that he wanted to do with his newfound freedom, enjoying the last few months in his small hometown before they ventured out together.

Hopping on one foot, he struggled to put on his socks, then shoved his feet into his running shoes.

"See? Ready," he told his dad. His father was stressing about nothing. He still had ten minutes to make it to the school football field and it was only a three-minute drive away. Nothing was far in Port Serenity.

"Almost ready," his mother amended. She turned her cheek toward him and he kissed her, wondering if she could smell the sweet, definitely female scent still lingering on his clothes, in his hair, on his skin. *He* could and he hated that in twenty minutes, his own sweat would overpower the nicer fragrance.

His mother studied him a fraction of a second, then a knowing gleam reflected in her eyes.

Shit. His mother knew where he'd been and who he'd been with. She always knew. As kids, he and Isla believed that she was psychic. They couldn't get away with anything under her watchful eye.

She held him a second longer and said, "Be careful."

He nodded as his father tossed his football gear at his feet. "Let's go."

Dex bent to pick up the bag, oddly comforted by the thought that she did know and obviously wasn't upset...just cautioning him. She didn't have to worry. He would always be careful with Skylar. Her body, her heart, her feelings.

He loved her and that day had only intensified their connection.

He bent to pick up the bag, a new smile forming on his face.

And then everything went black.

He preferred his father's angry expression to the one he was wearing when Dex opened his eyes. He blinked to focus as both of his parents moved closer to the...hospital bed?

He'd passed out. The last thing he remembered was reaching to pick up his football gear. He tried to sit up, but his mother quickly touched his shoulder. "Just relax, sweetheart."

He was hooked to monitors and an IV.

What the hell was going on? He'd just passed out. Low blood sugar or something, it was no big deal. He had to get to the game. While he wasn't planning on accepting the football scholarship, as star quarterback, he still had a team to carry to the state championships. He wouldn't let them down.

"What happened?" He touched his aching head and discovered a bandage around it. Had he hit his head when he fell? He'd had worse head injuries playing football. Why did his parents look so freaked out?

"You blacked out," his mother said slowly.

He nodded. "Yeah…weird. Low blood pressure or something? I hadn't eaten much today." He'd been far too nervous that morning to have breakfast, and although they'd packed a picnic lunch, he and Skylar had been occupied with other things…

His mother looked apprehensive. "The doctors want to keep you in for a few hours though, to run a few tests."

"Dad, sorry I missed practice," he said, watching his father pace the room. His father always said there was no excuse not to follow through on commitments. He'd instilled the importance of showing up from a young age, and Dex suspected his dad was pissed about the important end-of-season game.

So, when his father approached and laid a hand on his shoulder and said, "Football's not important right now, just rest," Dex knew something bad must have happened while he'd been out.

Something really bad.

And sure enough, he learned soon what it was. Seizures. Not a blackout. A CT scan, an MRI and a very unpleasant lumbar puncture later, they'd discovered the suspected cause: a tiny lesion on his temporal lobe.

It explained a lot. Apparently he'd been suffering mini seizures they called auras for weeks without realizing it. He'd been feeling dizzy and nauseated and had a few headaches lately, but he'd assumed it was just the pressure of having to tell his parents and Skylar's parents the truth soon. The pressure of the upcoming end-of-term exams and graduation, applying to the academy, the football championships. He'd thought it was normal.

The last action movie he'd watched with a ton of explosions had triggered an aura and he hadn't realized what had happened at the time. But now it all made sense.

"We'll set up an appointment with a neurologist, but in the meantime, we will start treatment with medication right away," his doctor said. "It might take several months to find the right one and the right dosage, so we need to be patient."

He needed to be patient.

"Will he experience more seizures in the meantime," his mother asked.

The doctor nodded. "Likely. The auras will probably continue but hopefully the grand mal seizure he experienced will be the only one. Many people have at least one in their lifetime without even knowing it. We will monitor Dex and see how the condition progresses."

"Are there side effects to the medication?" His mother's worry was putting Dex even more on edge. She sat wringing her hands, perched at the edge of the chair as though she was fighting the urge to flee.

Dex was numb.

"The medication has been known to cause fatigue, body rashes, speech confusion…"

As the doctor rattled through the list of possible side effects, Dex's pulse raced. He didn't want rashes covering his body. He'd look horrible. What would Skylar think? He wouldn't want to take his clothes off in front of her and they'd just started getting naked together and he really didn't want that to stop.

And speech confusion? That sounded worse than the blackouts.

He blinked. "Can I go back to playing football?" he asked, interrupting.

The doctor shook his head. "I wouldn't advise it."

"But he can?" his father said.

"Brian!"

His father stood and sighed. He ran a hand through his hair as he paced behind their chairs. "I'm just saying— I'm sure Dex doesn't plan on letting this derail his plans... He has a huge football scholarship," he told the doctor as though that might change his prognosis. "I'm sure he doesn't want to throw that away."

At least his condition would be to blame for breaking his father's heart, not Dex's decision to go into the academy with Skylar...because that wasn't happening anymore. Football might still be an option, but he knew without asking that any application to the coast guard wouldn't be approved now.

His stomach turned, and this time his nausea wasn't from an aura, but dark, crushing disappointment.

The future his father wanted for him was disappearing right alongside the future Dex had wanted for himself.

After that day in the doctor's office, it had taken over a year to regain the motivation to continue his life as best he could. With the support of his family and Marcus, he'd realized he could still do anything he wanted…

In a different way.

The volunteer rescue boat had been a step in living his life the way he wanted. On his terms. The new dog was another one… He still needed his meds, and he would always have restrictions on what he could do, but he'd overcome his grief. He'd accepted things as they were and he'd discovered a different way to be happy, to live the life he wanted.

Could he find a different way to make things work with the love of his life as well?

CHAPTER EIGHT

SITTING AT HER desk later that day, Skylar scanned the job posting board on the coast guard's internal site, just as she had every day since receiving her post in Port Serenity. This time her stomach twisted slightly, and she wasn't sure why. She forced the uneasiness away as she scrolled through the available positions. Mostly higher-level opportunities or civilian postings...

But her heart nearly stopped seeing one posted just three hours before.

Captain position on a ninety-foot cutter in California.

She clicked on the link and reading the description quickly, she knew she met the qualifications. This was exactly the opportunity she'd been hoping would pop up. Instinctively, she clicked on the apply link and then hesitated.

Could she really apply? She wanted to, but she'd only been on active duty for a few weeks. Would it seem presumptuous or viewed as not being committed to her postings if she jumped ship this quickly? Would it seem as though she wasn't loyal? Or would it seem ambitious?

And what would her crew here think? She'd just started settling in, gaining their trust... But this happened all the time. People were transferred, they moved, they advanced in their careers often not in the same place. Everyone would understand.

Three days ago she'd never have doubted herself. She

knew what was really holding her back. She couldn't let whatever this was with Dex throw her off course. This was what she'd wanted. It was *still* what she wanted.

And applying didn't mean she'd get it or have to accept it if it was offered...

Clicking on the first field, she typed in her information, refusing to overthink it further.

"Knock, knock," Doug's voice in the office door behind her made her minimize the site quickly.

She felt a tug of guilt as she turned to face him. "Hey, what's up?"

"Sorry if I interrupted you," he said, nodding toward the computer screen.

Shit, had he seen the site?

She cleared her throat and shook her head. "Not at all. Door's always open." Though maybe when she was applying for a new posting, she should close it.

"I just wanted to invite you over. Sorry for the late notice, but a bunch of us are getting together to watch a movie at my place."

Skylar frowned. "Oh yeah?"

"Yeah, the indie thriller that my boyfriend, Jay, shot here in Alaska. The crew and I were in a few scenes."

"Oh right!" She'd heard about the movie and how well it had done on the film festival circuit.

"Anyway, Jay's in town and we thought we'd have everyone over to watch it together. I've seen a director's cut, but most of the crew haven't seen it yet."

"Sounds great," she said.

Doug smiled. "Great. See you around eight?"

She nodded. "I'll be there."

Doug went to leave, but turned back. "Oh, uh... Dex will

be there too. Hope that won't be awkward with your family history," he said, studying her. He looked a little suspicious, as though he knew there was something going on and he was weighing her answer to confirm it.

She shook her head a little too quickly and forced the most neutral expression she could muster. "No...that's totally fine. Dex and I can be in the same room together." *And keep our hands off one another*, she hoped. "I mean, he's always around...like a persistent fly..."

Doug eyed her with a hint of amusement. "Right...so it's cool then."

"Absolutely. So cool, it's cold." *Oh my God, shut up, Skylar!*

"Perfect," Doug said as he walked away.

Skylar released a deep sigh and let her head fall forward onto her desk. She had to talk Dex out of going or the crew would be onto them within seconds. Doug had clearly not been fooled.

How they'd successfully hidden their relationship years before was a mystery.

"I DON'T THINK you should come," Skylar said, climbing onto the stool across from him in the empty bar. Dressed in her uniform, she'd obviously rushed over to the Serpent Queen Pub on her lunch break to talk him out of attending that evening. He'd been expecting her since receiving Doug's text giving him a heads-up that Skylar would be in attendance as well.

And damn, if she wasn't hot as hell. He'd never get tired of seeing her in uniform. The silent authority radiating from her was a huge turn-on.

He grinned as he unloaded the dishwasher behind the

bar. He wasn't an official employee, but Dollie often put him to work whenever he stopped in. "I was invited."

She bit her bottom lip. "I just think it will be hard to act like we're not together. Not give off a vibe. I think Doug already suspects there's something going on."

"The guys will think it's weird if I don't show up." He didn't care if everyone knew about them. And she was right, it was going to be difficult to conceal his attraction to her. He couldn't promise to try very hard. "*You* don't go."

She frowned. "I have to. The movie features *my* crew."

"They weren't your crew when the movie was made."

She looked like she wanted to lean across the bar and strangle him. "Still, I have to be supportive."

"Guess we're both going then," he said with a wink.

"You're infuriating," she said.

"That's what you love about me," he said leaning on the bar and gripping the front of her shirt to pull her in for a kiss.

Her eyes widened slightly, but the bar was empty, so she quickly gave in, wrapping her arms around his neck and pressing her lips to his.

Damn, he wished there wasn't a bar between them. She smelled and tasted so good as he deepened the kiss and separated her lips with his tongue. She was right. Being together that evening among the group, it was going to be impossible to conceal their attraction. It was going to be torture not being able to touch her, kiss her, hold her... He pulled away and stared into her gorgeous, flustered expression.

"Or we could both not go?" he said with a suggestive grin.

She looked severely tempted, but then sighed as she moved away. "I guess I'll see you tonight."

He appreciated the sight of her hips swaying as she headed toward the door. She turned back as she reached it. "Just try to behave, okay?"

"Where would be the fun in that?"

"Dex…"

He laughed. "Don't worry. I'll behave, but I won't like it."

A TON OF PEOPLE were already crammed into Doug's small living room hours later when she entered. She counted seventeen sitting on sofas, chairs and cushions on the floor, and everyone looked eager to see the film. Bowls of popcorn were placed on the tables and a cooler of drinks sat in the middle of the floor.

This movie was a big deal. The indie film had won dozens of awards on the film festival circuit. The leads had won for best actors and the director, Jay Kline, was an overnight success now.

He must be the man cuddled next to Doug on the loveseat, wearing leopard print leggings and an oversized orange sweater.

Skylar smiled. She knew how difficult it had been for Doug to come out and she was so happy he was happy. He was with the love of his life. The long-distance relationship seemed to be going well with Jay traveling to Alaska from LA whenever he wasn't filming a new project. He'd been getting busier lately though according to Doug and Skylar sensed it might eventually take a toll.

Long-distance relationships weren't impossible but they weren't easy…

She glanced at Dex who was pretending not to notice that she'd arrived. Could they make something like that work?

It would be easier to hide their relationship…but based on how the sight of him in his ripped jeans and sexy, worn black T-shirt had her wanting to tear his clothes off, she suspected thousands of miles between them wouldn't work in their case. Not that there weren't other layers to the relationship, but the physical was a big part of it.

"Hey, you made it," Doug said, noticing her.

She forced her gaze away from Dex and smiled at her host. "I'm excited to see the film."

"We're just about to start. Find a seat."

Skylar scanned the room. The only available spots were on bean bag chairs in the back. Two of them, side by side. She narrowed her eyes at Dex as he made his way toward one and motioned that the other was hers for the taking. The grin on his face was infuriatingly sexy. He was enjoying this way too much. So much for behaving himself.

He'd obviously orchestrated this, though he shot her an innocent look as she plopped onto the beanbag next to him.

"Did you have something to do with this?" she whispered.

He shuffled his seat closer. "Yep."

"I thought we were trying to keep things on the downlow."

"News flash—no one's paying attention to us," he said.

Skylar looked around. He was right. Everyone was caught up in their own conversations, laughing and drinking, eating popcorn. It felt kinda egotistical, the more she thought about it. Their relationship might be a big deal to them, but maybe people in town wouldn't care as much as she'd always thought. Not everything revolved around the Wakefields and Beaumonts and the silly family feud.

She released a deep breath and sank back into the chair,

but then her heart stopped when she saw someone with light pink hair on the sofa. It could only belong to one woman. She grabbed Dex's sleeve and whispered, "What is Isla doing here? I thought this was a movie premiere for the crew."

Dex shrugged. "She's dating Dwayne."

Of course she was dating the playboy bachelor helicopter pilot. Isla had always been drawn to the bad-boy adventurous type. In high school she'd dated every single guy that Dex warned her against. It was like she felt a magnetic pull toward drama.

And there would definitely be drama now if Isla saw her.

Luckily, she hadn't seemed to notice Skylar's arrival as she was currently involved a verbal sparring match with Aaron Segura about BASE jumping. A familiar sight. Since grade school, the two seemed to bicker whenever they were forced to share the same air.

"It's just ridiculous to put yourself in these dangerous situations," the coast guard rescue swimmer said. He was leaning forward, elbows resting on his knees as he debated the issue.

"It's called extreme sports for a reason," Isla countered. "It's no different than sky diving or parasailing, bungee jumping..."

Aaron nodded. "Exactly. *All* a bad idea."

"Oh my God, be more boring!" Isla rolled her eyes.

Aaron's jaw clenched as he inched even closer to her. "Hey, I'm the one who has to put my neck on the line to rescue your ass when things go sideways," he said jabbing a finger into his chest.

Isla raised her chin defiantly in challenge. "And when have you ever had to rescue me?"

Aaron's jaw tightened. "I'm just waiting for the call."

An intense stare down had the entire room expecting the argument to escalate to either a fist fight or a make out session. The tension simmering between the two was thick in the air. And Skylar had been worried about her and Dex's sexual chemistry being a focus. They had nothing on Isla and Aaron.

"Okay, you two, we get it—you love to disagree," Dwayne said with a tense-sounding laugh, wrapping an arm around Isla that looked more possessive than affectionate.

Obviously, Skylar wasn't the only one to notice the chemistry.

Isla shot her date a quick smile, but Skylar suspected she wasn't loving having her spirited debate cut short by the man. Isla wasn't the type to take shit from anyone. No doubt, this would be the last date with Dwayne.

Doug stood to address the room and everyone turned their attention to him.

"Thanks for coming everyone! I know some of you have seen the film already, but this is the new theatrical cut that Jay and his team have created for release later this year." Doug looked so proud of his partner and Skylar's heart swelled as they all applauded.

Jay stood and gave a mock bow. "It includes more of the coast guard scenes as well because they definitely made the movie feel authentic. Big thanks to all of you."

A silence fell over the group as the lights were dimmed and Doug started the movie—a thriller about a woman on the run from her abusive husband. Selena Hudson, the former rom-com queen, was starring in her new genre debut.

Skylar tried to relax but Dex's leg leaning casually against hers created tingles throughout her entire body.

He looked amazing in those ripped jeans and black tee. The smell of his cologne filled her senses, tempting her far more than the scent of popcorn.

She glanced his way at the same time he glanced toward her and their eyes met. His expression said he'd rather be somewhere alone together. The feeling was mutual.

But she turned her attention back to the screen, determined to pay attention. They were there to support Doug and Jay. She could keep her hormones in check for…two hours and twenty-seven minutes? Damn, why did this version have to be the extended director's cut?

She felt Dex reach for her hand. She swallowed hard as his thumb gently rubbed the back of her hand, before his fingers slowly interlaced with hers.

This was a bad idea, but they were seated in the back and everyone was watching the movie. The simple sensation of holding his hand in the dark filled her with an intense intimacy that went even deeper than their frantic make out session in his car. She'd always loved holding his hand. So big and strong, hers felt so tiny in comparison. It had always made her feel safe and protected. That same feeling enveloped her now.

Dex squeezed tight and she returned the gesture. Then he made a series a small squeezes in succession. One. Pause. One two three four. Pause. Then, one two three.

Her heart raced at the familiar code they'd used in private in situations when they couldn't talk, like at a school assembly. The code meant a one-letter word, followed by a four-letter word, followed by a three-letter word.

I love you?

Her mouth was dry as her mind reeled. Was he serious, or was he simply testing her to see if she remembered the old gesture? Should she signal back? Was she ready to say those words to him again?

Before she could contemplate her move, Doug stood and paused the movie. He addressed the crowd. "Here it comes," he said excitedly. "This is our scene." He resumed his position next to Jay and hit Play.

Skylar released Dex's hand and sat forward, desperate to focus on the action and hoping he didn't recognize her chickening out. She needed time to process. If they kept going at this breakneck speed, they were headed straight for a crash.

She watched as the crew and the cast acted out Alice's getaway scene. A real emergency had occurred during the filming and they'd used some of that footage. Pride swelled in Skylar's chest as she watched.

This was her crew.

For how long? Her gut twisted.

She hadn't wanted to be back in Port Serenity, but now that she was here, she realized she was proud to be stationed in her hometown. She liked her crew and she knew her surroundings, the ocean in Alaska and the coastline, better than anywhere else in the world.

What would it be like in a different state, on a different ocean? With strangers as crewmates and different people to protect?

She'd been eager for that experience before, but now... maybe there was a comfort in the known.

Was it a comfort that she wanted?

The sound of everyone cheering an hour later had her blinking alert. It was over. She'd barely paid attention to the rest of it.

"You okay?" Dex whispered as they stood. He looked uneasy as he studied her.

She nodded. "Yeah. Fine." No doubt he thought her pensiveness had to do with the hand squeeze. She'd practically ignored him after the rescue scene as she'd battled her unexpected uncertainty. She wanted to reassure him that it wasn't him…or at least not all of it, but everyone was dispersing so she tried to act casual as she said her goodbyes. She avoided Isla's pointed glare and escaped the house.

Predictably, Dex was right on her heels as she walked down Doug's driveway. "Meet you on the pier in ten minutes?" he whispered.

She wanted to say no. She was a bit of a mess, suddenly unsure of the life plan she'd been certain of.

"I have an early morning crew meeting…" A weak excuse said with absolutely no conviction.

"Please. Just a quick walk," Dex said with concern.

She sighed and nodded. "One quick walk."

ONE QUICK WALK.

Dex paced the pier eight minutes later, waiting for Skylar. The marina was quiet at that time of night and only the sound of the gently lapping waves competed with the pounding of his heart. He scanned the street for headlights approaching.

Would she show up? What the hell had happened? Was it because of the old hand squeeze? It was the first way he'd told her he loved her when he was too nervous to say the words out loud. She'd easily broken the code and understood what the series of squeezes had meant. That first time years ago, she'd returned the message. But this time, she'd gone cold. He'd felt the sudden change in her, seated next to him on the bean bag chairs.

Too much, too soon. Unfortunately, he wasn't sure how to slow down. He had the same feelings for her he'd always had. Now, they were even more intense. He'd had six years to get over her and it seemed like his heart hadn't even tried.

He wanted to be with her. In every way.

He checked his watch. Twelve minutes. Skylar was never late for anything, and Doug's house was only five minutes away. She wasn't coming.

Head down, Dex started walking alone along the pier. He still needed the walk to clear his head, attempt to put things into perspective, fight the tightness that was gathering in his chest.

"Giving up on me?" she asked.

Her voice behind him made him stop and turn. "Never," he said with a light smile that belied the thick emotion threatening to strangle him. "Thought maybe you'd changed your mind," he said.

About the walk. About them.

Her chest rose and fell in a deep sigh. "No."

That wasn't entirely convincing, but she was there and he hoped she'd open up about what was going through her mind.

She fell into step next to him as they headed down the deserted, tranquil pier, only the moon and the beam from the lighthouse lighting their way.

Reach for her hand?

Better not. He'd let her make the first move this time. But he let his hang at his sides, just in case.

"Nice night," she said, her gaze drifting out over the ocean.

He nodded, surveying the boats along the dock in the distance. "This time of year is just right. Not too hot, not too cold. No tourists yet." It was the perfect pace before the busy tourist season. His favorite time of year. Though, the last six years, this time had always held a faint feeling of loss and longing. A reminder of this time six years before when his life had changed.

But this season, Skylar was here with him again and he was once again taking steps toward changing his life.

Should he tell her what happened back then? The longer he kept it from her, the harder it would be to open up about it. He was ready to be completely vulnerable with her. It was what was needed if they could really move forward with a relationship.

He cleared his throat, but she spoke first.

"I applied for a position in California," she said.

His stomach dropped, even though he'd suspected it was her plan. He *was* surprised that she was telling him. Was she warning him that things between them had to remain casual because she was leaving? Or letting him down gently now before things moved further?

"You've always wanted to go to California," he said, unsure how else to respond.

She nodded. "I did, yeah… Do," she corrected quickly. There was definitely apprehension in her tone now.

"But…" He held his breath. Could this thing with them be causing her to have doubts?

"It's just…the crew."

Right, the crew. This wasn't at all about him and he had to stop getting his hopes up.

"I've gotten close to them and I feel like I'm making headway gaining their trust and respect."

"I'm sure that would be true wherever you were. You're great at your career, Sky, and you'd do great anywhere." Not that he wanted her to go but he needed her to feel supported in any decision she made. And it was the truth. Skylar Beaumont would succeed anywhere.

She glanced appreciatively at him. "But I just don't want them to feel abandoned, you know... I don't want to hurt... anyone."

Were they still talking about the crew?

"I mean, I'm applying for a transfer because it's something I've always wanted to do...not because I'm unhappy here," she said.

"I'm sure they'll understand."

She stared at the ground. "And of course there's my dad to consider. I know he wants me here, but I've always wanted to create my own path."

"I know that. And so does your father. He won't be surprised that you want to try something different, explore other places. That's always been the dream." One he'd shared with her. One he'd still share if he could. He paused. "Bottom line is, you're ambitious and career driven and no one could or would fault you for that."

"You sure?"

"Absolutely." Her rare showing of self-doubt made him forget all his own concerns, desperate to make sure she didn't lose faith in herself. He stopped and took her hand. "Everyone is happy you're back. I'm happy you're back. For whatever amount of time it is, I'll take it." He cleared his throat. "And so will everyone else." He added because this wasn't just about him. Not entirely at least.

Her eyes held so much uncertainty. He felt it too. Where they went from here was a mystery. He knew what he wanted, what he'd always wanted, but as before, he couldn't and wouldn't stop her from living her own life. Even if that didn't include him. He stared into her eyes, waiting for her to decide what came next.

"Should we head back?" she asked.

His heart sank, but he hid his disappointment. "It is getting late. I guess we should call it a night." He started walking back toward the pier, but she reached out for his arm. He turned and saw her usual confidence again. And the attraction.

"I meant back to the yacht," she said softly.

He swallowed hard. "Yeah, that's definitely a better idea."

CHAPTER NINE

WAS IT A better idea?

Skylar had no idea. That day it seemed impossible to make a decision regarding her career—or her heart. There were so many emotions involved in both, and she didn't know which ones she should listen to.

Her career was only partially in her hands. She'd applied for the position earlier that day, now she had to wait. She wouldn't need to decide unless she got offered the transfer.

Her heart was another matter completely. When she wasn't with Dex, it was easier to keep a clear head. They had a shared history. They still had attraction for one another. And she still had deep feelings for him. But the things that had kept them apart years before hadn't evaporated.

They seemed to still be at the same standstill.

But when she was with him, none of that seemed to matter, as the attraction overwhelmed her, clouded her judgment.

Like now...

Sitting on the oversized plush lounger on the upper deck of the yacht, Dex pulled her onto his lap and draped a blanket over them. He nuzzled her neck and Skylar's eyes closed as she savored the sensations flowing. His hands on her body had the same effect they always had. She craved it all. Craved him.

She cuddled into him as she turned to stare at the cloudless sky above. A million stars as far as the eye could see. She'd missed calm, clear Alaskan nights like this. There was something magical about the salty air, the gentle sway of the boat and the sky and ocean meeting on the horizon. The dark shadows of mountains and the wilderness surrounding them gave her a sense of peace. This was once her home.

Though the feel of Dex's body beneath her was rivaling the relaxing environment.

He gripped her waist, holding her close to his and she felt the reaction she was having on him. She pushed her hips harder against him and he bit her earlobe. Her body instantly heated and she turned her face toward his, lifting her chin to invite the kiss she'd been wanting all evening.

He lowered his head toward her and when his lips met hers, she stifled a moan. He tasted so good and smelled so good and felt so freaking good. She pressed her hands against his sculpted chest, enjoying the feel of his muscles beneath the thin shirt.

The kiss was soft, gentle at first, but quickly became more desperate, filled with the passion that always ignited when they were together. She couldn't get enough of him as she deepened the kiss, exploring his mouth with her tongue. She longed for satiation, but the more she kissed him, the more she wanted. He was dangerously addictive, a habit she never wanted to break. She wrapped her arms around his neck and pressed her body into him as her hands tangled in his hair.

Sexual frustration was something she'd never experienced with anyone else, but it was driving her to the brink right now. This desperate need to be fulfilled. The satisfaction of release eluding her despite the kissing and touching.

She needed more.

Dex pulled away and sucked in a deep breath. "Damn, Skylar, you are driving me wild," he growled. "I can't get enough of you."

She swallowed hard. "Tell me about it," she said almost grumpily. Why couldn't this intense longing and desire ease up?

He rotated her body and slid his hands up under her sweater as she lay back against him. His fingers inched higher over her stomach and rib cage, then fondled her breasts through the fabric of her silky bra. She swallowed hard as her body vibrated with a newfound awakening. Every nerve ending seemed to be tingling under his touch. He pinched her nipples and she felt herself grow wet between her legs. She moaned as he pinched harder, the pleasurable pain making her breath escape in small, frantic pants. It had been so long since she'd been this turned on and she knew it had everything to do with this man. No one had ever had the effect on her that Dex did. The power to command her body and heart had only ever belonged to him.

Burying his face in the crook of her neck, he slowly slid one hand back down her stomach, to the top of her leggings. He wiggled his fingers under the fabric and continued to move lower. Beneath her underwear.

She opened her thighs wider to give him access and he took his time, inching so slowly.

"Dex, I need you. Need this." She couldn't conceal her desperation for him. She didn't want to. She might not have her emotions figured out, but what she wanted physically was pretty damn clear. There was no denying herself this pleasure.

He continued to kiss her neck and squeeze her breast, but his other hand stilled on her mound. He applied pressure there with the heel of his hand, but didn't go any lower.

She swallowed hard, desperate for the feel of his fingers inside of her. But he kept teasing, circling the skin just above the opening with his thumb.

"Dex, please…"

He pinched her nipple as he slowly continued his trek lower with the other hand. He sucked gently at her collarbone as his finger slid along her folds. "So wet," he whispered, his voice thick with desire.

"Oh my god…" The feel of his touch was incredible. She was so wet and ready for him, but he took his time. Tightening and releasing her vaginal muscles did nothing to ease the throbbing intensity. She reached for his hand to guide him, but he gently shook her off.

"Not so fast," he whispered in her ear and his breath on her skin made her shiver. "I want to drive you wild, make you crave this."

She was already there. Her body was aching with the insatiable yearning. She tried squeezing her thighs back together to ease the ache, but he slipped his legs between hers from underneath, interlocking their ankles, holding her wide open.

"How badly do you want it, Skylar?" he asked.

"Bad. Very bad," she said. She reached for his hand again and covering it, she maneuvered his fingers to where she needed them most.

Finally, he slid one inside her body and a moan escaped her. She turned her head to him, and his mouth instantly crushed hers. He kissed her with urgency as he plunged another finger into her.

She explored every part of his mouth with her tongue, pressing her body as close as she could, driving her ass and hips down into him, feeling his erection build under her.

Dex inserted a third finger and moved in and out of her body, almost urgently. Frantic.

She was panting against his mouth as she felt the orgasm rise within her core. "I'm close, Dex," she said against his mouth.

He slowed to a torturous tempo. In and out. His thumb pressed against her clit as his fingers continued to fuck her slowly. She was dizzy with the overwhelming sensations flowing through her. She wanted him so badly. Now. Forever. Over and over again. She'd never get enough of him. How on earth could she walk away from him? But how could they make this work? Was there a way she could have everything she wanted?

"Please, Dex…faster."

He picked up the pace again, plunging deeper, harder into her. "Damn, Skylar, you're so wet, so sexy. I want to be inside of you so bad." He took her hand and placed it over his straining cock, still hidden in his jeans. The idea that he was as close as she was with barely any touching, only through what he was doing to her, made her that much more turned on.

She massaged him through the fabric of his jeans and he quickened his pace even more.

In and out. Hard and fast.

She clung to him and kissed him ravenously as her orgasm erupted and she let out a muffled scream. She trembled with release as she collapsed against him and he slipped his fingers out of her.

She expected a sense of relief, but all she felt was more

desire. Wanted to touch him, kiss him, pleasure him as much as he'd pleasured her. She kissed him again before pulling back and looking at him. Staring deep into his eyes, she unbuttoned his jeans and slid her hand beneath his underwear.

He was so hard, the tip of his cock wet with precum.

It was so sexy and she felt herself instantly ready for him again. She wrapped her hand around the base of his cock and slowly stroked up and down. Gently, applying a light pressure to tease him as he'd teased her.

"Skylar, this is torture," he groaned.

"Now you know how I felt," she said with a wicked grin as she continued to tease him with her touch, pulling his underwear down.

She rolled her thumb along the tip, using the precum as lubricant as she tightened her grip and continued to stroke up and down over the shaft. He was so big and so hard. She wanted him inside of her. It had been far too long since she'd had him… If she left, when would she ever have him again?

"Skylar, please go faster."

She quickened her pace and he gripped her waist tight as he tossed his head back against the lounger and closed his eyes.

She pumped up and down, unable to tease him any longer. She needed him to come, needed to regain some control. Dex left her defenseless and she wasn't sure she was strong enough to fight the feelings she'd repressed for so long. The idea was terrifying.

Her hard rhythm had him panting and swearing softly.

"I'm coming, Skylar," he said as she felt the first tremor

against her hand. She continued quickly, rhythmically, not breaking the pace.

He held her tight and his head fell toward hers. His forehead rested against her cheek as he came. She felt him shudder and his cock throbbed hard in her hand as he orgasmed.

She smiled at him when his gaze met hers and he kissed her gently. "You are too fucking sexy," he said.

"Likewise," she said, removing her hand from him and snuggling closer under the blanket, savoring the feel of his body close to hers, his arms wrapped tightly around her.

The stars in the sky overhead and the light breeze blowing was perfect. The gentle rocking of the boat was peaceful…but nothing calmed the swirling emotions throwing her off balance.

This moment, right here with Dex was perfect. The only place in the world she wanted to be. Now. Forever.

But what did that mean?

I love you was on the tip of her tongue, but she hesitated. Could she say it? Was she ready to open herself up like that to him again? There would never be a more perfect moment for the confession…if only she could be brave enough to trust in her heart.

"I love you, Skylar," he whispered, so softly she almost didn't hear him.

Her heart soared and in that moment there was only one response, one thing she knew for sure. "I love you too."

CHAPTER TEN

FOCUSING ON WORK the next day was a struggle.

"That's salt you just added to your coffee," Doug said behind her as Skylar absently stirred the liquid in her Sasquatch coffee mug.

Okay, focusing on *anything* that day was a challenge.

"Man, I must be tired this morning," she said with an embarrassed laugh as she dumped the coffee into the sink and started over.

She had to pull it together and get her mind off Dex. Not an easy feat after the night before, when they'd crossed a physical barrier and confessed their feelings too.

He'd said *I love you* first and thank God, because she'd hate to have misread what was happening between them. Knowing the spark, the connection, the deep feelings of love had lingered for him after all this time made her feel good. It hadn't been a one-sided longing all these years.

It was a relief to know they were on the same page... until she thought about what the hell she was going to do now. She took a deep breath.

One thing at a time.

Get her coffee right.

Pushing thoughts of Dex away, Skylar made it through the rest of the day. Her crew meeting went better than the first one, confirming her thoughts that she was developing a good rapport with the team. This time no one questioned her decisions or challenged the changes to the shift rotation she'd presented—longer days with three on, two off—to give everyone more rest between shifts and help provide a better work/life balance than the four days on, one day off schedule had provided.

Her father hadn't been present, and that had taken some of the pressure off. She hadn't felt as self-conscious. The crew had seemed more receptive, too, which unfortunately only confirmed that working in an environment without him would be a little easier. Maybe she and her father could plan on having opposite shifts. He was only working part-time these days anyway. That way in a rescue scenario, there would be only one Beaumont calling the shots.

Humming to herself as she entered the ship's deck later that evening, she stared out the window toward the marina, allowing a few moments of downtime to think about the man she couldn't wait to see that night.

She wasn't fighting it anymore.

While she still didn't want the entire town to know about their relationship, she was starting not to be so worried about it. They weren't the center of the universe her teen-age mind had once believed them to be. People in town had their own lives, their own drama.

Unfortunately, the call for assistance coming into the control center an hour later had to be Skylar's least favor-ite kind and her euphoria was replaced by focus.

Two local men had gone out earlier that day in a small fishing vessel and hadn't returned. They'd told their fami-lies they'd be home by 3:00 p.m. but it was after 6:00 now. Calls and texts to their cell phones went unanswered and a quick tour of the inlet by a friend had revealed their boat was still not back. They must still be out on open water.

The weather had been mild, but the wind had picked up and a light rain had started as night fell. Fog drifted in from the east, making visibility a lot more challenging, especially for a small boat without a lot of technical equipment on board.

Skylar and her team gathered quickly. Limited daylight hours meant limited time for the search. By nightfall, things would be significantly more difficult.

"One of the wives said they always take the same route," Dwayne said, pointing to the map on the briefing table. Using the digital pen, he highlighted the route. "From the inlet, they head west toward Fishermen's Peak, then along the south toward Jameson's Landing... Their last known position was 39 degrees north and 40 degrees west."

With a search path plotted, Skylar and the crew navigated the cutter out of the marina within an hour of the call.

Dwayne and Aaron in the rescue helicopter had headed out moments before to try to get a visual. Unfortunately, the radio conversation with the air crew wasn't promising.

"Whitecaps on the ocean are making it difficult to spot the white vessel," Dwayne said.

White boats should be outlawed. They were hard to see even when the water conditions were clear as glass, which was rarely the case in the North Pacific. Unfortunately, boat owners usually chose beauty over safety, so manufacturers weren't about to start making bright yellow or orange reflective vessels.

"There's no sign of them along the coastline," Skylar reported. "Going to head south." She commanded the vessel as close to the shoreline as possible, hoping that the men had docked somewhere when the fog had rolled in. Even with *Starlight*'s fog lights and equipment, it was difficult to see beyond a hundred feet.

The crew on deck scanned the area, but there was no sign of the small fishing vessel or the men.

Hours later, conditions had gotten worse and time was running out. The crew's anxiety could be felt as thick as the fog enveloping the rescue boat.

"It's difficult to see even with night vision goggles," Aaron reported, sounding annoyed by the weather. "We're about to head back."

The drone had already returned to base. The helicopter couldn't safely stay out much longer. There was nothing they could do. They all knew the search was coming to an end for that evening. Hearts were heavy and tensions were high as Skylar made the call just before midnight.

Not all rescues ended well, but that didn't make Skylar feel better as she climbed on board Dex's yacht, exhausted but on edge an hour later.

Her hand trembled slightly as he handed her a hot cup of tea and ushered her toward the table.

She sat, then stood again. Nervous energy making it nearly impossible to stay still. Her body was vibrating with a fight-or-flight instinct that she could do nothing to calm. Her stomach churned, and the idea of trying to eat or sleep was laughable. She knew nightmares would plague her. With an unfinished rescue and men alone at sea, personal comfort didn't seem fair.

"I hate that we couldn't do more today," she said, pacing. If only the call had come in sooner, they could have had more daylight hours, the men may not have drifted so far away, the rescue crew could have gotten ahead of the fog and rain…

Dex touched her shoulder and she almost jumped. Lost in her own whirlwind thoughts, she'd almost forgotten where she was.

"You did what you could," he said gently and rationally. "According to their wives, they have enough provisions and water to last a few days. The search will resume at daybreak, as soon as it's safe." He held her tight, and though his words were meant to reassure, Skylar couldn't calm her overactive mind. The boat could have drifted miles off course... With limited visibility, the men could have gotten misdirected or disoriented.

Surviving the night on the open ocean this time of year in a small boat was...

Maybe the rescue crew needed to expand their search pattern.

"Hey, try to take a breath," Dex said, rubbing her back gently.

The soothing gesture just irritated her. She didn't want to relax. How could she when two men—local people— were lost at sea? Her job was to save people, and now she was expected to just sit calmly and wait.

Impossible.

"You need rest to be alert for tomorrow," Dex said.

She sighed as she gently stepped out of his embrace. "I think I'm going to go see my dad," she said, hoping he didn't take offense. She set the cup on the table and reached for her jacket.

If Dex was upset, it didn't show. He kissed her forehead quickly and helped her into her jacket. "Of course."

She hesitated near the door. "I'll see you tomorrow night, okay?"

"Absolutely. Drive safe."

She nodded, lingering a moment. She wanted to stay,

but there was no point being there when all she could do was stress about the unfinished mission. There was only one place, one person, that could help her survive these uncertain hours.

Dex stood on the upper deck of the yacht watching Skylar's taillights disappear in the thick fog as she pulled away from the marina. He sighed as he stared out at the ocean, covered by the thick blanket of white.

He knew her leaving had nothing to do with him. She didn't want comfort. She didn't want to relax or rest or take her mind off the men lost at sea.

And that made her so wonderful at her career. Her compassion was just as strong as her competency.

He'd wanted to be there for her, but that also meant knowing when *he* wasn't what she needed. She was going home, to see her dad. And if there was one person who could help Skylar at all that evening it would be him and Dex was happy Skylar had the man to rely on.

Dex never wanted to do anything to jeopardize that relationship. He never wanted Skylar to have to choose between him and her family. He'd been ready to change, adapt, prove himself so that she never had to.

He was still ready to do that.

Unfortunately, that decision wasn't his.

The night before, he'd battled so many conflicting thoughts and emotions. She'd applied for a transfer, but then she'd told him she loved him.

The two confessions had him swinging between two opposite emotions. Despair at the thought of losing her again, euphoria that she still loved him. Their evening together had been magical and he was desperate to move forward with her.

But right now, those lost men were occupying Skylar's mind. *All* of the minds of the community. The interior lights of the homes along the water's edge would be left on all night…everyone hoping, waiting, praying. Along with the lighthouse beam, the lights along the shore would serve as a beacon for the lost men to find their way home.

Dex sighed as he lay on the damp deck lounger and folded his hands behind his head, knowing he'd get no sleep either. He took several deep breaths and said the fishermen's prayer.

"God grant that I may live to fish for another shining day. But when my final cast is made I then most humbly pray, when nestled in your landing net as I lie peacefully asleep, you'll smile and judge that I'm 'good enough to keep.'"

IT WAS ALMOST 2:00 a.m. but the kitchen light was still on inside the house.

Throughout Skylar's childhood, her dad had never slept when confronted with an unfinished mission or an unsuccessful search. Sitting at their kitchen table, he would sip decaffeinated tea as he'd stare out the window toward the water. He'd always hid the restlessness and disappointment that had to have been consuming him, as he'd sit pensively, reflecting and ultimately letting go.

As a child, Skylar used to sit with him. She'd always felt that he'd needed the company, that she could offer at least a little peace. They'd sit for a long time in silence, then he'd tell her stories about previous successful missions to help ease her mind… Listening to the stories she'd cherished a million times before was *her* way of easing his.

Her legs felt like lead as she climbed the front steps and entered the house. No one locked their doors in Port Serenity. The close-knit community knew they had nothing to worry about.

She shut the door quietly and made her way down the hall. As she entered the kitchen, she saw the extra mug on the table in front of her usual chair. Her heart swelled and she swallowed hard as her dad turned to face her. "You knew I'd come by?"

"Thought I'd be prepared, just in case," he said with a tired smile. "How you doing, darlin'?"

She slumped into the chair and took a sip of the still-warm tea before answering. "I don't know. Not good obviously. Unsettled." This was the first time the roles were reversed. She had never realized the magnitude of the pressure her dad had always felt on nights this like. Counting the seconds, waiting for the next opportunity to try again.

"That's about right," he said, touching her hand on the table.

They sat in silence, staring out the big bay window at the barely visible rocky shore. They couldn't see the dock or the boats in the marina through the heavy fog. The only visible light was the beam from the lighthouse rotating up high on the hill, cutting through the mist.

Minutes felt like hours passing before he turned to her.

"Did I ever tell you about the rescue in the fall of '87 when two vessels collided off the south side of Elise's Bay?"

A dozen times at least.

"I don't think so," she said, leaning back in the chair to hear his story of hope and optimism, an adventure with a happy ending.

A story she desperately needed while she waited out the night.

CHAPTER ELEVEN

FIRST SIGN OF DAYBREAK, the crew was back out on the search. The rescue helicopter lifted off the landing pad just as Skylar arrived at the dock. No one was wasting any time. The fog had disappeared and a clear, sunny day was dawning.

Skylar sighed as she saw Pam Jenkins, a reporter for the *Port Serenity News*, interviewing two women who looked more than a little distraught, with dark circles under their eyes. Hunched slightly and leaning on one another, the wives of the missing men recounted the story to the news outlet.

This was the toughest part of all. Her father always said he preferred the search to having to talk to the families of the missing when the news wasn't promising. Lieutenant Miller had been the point of contact for the women throughout the search and would keep updating them.

One of the women turned to look at her, and Skylar felt her palms sweat as she sent what she hoped was a reassuring look, one that didn't show how her confidence was dwindling.

She shook her head and straightened her shoulders as she joined her crew. She'd do everything she could to ensure a positive outcome and pray it was enough.

Ten minutes later, Skylar commanded the cutter out through the inlet. Despite the stressful night with little sleep, the crew was on high alert. Everyone knew what was at stake and that with each second ticking by, the stakes grew higher.

On the upper deck, Captain Fields and Lieutenant Miller scanned the water with binoculars for the boat or either of the men floating in the water. They looked for flares or any sign of motion in the distance.

But all was still out on the ocean. Hours in and it was as if they'd vanished. Reports from the circling helicopter revealed they were having no luck with a visual either.

Where the hell had the men gone?

Skylar reviewed the search path and analyzed the previous day's weather conditions. Wind from the north could have carried the boat farther south than they'd anticipated, so if they'd gone as far as Franklin's Pass, the stronger current in that area would have taken them farther west...

It was a long shot, but her gut was telling her they needed to check it out.

After relaying her plan to the crew, she abandoned the original search area and headed west along the shoreline. In the helicopter overhead, Dwayne sounded reluctant. "You sure you want to change course?" he asked.

Was she?

They'd searched this area for hours with no luck the day before. Abandoning the original plan was risky, but she believed it was the right thing to do.

Maybe she should consult her father. He was standing by but leaving this mission in her hands. Skylar squared her shoulders. This was her rescue. Her decision to make.

"Yes," she said, sounding far more confident than she felt.

"Copy," Dwayne said and she instantly heard the sound of the helicopter moving away.

The search continued along the shoreline as far west as Franklin's Pass and Skylar's heart raced as they sailed farther away from Port Serenity with no sign of the fishing vessel or the two men.

Maybe this wasn't the right call…

"I think I see them." Dwayne's voice over the radio a moment later had her pulse racing.

"Location?"

"Two miles south of Franklin's Pass."

She swallowed hard. "Condition of the vessel and the occupants?"

"Boat is stalled but upright. Occupants are standing, flagging us down. No visible injuries."

It sounded too good to be true.

"We got them. I'm going to drop in," Aaron said a moment later as the cutter drew closer and Skylar saw the boat and the two men. She released a deep breath as she listened to the rescue over the radio as Aaron was lowered down to the boat. She watched from the deck as he swam toward the boat.

"Would you like to stay with your boat or be hoisted up? We have a coast guard vessel standing by to tow," she heard him tell the men.

Both men opted to be hoisted into the helicopter. She didn't blame them. Over twenty-four hours out there had to be terrifying.

"Bringing them up," Aaron said after the cage was lowered from the helicopter and the men were secure inside.

As the men were lifted to safety and the helicopter changed its course back toward the harbor, Skylar's felt her body shake. She slumped into her chair, feeling the surge of adrenaline drain and an overwhelming relief at just how close this one was.

"THEY FOUND THEM," Dex told Isla as the two sat at the kitchen table, listening to the radio reports from the station. He clutched his coffee cup tightly as his shoulders sagged in relief.

Dex had been out on the original search path for several hours along with other boats who'd joined the volunteer effort that morning, but they'd all returned to the harbor when there had been no sign of the men and Skylar had changed course.

He'd been uneasy about her decision, but she'd been right. Only someone with as much knowledge of this area, the wind drifts and the currents in this part of the North Pacific Ocean could have made that call successfully.

Those men had been rescued because Skylar was a local who'd lived on these waters.

"Thank God," Isla said, looking just as relieved.

Everyone in the community had been on edge and now they could all breathe a collective sigh of relief. The men were safe. Their wives were getting the good news now.

Dex drained his coffee cup and grimaced at the now-cold coffee.

"Skylar did good," Isla said begrudgingly, twirling her own empty cup between her hands on the table.

"Yes, she did." He was so proud of her. He knew the night before had been hard on her. He'd resisted texting, knowing she was where she needed to be, processing and preparing for that morning's search. He didn't want to steal her focus.

But he'd thought of her all night. Worried about how she

was holding up and hoping she wouldn't lose faith in herself. He hoped she realized just how capable she was, how much of an asset to the crew here in Port Serenity.

Isla eyed him. "So, you two are really doing this again?"

He'd dodged the conversation for days, but he couldn't avoid it forever. His sister deserved his honesty. "I think so. I hope so."

Isla looked worried. "Listen, she's a great captain, I won't deny her that. But I can have a say about this relationship. I love you and I'm concerned about you. I know what she meant to you back then, but she broke your heart. What's to say she won't again?"

That was a chance Dex was willing to take. A heartache he was a hundred percent willing to endure. "Problem is, sis, there's nothing I can do about it," he said. "And besides, I pushed her away. I broke her heart first."

Isla shook her head, not buying it. "She should have been there for you."

They'd had this argument far too many times. His sister had been pissed when Skylar left Port Serenity for the academy rather than standing by Dex. Despite his insistence that he didn't want Skylar putting her life on hold. He'd begged his parents not to tell anyone about his condition…and Isla from telling Skylar. But his sister had thought he hadn't told Skylar the truth because he knew deep down she wouldn't be there for him. Isla had never trusted Skylar's intentions. She'd always said if Skylar loved him, she wouldn't be so adamant about keeping the relationship a secret. Maybe she'd always been a protective younger sister…

"The past is in the past."

"Have you told her yet?" she asked.

He sighed. "No."

"Why not?"

"Timing hasn't been right." He was terrified to tell Skylar, but he knew he had to and soon. As much as they agreed not to reopen past wounds, he needed to rectify the hurt from before. Explain and hope she understood why he'd done it.

"Are you going to?" Isla pressed.

"Yes."

"When?"

A strangled-sounding laugh escaped him. "Soon. Stop with the interrogation."

Isla looked annoyed, but she conceded. "Fine. I won't bring it up again, because I know you're not going to listen to my advice anyway...but don't say I didn't warn you."

"You are relieved of all responsibility if I get my heart trampled on."

"*When.* Not if," she said, standing and putting her coffee cup in the dishwasher.

His sister might be right, but when his phone chimed with a new text from Skylar two minutes later saying she couldn't wait to see him that evening, there was literally nothing that could prevent him from leaping off the ledge and free-falling straight into potential heartache.

CHAPTER TWELVE

EVERYONE IN TOWN seemed to be crammed inside the Serpent Queen Pub hours later when Skylar entered. The temptation to sneak back out was strong. It wasn't that she didn't want to celebrate the rescue, but it had been a stressful forty-eight hours and she still hadn't gotten off the emotional roller coaster.

She wasn't sure this strangely exhausted high of anxiety and relief would ever go away. Her father always needed time to decompress after rescues like this one. After sending her a quick congratulatory text, telling her he was proud of her for following her instincts, he'd conveniently gone golfing to unwind as soon as the men were reported safe. Skylar suspected she might have to adopt a similar hobby to escape as needed.

The only person she wanted to see was Dex.

She wanted to talk to him about the night before, explain how she'd needed the comfort and reassurance from her dad. But it made her stomach knot to think that she'd gone to her family instead of Dex. Her father had experience with situations like these and she'd wanted the security of his expertise to guide her through it. But she worried that deep down, she also didn't trust Dex fully.

She was trying to guard her heart, but now she wondered, if there was a choice to be made, would she pick her family or Dex?

All Skylar knew was she was desperate to make it up to him, to reconnect physically and hope it would reaffirm her feelings for him.

Maybe she should slip out and text him to meet her at the pier.

But too late. Doug and Dwayne had spotted her and were waving her toward their usual tables. Everyone not on shift was there already. And she saw Dex was there too, playing darts with Aaron. Her heart raced as it always did at the sight of the love of her life.

He was dressed in black pants and a light blue sweater that evening, his hair gelled in a controlled spiky mess and just the right amount of stubble along his jawline. She wished they could go somewhere alone.

But she knew it was important that she be there that evening. Part of her crew's success was dependent on their building relationships outside the job. She knew a lot of her crewmates personally already, having grown up in the small community. But if and when she received her transfer, being able to connect on a personal level with a new crew would be important.

She nodded her acknowledgement to the group but pointed to the restrooms. She would stay but she needed a minute to regroup, try to let go of the tension still trapped between her shoulder blades. The men were safe. Her quick thinking and knowledge of the area had turned a threatened mission into a successful one. Hopefully they wouldn't face challenges like this anytime soon and she'd have time to recover from this one.

She pushed through the restroom door and halted.

So much for a moment to decompress.

Isla turned to look at her as she hovered in the doorway. "Deciding whether or not you still have to pee?"

Skylar swallowed hard as she entered. They could be in the same restroom at the same time. Running into Dex's sister was going to happen...especially if she and Dex were together. If they built a life together, she and Isla would need to find common ground.

"Hey, Isla," she said tightly as she pushed open a stall door.

"Hey, Skylar..."

Skylar held her breath, sensing there was more to come.

"Good job on the rescue."

She released the breath, the compliment taking her by surprise. How much it meant to her surprised her even more. She'd always wanted Dex's family to like her but always got the sense that they didn't. She'd always felt the weight of judgment whenever they looked at her for being a Beaumont. Isla's words warmed her in an unexpected way.

"Thank you," she said. "I'm just glad things worked out."

Isla nodded. She seemed to hesitate, so Skylar waited.

"And whatever is going on with you and Dex is none of my business," she said. "Just remember that when you leave, it's the rest of us left behind who have to pick up the pieces."

Her spine stiffened. "Who says I'm leaving?" Had Dex told his sister that she'd applied for a transfer?

Isla shrugged. "Everyone knows you won't stay here."

The note of regret in Isla's voice made Skylar feel even more conflicted. Did everyone know that, including her crew?

It must be hard for them to put their trust in her if they thought she was ready to bolt. She needed to work harder to reassure them that whether she stayed or left, she was there now. Fully committed. She hoped she'd proven that over the last two days. Two rescues where she'd put the community first before the rule book had to count for something, right?

Would she get away with following her gut and not the rule book if she was stationed in California?

"Well, I'm here now...so..." she mumbled, entering the stall and closing the door.

Why was it always Dex's sister who could put Skylar on edge like this? She thought of their confrontation before she'd left.

Only in a small town like Port Serenity would the community high school get permission from the local hotspot to host a prom after-party. It was the school's way of ensuring a dry grad, giving the students a fun place they'd otherwise never be allowed to enter after 8:00 p.m. instead of drinking near the pier or at one of the local parks after the prom ended.

Skylar had gone to the prom only reluctantly and had zero intentions of going to the after-party. Alone, dateless and still reeling from Dex's rejection, she'd wanted to stay home and watch *Walking Dead* episodes, but being part of the planning committee and on school council, she couldn't avoid the prom.

So she'd put on the light blue gown she'd picked out specifically with Dex in mind, wanting to wow him with the princess cut and sweetheart neckline. But as she'd entered the beautifully decorated school gym, surrounded by all her friends celebrating their upcoming freedom and scholarly accomplishments, she'd only felt anxious. The urge to run out of the school had been overwhelming, but she'd powered through. She'd danced with her girlfriends, sipped the punch, pretended to laugh and then cried alone in a bathroom stall during the slow songs when the sight of couples swaying on the gymnasium floor had been too much to take.

Dex hadn't shown up.

And that had been so much worse than if he had, even if he'd brought a date. She'd really been hoping he'd snap out of whatever he was going through…

Which was why she was plastering on a fake smile for the after-party at the Serpent Queen Pub. Despite being underage, Dex had held a part-time job at the pub that year to make money. He'd told his family it was for university, even though they'd decided to go to the academy together. She hoped that he'd been forced to work the event so she could see him.

She needed to see him. He'd been avoiding her calls and texts and skipping classes, only showing up to school for his finals, then hibernating at home. She needed one last face-to-face, a final goodbye for closure before she could move on. Without looking back, without wondering.

Hip-hop blasted from speakers that normally played country or classic rock and strobe lights flickered on the wooden dance floor as she scanned the crowded pub. The Congrats to Class of 2016 banner hung across the bar and her chest tightened.

She'd gotten her acceptance letter that day. It should have made the prom even more special. Instead, it darkened her mood further.

Indecision had plagued her and her father's happiness only irritated her. Of course he assumed she was happy about it. This was what she'd always wanted.

Having second doubts was unexpected…

She surveyed the crowd and found Carly behind the accessories table of the zany photo booth they'd brought in for the event. Her older cousin was chaperoning, and she sent Skylar a sympathetic smile. Carly was the only one who knew about Skylar's heartache, her indecision. Her cousin had been there to comfort her the last few weeks and dry her tears.

She waved quickly and then headed through the sea of her friends toward the bar. She swallowed hard as she approached. If he was there, what would she say to him?

"Wow, look who actually showed up."

At Isla's voice, she turned. "This is *my* grad, after all," she said tightly. What was Isla even doing there?

Then Skylar spotted Alex Sharp watching them, and she sighed. Of course, Isla was dating the class bad boy. Neither of them had been at the actual prom—Alex was too cool for that, but of course he would be at the pub. Though, Skylar assumed he'd keep partying after the pub, which defeated the purpose of the safe grad.

Not her problem…

Isla gestured vaguely around her. "I thought Wakefield establishments weren't up to Beaumont standards."

She refused to take the bait. Isla had never been on board with Skylar dating her brother in secret or at all… She was constantly holding the knowledge over Dex's head to get her own way, threatening to out them when she and her brother had an argument. Skylar would have thought Isla would be thrilled that they'd ended things.

"Enjoy yourself, Isla," she said, turning to walk away.

Dex wasn't there and Skylar didn't want to be either. She caught Carly's eye and gestured that she was leaving. She'd done enough to satisfy the school and her parents. Now, she just wanted her pajamas and a tub of ice cream.

She didn't care if she never left the house again until it was time to drive to the Anchorage airport.

But Isla stopped her with a hand on her arm. "I'm not done," she said.

Skylar's jaw clenched. She wouldn't give Isla the argument she was looking for. The little tyrant's opinion meant nothing to her now.

"I suppose you'll be leaving soon?" Isla mocked. "Headed to the academy like all previous generations?" She said it as though following in Skylar's father's and grandfather's footsteps was a bad thing. As though the Wakefields didn't all follow the same beaten down path their ancestors had paved for them, taking over the local businesses or living on trust funds.

Skylar held her head high. "Yes, I am."

The briefest flash of disappointment reflected in her eyes before she said, "How predictable."

"What I choose to do with my life is my business and I don't care what you think."

"Of course you do," Isla said. "Appearances are everything to the Beaumonts. Look at us how perfect we are. Valiant heroes..." She rolled her eyes.

Skylar fought to control her sudden anger as weeks of pain and disappointment, confusion and uncertainty came bubbling to the surface. "And your family of thieves is better?"

The shot hit its mark. Isla's face reddened as she took a step toward her. "My family saved this community. We created all of this."

Skylar scoffed. "Created a fake sea creature who takes the credit for every successful coast guard rescue?" It maddened her that grown adults could actually believe in this stuff. She could understand catering to the tourists, and enjoyed the stories as a child. The idea of a serpent queen protecting sailors had made her feel better when her father was out on the water, but then she grew up. And locals actually believing in it? Ridiculous.

"Sealena was rumored to be in these waters for generations. My family just gave her the recognition she deserves."

"Recognition? Exploited the myth, you mean? Turned the town into a tourist trap?"

"What do you care? You've never wanted to stay here anyway. You're too good for Port Serenity." She paused, her expression hardening. "Too good for a Wakefield."

Skylar glanced around quickly. How many people had heard that? Skylar swallowed hard and held her head high as she nodded. "You're right. A Beaumont would never fall for a Wakefield."

Saving her pride had felt like her only option in that moment, but the words—the hurtful lie—had plagued her for a long time.

Leaving the safety of the restroom stall now and heading back out, she joined the others just as the waitress placed a tray of beers in the center of the table. Dex's gaze met hers from where he was throwing darts a few feet away. He smiled and she returned it as best as she could.

You okay? he mouthed, a concerned look on his face.

She forced her smile wider, brighter as she nodded, then turned her attention to the crew.

"Hey! There's the men on TV," Dwayne called out as she took a seat and accepted a beer from Doug.

The crowd quieted as Dollie reached for the remote behind the bar and turned up the volume on the news broadcast. Skylar was relieved to see the two men looking rested and cared for. Now out of the local hospital, they had a great story to tell and an audience eager to listen.

"It was terrifying out there," one of the men, Jim, said. "The darkness and thick fog made it impossible to see anything around us."

"The waves got pretty rough during the night," the other man, Bill said. "We'd drifted so far off course, we had no idea which way to navigate back toward the harbor."

"Was there any point when you thought maybe you wouldn't survive it?" the reporter, Pam Jenkins, asked.

The shorter man nodded. The taller one shook his head. They glanced nervously at one another then the first one spoke.

"Well, there was a moment when the boat was being thrashed about, sometime around three a.m...." Jim said.

"Supernatural hour," Bill interjected.

"...our supplies fell over the side and the vessel nearly capsized..." Jim paused. "Then it was righted as though being lifted off the water." He nudged the other man to take over.

"Yeah, it was as if someone was holding us up out of the danger." Bill cleared his throat. "Then the water instantly calmed. The fog even seemed to lift. The waves turned into just gentle rocking and everything was peaceful almost."

The reporter leaned closer, shoving her microphone into the taller man's face. "What do you think it was? What do you think happened?"

Obviously, Pam Jenkins knew where this was heading. They all did.

"Well...it might have been... I mean, it could have been Sealena," the second man said, looking embarrassed but also thrilled that he and his friend had had a rare encounter with the creature.

"You think our local serpent queen saved you last night?" Pam Jenkins said, delighted at the way the interview had taken this turn.

The two men nodded, smiling at the camera, enjoying their few minutes of local fame. One waved and the other said hello to his wife as Pam Jenkins turned to the camera with her award-winning smile. "Well Port Serenity, there you have it. Further proof of the existence of our fearless ocean protector. From all of us safe here on the shore, thank you Sealena!" she said as the broadcast went back to the station's weather report.

Skylar sighed. Geez. No mention at all about the coast guard's part in the rescue. The fact that it had been the crew who had relentlessly searched, that it had been their knowledge and quick thinking that had located the stranded men and Dwayne and Aaron's skill and bravery that had brought them to safety on the helicopter.

Nope. Only another Sealena story for the generations.

As Dollie turned off the broadcast, Dwayne held up his beer mug. "To Sealena!"

The rest of them laughed and raised their glasses and Skylar reluctantly clanked hers and took a huge gulp of her beer.

Dex sidled into the booth next to her. "Still don't believe in all that serpent queen saving lives thing, huh?"

Something brushed against her, forceful and strong, but instead of hindering her ascent, it accelerated it. She scanned the water but saw nothing at first. Then another shadow...

Skylar took another swig of beer. "I don't know. Maybe

there is something to it. Not necessarily an *actual* sea creature, but something out there that brings a sense of calm to people who are panicking which allows them to think clearer, help themselves survive the danger?"

Dex nodded. "Well at least you're not completely shutting down the idea. But don't worry, I think everyone knows who the real hero of the day is," he said, admiration and affection in his tone making her once again eager to be alone with him.

Her gaze locked with his as Skylar leaned toward him and whispered, "Hurry up and finish that beer so we can get out of here."

"Don't have to tell me twice." He tossed back his beer, climbed out of the booth and extended a hand to her. "Let's go."

"You okay?" Dex asked twenty minutes later when they were alone on the yacht. He carried two glasses of wine to where she sat on the sofa. "You seem a little quiet tonight."

While Skylar had joined the crew briefly at the pub, there had definitely been something a little off with her. Understandable. She was no doubt still processing the last forty-eight hours. There had been a lot of responsibility on her shoulders.

Hopefully that was all that was weighing on her.

"I'm okay. Just coming down off the adrenaline high of the last two days," she said with a tired smile as she accepted the glass of wine.

He sat next to her and set his glass down on the table before reaching for her legs tucked under her on the sofa. He placed them over his thighs and began massaging her feet gently. "Let me help with that," he said.

Skylar closed her eyes and settled back against the cushions. "I won't argue," she said with a laugh. She cleared her throat as though to continue but remained silent.

"What is it? What else is going on?" he asked, moving his hands up to her calves. Touching her felt amazing, her shapely legs a huge turn-on, but he wanted to go for a soothing rather than sexy massage. She obviously needed to talk and communicating was as important to him as their physical connection.

"It's nothing important," she said, but she bit her lip. "Just something Isla said tonight."

Ah. She'd ignored Skylar at movie night because she'd been respecting Doug and Jay, but he should have known his sister would catch Skylar and lecture her at some point.

"You know not to pay any attention to her. She suffers from a nonfatal case of obnoxiousness," he said with a grin, but his chest tightened as he wondered what his sister had said.

There were a lot of things *he* needed to say.

Skylar studied him pensively. "Isla can be…overbearing, but this time she may have been right."

"I can assure you she wasn't, but tell me what she said."

She hesitated. "Just that if and *when* I leave, there would potentially be pieces that needed to be picked up."

He nodded as he continued the massage, taking a moment to find the right words. "Maybe, but that's not on you. We talked about this the other night." He'd hoped he'd put her at ease then, but it was obviously still plaguing her. "You have to do what's right for you. Everyone else…the crew will adjust."

"The crew? What about you?"

"That's for me to figure out," he reassured her. He didn't

want what-ifs to detract from what they had now. He didn't want her retreating on his behalf. "I survived once before, right?" he said, aiming to sound casual, but her gaze only darkened with regret.

"Were you really that hurt when I left?" she asked.

It had been all his doing, the way things ended. He'd pushed her away. She'd left, the way he'd wanted her to. But that didn't mean his heart hadn't broken. She needed to know how much she'd meant to him back then.

How much she meant now.

He took a deep breath. "Yes, I was." He turned to face her. "I was lost and heartbroken. You were more than my girlfriend, you were my *best* friend. I missed seeing you, talking to you, having your support as I went through… some things. I was confused and messed up about a lot of stuff back then." Now would be the time to tell her. But still the words refused to surface.

He touched her cheek and said, "But, that was on me."

"I could have tried harder to get you to open up about whatever was going on," she pointed out.

"I would have only retreated harder." He moved closer and wrapped his arms around her. "Look, Skylar, we were both young. We were in love, but that didn't mean it could solve all our problems back then."

Her big blue eyes looked at him questioningly. "Love doesn't conquer all?"

"Love helps," he said. "But it's just one part of life. There's happiness and sadness and stress and anger. We can't feel fulfilled by one thing. I didn't want you to choose me and then feel regret or resentment for not chasing your own dreams. That wouldn't have made us very strong as a couple or as friends. I think people need more, that's all I'm saying."

"So, love is *not* all you need?" she asked with a slow grin.

He groaned. "Okay, enough with the clichés." He pulled her close. "*You're* all I need right here, right now." Always. He wouldn't tell her that. He refused to put pressure on her for any commitment beyond what they had right now. He meant what he said about people needing to be balanced in their needs and wants.

Skylar deserved everything. And he might only be a portion of what would ultimately make her happiest.

"What if I disagree?" she murmured against his lips. "What if I think that love is the most important piece of the puzzle and everything else should fall into place around it?" She stared deep into his eyes and in that moment he didn't regret his actions years ago. Her words only solidified his trust in them. He'd let her go and she'd found a way back to him, even if she hadn't planned to. Their connection was stronger now because of the time apart, knowing their love hadn't faded for either of them.

"Then I'm glad things played out the way they did because you mean too much to me to have been the cause of you not fulfilling this lifelong goal."

"You loved me that much?" she whispered, leaning closer.

"I *love* you that much," he said before kissing her gently and holding her close.

WAKING UP IN Dex's arms the next morning, where they'd fallen asleep on the sofa, Skylar felt the weight of her life choices a little differently. She'd been so confused leaving

Port Serenity as a heartbroken teen, then over time she'd convinced herself that she'd made the right choice. She'd thought she'd moved on from Dex, but she'd only repressed her feelings.

Coming back, reconnecting with him, put everything into perspective. She didn't want to change the past. She was where she was now because of it and she was where she wanted to be with a deeper, more profound appreciation for the love they shared.

Dex's take on love however, confused her, but she suspected he was once again saying what he needed to to make sure she always followed her own heart and didn't make decisions based on his.

And that only made her love him that much more.

She rolled toward him, noticing the quilt draped over them. That hadn't been there when they'd fallen asleep. Had Isla come home the night before? Her pulse raced a little at the thought that Isla might have seen them together like this, but she forced the uneasiness away. The only way she'd ever be able to change Isla's opinion of her was to prove that she and Dex could last.

And if only Skylar could promise that would be the case, she'd feel a lot better about things. Right now, she was taking the relationship day by day.

She snuggled into Dex, who was so warm and smelled so good. She stared at him, still sleeping beside her, mouth open, one arm around her, the other draped overhead. He looked so adorably sexy, she could lie there staring at him all morning. It was her day off and she had nowhere else to be.

She gently touched the scruff along his jawline.

One eye opened and a lazy smile stretched across his face. "Are you watching me sleep?"

"Maybe…"

He rotated them and grabbing her waist, he positioned her on top of him. "Sorry we didn't make it to the bed," he said, kissing her.

"I slept like a baby." In fact, this was the best sleep she'd had since moving home. Even on a couch with no pillow, being in Dex's arms had been all the comfort she'd needed.

"Good, because I have something planned for today and you're going to need your strength."

She frowned. He hadn't told her about any plans.

"What is it?"

"You'll see," he said with a grin, kissing her again before sitting them both up so he could stand and stretch.

"We're heading out now?" So much for a lazy day. Though, she was intrigued about what he had planned. "We're not going somewhere where there will be lots of people, right?" Isla, Dollie and Carly knowing about their relationship was enough for now. Baby steps.

Dex grinned. "Trust me. We will be completely alone," he said, reaching for her hands and pulling her to her feet.

She laughed uneasily. "That doesn't sound menacing at all."

He pulled her in for another quick kiss and she pressed her body to his. "Sure you wouldn't rather stay here all day?"

He gripped her waist and groaned, looking seriously tempted, but then released her. "Don't worry. You're going to love this. You have an hour to get ready, then meet me at the pier."

"And you're not going to tell me where we're going?" She tried again as he ushered her gently toward the door.

"Nope. Wear good shoes."

She shot him a sideways look as he opened the door and she stepped outside into the beautiful, warm sunny day. "I'm trusting you," she said.

"You won't regret it," he said.

Two hours later, Skylar wasn't so sure about that. Covered in sweat from a not so easy hike through the mountain trails fifteen minutes outside of town, she put her hands on her hips and struggled to catch her breath. "I thought I was in better shape than this." She ran all the time, but inclines were a different beast.

Dex grinned as he took her hand and practically dragged her higher up the trail. "We're almost there."

"Almost where?" So far there were trees and overgrown trails. Pretty, but no different than most of the other, easier trails in Port Serenity.

"Just keep going," Dex said, positioning himself behind her and placing his hands over hers on her hips to propel her forward.

She laughed as she trudged on and a few minutes later, she stepped through a clearing at the top of the trail. Her eyes widened and a smile formed on her lips.

"See? What did I tell you? Paradise," Dex said, not at all winded as he gestured widely at their surroundings.

Surrounded by mountains in the distance all around them, this untapped part of the Alaskan wilderness was breathtaking—lush vegetation and a beautiful cascading waterfall below that flowed into a small river and lake. "It is incredible," she said. She couldn't remember ever being here before. As much as she wanted to see the world, she couldn't deny that her hometown was one of the more beau-tiful places in nature. They had it all in Port Serenity—the ocean, waterfalls, mountains, spectacular trails and camp-grounds; the fishing in both winter and summer was sec-ond to none and the peace and slower pace easily rivaled the thrill of a fast-paced city.

"Should we hike down to the water?" she asked, wiping sweat from her forehead. Dipping her feet into a refreshing stream sounded amazing right about now.

"I have a better way down," Dex said, kicking off his running shoes.

Her eyes widened. "You're out of your mind. That water is going to be freezing," Skylar said, shaking her head as Dex removed his sweater and T-shirt together. The sight of his bare torso made her mouth go dry. He was so irresistibly sexy and only the fear that he was actually suggesting the jump off this cliff to free-fall about fifty feet into freezing cold water could distract her from thoughts of what she'd like to be doing with him.

"There's a warm current that flows through here. The water is like taking a bath," he said.

"I bet that's what you tell all the girls to get them down to the undergarments," she said. She wondered if he'd brought anyone else here and couldn't help a pang of jealousy.

He grinned at her. "Is that your way of asking if I've brought anyone here before?"

Damn, he could see right through her. "Well, have you?"

He laughed as he walked toward her, unbuttoning his shorts as he approached. He stepped out of them and stopped in front of her in his underwear. Skylar's gaze dropped to the bulge in the front of the boxer briefs and her body temperature rose even more. Damn, he was so sexy.

Dex reached for the base of her T-shirt, lifting it off over her head. His fingers tickled as they brushed against the heated skin along her stomach and over her rib cage. She trembled. His touch felt so incredible...

She shook her head, snapping out of it. "You're avoiding the question, Dex!" she said, stepping back and folding her arms.

He reached for her arms and unfolded them. "No. You are the first," he said.

She shouldn't feel so thrilled. Dex had been entitled to date whoever he wanted over the years. She had. But somehow this felt more special now.

He gestured for her to gear down and Skylar sighed and removed her yoga pants.

A moment later, they were in their underwear, standing at the waterfall's edge. She looked over the side at the cascade. It did look refreshing after the long hike, but...

"You've done this before?" It was impossible to judge the depth. The water below was dark and she couldn't tell if there were any rocks or other dangers below the surface.

"A million times. Don't worry, it's like forty or fifty feet deep," he said. "And no rocks."

"And the water's warm?" She narrowed her eyes at him. Alaska water was rarely warm. The most they could hope for was less than hypothermic...

"Would I lie to you?"

She sighed.

"On three?"

She nodded. She would never back down from a challenge from Dex.

Perched at the edge, he counted. "One...two..."

She jumped.

Closing her eyes tight, she plugged her nose as she free-fell a long three or four seconds until her body submerged below the surface of the water.

He'd lied. It was fr-freezing.

Her body instantly chilled as she made her way to the surface in time to see Dex's body plunge below. Her teeth chattered and goose bumps covered her skin. It wasn't as cold as the ocean, but it wasn't the bath water he'd promised.

She treaded water, hoping the movement would help. And a second later when Dex resurfaced, she lunged at him, dragging him below again with the weight of her body.

He struggled against her and easily won with his powerful muscular frame. He wrapped his arms around her tight as he surfaced again.

"Apparently, you *would* lie to me. It's freezing," she said, glaring at him. Though their bodies pressed together beneath the water was definitely adding to her warmth.

He held her close, keeping them both afloat with one arm as he ran a hand through his wet hair. "I swear it was warmer before."

"When? August?"

He grinned. "Maybe." He put his hand under her chin and drew her face toward his. He kissed her gently, his lips tasting fresh and crisp.

"You jumped without me," he said.

"You took too long." In truth, she knew if she'd waited, she might not make the leap off the cliff. She'd needed to do it without him as a security blanket.

"I love how brave you are," he said with a deep sincerity that resonated with her. "You never back down from a challenge."

She heard the intention in his tone. "Why do I feel like there's another one coming?" she murmured against his mouth.

He gripped her waist tighter and she wrapped her legs around him as they bobbed on the surface. The noise from the waterfall drowned out the sound of her thumping heart as she massaged his shoulders. The feel of his body had hers tingling.

He kissed her softly, teasingly running his tongue along her bottom lip, then demanding entry as he deepened the kiss. Her mouth ravished his with a hunger and passion only he brought out in her. She loved the way he kissed. They were in perfect sync.

When he pulled back, his gaze burned into hers. "You up for this?" he asked.

She nodded quickly before crushing his mouth with hers again. There was no one around. They were completely alone, surrounded by natural beauty. It was as though they were the only two people in the universe.

Being with him was all that mattered.

Reaching below the water, he moved her underwear to the side and then freed his cock from the constraints of the fabric of his boxer briefs. He took her hand and placed it on his already hard cock before sliding his fingers along her folds.

Her body vibrated with yearning as pleasure flowed through her at his light teasing touch against her clit.

She gently stroked the length of him, up and down, allowing the water to act as a lubricant as she circled the tip with her thumb.

Her breathing became labored and she broke the kiss. He buried his head into her neck, kissing along her earlobe, her neck, her shoulder and collarbone. "You are so sexy, Skylar." His finger dipped inside her and she moaned, gently biting the flesh on his shoulder as she clung tight.

"These have to go," he said, ripping her underwear free of her body and tossing them onto the shore.

Hiking back commando. She could live with that.

"Do you trust me?" he asked.

"I probably shouldn't, considering you just lied to me about the 'warm' water," she said shakily, her heart racing, "but yes, I trust you."

He took her legs and placed them onto his shoulders, easing her body back onto the surface of the water. He moved closer until her legs dangled over his shoulders and he supported her ass with his hands. "Just relax and float," he said before lowering his head to her stomach.

He licked the water droplets from her skin and Skylar's body radiated pleasure from the simple, sexy gesture.

Relax and float.

Right. Easier said than done when his hands were gripping her ass cheeks and his head was between her legs.

He kissed along her inner thighs, torturously slow. His tongue collected the water along her groin. His tongue flicked against her clit beneath the water and she took a deep breath.

One hand supporting her lower back, he fingered her folds, massaging and playing gently. His mouth pressed against her opening and his tongue plunged inside. He resurfaced, took a deep breath, then went back under. He sucked and licked as his fingers traveled in and out of her body.

Her muscles squeezed around him as she reached out

around her, gripping nothing, floating weightlessly and struggling not to come too soon.

The blue cloudless sky above her and the cascading waterfall an arm's length away was the most breathtaking place she'd ever experienced such intense pleasure, such intimacy, such a connection.

He made love to her with his mouth with a desperation and urgency as though she were a source of life. Each time he surfaced for air, his gaze was more lustful, more longing.

She desperately wanted to wrap her mouth around him and pleasure him this way. Just the thought had her toppling over the edge. Her body pulsated and trembled its release as Dex resurfaced and slid her legs off his shoulders as he pulled her into his body and pressed his hard cock against her opening.

"That was the sexiest thing…" she said, still fighting to catch her breath, enjoying the ripples of pleasure flowing through her.

He kissed her and then captured her bottom lip between his teeth. "Damn, I want to be inside of you," he said.

She took a deep breath and wiggling free of his embrace she dove below the surface. The freezing water was a momentary shock before her mission made it irrelevant. She gripped his ass and took his cock into her mouth. Air escaped slowly from her lungs as she sucked and licked.

She felt his hands guiding her to the surface. "Let's take it to safer ground," he suggested, guiding them toward the shore. He climbed out of the water and took her hand to help her walk over the slippery rocks.

Moving to a grassy area, Dex lay on his back. Skylar opened his legs and knelt between his thighs. She cupped his balls with one hand and gripped the base of his shaft with the other as she lowered her mouth to his cock.

He moaned as she licked the top, the taste of precum on her lips. She slowly took him into her mouth, sucking gently at first, then harder and faster. He tasted so good, like the fresh waterfall, and she savored it. This was the first time they'd pleasured one another this way and a brief moment of self-consciousness gave her pause. She glanced up at him, feeling unusually shy. "Is this okay?"

"Are you kidding? Skylar, you are driving me wild," Dex said, gently guiding her head back down to his cock. Gripping her hair, he guided her head up and down, pushing his hips up to fuck her mouth. "This okay?" he asked.

She nodded quickly. It was more than okay. The dominant gesture had her instantly turned on, getting wet again. She loved the way he was controlling the moment while knowing she was the one still fully in control of his pleasure. His fingers tangled in her wet hair and he pulled more, while forcing her to take him even deeper. The tip of his cock reached the back of her throat and she gagged slightly, before he slid back toward her lips. He continued to plunge in and out and she sucked harder, frantically, just as hungry to feel his release as he was.

She tingled between her thighs with mounting tension as she tightened her squeeze on his balls and applied more pressure to the base of his cock as he held her head right where he wanted it.

"I'm coming," he said in warning.

She nodded and moaned as she licked around the top of him, inviting his release.

She felt his entire body spasm as his orgasm took hold. His grip on her head relaxed as he came. She felt her own second orgasm course through her. Never before had she orgasmed only by pleasuring someone else.

She lifted her head and the look of satisfaction on Dex's face as her eyes met his made her feel sexually empowered. She couldn't wait to try new things with him, be physical in all the ways she'd only ever fantasized before.

She climbed up to lie against his chest and breathed a huge sigh of satisfaction as he wrapped his arms tight around her and kissed the top of her head. "That was amazing," he whispered.

"Definitely the best hike I've ever taken."

How on earth was he supposed to concentrate on his first training session with Shaylah when his thoughts kept returning to the hike with Skylar the day before? It had been the sexiest experience of his life. He was glad he'd decided to take her there. The hidden waterfall had been his special place he'd go to whenever he'd needed to clear his head or just get away to be alone.

Now it was *their* special place.

As Dex walked toward A Helpful Paw, he felt like skipping. When was the last time he'd felt so completely happy? So sexually satisfied, but also so incredibly in love that he was practically floating. He never wanted to come down from this high. He had to figure out a way to hold on to her.

Entering the building he looked around. As before, dogs and trainers worked together in separate pens. Some played games, while others worked. Dogs barked and commands were issued, balls and toys flew through the air. Dex's heart raced. It was a little intimidating. Could he really do this?

He stood there awkwardly, scanning the room and then waved at Kendal as she approached.

"Hey Dex, ready for your first training session?" At her warm smile, he felt some of the uneasiness subside. They'd worked with hundreds of people. They knew how to make the best human/canine connections. He just needed to put his trust in Kendal and her team.

He cleared his throat. "Absolutely," he said, hoping he sounded confident. "This is just a little nerve-racking."

"Totally understandable, but you'll relax in no time, I promise," she said. "Let me introduce you to Shaylah's trainer, Lee. He's going to be working with you both here at the facility and then he will work with you at your own home when we move to the next level."

The next level, when they started training outside the facility. When they brought her to places Dex often went and taught her the appropriate behavior in everyday situations like movie theatres, restaurants, businesses. When she was introduced to Dex's family and friends and the people Shaylah would need to bond with other than Dex.

His palms sweat. This was a big commitment.

One step at a time.

Kendal led the way to the pen where Shaylah and Lee waited.

"You must be Dex," Lee said, extending a hand in welcome. He was a tall, thin man about Dex's age wearing a T-shirt with the facility's logo.

Next to him, Shaylah—fifteen pounds, golden fur, wearing her therapy dog vest—sat patiently, but her tail wagged in excitement.

"Great to meet you," Dex said shaking Lee's hand. Then he bent to pet Shaylah. "Hey, girl."

The dog looked at Lee and Lee nodded his approval before she approached Dex and licked his hand. Dex pet the soft fur and the pup danced happily, enjoying the attention.

"Ready to get started?" Lee asked Dex.

Dex stood and nodded and his training officially began. They started by playing with Shaylah's toys—a game of fetch, then a tug-of-war with her chew toy. Dex laughed at her determination and strength. The dog was really committed to doing her best, even at playtime. She was aiming to impress.

Then, Lee taught him several simple commands and Shaylah responded perfectly. Dex hadn't expected such a young pup to be so advanced in her training, but she was alert and knew when playtime was over serious work mode had begun.

Lee looked suitably impressed.

"She's responding really well to you," he said.

Dex was responding well to her too. He hadn't expected it, but the bond he was forming so quickly with the dog was overwhelming. This was more than adopting a pet. They were learning to work as a team for his health and safety. In just one session, they were learning to read one another, react to the other's motions. It was truly life changing and he didn't take this opportunity for granted.

"Shaylah's been working on her response plan for emergency situations by witnessing seizures in patients. She's doing really well learning to identify the person's needs and offering comfort. Kendal and I are confident she can be the support you're looking for," Lee said an hour later as the training wrapped up for the day.

"After just one session with her, I already feel confident of that," Dex said, sitting on the floor, petting the dog's belly as she lay next to him, sleepily. He hated to end the session and leave her there.

Lee checked his watch. "Well, it's nap time and then lunch for this girl, but we'll see you again in a few days?"

Dex nodded as he stood. "Absolutely. Thanks again, Lee." He waved goodbye to the trainer and Shaylah, his heart tugged by the pup's sad look to see him go.

"See you soon Dex!" Kendal called out from her office.

"You bet," he said, feeling a lot more at ease. This was the right thing and he was more confident in his decision than ever.

He pushed through the door and his phone chimed with a new text message from Isla as he stepped outside:

Thought you might like the yacht to yourself this weekend. I've decided to go on that hiking trip after all. I assume you're okay with that?

Obviously, his sister had seen him and Skylar together the night of the rescue... That was where the quilt had come from. He grinned. His sister might act like a badass, but she was really a softie beneath the tough exterior.

More than okay with it.

A full weekend with Skylar alone on the boat to further explore each other, their connection, trust and boundaries. His sister was giving him the perfect opportunity to deepen their connection...and tell Skylar the truth.

His heart raced at the thought. Would Skylar want this too?

There was only one way to find out.

Texting her, he tried to make the invite as casual as possible, despite what he knew her acceptance would mean.

Isla's away this weekend...wanna sleepover?

He hadn't expected the phone to chime immediately with her response. He'd thought she'd need time to think about it. Maybe she didn't need time to say no...

He held his breath as he read her one word reply:

YES!

Tucking the cell phone away, he did skip as he made his way to his car. This day just kept getting better and better.

CHAPTER THIRTEEN

JUST WHEN SHE thought things were better, the lines drawn between her and her father on the work front, he proved that there were still boundaries that needed to be set.

Skylar sighed as she opened an email on her computer and saw the new training schedule her father had drafted for that spring and summer.

Including her team's schedule.

One already approved by the department.

Wonderful.

Putting together the training program for her crew was *her* responsibility and something she'd been looking forward to. She had some new ideas she'd wanted to implement and rescue practice drills she'd intended to add to the regular program.

Reviewing the schedule, she wasn't surprised to see the same old exercises. Helm command, adverse weather rescues, physical fitness assessments… While they were effective, Skylar believed there were other ways to help the team train for the dangers they encountered out on the ocean.

Her father hadn't given her the chance to present them.

Leaving her office, she headed straight to his. She knocked once on the open door and he waved her in.

"Just saw the training schedule…"

"You're welcome. It was nothing. Been doing them so long now," he said with a wide smile.

She could appreciate him wanting to help, but she needed to put a stop to the interference now. Early, before it got out of hand. "I was actually hoping to do it myself. For my crew at least," she said.

"One less thing to worry about."

She gritted her teeth. "It's my job."

"The training schedule is basically the same every year."

"Exactly. I'd been hoping to make some changes but I see you've already sent it in for approval," she said tightly.

He frowned as though not understanding her obviously not so concealed frustration. "Changes?"

"Yes. With Aaron trained in vertical rescues now, I was hoping to involve him more. Have him take us through the things he learned." They were lucky to have him—with his special skills and additional training—on the crew. Not utilizing him to educate the rest of the team would be a waste. She didn't expect the team to put the skills into practice on a regular basis like Aaron did, but having the knowledge and understanding their crewmate's advanced training would be an asset.

But her father scoffed. "Aaron's a young, fit member of an elite team of rescue swimmers. The rest of the crew isn't up for that level of training." He tapped his hip and grinned. "Joints aren't what they used to be."

"Dad! You're not listening to me and you're missing the point." She took a deep breath. "The training schedule for my crew was mine to make." Plain and simple.

He sobered and cleared his throat. "Right. I overstepped." He looked slightly sheepish. "I was just trying to help."

Damn, why was this so hard? He looked disappointed in himself and she felt guilty for making him feel bad. But this was work and if they were going to work together, she couldn't be afraid of hurting his feelings.

"I know," she said a little more softly. "But from now on, please let me do my own work, okay?"

He nodded slowly. "Understood."

"Okay," she said, leaving the office. She refused to feel bad. If it was anyone other than her father, these conversations would be necessary.

They'd also be a lot easier.

Just like another important conversation she was dreading. But she refused to think about that one right now, the text from Dex inviting her to spend the weekend helping to alleviate her work frustrations.

A few hours later, Skylar held a ladder for Carly, who was hanging a new collection of Sealena paintings in the gallery portion of the store. On the inside, she was practically vibrating with excitement. "So... I won't be here this weekend."

Two full days and nights with Dex. No interruptions, no one else around. Waking up together in the morning, cooking and eating together, cuddling on the sofa drinking wine and binge-watching Netflix and going to bed together...

Her mouth went dry at the last part. She couldn't wait to do all those things with him, but she was most anticipating the sex. She couldn't get thoughts of their waterfall date out of her mind, which was inconvenient when she was trying to focus on work or a conversation with her dad.

Carly glanced down at her with a knowing grin. "You're a grown woman now so I'm not going to ask if you know what you're doing." She paused. "But do you?"

No. Spending an entire weekend with Dex was likely not a smart idea. Being with him, opening up to him even more, being vulnerable and letting her guard down could and most likely would lead to heartache. Another heartache.

But they were both adults. They were both insanely attracted to one another. They could deal with whatever happened...

She waved a hand. "It's nothing, really. Just a physical thing this time."

Liar liar pants on fire!

Carly eyed her dubiously, but nodded. "Good."

Skylar frowned. "Good? What do you mean good?" Her cousin was the ultimate romantic. She fell hard and fast, physical relationships weren't Carly's thing.

Carly had been with one man her entire life so far. Her boyfriend of five years who'd ended things two years before. She'd been single and celibate ever since.

But she was nodding as she climbed down off the ladder. "You know I think you and Dex are soul mates. I'd love nothing more than for you two to fall back in love and for you to settle here permanently and make me favorite Aunt Carly to a dozen adorable kids..."

"But..."

"But, I also don't want to see you put it all on the line again for someone who broke your heart." She handed Skylar the hammer as she repositioned the ladder. "At least not without major groveling."

Skylar laughed at the joke meant to soften the truth of the words, but her heart lodged in her throat.

Dex *had* broken her heart, and worse, she'd never really known why...

During the two weeks leading up to graduation Dex's mood had completely changed. Out of nowhere, he'd gotten grumpier, darker. He was quick to get annoyed over little things and he was distant and cool toward her whenever they were together. Which was, oddly, not very often. Sure, they were sneaking around, but they'd never gone more than a few days without seeing one another... But lately, he seemed uninterested in being with her.

He refused to open up about whatever was bothering him, so Skylar had no idea how to pull him out of it.

Worse—it didn't seem like he wanted to be pulled out of it.

And it was killing her. This should have been the most exciting few weeks of their lives. Graduation and freedom were only days away. And then they would tell everyone they were seeing one another and announce their plans.

But Dex refused to even talk about their applications. Skylar knew he hadn't taken any of the necessary steps. He hadn't filled out the paperwork or completed a medical exam or gotten any letters of recommendation from teachers or his football coach. The more she asked him about it, the more annoyed he got. Until he'd shut down completely and refused to discuss it at all.

He wasn't going to football practice. He wasn't going to the gym or running with her anymore. He was even skipping classes. He didn't want to go out with his friends, and his sister seemed to be upset about something, not her usual bubbly, annoying self. It was a struggle to get Dex to leave the house at all. He was depressed and Skylar had no idea of the cause.

Unfortunately, it had all started after their day on the island. Since the first time they'd had sex.

She refused to believe that Dex was *that* guy. The type to lose interest in her after he got what he wanted. He loved her. And she knew their time together had been special.

There was no way he could have been lying or faking their connection. She'd felt it deep in her core.

Right where she felt the pain that day everything had fallen apart.

"Want to go to a movie?" she'd asked, sitting next to him in the basement of the Wakefields' massive house, which they'd transformed into a small apartment for Dex that year to give him more privacy.

"Not really." The television remote control in his hand, he absently flipped through the stations.

"We could take the kayak out?" she asked carefully, shyly. Since the first time they'd been together, they hadn't done it since and it was torture. She wanted him bad all the time, but he didn't seem interested in sex or her. Her ego was taking a huge hit.

Had she not been good at it? It had been her first time. Neither of them had really known what they were doing. They'd fumbled their way through it together, learning and experiencing together. Practice made perfect, right? It was odd that he didn't even want to try. Most of the couples they knew were going at it all the time. They couldn't keep their hands off one another. She and Dex had been the same way. Teenage hormones were no joke—where had Dex's gone?

"Sorry Sky, just not in the mood. I think I'd like to just stay in."

Like every day. She sighed. What else could they do here in his basement? She was going to go crazy if they just sat there like this in the musty cave all afternoon, but she wanted to be with him.

"Okay, well do you want to go online and find a tux for grad? We could figure out which one you want and then call to reserve it." If there was even anything left at the local formal wear store. He'd left it to the last minute. "I mean, you may end up with powder blue this late in the game." She brushed her shoulder against his with a teasing grin.

But he just shrugged, her joke not changing his mood one bit. "Maybe later?"

She sucked in her lower lip and nodded. Her patience was wearing thin. Obviously, there was something wrong, and she couldn't help if he didn't tell her what was up.

"Do you want to talk about whatever is going on?" she asked carefully. He normally bit her head off whenever she suggested there was something wrong. He insisted he was fine. He claimed he was entitled to a bad day every now and then. He asked her to not read anything into it.

He paused and she held her breath. Maybe today was the day he'd finally tell her what was going on. She waited, but he ran a hand through his hair, looking even more on edge. "No."

Shit. So close.

"Dex, you know you can tell me anything, right?" she asked gently. He was the love of her life. She wanted him to know that nothing he said could ever change that.

"There's nothing to talk about." He started clicking through the stations again, but she took the remote control away.

She'd had enough.

"Obviously there is!" She stood and blocked his view of the television. "It's two weeks from graduation and you haven't gotten your application ready yet." She'd applied long ago. At this point, she wasn't even sure he'd make the late-application deadline. Was that it? Was he getting cold feet? Was he nervous he wouldn't be accepted?

She understood the self-doubt, the apprehension… She'd

battled through it too. She could encourage him out of this fear of failing.

"I'm not going," he said.

And Skylar's world crumbled all around her.

"What do you mean?" she asked nervously, feeling as though her head might explode.

"Exactly what I said." His voice was cold, distant. Worse—resolute. "I'm not applying."

She frowned. "Why not?"

"I changed my mind," he grumbled, gesturing for her to get out of the way of the television.

She didn't. "When?"

"A few weeks ago."

"And you didn't think to tell me?"

"It's my decision."

His decision? What about their mutual plans? Tell their families together? Apply together? Go together? Start a life together? Her palms sweat and her knees felt shaky beneath her. "I thought it was something we were doing together?" she asked quietly, feeling like the wrong words, the wrong tone would completely set him off. This walking on eggshells around him was a foreign, unsettling feeling.

"I'm just not into it," he said with a shrug.

Into *it*? Or into *her*? A lump rose in her throat as she rejoined him on the couch. She reached for his hand but he didn't hold hers.

"What's going on, Dex?" It was more exasperation than she intended, but she was completely lost right now with no idea what was going on. Her life plans—their life plans— were being dismissed with no warning, no explanation… She needed a concrete reason for this change in him, his change of mind, change of heart. "Just tell me. Please," she pleaded.

"Nothing! Jesus, Skylar, just leave me alone!" He yanked his hand away from hers.

She blinked. She'd never seen him lose his cool. An outburst like this was so far out of character she had no idea who she was staring at.

His shoulders sagged as he stood and paced. "Look, I'm sorry to yell. I think I should be alone."

"No way. I'm not leaving you until you tell me what's going on?" He might be trying to push her away, but she wouldn't allow it. She loved him. She cared about him. She'd stay strong and be there for him. No matter how much it hurt. She wouldn't walk away from him when he obviously needed her the most. He could lash out, but she wouldn't break.

"I don't want to talk to you about it," he said. "Not right now."

"Then when?" Time was running out. She was being selfish, maybe, but her own life decisions needed to be made too. And they'd depended on him. From the big thing of applying to the academy to all the little things regarding the prom—everything hinged on him making decisions too. Decisions he'd been ready to make two weeks ago. How had everything changed so quickly?

"I don't know, Skylar. Quit pressuring me."

"I'm not trying to pressure you," she said, fighting to keep any annoyance or confrontation out of her tone, but it was hard. She'd allowed him to wallow in whatever this was for weeks. He was being stubborn and unreasonable and she wanted to grab him and shake him. "I just want to help."

"I don't need help."

"Well, then snap out of it!" She couldn't help it. He was infuriating. This Dex wasn't the Dex she knew. The funny, caring, loving Dex. Where had *he* gone? She wanted him back. Desperately.

He looked pained and for a second she thought he might *actually* snap out of it. A look of deep remorse stretched across his features and he took a deep breath. For a second she thought he might sigh and say, "You're right. I'm an asshole. Let's buy a tux." Or smile or laugh or anything...

Instead, he walked toward her and touched her cheek. Quickly. Gently.

A shiver ran through her despite the stuffy basement air.

"I don't want to go to the academy anymore," he said, dropping the bomb with such conviction, it left no room for argument.

Still, she tried. "I don't understand. This was the life you said you wanted." Her mouth was as dry as a desert and her hands shook slightly at her sides.

"Not anymore."

Her chest tightened so much it hurt to breathe. "Why didn't you tell me?"

"I didn't know how," he said simply.

Anger bubbled up inside her. "So instead you moped around for two weeks, having me worry to death about you. Having everyone worry about you. You refused to talk, go out, do anything... I was going out of my mind trying to figure it out. Figure out if I'd done something wrong, said something wrong...hurt you somehow." She paused for a quick inhale. "And you can simply say you've changed your mind without telling me. Not only did you keep me guessing, but you delayed *my* plans too."

He looked genuinely remorseful about that at least. "I know. I'm sorry."

"Why, Dex?" It was the only thing she really wanted to know. There had to be a reason. If there was a good reason, she could accept it. Maybe. But just a sudden change of heart with no obvious explanation—no.

"I just don't want that life. I don't want to leave Port Serenity. I never did."

She blinked. That was news to her. They'd talked all the time about traveling the world. They'd researched places they'd like to go. They planned a future together. In places people would readily accept them as a couple. Away from their family feud and the history that threatened their love. "Ever?" she whispered.

"Ever," he said.

She took a deep breath, her mind racing. Okay, he didn't want what they'd talked about. He didn't want the academy. He didn't want to travel. He didn't want to leave Port Serenity. That was a lot of revelations about what Dex didn't want in the last two minutes. It was hard to keep up, impossible to process. But she needed to know what he *did* want. She needed to know if there was a part of him that still could be persuaded in changing his mind again. Maybe it was fear or hesitation. Maybe he was worried or second-guessing her commitment to him.

She wrapped her arms around his neck, desperate not to let her own disappointment enter at the moment. He was clearly going through something and she wanted to help guide him out of it. "I love you. I understand you might be freaking out, but I'm here. Let's talk." She paused, aware that he still hadn't wrapped his arms around her or kissed her. "If you still don't want to go. I won't pressure you to change your mind."

He looked pained as his gaze burrowed into hers. So much conflict and pain there.

"I don't want to talk about it, Skylar."

"Dex…"

He unwrapped her arms from around his neck and backed away, hands plunging deep into his pockets. "I don't think…" He cleared his throat. "I don't think we should see each other anymore."

She scoffed. "That's just crazy." He might be serious about not wanting to go to the academy, but they were in love. They were amazing together (besides the last two weeks), they wanted to be together. That, she was certain of…

As certain as she'd been about his desire for the academy?

Her heart pounded. "Dex, we love each other. We will figure this out." If he was worried about her going away and not remaining loyal, he had nothing to worry about. How much had he worked himself up in the last two weeks? What lies had he told himself?

"There's nothing to figure out. I don't want to be with you."

Her heart broke and she swallowed the emotions strangling her.

"Dex…"

"Just go, Skylar," he practically begged. He stared at the floor as he said, "I'm not into this—into you—anymore."

She stood there for a long horrible moment, allowing the words to settle in, trying to comprehend… He didn't love her. He didn't want to be with her. Weeks before they were about to start a life together, he was ending things.

She squared her shoulders, fighting not to break until she was away from him, desperate not to let him see just how much he'd hurt her. "Well, you should have been man enough to tell me before I put my trust in you," she said before rushing past him, out of the basement, out of his house and out of his life.

Dex had never told her what had happened back then... but Skylar knew one thing. Before she could fully trust him, she needed the answers he hadn't been willing to give before.

Maybe if she knew what had caused her first heartache, she could somehow prevent a new one.

CHAPTER FOURTEEN

"YOU WANT TO interview me?" Dex was hesitant and he stared at Rachel. She nodded eagerly as she followed him around the deck of the yacht. "Yes. It's for my new blog about Port Serenity's history."

Dex eyed her. "You still trying to prove we're all a bunch of con-artists?" he asked teasingly, but with slight annoyance that at one time Rachel had been out to do just that.

Since coupling up with Callan Parks, she'd quickly changed her viewpoint to be more open-minded, but Dex wanted to be sure this wasn't some sort of trap.

"No. I promise. This is more about the Beaumonts and Wakefields and the long standing family feud."

Ah...

"Sorry. No comment," he said, getting back to work checking the rescue equipment on board. With tourists arriving soon, he wanted the boat in the best shape possible.

"Oh come on, it will be fun and informative."

"No thanks."

Rachel shrugged casually. "Okay...well if you don't want your side of the story told..."

He paused. "What do you mean?"

"Just that Skylar's more than willing to share her viewpoint on the subject."

Dex frowned. Skylar had actually agreed to be interviewed on this? He thought they were trying to move past this silly feud thing. Perpetuating the story, reminding the town and Rachel's readers about the family divide certainly wasn't going to help their relationship. Or have the town accept them together if they did finally come out.

"Skylar's participating?" he asked.

Rachel nodded. "But if you're not interested…"

Damn, she was calling his bluff and it was working.

He sighed as she turned to leave. "Fine. I'll do it."

Rachel turned back to him with a wide smile. "Perfect! Three o'clock today at the Serpent Queen Pub?"

"Skylar will be there?"

"Yep."

"Then three o'clock it is."

CARLY HAD GIVEN Rachel her cell phone number.

So much for avoiding the blogger and her request for an interview. If Rachel was close with Carly, Skylar would have to see her frequently as well.

How could she say no to the interview without making things awkward?

In her office, she stared at the text requesting a meet-up at the Serpent Queen Pub that afternoon.

A little white lie would at least postpone it, and she could try to explain to Rachel how the family feud wasn't something she really wanted to publicize once she got to know the other woman better. Blissfully in love herself, Rachel would have to understand once Skylar explained she was refusing in the name of love.

Sorry, I have to work.

Carly said you were off at two thirty today.

Damn, Carly! Skylar sighed. She'd just have to be blunt and honest.

I'd like to help but I'm not sure I want to continue talking about this. I think it's time to move on. But thank you for your interest in our families.

There. Straight to the point. No bullshit.

I understand...but just a heads-up that Dex will be sharing his family's side of the story.

Skylar's mouth dropped. Seriously Dex? What the hell? She thought they'd both agreed it was best to move on for the sake of the relationship? Now, he wanted to battle it out on Rachel's blog?

Her spine straightened and her fingers flew over the phone. There was no way she was going to allow a one-sided version of the story to be published.

I'll be there.

DID SHE FEEL bad for playing Skylar and Dex off of one another?

Sure. But good journalism required getting information straight from the source. Besides, they both obviously wanted to tell their stories or they wouldn't be here right now...sitting across from one another at a table in the Serpent Queen Pub...glares locked on each other. The tension simmering between them was exhilarating. If only there was a way to capture this intensity in the blog.

Damn, she should be doing a vlog.

Too late now. She doubted she'd get these two together again if she suggested rescheduling and camera equipment.

"Well, thank you both for agreeing to this interview," she said, placing her cell phone on the table. "I'm going to record it so I get the direct quotes right in my post. You two ready?"

Skylar nodded and Dex cleared his throat. "Let's do it."

Rachel hit the record button. "Okay, let's start with a little bit of backstory about your ancestors. Who wants to go first?"

Dex gestured to Skylar. "Ladies first."

Skylar sat straighter. "My great-great-grandfather was an Alaska State Trooper. He was responsible for protecting Port Serenity and Sirens Bay. He won a medal for bravery for helping to apprehend suspects in a smuggling operation along the coast."

"You come from a long line of law enforcement," Rachel said.

"Yes." Skylar said simply.

Rachel waited, but Skylar didn't embellish further.

Okay, she could tell she was going to have to coax the drama out of these two. She turned to Dex.

"And your great-great-grandfather was the legendary Earl Wakefield."

"Legendary." Skylar scoffed.

Dex sent her a look. "I believe the question was directed at me," he said to Skylar.

She folded her arms across her chest.

Dex turned to Rachel. "Yes. Earl was famous for transporting goods into more remote areas of Alaska, taking on the challenges of the open sea that a lot of other captains weren't brave enough to tackle. He brought in provisions from suppliers throughout the United States and Canada for the communities along the coast."

"Among other things," Skylar mumbled.

"I'm sorry, did you say something?" Dex asked her.

"Just that not everything Earl imported was legal," Skylar said.

Rachel had heard that, but she feigned surprise. "You mean Dex's ancestor was one of the smugglers?"

"Smuggler, pirate…"

"And your ancestor was a traitor," Dex countered, leaning his elbows on the table, challenging Skylar.

Skylar's mouth gaped as she leaned closer. "For upholding the law?"

"For arresting his best friend."

"Earl was an unmotivated criminal, taking the easy route instead of making his fortune from honest hard work."

Dex scoffed. "He was bringing in alcohol and cigarettes, not cocaine or guns."

Skylar looked slightly lost for a retort and Dex sent her a smug look.

Not wanting to lose momentum, Rachel asked, "Okay, let's talk about the next generation of Wakefields who created the Sealena town we all love. Dex, your family was responsible for that, right?"

He nodded. "Yes, my great-great-grandparents helped to build the community…" He paused. "But it was the hardworking, determined spirit of everyone here that made the efforts a success."

Rachel consulted her notes. She'd done her research. "But didn't the Wakefields also drive a lot of people out of business?"

Dex shifted uncomfortably. "Well, a lot of the local

shops were struggling and buying them out was the only way for progress."

"Was it though?" Skylar asked. "Couldn't the Wakefields' have supported those previous owners and helped them succeed instead of putting their own name on the awning?"

Dex sighed. "I guess they could have."

It was Skylar's turn to look smug.

"Okay," Rachel said. "So, obviously the families hold different views about the way this community was built. Neither one is wrong, just maybe a little misguided and steeped in a sense of pride and prejudice." She paused. "But the thing I find most interesting is how Sealena seems to represent the Wakefields and the coast guard represents the Beaumonts."

Skylar and Dex turned to look at her, confusion mirrored in their expressions.

"I just mean it seems like the two families are both just trying to protect Port Serenity in their own way and I think they do. Trying to debate which one is more important is like trying to debate between sugar and salt. Each adds to the community what the other can't."

Their expressions changed to one of long overdue realization.

Was it possible that neither of them nor their families had ever thought of that?

Now, Rachel grinned as Skylar and Dex's gazes met and the challenge they'd held five minutes ago now turned to a look of...respect maybe?

Funny how it took an outsider to explain how the two families might finally co-exist.

She was better at this journalism thing than she thought.

As RACHEL LEFT the bar half an hour later, after asking yet more questions about their great-great-grandfathers and that tumultuous relationship, Dex cleared his throat. "Well that was..."

"Enlightening," Skylar said.

Dex carefully reached across the table and took her hand in his. "Do you really think my family are unmotivated criminals?" It would make sense that her family had always held that opinion, but he hoped she could see that by today's standards what his great-great-grandfather did wasn't so illegal and that he had risked a lot to bring the good things into the community.

"No," she said. "Do you really think my family are traitors?" Her gaze burned into his. Obviously, she was referring to her own fierce loyalty to her family name and the fact that she'd left Port Serenity before.

"No," he said, kissing the palm of her hand.

"So...truce?"

He grinned as nodded. "Truce. Still want to spend the weekend with me?"

She smiled. "After that heated foreplay—you bet your ass I do."

CHAPTER FIFTEEN

EVERYTHING NEEDED TO be perfect.

Pulling the fitted sheet off his mattress, Dex bundled all the bedding together and dumped it in the washing machine. He put away the clothes in his bedroom, lined his shoes up neatly on the floor, dusted all the surfaces and washed the round porthole window. He swept and mopped the floor and repositioned the rug next to the bed.

Then he opened the bags from the bed and bath accessories shop in town and strategically placed the new sensual-scented candles all over the room. He sniffed one and coughed.

A little strong...

He took a couple and tossed them back into the bag.

"Why does it smell like an incense shop in here?" Isla asked, wrinkling her nose as she appeared in his bedroom doorway.

"Too much?"

She sighed. "You're trying way too hard."

Maybe, but it was Skylar and he wanted to make that weekend special. Make her want to have more weekends together.

Maybe a lifetime of weekends.

"You heading out?" he asked, eyeing her hiking clothes and her sleeping bag/backpack on her back.

"You in a rush to get rid of me?"

"Yes," he said, checking his watch. He had two hours before Skylar was off shift and he wanted to get their weekend started as quickly as possible.

"And you're sure you're sure about this?" his sister asked, looking deeply concerned.

"Absolutely. Please leave." He grinned. "I mean, go, have a great time. There's nothing to worry about here."

Still, she hesitated. "What if..."

He knew what she was referring to. The thought had crossed his mind as well. What if he had a seizure that weekend? "I haven't had one in months. I'll be fine." Besides Skylar had first aid training. He was probably safer with her than just about anyone else. Not that he wanted her to learn about his condition that way. "I'm going to tell her right away, just in case." He left the room and gently nudged his sister toward the stairs. "Go. Have a good time."

She sighed, but descended in front of him. She opened the front door and paused. "Okay, well if you need me..."

"I won't."

"If you do," she said, "just text and I'll be back right away."

"I won't be texting," he said.

She rolled her eyes. "Bye, Dex." She left then reappeared, popping her head back around the door. "Lose the candles. I have battery operated tea lights in the top drawer of my desk—use those instead."

He grinned. So, she wasn't completely against this idea of him spending the weekend with Skylar. "Thanks, sis."

"Stop grinning like an idiot. I just don't want you burning the place down," she said before closing the door.

Dex hummed to himself as he finished speed-cleaning

the entire yacht… By the time he was done an hour later, the place had never looked so good.

Going into the kitchen, he opened the fridge. Shit, it was practically empty.

"Okay, that could be a problem," he said to himself.

Then he grinned as an idea formed in his mind and reached for his phone and texted Skylar.

DEX'S IDEA TO meet at the grocery store in town had Skylar immediately texting back a "no f-ing way."

Was he out of his mind?

They'd driven outside of town for a dinner date, which had been tricky enough to navigate and they were trying to play it cool around town and at the Serpent Queen Pub with the crew. How could he suggest they go grocery shopping together?

I have a plan. Just trust me.

She read the text and sighed. That was the hard part. Trusting him.

She'd agreed to the weekend because she really had no other choice. Her feelings for him were already overshadowing all common sense. But since her conversation with Carly and the memory of their breakup years before resurfacing, she'd grown more and more concerned about it.

What's the plan? She texted.

I'll grab dinners, you grab desserts.

At 4:58, she finished her rounds and reached for her

purse from under her desk. Still uneasy about the grocery shopping, but eager to get their weekend together started.

"Heading out?"

The sound of Doug's voice in the doorway startled her and she bumped her head on the underside of the desk. "Ow!"

"Geez, sorry. You okay?" He was just starting the evening shift, relieving her, and he'd yet to change into his uniform.

She laughed awkwardly. "Fine. No worries." The idea of sneaking around had her already on edge. How much longer could they really keep it up?

"Did you need me for something?" she asked.

"Can I close the door?" Doug asked.

Skylar nodded. "Of course." She put her purse back down and gave him her full attention.

He closed the door and took a deep breath across from her. "There's no easy way to say this so I'm just going to blurt it out," he said.

She clasped her hands on the desk in front of her and waited.

He didn't blurt it out. He opened his mouth to speak, then quickly shut it again.

"What's going on, Doug?" she coaxed.

"It's just… Well, I applied for a position in California," he said.

She swallowed hard and nodded. That had to be the same one she'd applied for. "Okay…"

"It's not that I don't love it here. I do."

It made sense that he was applying. He was more than qualified. He'd been part of the crew for six years and he was one of the best captains they had. He'd been trained in all aspects of the job—he could navigate the boat and command a crew probably better than she could.

"The idea of leaving Port Serenity is tough, but I just want to be closer to Jay," he said, running a hand through his hair.

Skylar's heart dropped. Now she felt even more guilty having applied herself. If she got the position over Doug, it would also keep him apart from the man he loved.

Her mouth was dry as she spoke. "Yeah, no… That makes sense."

He looked relieved. "So, you're not upset?"

She shook her head. Guilty, conflicted maybe but not upset. "Not at all. You have to do what's best for you and your career."

Doug smiled. "Thanks, Sky… Captain Beaumont." He stood to leave.

She nodded, forcing a smile. "No problem."

He opened the door. "Sorry again about your head. Have a nice weekend off."

Sighing, she picked up her purse and left the office.

There was nothing she could do about it right now. It would be up to their superiors to decide who was better for the position. She'd worry about crossing that bridge when she got to it.

Right now, she had to survive a covert trip to the grocery store.

Five minutes later she pulled into the Super Save parking lot, seeing Dex's car already there. He smiled and winked at her as she parked the car several spots away from him. The simple gesture had her heart racing and she forgot all about the Doug situation.

Her phone chimed with a text.

You go in first. I'll wait ten minutes then come in.

Instead of texting back, she nodded at him as she got out of the car. She could feel his gaze on her as she made her way toward the store. She swallowed hard, feeling her excitement for the weekend returning.

She wasn't even sure why they were wasting their time grocery shopping. She knew she'd be hungry, but not for food.

Inside, Skylar grabbed a cart, looking around. It was quiet in the late afternoon. She relaxed a little until she saw Dex enter with a cart behind her.

What happened to waiting ten minutes?

He avoided her glare as he headed toward the produce section, humming to himself. He was obviously enjoying this.

She couldn't help the tug of a smile, remembering how they used to pull a similar move at the convenience store when they'd go in search of treats to watch movies together on Friday night.

She headed toward the bakery and scanned the selection. She loved angel food cake with strawberries and whipped cream…but Dex was a huge chocolate fan. Anything chocolate, he devoured.

She reached for the chocolate cake, but her phone chimed:

Go with the angel food… I can think of a few uses for the whipped cream.

Damn. She swallowed hard and grabbed both before texting back.

Stop spying on me.

Can't help it. Those jeans look painted on.

Changing out of her uniform into the jeans in the car had been a last-minute decision, but now she was happy she had. She knew this tight-fitting, low-cut pair would get Dex's heart racing. He'd always said she had a fantastic ass and that he loved her in denim.

Hurry up and shop or you'll never get them off, she texted back.

She heard his cart tires squeal as he turned in the opposite direction and headed toward the meat section.

Skylar hid a giggle as she headed to the coolers and retrieved a can of whipped cream, then grabbed two more. They had an entire weekend, after all. Her body ignited at the thought.

She went to the produce section, where she saw him perusing the vegetables. She hesitated, but grabbed a carton of strawberries. Then she purposely rolled the cart past him as he bent to reach for some lettuce. She quickly glanced around her before pinching his butt.

He whipped around, but she avoided his gaze as she nonchalantly kept going down the aisle. This was fun.

A few minutes later, she had everything she needed.

Headed to the counter now. This time, actually wait ten minutes, she texted Dex.

Of course, he didn't listen.

She reluctantly pulled her cart up behind him in the only open lane and shot him a look. Which he pretended not to see as he loaded his items onto the conveyer belt and chatted up the cashier, a young woman Skylar didn't recognize.

She was grateful for that at least. Someone familiar might definitely have their suspicions seeing her and Dex there at the same time.

"Settling in okay?" Dex was asking the cashier.

Ah, so she was new to town.

She nodded. "Getting there. Just need to enroll Sebastian at school, but there's still time."

"Yeah, let him enjoy the summer here first. He'll love it. So much to do," Dex said.

Dex truly believed that. He loved their small hometown. She'd always assumed it was because of his family's popularity...but being home again after being away, Skylar had a better appreciation for her hometown. Especially after the hike to the waterfalls.

The woman noticed her listening to the conversation and smiled. Skylar returned the smile politely, then quickly turned her attention to the magazine display. She picked up the latest issue of the 'Gossip Mill' and was relieved to see her and Dex's dinner date at the steakhouse hadn't made headlines.

As Dex's items moved forward, she put the magazine back, reached for a divider and unloaded her desserts from the basket, setting it back under the counter.

The cashier eyed their individual items and laughed. "Between the two of you, you have a pretty delicious meal."

"Oh, we're not together. Why would you think we were together?" Skylar said quickly.

Dex pretended to notice the items on the conveyor belt for the first time and winked Skylar's way. "Kismet."

Skylar was going to strangle him as soon as they were alone.

"I'll buy the lady's things as well."

"Oh no, I couldn't let you do that," Skylar protested, her cheeks flushing.

The cashier looked in love with Dex as she tsked. "Nonsense. Of course you can," she told Skylar. Then turning back to Dex, she asked, "Is everyone in Port Serenity so neighborly?"

"I'd like to think so," he said as she continued to scan Skylar's items, adding the cost to Dex's bill.

"Thank you," Skylar mumbled awkwardly. She stood there refusing to meet Dex's gaze as he paid and then insisted on carrying her bags to the car for her.

Yep, going to kill him.

"What the hell was that? You did not stick to the plan at all," she hissed the moment they were outside and out of earshot of the cashier.

He leaned dangerously close to her as he murmured, "Not planning to stick to any rules this weekend. You still in?"

Damn right she was in.

"I'll race you there."

THE DOWNPOUR THAT had started unexpectedly on the drive from the grocery store to the dock provided the perfect cover for Skylar to sneak on board without anyone seeing. The dock and pier were cleared out as fishermen had all packed up and called it a day and all the sailors at the marina were cozy inside their cabins.

Rain pelted Dex as he waited on the deck for her, watching her pull her hood up before hopping puddles to meet him on the yacht. Struggling with the grocery bags, he got the door open and nodded for her to go in first.

"Wow, the weather turned quick," she said, lowering the

hood and shaking water from her hands. She peered out the nearest window. "Hope no one's out there."

"Same." He'd hate for an emergency call to interrupt their time together. He wanted Skylar all to himself for the next two days.

Starting now.

He dropped the grocery bags onto the counter in the kitchen and reached for her waist, drawing her into him. "Let's get these wet clothes off," he whispered against her neck. Damn, she smelled incredible—her soft body lotion mixed with the freshness of rain. He wanted to breathe her in all day.

She turned in his arms and gently removed his hands from her waist. "First...we should put the groceries away," she said moving away from him.

He frowned. She avoided his gaze as she opened the bags on the counter. Uh-oh. Was she starting to freak out about this? As much as he wanted to rip her clothes off, he could be patient. He cleared his throat, joining her in the kitchen to unload groceries. "Everything okay?"

"Just wanted to...chat," she said.

Something was definitely bothering her. "Okay. Sure. What do you want to talk about?"

"Doug applied for the California posting as well."

"That doesn't surprise me," he said. "He told you he applied?"

"Yes. And I feel bad for not telling him that I applied too." She removed the three cans of whipped cream and it took all his strength to concentrate on the conversation. The things he planned to do with it started turning over in his mind and he absentmindedly licked his lips.

"Should I have?"

"I don't think there was any reason to."

She bit her lip and nodded. "Yeah…and anywhere else, with a different crew, the thought of telling anyone wouldn't even occur to me as a good idea, but here…" Her voice trailed.

"They're friends too?"

She nodded, taking the empty paper bags and looking for a place to stash them. "It just feels deceitful somehow. Like I'm planning to ditch them, or in this case, be their competition and don't have the courtesy to tell them…" She looked around the kitchen. "Where do these go?"

Dex was still stuck on the last thing she'd said: Ditch them. Ditch *him*.

He knew her plans; he wouldn't let thoughts of what could and possibly would happen down the road ruin the weekend.

He took the bags from her and opened the pantry in the corner of the kitchen. "I don't think they'll see it that way. Don't worry about it. You're right to keep your plans to yourself until you've secured the position," he reassured her. He almost wished she hadn't been so open with him about applying to leave either.

What he didn't know…

"Okay…" Her gaze landed on something beyond him and she pointed to a poster on the inside of the pantry door.

"Stay. Safe. Side. Stay," she read. "What is that? I noticed the same thing in Isla's room."

His mouth went dry. It was probably a good thing that Skylar had seen the reminder. As much as he wanted to tell her the truth this weekend, he wasn't sure he'd have had the balls to bring it up.

This way he hadn't had to. The conversation was started

for him. He took a deep breath. It was a part of his life, something he was no longer frightened or ashamed of. Skylar deserved to know everything. She also deserved an apology for the way he'd treated her years ago.

"It's a seizure action plan," he said. "It means, Stay calm, stay safe by removing harmful objects, protect the head, but don't restrain." He paused. "If the person is not awake, turn them onto their side, and stay with them." He knew the drill by heart. So did Isla. But his sister always insisted that in an emergency, if she had to apply the steps, she might panic and forget something, hence the posters.

"Was your grandpa epileptic?"

It would be easy to simply say yes, take the coward's way out, but that would be wrong. He cleared his throat. "Grandpa had a lot of different ailments in the end," he said honestly.

Skylar nodded as though it made sense.

"But he didn't have epilepsy. I do. That chart is for me."

Skylar's heart raced as she swallowed hard, processing what he was saying. Dex had epilepsy. He looked just as healthy as always. So many questions spiraled in her mind, so she started with the easiest one.

"When were you diagnosed?"

He stared into her eyes and the look of remorse was so strong it nearly stole her breath away. "A few weeks before graduation."

Her stomach dropped. It all made sense now. The moodiness, the irritability, the change in life plans. Dex hadn't changed his mind about his future, about them. His options had been taken away. Or at least that must have been how it felt.

And she'd been so angry, so disappointed. She'd been irritated by his attitude and so incredibly brokenhearted. She'd had no idea…

"That's why…"

He nodded before she could finish the sentence.

"Why didn't you tell me?" she asked so softly it was almost a whisper.

He opened his arms and she immediately stepped into them. He held her tight as he looked into her eyes and sighed. "I was upset, confused. I wasn't sure what it meant for my future, for my life."

Her heart hurt as she thought about those last few weeks. She could have helped. She could have been more understanding. Would she have still gone to the academy? "I wish I'd known."

"I'm sorry I didn't tell you. I know it made you think I didn't love you anymore. Nothing was further from the truth. I loved you with all my heart, and hurting you was the hardest thing I'd ever done. But I don't regret keeping it to myself. You had enough going on at home with your mom being sick."

It had been a tough time, made even harder by his rejection. She'd known something was wrong with him, had wanted to beg him to let her in, but her pride had finally won out. When he hadn't been at the graduation or afterparty, she'd finally given up hope. Given up on them. Given up on him.

Damn, that feeling had been awful for *her*. She couldn't imagine what it had done to Dex.

"I'm sorry, Dex. For not understanding…"

He silenced her with a soft kiss. "None of it was your

fault. You couldn't possibly understand something I'd re-fused to tell you."

That was true, but it didn't erase the deep regret she felt for not having tried harder, tried one more time.

She sighed. It was in the past. They couldn't go back and do things differently.

"What's your prognosis?" she asked nervously.

"How bad is it, you mean?"

She nodded. In the few weeks they'd been together, there hadn't been any signs that he'd been hiding the illness.

He turned and lifted her up onto the counter, settling be-tween her thighs before answering. "In the last six years, I've only had eight seizures, three of them in the first year before doctors could fully diagnose the condition and work out my medication dosage."

Eight seizures. Fear gripped her chest. She couldn't fathom how terrifying that could be. She hesitated. "We don't have to talk about this… You don't have to tell me…" She desperately wanted to know more, but only if he was comfortable. He hadn't said anything since they'd been spending time together. Would he have told her now if she hadn't seen the safety chart? She hated to think that he'd felt like he couldn't tell her—then and now…

"No, I want to talk to you about it. I was planning to this weekend anyway." He held her face and kissed her gently, but confidently. "I'm ready to talk about it, so ask away."

Still, she was unsure how to broach the subject. She didn't want her questions to be insensitive. "What are they like?"

"Mine are essentially similar to blackouts, but I have some awareness of it. I asked my parents to describe what happens…from their point of view and they said I faint and am essentially unconscious for a length of time. Some mild shaking, but nothing too severe."

"The safety plan is how to care for you?"

He nodded. "Yes. All I really need is someone to make sure I don't injure myself while I'm unconscious."

Her heart was racing as she nodded. She'd read about a famous actor's brother drowning from having an epileptic seizure in a swimming pool. The idea that Dex could be somewhere and experience a seizure that put him in danger made her mouth go dry and her palms sweat.

She was overwhelmed by a desire to help him, to protect him, but she resisted. She knew Dex didn't want sympathy.

"And now things are controlled?" He'd mentioned medication.

"Better controlled, yeah. They are still unpredictable and I'm working on that..." He hesitated, but then moved away and nodded for her to join him at the table. He opened his laptop as she took a seat next to him.

Skylar reached out and placed a trembling hand on his thigh as he logged into an epilepsy organization website.

He moved the laptop closer as he took her hand in his and she saw an online journal of sorts.

"I record everything that happened the day of a seizure," he said. "What I ate, drank. Any activities I did that day. How I felt—if I was tired or sick or under more stress than usual. If I'd been exposed to any possible triggers like flashing lights, even something like gunshots or explosions in action movies."

"Rom-coms only from now on," she said, only slightly joking.

Dex laughed. "Deal." He gestured toward the screen.

"I'm looking for patterns. Things to avoid, ways to better take care of myself."

"Wow." A lot of his time was obviously devoted to working on his health. She realized how much she took hers for granted. It was humbling. "What have you found?"

"Not much." He sounded frustrated and she touched his hand. "Eight seizures don't provide a lot to go on and I'm not exactly trying to induce more."

"When was the last one?"

"A few months ago. The one before that had been two years before, so I actually thought I'd maybe somehow gotten over them." He shook his head. "I think this is something I'll always have to deal with."

Skylar studied him. "That's why Isla came back?"

"Yeah. After Grandpa died she insisted on being here, since my parents spend half the year in Florida," he said tightly. "It's the most frustrating thing about all of this. She's putting her own life on hold to babysit me."

"I'm sure she doesn't see it that way," she said gently. They'd always been close and Skylar knew if the roles were reversed, Dex wouldn't hesitate to do the same for Isla. Though she suspected that didn't make him feel any better about it.

"It's not as though I need someone around the clock or anything," he said. "I'm quite capable. I can cook and clean and drive...until it gets dark." He sent her a sheepish look.

The early dinner date at the steakhouse. Made more sense now.

"I can even work," he said.

Her hope rose and he must have sensed it.

His gaze met hers and there was definitely a note of disappointment in his voice as he said, "No emergency personnel jobs or operating heavy equipment."

Right. Meaning no coast guard positions.

A long silence fell between them and she squeezed his hand. "Thank you for telling me," she said. It meant so much that he could be open and vulnerable with her.

"You needed to know. You deserved to know."

She gave a weak smile as he squeezed her hand again. He hesitated, then taking a deep breath, he opened another tab on the laptop.

A website loaded with an image of an adorable little German shepherd pup. Beautiful golden fur and the most incredible blue eyes Skylar had ever seen on a dog. Intelligence and confidence radiated from the canine.

Shaylah, the name underneath read.

"Who's this?" she asked, squinting to read the caption below.

"Isla's soon-to-be replacement."

IN OPENING UP to Skylar, revealing the truth and apologizing for hurting her, it felt like a huge weight had been lifted from Dex's chest.

But had he transferred that weight to Skylar?

He studied her expression as she read all about the seizure response dogs and A Helpful Paw. He could tell she was interested, but he also sensed she was putting off responding emotionally.

He was desperate to know how she felt. After all, he'd had six years to digest what all of this meant.

A few moments later, she took a deep breath and slowly turned to face him. "Wow."

That simple word could mean so much.

"Wow," he agreed.

"She's definitely adorable," she said, glancing back at the photo of Shaylah.

"Adorable and very impressive," he said.

"You've met her already?"

How much did he tell her about his sudden renewed motivation to get the therapy dog? He didn't want her to freak out, but… "Yeah…a few weeks ago. I'd been thinking about it for a long time, but kept putting it off. But… um… I decided it was definitely time to take this step to more independence."

She nodded slowly. "A few weeks ago."

"Basically since you've been back," he said staring into her eyes. He was tired of hiding things from her, tired of pretending that he wasn't all in. He wanted a future with her, a life together…no matter what that looked like.

A thick tension-filled silence lingered between them and then she reached for him. Her hands tangling in the fabric of his T-shirt, she pulled him closer and her mouth met his.

He moaned as he grabbed her waist and pulled her onto his lap. Kissing was definitely better than talking. They'd eventually have to, but right now he was getting all the reassurance he needed from the passion in her kiss.

She hadn't retreated. For now, that was enough.

He stood and pulled her to her feet, then lifted her into his arms. She wrapped her arms around his neck and snuggled closer as he made his way toward the stairs and carried her up to his bedroom.

Talking could wait. Food could wait. The whipped cream could wait.

Right now, he just wanted to be with her. As close and as intimately as possible. His confession had made his heart lighter, but his emotions that much deeper. There were no more secrets between them.

He was fully vulnerable to the love of his life.

He carried her into the bedroom, where only the white tea lights flickered, casting a warm, romantic glow and laid her down on the bed. Without speaking, she reached for him, pulling him down on top of her.

Propping himself on his arms, his lower body pressed into hers as he dipped to kiss her. Her hands entwined in his hair, drawing his head closer, holding it in place.

She still held the faint scent of the springtime rain and he couldn't breathe her in enough. He sat up and removed his T-shirt and then reached for hers. She raised her arms overhead to allow him to remove the shirt up over her head. He tossed both shirts aside onto the floor as she reached around and unclasped her bra, flinging it aside.

His mouth went dry at the sight of her breasts, round and soft with erect nipples. He massaged them, flicking his thumb over the buds, before lowering his head between them and kissing them gently. Skylar's arms around his neck held him closer as she moaned in pleasure.

He eased her back down and reached for the button on those painted-on jeans. He lowered them down over her hips, down her long, slender legs. Her jeans and his joined the pile of discarded clothing on the floor.

Taking in the silk panties she wore, he climbed back on the bed between her legs and ran his hands along her inner thighs. He felt himself get hard as he brushed the fabric.

She arched her back and closed her eyes as goose bumps surfaced on her skin.

He reached higher to cup her breasts as he lowered his mouth to her toned, sexy stomach. He kissed along her rib cage, down toward her belly button, and her legs trembled on either side of him. He knew without words that she was craving more, her desire evident in the way her body reacted to his touch, his kiss.

He loved having this effect on her. There might be limitations to the life he could offer her, but he knew he could meet her every desire physically. There was nothing he wouldn't do to please her.

She reached down to take off her underwear, and he took over, removing them and tossing them to the floor. He stood and removed his own underwear before rejoining her on the bed.

The look of desire and appreciation in her eyes as she took him in gave him all the confidence in the world. He was the man for Skylar and he wanted to prove that to her.

He reached into the bedside drawer for a condom and slid it on quickly, desperate to be inside her, desperate to feel as close to her as possible. She opened her legs and he settled between them. He stared down at her and she reached up to cup his face, the love he felt for her reflected in the depths of her intoxicating eyes.

Overwhelmed with emotions so strong, he made love to her with nothing left between them, except the uncertainty of a future he knew he was prepared to fight for.

A LONG TIME LATER, Dex still couldn't sleep, and he knew Skylar was still lying awake in his arms.

"What are you thinking about?" he asked. It was hard to read her mood.

"I was just thinking about Doug," she said.

"That's flattering," he said teasingly.

She slapped his chest lightly. "Not like that. I just mean his relationship with Jay. The long distance thing."

Ah. "They seem to be making it work."

"Not as well as they'd like though." She trailed her fingers over his chest and glanced up at him. "Not being intimate as often as they'd like must be difficult."

He nodded. "I'm sure it is."

"I'm not sure I could do it," she said.

He'd known that's where the discussion was headed and he appreciated the honesty. He took a deep breath. He wouldn't love it either. This time with Skylar was everything. He loved holding her, kissing her. He couldn't keep his hands off her and he knew that attraction and passion would never fade. It wasn't the only important element in their relationship, but it was important. "I'm not sure I could either," he said softly.

Her eyes searched his. "So, what do we do if I get the position in California?"

He had no answers to that question, so he held her close and whispered, "We'll figure that out together if it's a bridge we need to cross."

For now, he'd just appreciate every moment they had together.

CHAPTER SIXTEEN

DEX WAS GETTING a therapy dog.

Dex *needed* a therapy dog. Skylar was still trying to wrap her mind around that as she showered the next day, the smell of breakfast cooking in the kitchen making her hurry. They hadn't eaten dinner the night before, neither wanting to leave his bed. They'd both needed that time to just hold one another in full vulnerability. There was so much to process. For so long she'd believed Dex had ditched out on her, on the academy. That he didn't want to be with her, didn't love her.

Now all those years of hurt and anger disintegrated at the selflessness he'd hidden. He could have told her, drawn on her support and asked her to stay. She would have stayed willingly. She'd loved him and he would have taken priority over everything else.

He'd known that. So, he'd pushed her away.

She lathered her hair quickly and ran a razor over her legs. Then moments later, she turned off the water and stepped out of the shower. Seeing a cup of hot coffee sitting on the counter, she smiled at the thoughtful gesture. Normally, she did need copious amounts of caffeine to wake up, but that day she was already buzzing.

Dex had invited her to go meet Shaylah at A Helpful Paw and she was excited, but also terrified. He'd made this step toward more independence because of her. She wasn't sure what to do with that information just yet, but she was determined to take things one day at a time. She wanted to be involved with this huge life decision he was making. In whatever capacity he wanted her to be.

Moments later, dressed in her jeans and sweater, she quickly knotted her hair in a bun and applied a coat of mascara and a pale pink lip gloss.

She swallowed hard remembering their time together the night before. There had been no words, yet she felt their relationship reach a new level. They'd needed the tender lovemaking after the intensity of their conversation and their raw emotions. And afterward, things had gotten serious with the realization that a long-distance relationship wasn't what either of them wanted.

They'd figure it out together if it was a bridge they needed to cross, Dex had said. She knew they would.

Leaving the bedroom with her coffee, she descended the stairs and joined Dex in the kitchen just as he set their plates on the table. The bacon and eggs smelled so good, her stomach growled. And the sight of him in his jeans and sweatshirt, his hair still wet from his own shower had her heart swelling.

"There you are," he said turning and opening his arms.

"Looks and smells delicious. A girl could get used to this," she said, leaning into him.

He wrapped his arms around her. "A guy could only hope," he said casually, but she heard the intention in his tone. This weekend was more than just about sex and spending uninterrupted time together. This was Dex's way of showing her what a life together could look like.

She'd always envisioned one and had always loved what

she'd seen. But the version she'd thought of in the past had been slightly different. Actually a lot different.

Could this new version make her just as happy?

Sitting at the table, they ate quickly and then after sneaking off the yacht unnoticed, Skylar joined him in his car as they headed to A Helpful Paw. The excursion was unexpected, but this was important. They were both quiet as he drove and she sensed he was just as nervous about her meeting Shaylah as she was.

But that nervousness subsided the moment they entered the dog training facility.

"You brought a friend today?" a woman greeted them as they entered.

His hand clutching hers, Dex did the introductions. "Skylar Beaumont, please meet Kendal Riley, the coordinator of A Helpful Paw. Skylar is my..." Dex hesitated, glancing at her. Waiting for her to fill in the blank.

Friend? High school sweetheart? Soul mate?

Skylar swallowed the lump in the back of her throat as she extended a hand to Kendal. "His girlfriend," she said, sensing Dex's wide smile without even having to look at him.

And just like that, once again, she was.

THAT DAY COULDN'T have gone better. He'd sensed Skylar's hesitancy when they'd first arrived at A Helpful Paw. He understood. Skylar had only learned the truth the day before, but she was handling it well.

And luckily Shaylah was so adorable, it was easy to fall in love with her.

A lot of the pressure from the day before had eased and

he was looking forward to a more relaxed evening with Skylar.

His girlfriend.

He was still elated on the drive back to the yacht at hearing her label them that way. He'd known that was what he wanted and they'd seemed to be headed in that direction, but actually hearing her say it had made his heart soar.

She seemed to be on the same page as she headed straight for the fridge the moment they entered the boat. For a second, he thought maybe she was hungry...but nope, there it was—the can of whipped cream in her hand with a mischievous gleam in her eye.

Thank God.

After scooping her into his arms, Dex carried her upstairs, into the bedroom and gently placed her onto the bed. They disrobed in record time, and Skylar reached up and released her bun. Her pretty, wavy blond hair fell like silk around her shoulders.

Damn, the sight of her naked and as eager for him as he was for her was a major turn-on. He reached for her and then laughed as Skylar pulled him onto the bed, armed with the whipped cream.

"I'm kinda scared," he said as she shook the can, clearly on a mission. Scared but definitely up for anything. His body was already alive with anticipation.

"You should be," Skylar said, before spraying some of the whipped cream into her mouth. She swallowed the dollop and then licked the remaining bit seductively from her lips.

Holy hell.

His mouth dropped as he watched her. The woman was

going to be the death of him. She hadn't even licked the cream off him yet and he could feel himself harden.

Naked, she straddled him on the bed and he folded his hands behind his neck as he watched her spray a trail of the cool cream over his pecs. She tossed her long hair to the side as she bent her head to lick the cream off him. He swallowed hard as her tongue caressed his flesh and she lapped up every little bit.

She sprayed more along his abs and he reached down and gathered her hair in his hands as she continued her sexy quest to savor him like dessert. The way she pushed her ass up into the air as she bent over him, licking every inch with an eager hunger had his mouth going as dry as a desert.

He sat up and flipped their positions. He tickled her and she giggled and wiggled beneath him as he wrestled the can away from her. "My turn," he said.

He gripped both her wrists with one hand and held her arms overhead as he sprayed the whipped cream over her collarbone with his other hand. He lowered his head and licked the cream away. Skylar moaned and her body shivered beneath the feel of his tongue on her skin.

He sprayed more in a line from her collarbone, all the way down between her breasts and followed the motion with his mouth. He applied the cream to both breasts and hungrily licked every last bit, teasing her nipples with the flick of his tongue and gently biting them.

Skylar panted on the bed beneath him. Her legs wrapped around his waist and she squeezed tight. He pressed his erection against her opening and her eyes widened as he dared to dip the tip of his penis inside. He longed for a time when he could take her without any protection at all.

He pulled back out slowly and released her hands as he

moved farther down the bed between her legs. He sprayed whipped cream along her mound and folds and then handed her the can. She repositioned her body beneath him in a sixty-nine position and covered his straining, throbbing penis with the cream.

Her eyes met his as she tossed the can aside and lowered her mouth to him. The feel of her taking him in her mouth had him twitching with desire and when his mouth met her opening, licking and sucking the cream away, he knew he wasn't going to last long.

Thank goodness she'd bought more than one can.

By midnight, all three cans of whipped cream had been used and not one little bit was consumed in the kitchen on the angel food cake.

Satiated, for now, Skylar drifted off to sleep next to him as the moon streamed in through the bedroom window.

Dex couldn't remember a more perfect day. Skylar was still lying next to him. Naked, sweaty, and slightly sticky from the cream. He stared at her as she slept and couldn't resist touching her. Just to be sure she was really real. He was in love with her and they'd taken the next step in their relationship by labeling it.

She'd labeled it.

His girlfriend. Skylar Beaumont was his girlfriend. Again.

She was so beautiful. He'd always thought she was the most breathtaking girl he'd ever seen and time had only intensified that beauty. Her womanly curves, the shapely hips, ass and thighs and soft voluptuous breasts had him completely under her spell. The way she moved her body and the way she pleasured him… He was fully devoted to her. There was no one else he'd ever wanted as badly as he wanted her. No one else he'd ever needed in his arms, in his life, in his heart this way.

He'd do anything to keep her.

She stirred in her sleep and reached for him.

"You're sleeping," he whispered against her ear.

"Well then wake me up," she murmured, rolling onto her back and dragging him on top of her.

Damn, she was sexy. They'd both orgasmed three times the night before, but he could never get enough of her and it was such a relief that the feeling was mutual.

He lowered his head to kiss the crook of her neck, her shoulder, her collarbone. She tasted so good and felt even better. Soft skin and firm muscles. A tantalizing scent that filled his senses and drove him wild.

He was so grateful for this time with her. No sneaking around or pretending not to be together in front of their family and friends.

Alone together and able to be a hundred percent committed to one another.

She kissed him as she ran her hands over his chest and stomach. He lay between her legs and swallowed hard. He wanted to feel himself deep inside her body.

"You sure you don't want to sleep?" he teased, slipping a hand between her legs and feeling how wet and ready she was already.

"Dex, I've never been more sure of anything in my life," she said. "I love you."

She loved him. The very idea that after years apart, they still loved each other made his world. He'd never dared hope that Skylar would come back and certainly not back to him.

Yet, here she was. In his arms, always in his heart and she was telling him that she loved him too.

He opened the bedside drawer and took out a condom. He tore it open and slid it on over his erection.

Her eyes watching him were full of desire and when she licked her lips, he was tempted to pull it off and take her mouth again instead. But he knew this wouldn't be the last time they made love that day. He didn't care if they never left the yacht for the rest of their time together.

He lowered his hips as he wedged his body between her thighs. Supporting his weight on his forearms, he kissed her and she moaned as he pressed his cock against her opening. He wanted her so badly. He'd thought the yearning would decrease after multiple orgasms, but each time felt as desperate and passionate as the first.

"Dex, please get inside me."

He rubbed the length of his cock against her folds, feeling her wetness cover him. He picked up the pace, grinding faster against her mound and daring to dip the tip into her. Damn, she felt amazing. Better than he remembered.

He entered her slowly and she gripped his shoulders as she wrapped her legs around him, drawing him closer. "Deeper, Dex. I want to feel all of you inside all of me," she said.

God, he was barely going to last.

She lifted her hips to get even closer, take him even deeper.

Her tight, wet pussy was intoxicating. He felt euphoric as their bodies rocked together in sync.

Gripping her breasts, he squeezed hard as he plunged in and out.

Skylar moaned and her nails bit into his back as she rocked her body faster and tightened her muscles around his straining, thick cock. Desperate for release, but not wanting the moment to end, he slowed the pace.

"Dex…" she nearly pleaded.

"Not yet." He was torturing himself, but he wanted this time with her to be amazing. He wanted each experience to be better than the last, to push their boundaries as they explored one another's fantasies and limits. He slowly pulled out of her body and her eyes widened.

"Flip over," he commanded.

She did without hesitation and his heart pounded.

"Lift your ass in the air. Face down into the pillow."

He heard her swallow hard as she did as he commanded. Her ass high, the arch of her back accentuating her curves, she was mesmerizing.

He massaged her ass cheeks and slid a hand between her legs to rub her clit. She moaned against the pillow. He ran his thumb slowly along her butt crack all the way down to her opening. The taut little bud was so sexy, it nearly put him over the edge just thinking about it. He felt her tense slightly, but she didn't ask him to stop. Her fingers gripped the fabric of the pillow and she pushed her ass even higher.

"Open your legs wider," he said.

She did eagerly and he reached around and fingered her clit as he slid into her body from behind. This position gave him better access to go deeper, and he had to fight for control of the sensations building.

She was so sexy submissive, ass in the air, face buried into the pillow. It was hard not to come immediately.

He gripped her hair and pulled gently. Testing…pushing boundaries. She nodded her approval over her shoulder, allowing him to take her as he desired. Having such a strong, independent woman completely surrendering to him, completely at his mercy had him so close to the edge.

He pulled her hair and rode her hard. She clung to the pillow, crying out in pleasure as he pumped into her. He was deep within her and it was still not enough. Gripping her hips, digging his fingers into her flesh, he fucked her hard and fast from behind until they were both panting.

"Dex, please…"

"Come for me, Skylar." He wouldn't let go until she did. He slid in and out, tugging her hair, as she tilted her head to look at him as she came. She cried out one last time as her body trembled her release.

He came, shuddering with such intensity he thought his heart might actually stop. Damn, that was the hottest sex he'd ever had. He collapsed against her body and gently stroked her back. "Was that okay?" he whispered against her skin.

"Do it again," she said, her tone full of want and Dex felt himself grow hard once again.

He was so in love with this woman.

EVERYTHING WAS ABSOLUTELY PERFECT.

Right up until the moment Dex's radio sounded, waking them from a half sleep sometime before dawn. Skylar's eyes shot open and she sat up, as Dex rubbed the sleep away from his face.

"What's going on?" she asked, immediately tense. All the relaxation she'd finally given into evaporating in an instant. Hours of passion had finally led to sleep, but now she was fully awake.

"A call for assistance from the coast guard," he said.

Her father was on duty that weekend and he was requesting assistance from Dex?

"It's sent out to all nearby vessels," he explained, answering her unasked question as he got up out of bed.

Normally the sight of his incredible naked body would have had her heart racing and her body awakening, but Skylar was fully alert in a different way.

Shit, shit, shit. They'd almost survived the entire weekend together without something ruining it. But the illusion was being lifted, and she remembered how messy their situation was.

She was on Dex's volunteer boat. They were obviously going to answer the call, but if she assisted from Dex's boat, her father and everyone else would learn about the two of them together.

In the most awkward of ways.

They dressed quickly and she followed Dex down to the cabin as he started the boat and responded to the emergency assistance call. "This is *The Mariana* responding, what's the situation?"

"A little girl has been reported missing from her family's cabin on Marina Way," Skylar's father said over the radio. "She's known for sleepwalking and the family's canoe is missing from the dock. Her parents fear she may have taken it out alone."

A missing child meant everyone was on deck.

"Requesting *The Mariana* search along the south coastline as close to shore as possible."

Dex glanced at her as he responded. "Copy."

What the hell was she going to do? Skylar couldn't sit this one out. She also couldn't assist with Dex on his boat. Her father finding out about them this way would be disastrous. And she wasn't ready to have everyone in Port Serenity know they were together either.

She grabbed her jacket quickly and shoved her feet into her shoes as Dex continued to communicate with the coast guard regarding the search plan. She shot him a look as she opened the door. She wanted to go to him and kiss him, but the tension of the situation and urgency made the moment not right.

"Bye," she mouthed.

He looked disappointed, but nodded. They both knew what the priority was right now.

Skylar deboarded Dex's yacht just before he pulled away from the dock. As she hurried along the marina toward the coast guard station, she saw the lights of other vessels turn on and engines starting in the harbor and several already moving slowly out of the inlet.

The whole community came together in times like this and living in Alaska, these situations happened all too often. An overwhelming sense of pride wrapped around her, despite her fear. Port Serenity was a special place. One that she'd always thought she needed to get away from, but now she was questioning that decision. She swallowed hard as she headed toward the coast guard station.

What was she going to say when she arrived? How was she going to explain the fact that she'd heard the call for assistance? She was off duty. There was no way she should even know about this yet…

Her mind raced. Either way, she was going to help find this little girl.

As she picked up her pace, something caught her eye from under the pier about ten yards away. A brief flash of white, then it disappeared again in the shadows. She almost thought she'd imagined it, but then it reappeared. There was definitely something...or someone down there.

She ran down the boardwalk, careful not to trip on the uneven planks of wood in the dim, early dawn lighting. Reaching the pier, she climbed over the side railing and made her way down the side on the slippery, treacherous rocks as the ocean waves slapped against them.

How on earth had someone gotten down here? There were no stairs, no ramp.

Her pulse raced as she reached the bottom and she gasped as the shallow North Pacific Ocean reached her knees. Ignoring the chill, she scanned along the bottom of the pier. The parents had said the family canoe was missing. But she didn't see the boat anywhere...or the child.

Had she imagined it?

She'd been certain of the flash of white...

Skylar surveyed the area. She grabbed her cell phone from her pocket, turning on the flashlight to get a better view. She clung to the wooden pillars supporting the pier as she moved out farther, the deeper water and light current making it harder to tread through the choppy waves.

"Hello!?" she called out. "Anyone down here?"

Silence.

Her legs felt numb and she shivered as she continued to look. She had to be sure there was no one down here. She thought of calling Dex to let him know where she was, but there was no service beneath the pier.

"Damn it," she muttered as she moved through the water, now up to her waist. She turned in a circle, surveying the area. She squinted in the dark, searching.

There was nothing there. It must have been just a shadow or a reflection from one of the boats...

Then her heart stopped, seeing the flash of white again. A nightgown. She was sure of it. She peered through the dark and saw the small figure floating face down in the water.

Her mouth went dry as she powered through the deeper currents of water, then broke into a swim as she neared the body. A little girl. No more than seven or eight…

She grabbed the child, flipped her face up, then swam with one arm around the girl back to the safety of shallower water, before lifting the child onto the pebbled beach.

It had been months since she'd had to resuscitate someone, but her training kicked in as she applied chest compressions and gave oxygen to the limp, terrifyingly lifeless body.

How long had the child been in the water?

She couldn't be too late. Skylar was the only one who knew the child was there. She was the little girl's only hope. There was no time to call for help.

She continued the compressions and oxygen, her hope fading.

"Come on. Please, come on. Wake up."

Finally, the little girl spat water from blue lips, and her eyes opened slowly.

Relief overwhelmed her as Skylar turned the child to her side and the little girl coughed up what seemed like an ocean of water.

"It's okay. You're okay," she said. Her heart raced and her hands shook as she soothed the terrified little girl.

The child looked on the verge of passing out. "Where am I?" she asked tearfully.

"Under the pier at the marina," Skylar said, keeping her

voice calm and steady despite her body's trembling. "But it's okay. You're safe now. What is your name?"

"Rosa."

"Are you hurt, Rosa?" She quickly checked the child but saw no visible injuries.

The child shook her head. "Just co-cold," she said, her teeth chattering.

Her skin felt like ice and Skylar hugged the child to her to provide some warmth and comfort as she reached for her cell phone and prayed it was actually as waterproof as the manufacturer claimed. She hoped there was enough service as she dialed the coast guard station.

She gave no thought to how she would explain her knowing about the situation. Or why she was there. None of that mattered. All that mattered was...

"I found her. The missing child is alive, down under the pier," she said quickly when the control tower answered the call. "Request for immediate assistance and emergency services."

"Copy. Locating your position now," the attendant said.

Skylar's chest swelled with relief as she held the scared little girl tight and waited for help to come.

CHAPTER SEVENTEEN

SKYLAR WAS THE hero once again and despite Dex's conflicted heart about her hasty exit, he was so happy she had left when she did. They wouldn't have found the missing child in time otherwise. The coast guard and the rescue assistance boats were all out on the water, looking for the family canoe.

One that turned out to have been "borrowed" by a group of teenage boys, who were so distraught about their role in the incident, the family thought they'd been punished enough and weren't looking to pursue charges for theft. The parents were just happy to have their daughter safe again.

Rosa was recovering at the hospital, being monitored for excess water in her lungs. The doctors were confident of a full recovery. Her father had already put new locks on the exterior cabin doors to prevent her from further endangering herself with her late-night adventures.

As Dex rounded up the tea lights and replaced them in Isla's desk drawer, his thoughts were free to return to Skylar.

How was she feeling now? About them?

He knew the call had freaked her out for more than just the obvious reasons. She'd been on his boat. Her father was leading the rescue. She'd had a difficult decision—stay and let her father find out about them in a less than desirable way or leave the scene. He couldn't shake his frustration at how much she wanted to keep their relationship a secret.

If they were going to be together, really together, keeping things a secret couldn't go on much longer.

Unfortunately, he had no idea what that meant.

SKYLAR HESITATED AS she walked toward her father's office in the coast guard station hours later. She'd been at the hospital with Rosa until the doctors had confirmed the little girl was going to be okay and then she'd had to give a statement to police.

But now that the rescue was over, it was time for Skylar to face the music. Pausing outside the office door, she squared her shoulders and took a deep breath. She was a grown woman and this was her life. Who she chose to love was her decision.

If only she thought her dad would see it that way.

She knocked once on the partially closed door and he waved her in as he hung up his desk phone.

"Hi, Dad," she said somewhat meekly then forced more strength into her voice. "About last night or I guess it was actually this morning..." She avoided his gaze, trying to find the right words. What could she say?

I had just had a mind-blowing night of sex with a man you disapprove of when the call for assistance interrupted my night...

Probably not.

Luckily he spoke first. "Great thing you've stuck to those early morning runs," he said, looking at her with pride.

Early morning run. Of course.

That explanation—lie—was easier. "Just happy I was

in the right place at the right time," she said, her throat constricted.

"We all are."

She should tell her father the truth. Sneaking around was childish... But, she actually had something else she wanted to discuss with her dad. Maybe she would only fight one battle today.

"Hey, Dad, I was wondering—the coast guard health regulations have relaxed a bit over the years, haven't they?"

He nodded. "Yeah. When your grandfather started at the academy, even having less than perfect vision was a reason to be denied. Things have changed to be more accommodating and not as restrictive to ensure the best candidates get a chance," he said, nodding slowly. "Why do you ask?"

She swallowed hard. Did anyone in town know about Dex's condition? It suddenly occurred to her that she hadn't asked him if others knew. Maybe they didn't. Maybe it was something he kept to himself. Someone might have told her if it was something he'd shared.

Though getting the therapy dog would soon alert people to the situation.

Still, she kept the specifics to herself. "I just had a... friend..." Dex was so much more than a friend. He was her lover, her boyfriend, her *best* friend. "He's interested in applying to the academy, but he has some health issues."

Her father shrugged. "Well, depending on the condition and the severity, the risks it poses for crew and public safety...who knows? Every situation is different."

She nodded. "Thanks, Dad." Every situation was different. And there were other positions Dex could apply for. Ones that might be different than he'd originally aspired to, but maybe ones he might consider if it meant that they could move forward with their original life goals. Together.

Feeling a little better, but still guilty as shit, Skylar headed toward her office to do some research of her own.

"HOW WAS THE WEEKEND?" Isla asked, as she unpacked a stack of dirty clothes from her hiking bag later that day.

"Obviously cleaner than yours," Dex said, nodding toward a pair of brown socks that used to be white and plugging his nose against the mild, musty smell coming from the pile.

Isla laughed. "It rained the entire weekend, so the hiking trails were essentially mud." She pointed a finger at him. "But we're not talking about *my* weekend. We're talking about yours."

Dex sighed. "I took her to A Helpful Paw to meet Shaylah," he said, which should basically answer all her questions.

Isla's eyes widened. "So, she was cool about the whole thing? Didn't freak out at all? Wasn't upset about the fact that you didn't tell her in high school?"

Skylar had been fine about all that. It was the rescue call that had thrown them off course.

"She had a lot to process, but everything was fine," he said. He cleared his throat. "Do you have plans this evening?" he asked casually.

Isla shot him a look as she scooped up the heaping pile of laundry. "I was planning on laundry."

He sighed. "I'll do it if you'll disappear for a few hours." Skylar was coming for dinner. He didn't need his sister eavesdropping on the conversation or making Skylar even more uncomfortable.

As it was, he suspected the evening to be slightly strained.

So, he was pleasantly surprised a few hours later when Skylar wrapped her arms around his neck and kissed him when he opened the door to her. It was a quick peck, but it was better than the "I think we should cool it" speech he'd been preparing to defend all afternoon.

"Hello to you too," he said, hugging her tight. "Everything okay?"

She nodded and took a deep breath as she stepped back. "I'll admit I panicked this morning. When the call came in, I had no idea what to do and the thought of my dad finding out about us…in that way…well, I felt like a seventeen-year-old again, afraid of disappointing him." She paused. "But, after the rescue I had a lot of time to think and I don't think we should hide this—us—anymore."

Dex released a sigh of relief. They were on the same page. Finally. After years of trying to convince Skylar that their family feud and history shouldn't define their lives, she seemed to agree.

"I mean, we're adults. Our family's feud is their issue, not ours. You are not your great-great-grandfather and shouldn't have his former questionable decisions held against you, and I'm not the type of person to continue this grudge against your family."

It sounded like she was still talking herself into this, but Dex nodded. "I'm pretty sure I've heard all these fantastic arguments before," he teased.

She swiped at him playfully and he pulled her in close again. "So, you're sure you're okay with that? Everyone knowing? Your father knowing?"

Skylar nodded. "Yes," and damn if it didn't sound convincing.

He kissed her, savoring the moment that had been a long time coming. His heart soared and while he knew it wouldn't be an easy conversation for her, he'd offer to be there to support her and convince her father he was committed to her, to the relationship.

But when she slowly pulled away, Dex could sense there was something else on her mind. Something else she wanted to discuss.

"Should we make dinner? I'm starving," she said, avoiding his eyes.

Obviously not ready to broach whatever was on her mind yet.

"Sure," he said, taking her hand and leading the way to the kitchen. "Chicken pasta?" They still had all the ingredients as they hadn't done as much eating that weekend as he thought they would.

"Sounds delicious," she said.

They worked together on the meal, but she didn't say anything more about whatever was bothering her.

After the past week together, letting all their walls come down, there shouldn't be anything she should be afraid to tell him or ask.

Having her in his kitchen, cooking together, was nice. It would be nicer if he wasn't nervous about what she was struggling to say.

She cleared her throat again, but her gaze remained focused on the chicken in the frying pan when she finally spoke. "So, I was talking to my dad today about health restrictions in the coast guard. He says they've gotten a lot less restrictive over the years."

Dex frowned. "You mentioned me?"

"No!" Skylar shook her head. "No, I didn't know if any-one knew."

"They don't. I've kept it to just close family and friends."

She nodded and flipped the chicken. She was quiet for another moment before saying, "Did you know that Walt Benson, the senior lieutenant of *The Atlantic* has diabetes?"

Dex stirred the pasta. "Had no idea," he said, his spine stiffening.

She added spices to the meat. "Yeah, apparently it's under control with insulin and a healthy diet so he's been able to advance through the ranks."

"That's great."

"It just got me thinking that in certain situations, it might be possible for you to think about a career in the coast guard again. If you still want one," she added quickly.

Obviously, she was hoping he did. He sighed. "Diabetes and epilepsy are two different things, Sky."

"I know." She turned to face him, the hopeful expression on her face making his mood plummet slightly. "I'm not saying it would be an easy road, but I think it's possible."

He shook his head. "I don't think so. I looked into it be-fore and there doesn't seem to be a way around it with my particular condition." The pasta water started to boil and he lowered the heat of the burner.

"Things change all the time. Requirements change... I'm sure there has to be a way." Abandoning the chicken, her attention was now fully on the conversation. "I can help you look into it more. We can research options..."

His chest tightened at her eager excitement. "Skylar, can we not do this right now?"

258   SWEET HOME ALASKA

She looked ready to argue, but said, "Sure. I just thought I'd mention it."

Her disappointment broke his heart. He approached her and turned her to face him, then he took her hands in his. "Look, I'm sorry to shut the idea down. I know how badly you want this for me. I wanted it too. A long time ago. But I've come to accept it's not in my future. Not professionally anyway."

Unfortunately, she saw it as an open door. "I can make a few calls. Find out some answers from higher-ups. Online always gives it in black-and-white, but they make exceptions all the time," she spoke quickly.

He hated to let her down, but he knew this was not something he'd consider. Not again. The crushing realization that he couldn't go to the academy years ago had nearly destroyed him. He'd spiraled into such a depression that took months to climb out of with the love and support of his family, doctors and his online support group chats with Marcus. He'd made the best of it, accepted it, moved on. He wouldn't backpedal and undo all the healing and progress he'd made. Risk being hurt again if it turned out he still couldn't apply.

"It's a no, Skylar," he said gently.

"But you're doing it anyway on a volunteer basis."

"That's different."

"How?" she countered.

"It just is," he said simply, knowing she'd find a way to argue if he elaborated.

She seemed irritated by the dismissal. "Why won't you at least consider it?"

"Because it would be selfish."

She frowned. "To follow your passion? How?"

The pasta pot overboiled and the chicken sizzled in the frying pan. They both ignored them.

He cleared his throat. "What if I have a seizure on a rescue and someone gets hurt…or worse? How could I live with myself? Volunteering is a little different. I can control when I go out and no one is really depending on me."

She looked distraught as though finally getting it. Her argument seemed to fizzle out and die on her lips as she nodded slowly. "I guess I understand that."

If only he could try. If only he could give her this. But he couldn't.

"I'm sorry, Skylar. I can't revisit that option for my life."

"Okay, so maybe the position you wanted before might not be in the cards… But there are other options," she said carefully.

"Like?" He turned off the burners and struggled to deal with a conversation she obviously wasn't finished with. He owed her this opportunity to try to change his mind or come to terms with the facts.

"What about looking into civilian positions?" she asked, reaching into a cupboard for two bowls.

He'd thought about it over the years, but he was doing what he loved—assisting on a volunteer basis on actual rescues. Other positions didn't appeal to him. Sitting on the sidelines in a support role would only make him feel as though he were missing out, not doing enough.

He was silent for a long moment, thinking of how best to explain it to her. He knew she was trying to help and that for her, this was still an important part of them being together. If he was an active member of the coast guard it would gain him points in her father's eyes, making the relationship easier for them both. And admittedly he had been drifting these last few years. Helping out at the Serpent Queen Pub and being available to volunteer on the rescues suited him, but maybe it was time to follow a real career path.

When he turned to face her again, the look of hope reflecting in her eyes was too much to dash so he nodded. "Absolutely. I'll look into it," he said.

"You will?"

"I promise."

Dex swallowed the lump of anxiety rising in the back of his throat at the promise he was going to be putting himself at risk of heartache again to keep.

But it was better than risking the heartache of losing the woman he loved.

CHAPTER EIGHTEEN

WITH RACHEL'S BLOG post going live the next day, the Wakefield/Beaumont family feud was once again the talk around town. It was a fantastic post that portrayed both Skylar and Dex's positions fairly, while highlighting the importance both families had for the community.

But being in the spotlight once again didn't help her and Dex fly under the radar the way she was hoping, so Skylar weighed the options.

She could not tell her father directly about her and Dex and let him eventually find out through the *Gossip Mill* or she could have the tough conversation with him and be done with it. If he found out on his own, he'd be annoyed that she hadn't told him herself. But maybe he'd respect her for coming to him with the news upfront…or six years later, as the case might be.

Carly was of little help.

"If you tell him, you're making a big deal about the Beaumonts and Wakefields…comingling," she said as she plugged her phone into the store's music system and the sounds of the local folk band singing yet another song about the serpent queen almost made Skylar's ears bleed.

"But if you don't tell him, he'll know you were hiding it, which confirms that the feud is still alive and infiltrating the current generation," Carly said.

As Rachel had suggested in her blog post. Maybe Skylar should have told her that she and Dex weren't exactly enemies...

Skylar bit her lip. "So, which is worse?"

Carly sent her a sympathetic look. "Sorry, cuz, I think you'll have to trust your gut on this one. You know your dad and how he'll react a lot better than anyone."

If only her gut wasn't twisting at the thought of either option.

Skylar still wasn't convinced one way or the other as she climbed the stairs to the family home later that day. Knocking once on the door, she opened it and went inside. "Dad? You home?"

Please don't be home.

"In the den," he called from down the hall.

Skylar walked slowly, taking calming breaths. She wiped her sweaty palms on the legs on her pants.

This was ridiculous. She was in love with Dex and her father would just have to learn to accept it.

She entered the den and saw him standing over his desk, carefully gluing a tiny toothpick-sized piece of dark stained wood to a model boat he was building.

Behind him on the office shelves were the six other kits he'd built over the years. She'd helped him with each one. He was normally such a perfectionist, but he never got upset with the slightly off-centered pieces and imperfections resulting from her "help." Memories of hours chatting with him and building the model boats flooded Skylar's mind, making her rethink this conversation.

She swallowed hard when he smiled up at her. "Just in time to help me with the new kit," he said, waving her in.

She approached the desk and he handed her the box. She

studied the whaling boat on the cover and swallowed the lump of nerves in her throat.

"It's the latest in the collection. Carly ordered it in for me for my birthday." He smiled at her. "But I thought I'd wait for my helper before breaking it out of the box. Thought I'd start on the framework, since it's your least favorite part and you can work on the interior details."

She gave a strangled-sounding laugh. "I haven't built one of these in years."

He nodded toward the glue. "She's all yours."

Skylar hesitated before picking up the superstrength glue and a tiny piece of the boat's deck. She carefully applied the glue with a shaky hand.

She cleared her throat as she bent low and painstakingly lined up the piece to the edge of the one her father had just applied.

"You and Dex are not a good idea," her father said gently, knowingly.

Her hand slipped and the tiny piece went on sideways. Her eyes widened as she looked up at him.

"You know about us?" They hadn't been as careful the last few days. They'd gone to the Serpent Queen Pub together the night before and Dex had run with her the past two days. Not several feet behind or in the opposite direction to give the appearance of a coincidence.

Secretly, she'd been hoping her father would see them. Obviously he had.

He laughed wryly. "Darling, everyone knows about you two." He paused, removing the piece of wood she'd misplaced and realigning it. "Just like we all did years ago."

Her heart nearly stopped. Okay, *that* was a shock.

He shot her a look. "You were trying to be so secretive, but your mom and I weren't stupid."

She swallowed hard. All this time she'd thought they'd been deceiving everyone. Back then she'd felt guilty lying to her parents and all that time they'd known.

"If you'd known, why didn't you stop me from seeing him?" Maybe this whole family feud thing wasn't as big a deal as she thought it was. Maybe their parents wouldn't have cared. So much of her young anxiety may have been completely avoidable.

But her father waved a hand. "You were going away to the academy. I wasn't worried you'd change your plans for him. Grab the next piece."

His dismissal made her chest tighten. So, they hadn't been okay with it, they'd just thought it wouldn't last.

"That one, right there." He pointed at it.

She moved away from the desk and folded her arms across her chest. Building the model while having this conversation wasn't a good idea. She didn't want to ruin the wonderful memories.

"Dex had been planning on going with me."

"But he didn't. He backed out and bailed on you."

"It wasn't exactly like that…"

"And now, he continues to just cruise through life on the Wakefield money, involving himself in rescues when it suits him."

Suddenly, her annoyance with her father made defending Dex and the relationship that much easier. No more guilt or fear of his opinion. Just determination not to let him derail what she and Dex had. "He saved my life, Dad."

Where was her father's appreciation for that? And countless other rescues Dex had helped with?

"And I'm obviously very grateful for that. But the family history…" he continued.

"Is in the past. It was generations ago. Dex isn't his great-great-grandfather." It was time to leave the feud in the past where it belonged.

"This community holds on to things, Skylar."

"No, *you* hold on to things," she said with exasperation.

He frowned. "So…you actually have real feelings for him. This isn't just some sort of rebellion?"

"Rebellion? Dad, I'm twenty-five years old." And the fact that her feelings for Dex had never faded over time, distance, the strain of knowing this would be a disappointment to their respective families spoke volumes about the strength of them.

Her father's jaw tightened. "I think you could be putting your career at risk being with him."

"I don't see it that way. Everyone on the crew admires and respects Dex." She paused. "I love him."

There, she'd said it. Couldn't get much clearer or more honest than that.

Her father's face fell and he lowered his gaze as though he was unable to look at her. "The boy hurt you before, Skylar. I saw how devastated you were back then. Losing your mom…and Dex disappointing you." He paused. "What makes you think he won't do it again?"

Her father didn't understand. Dex had let her go for her benefit. "Things were complicated for him,." It wasn't her place to tell her father about Dex's epilepsy. It was something he obviously didn't want to reveal, so she sighed and said, "Things are different now."

Her heart raced and her mouth was dry as she waited for him to say something. Anything. Desperate for him to understand, to give his approval, support or at least his understanding.

He slowly, silently collected the pieces of the model boat and put them back inside the box, placing it on the shelf, unfinished.

"Are you going to say something, Dad?" His silence was killing her.

His back still turned to her, she watched his shoulders rise and fall in a deep sigh. "You're an adult now, Sky. It's your life and you can make your own decisions."

And by decisions she heard what he really meant—she was an adult, she could make her own mistakes.

CHAPTER NINETEEN

"I THINK I know the answer to this, but are you sure you don't want to come?" Carly asked from the spare bedroom door, dressed in a light sundress and heels, a bottle of wine in each hand.

Skylar glanced up from the drone training manual she was barely reading and shook her head. "I'm sure. You look beautiful. Have a good time. Say hello to everyone for me."

Everyone except that pigheaded, stubborn old man.

Carly sighed. "How long are you two going to keep this up?"

"Until he can see how unreasonable he's being." It had been a few weeks since she'd told him about Dex.

Carly raised an eyebrow but Skylar appreciated that her cousin held her opinion to herself. She knew Carly thought that the apple didn't fall too far from the tree.

Skylar closed the manual and stood. "Look, he's the one who can't accept Dex and me being together. And if I can't invite my *boyfriend* to a family cookout, then I'm not going."

"I see your point, I do, but he's your father," she said simply. "Just because you can't have both men in your life at the same time, do you really need to cut your dad out?" She offered a sympathetic smile. "Just think about it okay?"

Skylar slumped into the chair at the window as Carly

left the room. She watched as her cousin got into her car and drove away, feeling a deep hollowness in the pit of her stomach.

The Beaumonts' annual backyard cookout was arguably the biggest family event of the year. Over forty family and friends attended for the reunion, her dad barbequed every kind of meat imaginable, there was a dessert table a mile long, drinks flowed and laughter and conversation often drowned out the sounds of the music being played by a local band they always hired to perform. Growing up, it had always been Skylar's favorite day.

Except the year she'd been seeing Dex and while her cousins had all brought their boyfriends to the event, she had been unable to invite Dex.

This sense of déjà vu was the major reason she wasn't going.

She wanted to reconcile with her father. Weeks of barely talking, except when they had to at work had been tough. Even when she'd been away at the academy, they had spoken two or three times a week. Not being able to communicate with him now after their argument was hard. If he was feeling the pressure and missing her too, he'd yet to cave and she refused to be the one to give in.

If he didn't accept Dex in her life, then he didn't fully accept her.

Her phone chimed with a new message and she felt a little better seeing the excited text from Dex.

Just picking up Shaylah now from A Helpful Paw. See you tonight?

Can't wait, she replied.

The puppy was going home with Dex that day. The team had completed their on-site training with Lee and they'd continue a few times a week at the facility, but now the focus was on their bond, their connection, becoming a team together. It was the next step and Skylar knew Dex was thrilled about it for more than one reason.

With the therapy dog living with him it meant Isla could move on, return to traveling or at least get her own place.

Dex hadn't come out and asked her to move in with him yet, but he'd definitely hinted at the idea and Skylar would be lying if she said it wasn't appealing. She was spending most nights on the yacht anyway whenever Isla wasn't there. Unfortunately, she'd yet to figure out a way to connect with Dex's sister. The two of them just avoided one another as much as possible.

Her father wasn't happy about the relationship. Isla wasn't thrilled about it.

Could she and Dex really make it work when two of the most important people in their lives weren't on board with it? That it might mean choosing one relationship over the other—the way she practically already had?

And did making a decision about living together truly make sense if Skylar might not even be there much longer? If she was still ultimately planning to leave?

She'd gotten the standard "we've received your application" email from the coast guard human resources department weeks before, but they hadn't contacted her for an interview or anything yet, so maybe she wasn't in the running for that one. Would she apply for others? And if so could she really move in with Dex?

She sighed as she stared out the window at the ocean

in the distance, her mind and heart fighting so many levels of uncertainty.

Decisions that had seemed so clear six weeks ago weren't so clear anymore.

DEX HELD HIS breath as he waited for the verdict from his sister later that afternoon.

"Okay, so she is kinda cute," Isla said begrudgingly as Shaylah danced around her feet, demanding attention. He'd just gotten home with her, and introducing Shaylah to Isla was a big deal.

He watched as his sister bent to pick her up and the dog licked her cheek. "Hey, let's not get carried away. We just met and I'm not sure how much love my antihistamines can tolerate," she said, but her tone suggested the pup had already melted her heart.

Instant, unlikely friends.

Dex was relieved. He hoped Isla could see it was for the best, especially after meeting the dog and getting to see how incredible Shaylah really was.

"Okay, put her down. She's a support animal, not a pet."

Isla reluctantly put the puppy on the ground and Dex issued several commands that the dog followed like a pro. Sitting at alert attention at his feet, only the slight wag of the tail indicated the pent-up energy the pup was suppressing.

Isla looked suitably impressed. "Okay...well, when she can make coffee, let me know," she said teasingly.

Dex's shoulders relaxed having Isla's official approval. "So, when do you move out?"

"Hey!" She playfully slapped him.

He laughed. "Kidding." He paused. "No, really—when are you leaving?" Now that Shaylah was staying with him, he was confident he'd be okay without his sister there. And lately Skylar had been staying over when Isla wasn't home, so it wasn't as though his sibling needed to stay any longer if she'd rather be traveling…and Dex was not so secretly hoping as one "roommate" moved out, another one might move in.

Skylar hadn't talked about the possibility of leaving Port Serenity, leaving him, in weeks, so he dared to hope she'd decided to stay.

Or that it was an option at least.

"There is a three-month summer hiking tour I'm interested in," Isla said as she sat at the table and curled one leg under her.

"Have you registered?" Three months would be a great trial period with Skylar. She didn't have to commit to "moving in" officially with him. But she could stay there and they could test it out, without too much pressure.

"Not yet," Isla said, twirling a piece of now–pale blue hair around her finger. "But maybe I will."

"You definitely will," he said. He'd register her for it himself.

She bit her lip and a worried frown creased her forehead.

He reached across the table and touched her hand. "What?"

"You sure about this? Being here alone with the dog? I mean, there's no rush."

Maybe not for her. But Dex was eager to take his relationship with Skylar to a deeper level. He was ready to commit to her in ways he hadn't thought he could. She'd shown her commitment by refusing to let her father's disapproval deter her from being with him. He hated that he'd come between father and daughter, so he wanted to make sure the decision had been worth it for her. In time he hoped to help her reconcile with her dad, even if the coast guard captain never fully accepted him.

"I'm sure," he told his sister.

"And you and Skylar?"

He knew that question had been coming. He took a deep breath. "I'm sure about that too."

Skylar eyed the German shepherd who was at least double her size from since the first time she'd seen her at the facility. "I can't believe how much she's grown," she said.

Dex laughed. "Yeah, they said to expect her to get double this size again. I may need to buy stock in dog food."

Skylar bent to pet the dog's head. "Welcome home, Shaylah," she said. Then she stood to wrap her arms around Dex's neck and kissed him, feeling some of the unease about an event happening across town that she was missing seep away.

Some.

Dex must have sensed it as he pulled back and looked into her eyes. "You can go, you know?"

She shook her head. "Nope. Not without you."

"You're being stubborn."

"So is he."

"Two wrongs don't make a right," he said gently, kissing her forehead.

She sighed. "I don't want to go. I want to be here for Shaylah's first day," she said, forcing what she hoped was a convincing smile. She did want to be there with Dex and that's all that mattered.

"I just hate that I've come between you and your dad," he said.

They'd had the same conversation multiple times over the last few weeks and Dex needed to realize this had nothing to do with him and everything to do with her father's inability to move on from the past. She pressed her body closer. "Do you think Shaylah would mind if we...took a nap?"

Dex's grip on her tightened. "I think she's fairly occupied at the moment."

Skylar laughed watching the dog growl and fight with a ball on a rope, lying on the living room rug.

Dex took her hand and the two sneaked upstairs into his bedroom. They took their time removing each other's clothing. After weeks of regular sex, the frantic urgency had relaxed somewhat. They still craved one another, but their lovemaking had evolved into a deep, meaningful connection. They still experimented and pushed one another's boundaries and now the trust between them made the experiences that much better.

Skylar felt cherished as they made love, letting all the conflict she was struggling with disappear. She was where she wanted to be. Where she was meant to be.

Afterward, she lay on his chest, savoring the alone time together and the feel of his body close to hers.

Dex cleared his throat and hugged her tight before slowly releasing her and climbing out of the bed.

"Hey, where are you going?" she said with a fake pout.

He laughed as he opened a box on his dresser and took something out. Then he sat next to her and held out a key. "Isla's going away for three months and I'd like you to stay here with me," he said, his gaze searching hers, hope reflecting in his eyes.

Skylar's heart raced at the invite she'd been expecting.

She ran a finger along his stomach, tracing the shape of the muscles as she contemplated the idea. Isla was leaving, Shaylah was there…they'd both chosen one another despite any consequences or family drama…

"I'd like that," she said, accepting the key and wrapping her arms around him, feeling as though she'd somehow committed to so much more.

CHAPTER TWENTY

TOURIST SEASON WAS in full swing and the marina was full of vacationers when Skylar arrived at the docks the next day. Kids played along the shore, daring to run into the cold waves and squealing with delight. Families enjoyed picnics along the rocky beach and the inlet was full of sailboats, Sea-Doos, kayaks, canoes—and farther out, tour boats were on constant rotation.

Skylar waved to Doug as she made her way to her office. He popped his head in a few minutes later. "Why are you acting so calm?"

She frowned. "Why wouldn't I be?" she asked slowly.

Doug looked at her as though she had a second head growing out of her neck. "The retirement announcement!"

"Who's retir..." Her heart stopped as the question died on her lips. "My dad's retiring?" She frantically searched her in-box for the news, but there was nothing there. No formal announcement from the coast guard. No email from him formally announcing it to the crew. "How do you know?"

"He announced it yesterday. You didn't know?"

Ah... So not only had she missed a fun family event, but also her father's huge important announcement. She swallowed hard, dismissing the pang of guilt.

Then she shook it off. No. He'd have known this was a big deal and something she would have liked to hear about before everyone else. She forced her tone to sound light, unfazed as she said, "Well, that's unexpected, but good for him."

Doug nodded slowly. "And good for you."

"What do you mean?"

He shot her a knowing look as he entered and closed the door slightly. "We all know working with him has been... stressful for you."

"That obvious, huh?" She hoped their tension the last few weeks especially hadn't caused too much hardship for anyone.

"I totally get it. In high school, I worked part-time at my dad's mechanic shop to raise money for school. It was torture."

Skylar laughed. "It's hard to imagine you in a dirty mechanic shop."

"Believe me, it was brutal. But my point is, I get it. Working with family is not easy. It can drive a wedge between people."

It hadn't been the job that had done that.

But she nodded. "It's been challenging," she admitted.

"Well, now it will be easier," he said, leaving the office. Then he hung back. "Sorry I was the one to tell you. I thought you knew."

She waved a hand. "My fault for not attending the cookout."

As Doug disappeared down the hall, she sat back in her chair and stared at the calm ocean outside her window.

Her father was retiring. That had to have been a huge decision. One he'd normally have discussed with her. Or at least told her. Her chest ached at the thought that she hadn't made herself available for that conversation.

But neither had he, damn it!

They'd been so close. She'd always respected him. She'd hoped those feelings would go both ways now that she was an adult and following in his footsteps. Was this Beaumont/Wakefield thing really worth losing his daughter over?

Her phone chimed with a new text message and she frowned seeing the unknown number on the display. Opening it, she read.

It's Isla. Are you with Dex?

Her mouth went dry and her pulse raced.

No. I'm at work. He was asleep when I left twenty minutes ago. Why?

I left my house keys at Dwayne's and I'm locked out of the yacht. He's not answering the door. Shaylah's barking her head off inside.

On my way.

Skylar jumped up from the chair and after grabbing her purse, she ran out of the office and off the boat. The four-minute run had to be her best record-breaking sprint, but it felt like an eternity before Skylar reached the yacht, where Isla paced nervously, her phone to her ear. "Damn, voicemail again."

"Maybe he went out," Skylar said, climbing onto the boat.

"His car is here and he's supposed to bring Shaylah with him wherever he goes."

The first few weeks were important to get the dog familiar with the people and the places in Dex's life.

Skylar moved past the other woman and her hand shook slightly as she unlocked the door. Isla looked surprised, but not entirely. "He gave you a key?"

"This morning," Skylar said. It was a conversation for another time. They entered quickly. Shaylah's barking grew louder, coming from the upstairs bedroom.

Isla passed her on the staircase and Skylar was grateful she wasn't alone. Despite their personal differences, she was thankful that Isla was there right now. She had no experience with this and she wasn't sure she was fully prepared for what they might encounter.

She followed Isla into the room where Dex was lying on the bedroom floor. Shaylah was beside him. She barked once more then settled in next to him, offering comfort now that help had arrived. The dog was truly a superstar and it made Skylar feel better.

Her mouth felt dry and her voice cracked slightly as she asked, "What do I do?"

Isla knelt on the floor beside her brother and lifted his head onto her lap. She glanced up at Skylar as she pet Shaylah to let the dog know she'd done good, alerting them. "Nothing. This is all we can do."

"We just have to wait?" Skylar stared at the man she loved lying on the floor. He looked like he was sleeping except for a mild tremble of his body.

Isla looked pained as she nodded. "Yes. I don't know how long it'll be so it's okay if you need to go back to work. I've got this." She brushed sweat off Dex's forehead. Silence echoed around them.

Skylar sat on the floor next to Isla.

The other woman sent her a grateful look. "Thank you," she said quietly.

Skylar felt absolutely helpless and she thought she should be the one offering thanks, so she just nodded as the two sworn enemies put aside their personal differences as they sat there to wait out the harrowing moments together.

DEX FELT MORE than a little stressed as he lay on the bed, trying to refocus and calm his thundering heart a half hour later.

Isla, Skylar and Shaylah were all next to him and he felt slightly claustrophobic at the doting. "I'm fine," he said, a little more gruffly than he intended.

Isla nodded, handing him a cold facecloth.

He turned to Skylar. "Sorry you had to leave work," he said.

She shook her head emphatically. "It was nothing. I'm just glad I had a key." She glanced quickly at Isla.

But for the first time there didn't seem to be the same tension radiating between the two of them. As much as he hated that they'd both had to deal with this that day, he was grateful for the apparent truce.

Shaylah sat on the floor next to the bed. Alert and attentive. She'd done her job well, according to Isla.

He petted her head affectionately. "Good girl. We'll get treats soon."

"Hey, I helped too," Isla teased. It helped to break the heavy cloud of tension around the room as they all laughed.

"You can have treats too," he told his sister. "And so can you," he said, turning to Skylar and reaching for her hand.

They stared into each other's eyes. Had she been completely freaked out by the episode? Did it make her rethink living here with him?

"Well, I just stopped by to grab my hiking boots, so if you don't need me, I'm going to go," Isla said awkwardly.

He barely heard her.

"Thanks again," she said to Skylar.

Skylar just nodded, her gaze still on him. Her *worried* gaze.

"You okay?" he asked as his sister left the room.

She gave a mirthless laugh. "Am I okay? Are *you* okay?"

"I'm fine. Really." He ran a hand over his face, using the cloth to wipe beads of sweat from his face and neck.

"Do you know what happened?" she asked softly.

"Nothing really. I just woke up and got up to go to the washroom and then lights out," he said. It was always the same. No real trigger. No warning. And afterward he felt fine. He was happy his condition wasn't worse, but not knowing what caused the episodes and their unpredictability made his seizures frustrating to say the least. "Sorry you had to witness that."

She shook her head. "You shouldn't be apologizing. I'm just glad I was able to be here," she said softly. "Grateful I had a key to get in."

He pulled her closer and she lay down next to him on the bed. "You're not freaked out?"

She sighed. "I won't lie, it was scary. Seeing you there like that and feeling like there was nothing I could do to help. But, no I'm not freaked out."

He breathed in the scent of her hair as he held her close. "Good. And you did help."

She tilted her head to look up at him. "And no, I haven't changed my mind about moving in," she said, answering the question he'd been too afraid to ask.

CHAPTER TWENTY-ONE

CONCENTRATING ON WORK was going to be impossible.

Back in her office an hour later, after Dex had basically pushed her out the door with a promise he'd lie on the couch and binge-watch TV all day, Skylar was still on edge.

The image of Dex out on the floor continued to haunt her. What if he'd hit his head? What if he'd been cooking and set the yacht on fire?

She hadn't let on to him just how terrified she'd been. How terrified she was.

But now she understood why he was completely closed off to the idea of trying for the coast guard career again. That day had been the very real wake-up call she'd needed to fully and truly accept his decision. She shouldn't have needed it.

She sighed as she opened her window and strained to hear across the lively, bustling harbor. Would she be able to hear Shaylah bark from this distance? Maybe they needed to teach the dog to use a two-way radio…was that possible? Dex and Shaylah's trainer, Lee, had mentioned something about teaching the dog to sound an alarm, but she knew that idea didn't appeal to Dex.

Skylar rubbed a hand over her face as she logged onto the coast guard site. Two new postings had been listed within the last three hours and she hesitated before opening the links. Both in Florida. One for an entry-level position on crew and one for a captain. Florida was another place she'd love to be stationed.

Should she apply? She hadn't yet heard anything on the last posting application, which had made things a little easier the past month. Not having to decide whether to stay or leave?

And after that morning's event, how could she actually leave Dex?

Being a million miles away from him if he needed her would make her crazy. She could barely be half a mile away without wanting to go back and check in on him. Though, she knew she had to repress that urge. Dex was quite capable of managing on his own. He'd been dealing with the condition for years without her help.

She checked her watch. She had a crew meeting starting in three minutes. She needed to clear her head quickly. She stood and poured some coffee into her Sasquatch travel mug, but before she could leave the office, a new email caught her attention.

The subject line from the US Coast Guard recruiting and human resources department read "Interview Request."

Her pulse raced as she slowly lowered herself back into the office chair and opened the email.

Yep, the subject line wasn't wrong. They were requesting a Zoom interview with her for the following afternoon for the position in California. The next day was her day off and she and Dex had planned to hike back to the waterfalls. She'd really been looking forward to it, to that time with him.

Could she request a different time?

"You headed to the meeting?" Doug asked, popping his head around the corner of her office.

She glanced up. "Yeah, I'll be right there." She hesitated. "Hey, Doug, can I ask, did you ever hear back on your application for the position in California?" she asked lowering her voice, as others passed on the way to the meeting room.

He glanced around and waited until no one else was in earshot before answering, "Yeah, actually, I just received an interview request this morning."

Skylar swallowed hard. "Great. That's great news."

Doug grinned. "I mean I know there are others up for the position too…so let the best person win?"

So, he did suspect that she'd applied as well.

"We should get to the meeting," she said, standing. "You go on ahead. I'll meet you in there." Staring at the email, she hesitated just briefly before hitting Yes to the "Will you attend this meeting?" question.

It made her feel better that Doug had an interview too. And maybe others. The job wasn't hers yet. And right now she wouldn't think about what she would do if it was hers to either accept or turn down. Because right now, she had no idea what she'd do.

DEX WOULD NEVER let Skylar know he'd been disappointed when she'd had to cancel their plans that day for her interview.

He knew she'd applied and despite everything, they'd never discussed her staying here in Port Serenity forever. Her life goals hadn't changed. His situation hadn't either.

"Come on Shaylah, this way," he told the dog as he walked through the empty bar. He was going to help Dollie with inventory today.

With his clipboard in hand, he entered the stifling stock room where Dollie had restocked all the alcohol the day

SWEET HOME ALASKA

before. He got to work counting the bottles and rearranging some new spirits behind the bar.

Skylar had said she needed time to prepare, so she'd stayed at Carly's the night before. He was desperate not to read anything into it. He knew she'd needed the space to think about the job opportunity without second-guessing herself.

As he worked, his mind continued to wander to her, but he refused to call or text to interrupt her. She deserved this time to get her head in the game. And he sincerely wished her the best with the interview. No matter what that meant for their relationship. They'd find a way to make things work no matter what. He didn't even want to contemplate a future without Skylar in it.

The pub door opened around two and he turned hoping to see her. Instead it was Doug. Dressed in his uniform, the man wore a distraught expression as he climbed up onto the bar stool across from Dex.

"Hey man, you okay?"

"Just completely tanked an interview," Doug said.

Dex swallowed hard. "For the position in California?"

Doug nodded, gesturing to the scotch.

Dex filled a glass with ice and poured the drink.

"How do you know it didn't go well?" He'd be lying if he hadn't been hoping that Doug's interview would have gone really well, but he felt guilty for wishing someone else might get this one.

Doug ran a hand through his hair. "It's the online thing. I freeze up on those stupid chats. Three executives sitting there on the screen spit-firing questions at me and there's no way to read the room like in a real face-to-face situation."

"Everyone gets nervous and awkward on those things."

If Skylar left town, video chats would be their main way of connecting. Dealing with different time zones and a computer screen as well as miles and miles between them was definitely not ideal. And they'd both admitted they didn't think it would work long-term with physical intimacy so important to them both. Doug knew all about that as his relationship with Jay had mostly consisted of similar challenges in recent months.

Doug drained the contents of the glass and gestured for another.

Dex complied, this time pouring one for himself as well. At his feet, Shaylah gave a disapproving look, which he ignored.

"Still, I'm sure you're being too hard on yourself," he told Doug. "They wouldn't have contacted you for an interview if you weren't qualified. I'm sure you did better than you think."

Doug shook his head. "I thought so too, until I stuck around and kinda eavesdropped on Skylar's interview for the same position. The office walls are paper-thin."

Dex's heart raced as he downed the scotch. "She did good?" He wanted to be happy about it. He did.

"She killed it. She even had them laughing a few times," Doug said, draining his glass again. "And these military recruiters never laugh."

Yep, sounded like she'd killed it. Which meant her leaving was going to kill him.

Unless he went with her.

THE HIGH OF knowing she'd crushed the interview was dimmed by the fact that she wasn't sure she wanted the position. Doug had been disappointed in his performance and that just made her feel worse. When she wasn't sure what she wanted anymore, she'd had to go in and do her best…in case the transfer was still what she wanted most.

But a part of her still hoped the decision wouldn't be hers to make.

Opening the door to the bookstore/museum, she waved at Carly as her cousin finished serving a customer at the counter. She perused the shelves, not really seeing anything in particular, but feeling a little less annoyed by the countless Sealena products on display. The last few weeks the items had been flying off Carly's shelves and everywhere she looked there were tourists wearing Sealena-themed shirts and hats, and marveling over the folklore.

Part of her own enjoyment over the stories and the mythology had returned and she knew it had to do with her reconnecting with Dex. Opening up to him again meant also opening herself back up to her hometown and she realized maybe her disdain for the tourist attractions was based on the wedge it had caused their families. Maybe she'd been annoyed at the implications the feud had had on their families as it related to her own inability to be with Dex than anything else.

But now that she was determined to be with him regardless, the Sealena stuff didn't seem to bother her anymore.

"How'd it go?" Carly asked as the customer left the store.

"Good, I think," Skylar said, joining her friend at the counter.

"That's good, right?" Carly studied her.

"Yes. Definitely. It just also makes things a little more complicated."

Her cousin touched her shoulder. "Complicated yes, but not impossible. I know you'll find a way to work this out."

"What if I don't want to go?" Skylar blurted out, voicing the thought for the first time.

Carly smiled. "Well, I think that depends on *why* you don't want to go."

Skylar frowned. "What do you mean?"

"If you're staying because of Dex, then you need to be sure that love is enough for you, that you'll be happy here and not always wonder what else may be out there." Carly paused. "But if you're staying because you realize Port Serenity is the place you want to be, where your fantastic cousin is and where there's an opportunity to protect the community that raised you and loves you, then I think you'll be a lot happier in that decision."

Skylar bit her lip. Her cousin's words echoed Dex's sentiments from a few weeks ago.

Love isn't all you need.

Skylar knew they were both right. Now she just needed to figure out if she was doubting her desire to leave because of her love for Dex or if it was because of a newfound love and acceptance for her small hometown.

And everything and *everyone* in it.

At home an hour later, Dex fed Shaylah, made himself a sandwich and then sat at his computer. Opening up the coast guard website, he clicked on the job postings page. The likelihood that there would be something suitable for him in California was low, but he had to at least start looking. The way he'd promised Skylar he would.

Being with her the last six weeks had only reconfirmed his love for her and the fact that he didn't want to be without her. He wouldn't ask her to give everything up and stay, and he didn't want to do long-distance indefinitely.

He scanned the regular positions, ignoring the slight sinking in his gut at his inability to apply for one of those, then he scanned the civilian positions. He was definitely capable of fixing machinery on vessels and installing different technical equipment.

Seeing a posting in California for an entry-level boat maintenance position working on the same cutters Skylar would be commanding, his heart raced. He read the job description and the qualifications quickly. He wasn't a hundred percent suited to the job, but with some resume embellishments, this one could definitely work.

He hesitated, absently stroking Shaylah's fur. Could he really do it? Give up everything he loved here in Port Serenity? This place had always been his home and at one point he'd been willing to leave it. For Skylar.

What if he followed her now and things didn't work out? What if she decided a life with him wasn't what she wanted? After all, she'd made it clear that staying wasn't really an option for her. Not even for him.

He stared at the job posting, his heart a mess.

It wasn't his dream job, it wasn't here in Port Serenity, but it would be near Skylar, the woman he loved and that was all that mattered. She was definitely worth the risk.

He opened the application file and completed all the fields to the best of his ability, embellishing slightly as needed, then paused at the last requirement. A letter of recommendation.

That part would be the hardest.

CHAPTER TWENTY-TWO

SKYLAR FOUGHT TO push aside her indecision as she got ready that evening. Once she was with Dex things would be clearer. She applied a pale pink gloss to her lips and ran her fingers through the loose curls hanging around her shoulders. It wasn't like she had to make a decision immediately.

In the living room, she heard Carly and Rachel talking, so she grabbed her purse and sweater and left the room. Her cousin was in the kitchen popping the cork out of a bottle of wine and the smell of popcorn made Skylar's stomach grumble.

"Which one will we start with? *Sleepless in Seattle* or *You've Got Mail*?" Rachel asked.

A Meg Ryan Marathon. Carly's favorite. Her gut twisted slightly. She'd yet to have that girls' night with her cousin since being back. "Hi," she said to Rachel. "Great blog post."

Rachel sent her a look. "Could have told me you two were hooking up. Definitely explains the heat between you two. I thought you were going to set the pub on fire."

Skylar laughed. "We were keeping things quiet."

Skylar's phone chimed with a text from Dex and she read quickly:

Still up for dinner?

Skylar paused, surveying the popcorn, the wine, the lineup of Meg Ryan movies and the two women in front of her. "Hey, you two mind if I crash your evening?" There was nothing like a good girls' night to help resolve a conflicted heart and she really wanted to stay in with them that evening.

Carly smiled and Rachel shook her head. "Not at all."

Skylar texted Dex:

Rain check? Girls' night with Carly and Rachel.

His immediate, understanding reply warmed her even more.

Talk about me ;)

"I recognize that look," Rachel said as Skylar tucked the phone away. "Seems I'm not the only one in love in this room."

Nope, but Rachel had already decided to follow *her* heart and move to Port Serenity. Skylar still had a choice to make. But not right now. That evening was all about Meg Ryan's quests for *her* happily-ever-afters.

THIS CONVERSATION WITH Skylar's father was long overdue. As a seventeen-year-old boy, Dex had immaturity as an excuse. But he was a man now. A man so completely in love with the coast guard captain's daughter that he was prepared to do anything to make the relationship work.

Including asking her father's blessing in the form of a letter of recommendation so he could follow Skylar wherever her heart led them.

Captain Beaumont knew all of the things Dex had done over the years to help with the rescues whenever possible, he'd seen the upgrades he'd made to the yacht and he knew Dex's commitment to Port Serenity. The two of them may not have been friends or always seen eye to eye based on their family history, but if there was one person who would be the right one to get the reference letter from, it would be Captain Beaumont.

And it would mean everything to Dex.

He took a deep breath as he led Shaylah up the front steps to the door and knocked.

It struck him that it was the first time he'd actually walked up to Skylar's family home and knocked on the front door. It had always been a fantasy, to be able to confidently walk up and ask the Beaumonts' blessing to be with their daughter.

Captain Beaumont opened the door, looking surprised.

"Hi, sir, I was hoping I could talk to you," Dex said, forcing himself to sound braver than he felt.

The older man glanced outside, obviously looking for Skylar.

"I'm alone," Dex said. "Except for Shaylah here… She can wait outside if you prefer."

On cue, the pup sat obediently.

Captain Beaumont shook his head and frowned as though just noticing the dog. His expression changed seeing Shaylah's therapy vest. "No, of course, bring her inside."

"Coffee?" Captain Beaumont asked as he led the way to the kitchen.

"Thank you." The Beaumont family home was exactly the cozy environment he'd expected. Unlike his own home, which had been big and impressive but lacking this level of warmth. He walked slowly, taking in the pictures on the wall of Skylar in each grade. His heart swelled at the sight of her growing from a toothless, grinning five-year-old to the beautiful picture of her from the winter formal dance with her fake date.

In the kitchen, her father gestured for him to have a seat at the table. "Can I get her some water?" he asked, nodding toward the dog.

"Thanks, she's okay."

He nodded as he poured a cup of coffee and handed it to him, then poured one for himself. He opened the fridge for the milk. "Milk, sugar?" he asked.

"Black is fine. Thanks." Dex clutched the coffee cup in his hands as he waited for the other man to join him at the table.

When he did, he was silent. Obviously waiting for Dex to start.

He cleared his throat. "I needed to talk to you," he said. "I know you know that Skylar and I are seeing one another. And I know our families have never seen eye to eye. But sir, I'm not my great-great-grandfather and while I can't change the wrongdoings of the past, I'd like to do my best to make things right. I want to be with Skylar, but I don't want our relationship to ruin the bond she has with you."

"I appreciate you coming to me." He sighed. "Truth is son, you both don't need my permission. You're both adults and the relationship is your business." He paused. "I may not have handled the conversation the right way when Skylar told me and it's my fault she's phantoming me."

Dex hid a grin at the terminology. "You could reach out to her. I'm sure she'd appreciate the opportunity to reconnect."

"It's the Beaumont stubborn streak. We are all affected by it, I'm afraid." Captain Beaumont leaned forward on the table. "The thing that concerns me is Skylar making decisions that she might ultimately regret."

Like turning down the position she wanted to stay in Port Serenity to be with Dex.

He nodded. "Me too."

"Don't get me wrong. I'd love it if Skylar decided that she wanted to stay here. It was actually one of the reasons I decided to retire."

It was? The man actually understood that Skylar was struggling to work with him so he'd made that big decision to make things easier for her. Make it easier for her to choose to stay?

"But I can't be selfish," he said. "If she wants to travel the world, that's her dream."

He heard the meaning. Dex couldn't be selfish either.

"Thank you. I feel the same and I want to prove to you that I'm worthy of her."

"Son, you're not your great-great-grandfather. I know that. You don't have to prove yourself to anyone. I may not have been supportive of you turning that yacht into a volunteer rescue boat, but you have to understand that was because I worried about your safety. Untrained in the position. But I recognize the support you've given the crew and if you hadn't been there that night to rescue Skylar..." He paused and lowered his head. "This town's obsession with this family feud has gone on far too long. I'm officially done with it. If you've come for my blessing to follow your heart in regard to my daughter-you have it, but you've never needed it."

He did more than the other man could possibly know,

but he appreciated the words. "Thank you, sir." He paused. "And I uh… I've decided to apply for a civilian post in California."

The older man's expression was one of respect mixed with sadness at the realization that it meant Dex was choosing to follow Skylar and not expect or ask her to stay. They both knew it was the right thing for him to do.

"Why a civilian post?" he asked, but his gaze drifted to Shaylah as realization dawned. "It's not too late to join the academy. You're only twenty-five, they'd accept the application I'm sure."

Dex cleared his throat. "The truth is sir, I can't join. I was diagnosed with epilepsy a few years ago. Before high school graduation."

The other man's face took on a look of recognition. Understanding. "That's why you didn't go back then, with her."

Dex frowned. "You knew that was the plan?"

Captain Beaumont stared into his coffee cup. "Yes, we knew all about you two. So did your parents. It was actually another source of tension between your dad and me. He wanted you to pursue football and we may have had words back then when I thought he'd had something to do with you not choosing the academy, which I believed was your passion."

"You talked to him? For me?" His father had never told him.

Captain Beaumont nodded. "Probably set back any progress we'd made toward resolving the feud."

"Thank you, sir. My dad was adamant about the football scholarship, but as it turned out, I couldn't follow his dream either," he said shaking his head. "It was the hardest time in my life but all I knew was that I had to make sure Skylar didn't stay. That she went anyway. Without me."

"You didn't tell her," he said. "You broke up with her so she'd leave."

He nodded. "But while I can't go to the academy, there are positions I could do. And there's one I'm applying for but I need a letter of recommendation." He paused. "I was wondering if you might consider writing one? It would mean everything to me."

Captain Beaumont stood. "Wait here."

"Oh, I didn't mean right away…you can think about it," he said.

"Just wait here one moment."

A moment later, the man returned with a slightly yellowed envelope. He handed it to him and Dex saw his name on the front. He opened it and took out a folded piece of paper.

He started to read the letter dated six years earlier.

…*Highly recommend Dex Wakefield for the academy based on his courageous spirit, determined work ethic, commitment to the community…*

He glanced up at Skylar's father in amazement. "You wrote me a letter?"

"I'll be happy to write you a new one for this position, but I thought you should know that I've always believed in you," the man said, standing and extending a hand to Dex.

Dex's heart swelled and a lump formed in his throat as he nodded his appreciation, not trusting his voice.

As he left the house, his heart felt lighter than it had in years. He'd gotten the approval and acceptance he hadn't had the courage to ask for years before.

Now he just needed to find the courage to go all in with the woman he loved.

CHAPTER TWENTY-THREE

THIS WAS WHAT she'd been hoping for when she'd arrived in Port Serenity. So why—a week and a half after she'd aced the interview—was her gut twisting at the sight of the email offering her the position in California?

San Diego Coast Guard. Her new position—if she accepted—would start in six weeks.

Six weeks.

The thought of leaving wasn't as appealing anymore.

Skylar closed the email without responding, her emotions a whirlwind. She needed a run to clear her head. She couldn't make this decision based on Dex or her father or her loyalty to Port Serenity. If she was going to be truly happy, she needed to base this decision on what she wanted. What she knew in her soul to be the right choice for her.

She changed into her running gear and headed down the pier. Dusk settled over the ocean and she stared out at the crashing waves, listening to the sound of them lapping on the shore, tasting the salty air on her lips, clearing her mind and hoping to find the answers on the air around her.

As she ran, she took in the sights and sounds of her hometown. The boats along the marina, the familiar faces she'd known since she was a child. The familiarity used to feel suffocating, when each person seemed a source of judgment, when she'd felt everyone waiting to see if she succeeded like previous generations of Beaumonts or if she'd fail. That pressure she'd felt leaving Port Serenity had made her reluctant to return. It had been that fear of letting down the people who really mattered to her that had made her think that someplace else might be better.

She didn't feel that same weight on her shoulders now. She'd come home. She'd proven herself. She'd stood up for the love and the relationship she wanted.

Her home felt like home.

She paused at the end of the pier and took a deep, cleansing breath. The statue of Sealena, standing proud and fierce in the water in front of her, made her heart race even more than the physical exertion as she read the caption engraved on the limestone.

She, who protects these waters, is capable, brave and strong. A force among men.

Maybe there wasn't a serpent queen below the surface rescuing sailors in their hour of need, but there was a woman just as strong, brave, capable and fiercely loyal who could try.

HIS RINGING CELL woke him from a deep sleep and Dex scrambled to find it in the bedsheets. On the floor next to him, Shaylah opened one eye grumpily. Turned out the pup wasn't exactly a morning person either. She growled at him as the ringing continued.

"I'm looking. I'm looking."

Locating it, his heart pounded seeing the number for the United States Coast Guard lighting up the display. "Hello?" he answered, trying to sound as awake as possible.

"Dex Wakefield?" a male voice on the other end asked.

"Yes."

"This is Alex Pierce from the recruiting office of the United States Coast Guard."

"Yes, hi, Alex."

"I'm happy to be offering you the position as a vessel maintenance engineer, stationed in California."

That was fast. He'd applied for the position a week ago and sent in his letter of recommendation from Skylar's father. Then he'd had a Zoom interview the day before. He hadn't thought he'd hear anything yet. He hadn't mentioned anything to Skylar and had asked her father not to say anything in case he didn't get it.

But here they were, offering him the position.

Was he interested? Taking a support position not on the water, not where the action was had never appealed to him, and he'd never been keen to leave Port Serenity. But Skylar would surely be offered the position she'd applied for and as much as he wasn't sure about what he wanted for his future, he knew he wanted her in it. He would be happy wherever she was.

That was the only real certainty.

"That's wonderful—I accept," he said with confidence that he was making the right decision.

"Welcome aboard. We will email you all the paperwork and the details for a commencement in three weeks. Will that be sufficient time to settle your affairs in Alaska?"

It was long enough to settle his affairs, but would it be long enough to say goodbye to the community he loved?

Being with Skylar was all that mattered. Home was wherever she was.

"Yes, sir. I'll be ready in three weeks."

DECISION MADE, LATER that day, Skylar drafted a polite email turning down the position in California and recommend-

JENNIFER SNOW   299

ing that they reconsider Doug's application on her high recommendation. She expected self-doubt or remorse as she typed, but she only felt more sure of her decision. She was staying in Port Serenity because this was exactly where she wanted to be. Protecting the ocean she loved and the people she loved.

Now, she needed to tell Dex the news.

She felt like she was floating as she approached the yacht later that evening. She couldn't wait to share the news with him.

He was pacing the upper deck as she approached and immediately took her into his arms as she boarded the vessel. His mouth crushed hers with such intensity, it surprised her. The passion in his kiss held a hint of urgency she hadn't expected.

He pulled back and looked slightly nervous as he said, "Sorry, I just needed that."

"I did too," she said softly. She studied him. He looked frazzled, with his adorably messy hair and his inability to stand still. "Everything okay?"

"Yeah…of course. Things are great," he said, but his tone was slightly higher pitched than normal. Even Shaylah seemed to notice as she sat near his feet, staring up at him.

"You're acting weird," Skylar said.

"Just…uh…it's nothing."

She cleared her throat. "Well, I have some news."

"You got the job," he said, his tone free of emotion. She couldn't tell how he felt.

"They offered me the position."

"That's wonderful," he said, wrapping his arms around her and squeezing her tight. "Congratulations. You absolutely deserve this opportunity. You're perfect for the position and California was always the dream. This is great news."

She frowned as she watched him ramble on. Since when was he happy about her leaving? Obviously, he was trying to be supportive. "Dex, can you stop talking for a sec?"

He clamped his lips tight.

"I turned it down," she said.

He blinked. "You what? Why?"

She wrapped her arms around his neck. "Because I refuse to let you push me away this time thinking it's in my best interests. I shouldn't have allowed you to let me walk out of your life and I won't do it again."

"Sky..."

"Shhhh. I love you Dex. And I want everyone to know it. I want to stay here in Port Serenity and start a life with you. And Shaylah," she said reaching down to pet the dog who was standing beside them, tail wagging.

"I want you too, Skylar but I don't want you giving up your dreams for me. You deserve this opportunity." He paused and took a deep breath. "That's why I applied for a civilian position in California."

Her mouth dropped. "You did?"

"I told you I would," he said. "And because of the amazing recommendation letter I received from your dad, I got it."

She tried to process everything he was saying. He was ready to give up the life he loved for her. He'd applied for a job to follow her, be with her...and he'd gone to see her father? And her father had written him a recommendation? Essentially giving his blessing for them to be together? Finally accepting Dex into her life. Into their family.

So many emotions strangled her. All wonderful, all

hopeful, all full of promise as she said, "You talked to my dad? And… But you love it here. You don't want to take that position. You belong on the water, rescuing…" She didn't want him giving anything up.

"I want to be with you," he said. "Whatever that takes."

She laughed. "So, let me get this straight. *I'm* staying and *you're* going?"

He nodded. "Apparently." He held her tight in his arms and kissed her. Soft and long and full of love before pulling back and looking into her eyes. "Unless one of us changes our mind?"

She looked around them, at the ocean, at the coast guard station in the distance, at his yacht—her new home—and took a deep breath. "I want to stay. With you and in this community where I belong."

"That's the best thing I've heard my entire life."

"I love you, Dex," she whispered against his mouth.

"Okay, I lied a second ago. *That's* the best thing I've heard my entire life," he said, as his lips met hers again.

Skylar released a deep, happy sigh as she kissed the man she had always loved. They were embarking on this new life journey together and she finally realized that she didn't have to go far to find new adventures.

The best ones awaited her here in her hometown, where she was meant to be, with the man she loved.

EPILOGUE

Three Weeks Later...

SKYLAR SQUINTED AS she carefully glued the last piece of the model boat in place and then stood back to admire their handiwork. "I think this may be our best one yet," she said to her dad as he put the cover back on the glue.

He smiled and nodded. "I have to agree."

"Helps that I'm not ten years old anymore," Skylar said with a laugh.

He dad wrapped an arm around her and kissed the top of her head. "You'll always be my little girl."

Skylar picked up the boat and placed it on the shelf with the others, then she cleared her throat. "You know, you don't have to retire so soon. Technically, you could work for another ten years."

Her dad looked surprised. "I thought working with me was challenging?"

"It is," Skylar said gently, "but not working with you will be just as difficult." In the last few weeks, she'd come to appreciate how special it was to have such an amazing mentor, someone she respected and admired to always have her back. She'd once viewed his pride in her as a hindrance, as a reason her crew and colleagues wouldn't take her seriously, but now she knew she deserved her father's pride.

She was a great captain and her last name had everything

to do with that. She'd come from a long line of capable, strong leaders and she wouldn't try to resist that anymore. She was lucky and she knew it.

Her father thought for a moment, then he shook his head. "It's time to hang up the hat, but... I was hoping to maybe secure a volunteer position on the yacht." He looked past her into the hallway. "What do you say, Dex?"

Skylar turned to see Dex standing in the office doorway, looking gorgeous in ripped jeans and a crew neck T-shirt, a grin on his handsome face.

"You're welcome anytime," Dex told him. He entered the room and gave Skylar a kiss on the forehead, then he turned back to her father. "You coming with us to the Serpent Queen Pub for Doug's going away party?"

Skylar's recommendation had helped him secure another shot at his interview and she'd rehearsed the questions with him over a Zoom connection for a week to help him conquer his fear of the intimidating process. He'd been offered the job in California the week before and was leaving soon. She was happy that they'd both gotten the best positions they were qualified for *and* hadn't had to sacrifice being close to the men they loved.

Her dad hesitated.

"You should come," Skylar said. "Doug would love to see you there."

Her father looked at Dex. "You sure a Wakefield establishment will serve us Beaumonts?" he asked, only half joking. It struck Skylar that neither her father nor grandfather had ever been inside the local pub.

"For Beaumonts, drinks are on the house," Dex said.

Skylar took his hand and squeezed it, overwhelmed with

happiness as the two most important men in her life shook hands, merging two families and ending the decades-long feud that had kept them all apart.

* * * * *

ACKNOWLEDGMENTS

Thank you to all the readers who enjoyed my Wild River, Alaska series and who have inspired me to write another fun series set in a different fictional small Alaskan town— Port Serenity. Thank you to my agent, Jill Marsal, for all your support and my editor, Dana Grimaldi, for giving me this opportunity to write a series featuring the Alaska Coast Guard and a warm, welcoming tourist town with its rich culture and history. Thank you to the HQN art department and marketing teams who continue to bless me with beautiful cover art and cover blurbs that make me want to reread the book (for the 6754 time ;)). Thank you so much to my Uncle Brian Legge, a Canadian coast guard captain, for all the insightful research help and to Katie, Diana and Wendy for their amazing guidance as I wrote about a hero with epilepsy. All mistakes are my own. So much gratitude and love, as always, to my family for allowing me the time, space and energy required to keep up with deadlines and for always being my fun, safe place after I hit Send.

XO
Jen

Love on the Coast

CHAPTER ONE

BREAKUPS WERE DIFFICULT anytime of the year. A breakup the week before a nonrefundable Alaskan cruise was worse.

Rachel Hempshaw sighed as she sat at her desk at *Dispelling the Myth*, a small magazine in Seattle where she worked as a blogger, researching mythical creatures and evaluating their legitimacy. She stared at the cruise tickets in her hand as her boss, Jaime, knocked on the open door.

"Wow, girl, that last article you posted about the swamp creature thing in the bayou was your best one yet. Funny in your usual sarcastic way, but very thorough and concise."

Praise was rare from her boss, so Rachel soaked it up. "Well, two-headed giant alligators do make my job a little easier."

"Still, you did research and due diligence before reporting what every rational being already knew—the thing doesn't exist and the tour boat companies promoting it are full of shit."

Right, but how many of those tour boat companies would suffer because of her article?

Nope. Guilt was something she refused to entertain. People were being taken advantage of by these false claims of creatures and phenomena that didn't exist. Families spent money on vacations hoping to see these wonders, only to be disappointed and in some cases—like Rachel's father—end up in debt in the search for things that weren't real.

Bills were real. A daughter needing school supplies and clothing was real. Eviction notices were real.

She shouldn't feel any remorse for wanting to provide her readers with the facts. Not overblown fairy tales. No one could fault her for wanting to be honest.

Brutally honest, according to her ex. In his breakup speech, Harry claimed she was a cynic who refused to believe in anything and he'd had enough of the negativity.

Maybe one day she would find a mysterious creature or paranormal phenomenon that she couldn't so confidently dispel. But that hadn't been the case for the Louisiana Swamp Monster or the dozen other research subjects before him.

And maybe one day she'd believe in happily-ever-after, but that hadn't been the case for her parents or in her own disastrous relationship history.

Jaime sat across from her, adjusting her tan pencil skirt around her legs, and nodded toward the Alaskan cruise tickets. "You're still going, right?"

"Alone? No way."

"Invite someone to go with you. Your mom could probably use a vacation."

Rachel shook her head. Her mom preferred not to discuss Rachel's career. She'd had enough talk of fantastical beasts with Rachel's father before she'd finally divorced him over his obsessions, and she wasn't thrilled that Rachel seemed to be fixated in her own way. "I think I'll pass on this one," Rachel said.

Jaime looked unimpressed as she instantly transformed from the old high school friend who'd given Rachel a job to the boss paying her salary. "Do I need to remind you that this wasn't just a pleasure trip? You expensed the tickets on the company's credit card claiming it would also be research for your next article."

Damn, Jaime remembered everything.

"You've already announced next month's topic on the magazine's site and your readers are looking forward to it," Jaime said.

Rachel had a surprising number of followers. She was a trustworthy source for those looking to distinguish between the places worth visiting and ones that were simply tourist traps. Her readers had been asking Rachel to visit Port Serenity, a community famed for a Serpent Queen residing beneath the surface of the North Pacific Ocean, for months.

There'd be no getting out of it.

"Come with me?" At least with her boss, it would truly be a work trip and she wouldn't feel so pathetic.

But Jaime scoffed as she stood. "Nope. Cold weather is definitely not my thing. That sea witch is all yours."

THE SKYPE CONNECTION glitched and all Callan Parks could see was the police uniform worn by his five-year-old's Barbie doll frozen on the screen. Apparently, Barbie had joined law enforcement and in doing so had given his daughter a new reason to follow in Callan's footsteps.

All he could do was hope the teenage years changed her mind.

He wouldn't wish this intense, dangerous life on anyone, especially someone he loved more than anything. A former active marine, Callan now worked on the coast guard's law enforcement boat stationed out of Port Serenity, intercepting drugs being transported through the North Pacific waterways. He'd accepted the job after his sister's death, when he was awarded guardianship of his niece, so he could spend more time in Alaska rather than overseas.

Even these relatively shorter missions made the job almost intolerable. Three months at sea, away from Darcy while she stayed with his parents in Port Serenity, had him contemplating his career choice a lot more frequently.

But he couldn't deny that he was good at his job. He'd been chosen for the coast guard's elite team based on his skills, and since joining the crew, they'd apprehended eighteen smugglers' boats. The drug enforcement crew was a unique blend of brains and brawn. This mission would be their biggest test yet. They were getting close to apprehending one of the major transporters, preparing to intercept on the boat's next trip the following week.

Catch the criminals and then go home.

Keeping the Alaskan communities free of drugs and the waters safe gave him a sense of purpose and pride. But Darcy needed more than just a "hero" to look up to. She needed a steady, secure upbringing and Callan was desperate to provide that. He'd promised his sister.

The connection resumed and now his mother's face appeared on the screen. "Callan, you still there?"

"Hey, Mom. Where did she go?"

"*PAW Patrol* just started."

Couldn't compete with her favorite cartoon.

"How is everything?" he asked, leaning closer.

"All good, darlin'." She'd never tell him if things weren't. She kept all bad news until his feet were safely back on the shore, claiming he had to be focused on the job and not have any distractions from home. But he did sense there was something on her mind as her dark eyes clouded slightly. "She misses you a lot this time," she said.

He sighed, running a hand over his face. "I miss her too." More than he ever thought possible. As her uncle, he'd always relished spoiling her and spending time with her, but since becoming her guardian, his role had changed to something so much more important, and with that came a feeling of deep obligation that he was honored to have. Honored but terrified. "Give her a big hug for me and tell her I'll be home soon."

Just another week at sea. One more bust.

"I will…" his mother said, and paused before asking, "Have you given any more thought to what we discussed?"

His aging parents had plans of their own and hadn't become Darcy's guardians for a reason. They loved their granddaughter, but they'd raised two kids already and weren't able to keep caring for her during these long stretches of time. They operated a fishing/tour boat out of Port Serenity that was busy during the summer months and they were struggling to keep up with the business. They planned to officially retire and sell the boat the following year, but they'd talked to him about taking over the family business. It had never been an option for him before, but now that he had Darcy to think about, maybe it made sense. Civilian positions in the coast guard in Alaska were tough to secure and he hated the idea of moving Darcy away from the small coastal town she loved.

He nodded. "I have. I still need some time to think about it." It had been the standard response for months. Soon, he'd need to give a more definite one. One way or the other.

"Okay, son, take care, stay safe," his mom said, blowing him a kiss as the Skype call disconnected.

Callan sat back in his chair and stretched his long limbs. Could he really take over his parents' business and be happy running a tour boat? Give up a career he was damn good at and settle into a slower, more predictable lifestyle? He still didn't know, but he needed to find a way to make his situation work.

Nothing mattered more than his daughter.

CHAPTER TWO

THE ALASKA-BOUND cruise boat *Sea Venture*, sailing from the Seattle port, was smaller than Rachel had expected. It would be better described as a hundred-foot expedition-style catamaran. However, despite its size, the boat was actually bright and spacious on the inside.

The company's website had boasted high-quality boutique cruises that offered authentic experiences. With multiple decks for enjoying the great views, outside dining, a cozy salon with dark wood and leather furnishings, and ten cabins that all had large windows and private decks to allow a lot of natural light, *Sea Venture* did not disappoint. Rachel was actually feeling good about the trip by the time the boat set sail that Friday evening.

As she unpacked her clothes and hung them in the closet, she eyed the hot tub she could see outside on the upper deck. That was where she planned on spending her evening. This work trip was definitely the most luxurious she'd ever taken, having planned it as a pleasure trip with Harry as well. Most times, she flew into a community for two days to talk to locals, explore the area, search for the mystery creature herself, and when it predictably didn't make an appearance, she'd head home. This trip would be five days at sea with two days docked in Port Serenity, giving ample time for the Serpent Queen to prove her existence.

Placing her empty suitcase in the closet, Rachel changed

316 LOVE ON THE COAST

out of her sweater and jeans into her swimsuit and headed to the upper deck. The hot tub was empty and she could see the other six passengers sitting at the long dinner table on the outside dining area below.

She'd eat later. Right now she wanted to soak in the inviting hot bubbles and enjoy this rare opportunity to relax. She closed her eyes as she sank below the water.

Maybe this trip alone wouldn't be so bad after all.

Drones scanned the wide-open seas with cameras and thermal imaging looking for targets of interest. They weren't what most people might suspect. Drug trafficking boats often didn't look suspicious at all. Not normally big, flashy operations that would draw attention. Often they were small fishing boats with fresh paint, traveling fast.

In this case, Callan and his crew were searching for two vessels they suspected would be meeting about ten miles off the coast of Port Serenity. A small fishing boat and a cruise ship, *Sea Venture*, sailing out of Seattle. They'd observed the suspicious vessels meeting once before and had significant reason to suspect the transfer of drugs from the cruise ship to the fishing vessel. The smaller boat would then complete the shorter trip to the docks, unnoticed.

A little before sunrise, they spotted the cruise ship. As predicted, the small fishing vessel was approaching from the opposite direction.

"We're moving out…" When Callan's commanding officer, Sanchez, gave the order, the crew sprang into action.

Callan's pursuit boat and mission responders picked up speed as they navigated the choppy ocean toward the cruise ship. Overhead the coast guard helicopter was on standby with snipers at the ready. Callan stood on deck, armed, poised and ready for anything they might encounter. As always, adrenaline coursed through his veins and all his senses were on high alert.

Idling the pursuit boat twenty feet away from the cruise ship, he used the radio broadcast to give them fair warning.

"This is the United States Coast Guard. Stop your vessel." He repeated the command several times, but the cruise ship picked up speed instead, confirming the crew's suspicion of illegal activity.

They had their warning.

"Noncompliant vessel. Permission to take out the engine," Callan said over the radio to the responding snipers in the helicopter circling above.

Two gunshots sounded as the snipers hit the marks, stalling the cruise ship. The response boat moved in a little closer and Callan radioed the suspicious vessel.

"This is the United States Coast Guard. Put your hands up!" Two crew members appeared on the deck of the cruise ship. But instead of complying, they started throwing things overboard. He suspected it was GPS units, cell phones, bags of drugs…anything to tie them to the illegal activity.

"Stop and put your hands up!" he said again.

The two men jumped off the boat.

"One over. Two over," Captain Sanchez said as they drew closer.

Shit. They had to move in fast. When there were jumpers, it meant the criminals might have set the boat on fire, and there were passengers on board. Callan stood with one foot on the edge of the boat as they closed in, ready to jump across on his captain's signal. His heart pounded and his training had him moving with instinct, no hesitation.

Now was where the real action began.

Rachel's eyes snapped open and she sat up quickly. She'd thought she'd imagined the sound of gunshots, but the sudden stalling of the boat had shaken her awake.

Was that a helicopter circling overhead?

She jumped out of bed and headed onto her deck. A fierce cool wind blew her hair around her face and ruffled her silk pajamas as she scanned the situation outside.

A helicopter hovered above and a coast guard police boat had stopped next to the cruise ship. There was yelling and commotion all around her. Several of the other passengers were watching on from their own decks, looking equally as confused. In the water, the cruise ship's captain and first mate were desperately trying to swim against the current caused by the helicopter as a pursuit boat followed and a coast guard officer dived in after them.

What the hell was going on?

In the room behind her, her cabin door flew open and a man wearing military cargo pants and a tight black T-shirt, holding a radio and a gun, entered.

"Hey!" Rachel said, going back inside. "What's going on?"

"Put your hands on your head!" he commanded.

What?

Confused, she slowly did as he said.

"We have position control," he said over the radio.

"You have what?" she asked as he approached, tucking his weapon into his belt.

He ignored her as he continued reporting over the radio. "Suspects in custody."

Suspects?

"Drilling through fiberglass has commenced, false deck expected."

Rachel frowned. Drilling through the boat? Whatever this was, it was not good. Not good at all. Her stomach sank as she scanned the cabin, taking in the big comfy bed and soaker tub in the bathroom, suspecting this would be her last view of it. So much for a relaxing solo trip.

"Seven passengers on board to be transferred." The coast guard officer's gaze swept over her silky pajamas. He frowned as though he had expected a different choice of sleepwear for a cruise ship headed to Alaska. "Grab only what's absolutely necessary and come with me," he said.

She lowered her arms and crossed them to hide as much as her body as possible. "I'm not going anywhere with you." How the hell did she know this muscular, gorgeous, intimidating armed man wasn't some pirate or something? She'd heard about these attacks on cruise ships before. Opportunists preying on unsuspecting tourists. Pretending to be law enforcement…

He looked annoyed. "A demolition team will be setting this boat ablaze in about six minutes. You probably don't want to be on it when that happens."

Her heart raced as she glanced at all her new clothing hanging in the closet and then she grabbed her purse and travel documents. "I've paid good money for this cruise and I'd like to know what the hell is going on," she said, sliding her feet quickly into her hiking boots.

"You are aboard a vessel suspected of smuggling cocaine across international waters," he said, the tiniest hint of amusement in his tone at her attitude. "Any more questions?"

CHAPTER THREE

PORT SERENITY WAS exactly how the travel brochure had described. Nestled among the mountains, surrounded by vast Alaskan wilderness was a touristy town with shops, restaurants and a surprisingly modern vibe. The shoreline along the marina was jagged in parts with pebbled beach areas where kids played and fishermen set up their poles. Docked along the pier were boats ranging in size from small fishing dinghies to one impressive-looking yacht named *The Mariana.*

As Rachel deboarded the coast guard rescue boat along with the other cruise passengers, she was still trembling beneath the oversize scratchy blanket the officers had given her.

The on-sea experience had been terrifying, but at least she'd have a great story to tell.

She had to try to stay positive. And avoid glancing at the officer who'd introduced himself as Lieutenant Parks. The guy was as gorgeous as he was intimidating, and she already felt embarrassed and slightly naive that she'd booked passage on a cover boat.

But how was she supposed to know the cruise ship hadn't been legit? She researched mythical creatures, not criminal organizations.

She'd felt his gaze on her several times as they'd sailed toward Port Serenity and now he was heading straight for her as she stood on the dock, contemplating the best next steps.

"Hey. Rachel, right?"

He should know. He'd had to verify the legitimacy of her travel documents and identification. He probably knew her credit score as well.

"More questions for me?" They'd interrogated her and the rest of the cruise ship passengers already.

"Just one. Do you have a place to stay in town?"

"Not since you set it on fire," she said, raising her chin slightly. She may be in revealing pajamas under this ugly brown blanket, her hair messy and her eyeliner smeared, but she was a US citizen whose vacation they'd destroyed.

"I *am* sorry that we ruined your vacation…"

"Work trip," she said quickly. "I'm not some loner who takes vacations by herself." She still had her pride after all.

"I take vacations alone. Does that make me a loner?"

Rachel couldn't imagine how this incredibly sexy coast guard officer could possibly ever be alone. Just the GI Joe–looking "uniform" would have women falling at his feet. Combined with his six-foot, two-hundred-pound, solidly muscled frame, dark hair, dark eyes and square, scruffy jawline, she'd bet that even if he went on vacations alone, he didn't necessarily spend them lonely.

"You were going to suggest a place to stay?" she asked, tearing her gaze from the biceps threatening to rip through the fabric of his T-shirt.

He nodded, pointing down the dock. "The Sealena Hotel. If you're here for the whole experience, you'll find it there." He paused. "And besides a few B and B's, it's really the only hotel in town."

Disdainfully, Rachel eyed the hotel with the sea green,

seashell exterior that featured an image of the Serpent Queen. "Wonderful," she muttered. No doubt the nightly rate was astronomical. She also needed to find new clothes and toiletries. Rachel seriously doubted she would get a refund on this trip or be compensated in any way for the trouble. And she couldn't expense any more to the magazine.

Lieutenant Parks frowned, looking slightly confused. "You were sailing to Port Serenity on a Sealena-themed excursion, so I assumed..."

She sighed. "This is a research trip. I work for a magazine in Seattle called *Dispelling the Myth*."

His expression darkened slightly. "Ah."

Ah. What the hell did that mean? Obviously, he had an opinion about it. "Something wrong?" she asked.

"Nope," he said, but his expression claimed otherwise.

"Okay, then. Bye." She shivered in the cool Alaskan breeze, feeling goose bumps surface on her bare legs. It was so much colder here than in Seattle. "I'm keeping this awful blanket," she said as she turned to head toward the hotel.

"Hey, Rachel," he called after her when she was a few feet away.

She turned with an exasperated sigh. "Yeah?"

He jogged toward her. "I know you're here to try to dispel the Sealena myth, but maybe I can show you some things off the usual path, away from the tourist attractions."

Her eyes narrowed. "Why would you do that?"

"Because I'd hate for you to base your article on whether our folklore is just a tourist trap based on...well, the tourist traps," he said with a grin.

A grin that left her unusually speechless for a second. Was it possible that there was a nice guy beneath the rough exterior? Her interest piqued, she raised an eyebrow. "You want to try to prove that there's some truth to the Sealena mythology?"

"I'd like to prove that Port Serenity is more than its brochure," he said, nodding toward the folded paper sticking out of her purse.

She hesitated, but she was here for a story and it wouldn't be unbiased journalism if she didn't explore all available information, so she nodded. "Okay. Deal."

"I'll let you get settled, find some clothing…" His gaze drifted over her and lingered a fraction too long on her bare legs. He cleared his throat as she caught his stare. "I'll meet you in the hotel lobby at eight?"

The idea of an evening out with a hot coast guard officer who had heartbreaker material written all over him gave her momentary pause, but it was in the name of journalism after all. "I'll see you at eight," she said.

WHY HAD HE suggested his tour guide services to the pretty folklore blogger (whatever that was)? He had more than enough on his plate. But something had twisted inside him upon learning that she was in town to prove that Port Serenity's history was a hoax and he hadn't been able to stop himself.

Sure, the Wakefield family had commercialized the myth of the Serpent Queen three generations ago, but accounts of the creature in these waters had been around since the 1800s.

His own parents had made a nice, modest living from Sealena's appeal and the stories they told tourists were ones Callan himself had memorized over the years. He may not know if he really wanted to run the tour business, but he certainly could. He knew the spiels, the points of interest and the best fishing places from working on the vessel alongside his parents and sister during summers growing up. He doubted Rachel would be interested in getting back on a boat anytime soon, so he was going to have to think of other ways to introduce her to the community.

As he entered the home he shared with his parents, after filling out all his reports and debriefing with the crew, he set his bag down in the entryway, and his spirits lifted when he heard the sound of tiny feet running down the hall.

"Uncle Cal!" Darcy leaped and he caught her in midair, spinning her around until they were both dizzy. She was in her Sealena-themed pajamas already, her long blond hair in pigtails, a streak of blue marker across her forehead. She was always drawing, coloring and making up stories. An artist like his sister had been.

"Man, I missed you, kiddo," he said, hugging her tight.

"Grandma and Grandpa are napping. They said they were just resting their eyes, but they're snoring really loud."

Callan sighed as he set her back on the floor. Five-year-olds were a lot of work. He couldn't expect his aging parents to keep this up much longer. It wasn't good for them or for Darcy.

He checked his watch. "It's 7:00 p.m. Almost bedtime for you as well."

She pouted. "But you just got back."

"And I'm home for a long time, so we will have lots of time to do all the fun things we talked about." He wanted to take her camping and to the waterfalls for hiking and swimming once the weather got warmer. Port Serenity had so much to offer an outdoor enthusiast with its unspoiled wilderness, and it was the perfect place to raise his niece.

"Grandpa says we might take over running the tour boat," she said excitedly.

He wished his father hadn't mentioned that possibility to Darcy until Callan knew for sure. The little girl would love it and he'd hate to disappoint her if he ultimately decided it wasn't the future he wanted. "Maybe. But we'll talk about it later. Let's go wake up your grandparents," he said with a wink, carrying her into the living room, where his parents were definitely not just resting their eyes—if the drool escaping his dad's mouth was any indication.

An hour later, at 7:58, he paced the lobby of the Sealena Hotel fighting the urge to leave. Truth was, he wanted to get to know this Rachel woman better and find out what was at the heart of her cynical nature. Why she had the desire to prove false something that a lot of people believed in and took joy in imagining possible. He'd googled her magazine and read several of her articles earlier that day. Her writing was fun and fresh and the articles themselves were entertaining, but she always claimed the myths weren't real. From the discussions in the comments sections, she seemed to relish the controversy her articles sometimes caused.

As someone whose career revolved around conflict, despite his constant search for peace, Callan was curious to understand her motivation for wanting to instigate it.

He checked his watch, and when he glanced up, he saw her exiting the elevator. She'd obviously bought new clothes as she was now in a pretty black jumpsuit and low wedge heels, a light sweater draped over her arm. Her dark hair was curled in loose waves around her shoulders and she wore simple makeup, a pale gloss shimmering on her lips. She looked slightly nervous, giving a small wave as she approached. "Hope I'm not overdressed. All I could find in the shops along Main Street was formal wear or work-out clothes," she said.

"You look great." More than great, but he kept the compliment to neutral territory. This wasn't a date after all. It was a tour. "Shall we go?"

She nodded and he led the way out of the hotel. She shivered slightly once they were outside and put on the sweater. "Wow, it cools off quickly once the sun goes down."

"It does." He hesitated. "Would you like my jacket?"

She shook her head. "I'm okay for now, but I'll be sure to take you up on that if the temperature drops further."

He nodded as they walked along the dock. "We won't be outside long."

"So, where does this tour begin?"

He stopped. "Right here." The Serpent Queen Pub was next door to the hotel, and while it wasn't on the tourist brochure, this place was a must visit. Owned and operated by the Wakefields since 1915, the local watering hole was home to many historical items from the days when the legend of Sealena was first claimed by the community. And Dollie and Zac, who manned the bar, were Port Serenity treasures in their own right.

Rachel raised an eyebrow. "The local pub?"

"Just trust me," he said, opening the door for her.

She scoffed, giving him a tiny glimpse of something deeper.

Were trust issues at the heart of her chosen profession? Might help explain why she seemed intent on proving fairy tales untrue.

He followed her inside, where dim lighting and loud local music greeted them. He waved to Zac behind the bar and the bartender sent him a curious look.

It must seem strange to see Callan in the bar with a woman. He hadn't dated since he'd become Darcy's guardian. Life was far too complicated to entertain the idea of bringing another person into the mix. He needed to figure out what the future held for the both of them first. He gave a quick shake of the head to gesture that it wasn't what it looked like, but Zac just grinned and sent him a look that said, *Sure, man. Famous last words.*

"That is one big statue," Rachel said, eyeing the fifteen-foot, thousand-pound hand-carved Sealena statue positioned beside the bar. The magnificent sea creature's arms were outstretched, but instead of holding up ships being tossed around the ocean, as she was usually captured doing, she held two large drink trays with martini glasses.

"Well, she's a big deal, as you obviously know," he said.

Rachel grinned as she turned to face him. "Pretend I don't and enlighten me."

Okay, this was his chance. He took a deep breath as he led the way to the back of the bar. "Sealena is rumored to be a half woman/half serpent who protects shipping vessels at sea." He paused, searching for the right words. "But she's more than just a sea monster and a way to lure tourists to Port Serenity."

Rachel listened intently, seeming to weigh his words carefully. "She is?"

"Yes—she represents the spirit of the community. As much as it might seem contradictory, she's actually a symbol for the coast guard and the men and women who protect the oceans."

"I thought she often stole credit for the work of the coast guard."

He laughed as he nodded. "That is true, but we've learned to share the praise."

"Surely not everyone," she said knowingly. "I mean, didn't her creation cause a generational family feud within the community?"

Ah, yes, the other thing that intrigued a lot of visitors. "The Wakefields and Beaumonts have been at odds for generations—it's true. But rumor has it, the feud started when Lieutenant Beaumont, a state trooper, had to arrest his best friend, Earl Wakefield, over the transporting of contraband. The charges didn't stick, but the two men never spoke again. That's what started it all."

She nodded slowly. "So, do you think this Wakefield guy started this whole Sealena thing as revenge?"

He shook his head. "Nothing as sinister as that. Let me show you something." He led the way to a pillar behind the tables and motioned toward an old letter framed beneath glass.

"This is the original letter that Earl Wakefield wrote to first pitch the idea of a Sealena-themed community back in the 1900s."

Rachel squinted to read parts of the spirally handwriting. "'A story children can understand. A way to make families feel better when their loved ones go to sea...'" She looked pensive as she glanced up at him. "Definitely a nice thought. Better than a spreadsheet of suspected annual revenue from a massive influx in visitors."

Still a skeptic. "You're tough."

She shrugged. "I've just got a good radar for detecting bullshit."

"Okay, well, let's take a look at the evidence, then," he

said, leading her to the wall of images capturing the Serpent Queen in action.

She eyed the wall of framed, mostly blurry, far-off shots of the ocean, the marina and several boats that held traces of the sea queen. Parts of a serpent's body was featured in one...a woman's shape coming out of the waves in another.

"I've seen better photos of Nessie," she said, hand on her hip as she turned to face him. "Look, I'm not saying with certainty that this thing doesn't exist. I'm not narrow-minded enough to suggest an absolute. All I am saying is that there is such a thing as expectant attention, the psychological phenomenon that suggests people who expect or want to see something are more likely to misinterpret visual clues."

"People see what they want to see?"

"Exactly."

He sighed. "Well, I guess the Serpent Queen Pub was a bust in altering your perspective." He paused. "But they do make a mean green serpent tail martini." Would she want to stay and have a drink with him? He glanced across the pub where several fishermen sat chatting. "And I think those men over there may have a story or two if you're up for it."

She smiled and his heart skipped a beat at the first genuine look of contentment on her beautiful face. Her smile really lit up the room. He'd always thought that expression was a cliché.

"A green serpent tail martini and other tall tales sound great," she said.

A SMALL PART of her had really hoped there'd be something at the Serpent Queen Pub to give her reasonable doubt, but so far all Rachel had seen were the same things that every other community capitalizing on a fake monster had. Memorabilia, doctored or out-of-focus snapshots, fishermen with fabricated, albeit entertaining, tall tales...

Port Serenity was a beautiful community surrounded by some of the best scenery she'd ever experienced. And this green serpent tail martini was the best drink she'd ever had. But unfortunately, the evening's expedition had failed to convince her of the existence of the Serpent Queen and any reason why tourists should choose this wild-goose chase over countless others.

It *had* however made her more curious about her self-proclaimed tour guide, who was sitting across from her in a booth in the corner of the pub. He was a gorgeous, brave, sexy hero who was giving up his first night back home after three months at sea to hang out with her.

Why? There had to be a catch. He seemed to be having a good time showing her around and introducing her to locals, but there had to be an ulterior motive. In her experience, there always was. Were flings with tourists his thing?

Would she be opposed to one if it was?

Feeling her face flush at the thought, she cleared her throat. "So, you've lived here your whole life?" she asked Callan.

He nodded. "My parents run a fishing/tour boat, and when I left the marines, I was lucky to be stationed with the Port Serenity Coast Guard."

"Why did you leave?"

"I traveled overseas a lot and it was time for a change."

"That must have been challenging on relationships," she said, aiming for casual but falling short. This wasn't technically a date, but she decided that if it turned into one, she wouldn't be opposed. There was a vibe between them.

The tension from earlier had been charged with a sexual chemistry—the way his gaze had drifted over the sight of her in her pajamas and then the appreciative look on his face when they'd met in the hotel lobby.

And he was definitely her type. A short-term thing with an expiry date even more so. No chance of developing real feelings and getting hurt.

"Relationships did take a back seat to my career," he said.

"Do you enjoy what you do?" she asked before taking another sip of her second martini.

He nodded slowly. "I do. I've always known I wanted to go into some sort of protective service position and I love the water, so the marines made sense," he said, but she sensed it wasn't the complete story.

"But…"

He laughed. "You really like to dig, huh?"

"Occupational hazard, I guess."

He hesitated, his gaze burning into hers as though weighing how much to reveal, how much to confide, and she leaned closer, hoping he was sensing a genuine interest.

"Well, the truth is—"

His phone rang, cutting off his next words as the image of a woman and little girl lit up the display. He looked slightly panicked and Rachel's palms sweat.

Oh my God. This guy was married with a kid. Did his family know he was out with her? Sure, it wasn't an actual date, but they were certainly flirting as though it was.

She grabbed her purse and started to slide out of the booth as he hesitated with the ringing cell phone in his hand. "Wait…let me explain," he said.

"No need." She hurried out of the bar as she heard him answer the call.

"Hi, sweetheart…"

Sweetheart. Wow. The guy was a complete jerk. She was in Port Serenity to dispel a myth about a half-woman/half-serpent creature and she was also receiving yet another reminder of how good guys just didn't exist.

She stepped out into the cold and pulled her sweater tighter around her body as she stalked down the pier toward the hotel.

Unfortunately, his footsteps echoed on the wooden planks behind her. "Rachel, please wait."

She kept going.

"Please, let me explain. I'm not married if that's what you're thinking," he said, slightly out of breath.

She slowed, but just a little. A live-in partner or girlfriend was the same thing in her mind. A commitment was a commitment.

"That was my niece, Darcy, who called."

She stopped and turned, placing her hands on her hips. "Your niece calls you at almost midnight?" Likely story, buddy. Who did he think he was fooling?

He sighed, as though he was being forced to confess something he wasn't ready to share. "She does when she's woken from a nightmare and needs me."

Rachel frowned. "I'm not following."

"I'm her official guardian. Have been since my sister—the woman in the photo—died two years ago."

Oh shit. She'd naturally assumed the worst and now her actions had shown that the attraction between them was mutual. That she'd hoped they were on a date. That she'd been upset to think he was unavailable and a slime bag.

Great, she'd shown her cards.

"I guess I should have let you explain instead of leaping to conclusions," she said awkwardly.

He nodded. "I take it you haven't had the best luck with men?"

She faked a look of shock. "And why on earth would you assume that? Because I spend my life trying to prove that fairy tales and myths are all horseshit?" Her honesty even surprised herself, but she didn't like to bullshit any more than she liked being on the receiving end.

He laughed. "Sorry you didn't get a chance to finish your drink, but I do appreciate you not throwing it in my face."

"I did consider it for half a second," she said teasingly.

"Unfortunately, I do have to go," he said, looking genuinely remorseful to see the evening end. "But I'd like to continue being your tour guide...if you're up for it."

She hesitated briefly. Things had somehow shifted very quickly from potential casual vacation hookup to deeper territory. In the matter of minutes, they'd both had to open up and let their guards down unexpectedly. That made her slightly uneasy, but she couldn't deny that she wanted to see him again.

"Nine a.m. tomorrow?" she asked.

"Works for me," he said.

"It's a date," she said, then shook her head. "I mean, not a date, but..."

"It's a date," he said, stepping toward her and taking her hand in his.

Surprised, but pleasantly so, she interlocked her fingers with his as they walked back to the hotel, slightly disappointed to be ending the best non-date turned date she'd ever been on.

CHAPTER FOUR

THE RINGING OF Rachel's cell phone woke her far too early the next day. She groaned as she rolled to her side in the queen-size bed and blindly reached toward the nightstand. She opened one eye and, seeing Jaime's number on the phone display, answered on the fourth ring. "Hey, boss," she said.

"'Hey, boss'? You were just part of the seizure of an international drug smuggling operation and 'hey, boss' is all you got?"

Rachel sighed. She probably should have updated Jaime the day before, but she'd been a little preoccupied. "It was quite the adventure," she said, an image of Callan in action playing in her mind. It had been hot as hell, and the night before had revealed more layers to the sexy, commanding coast guard officer.

A single dad was just about the most heartwarming—and panty-wetting—thing she could imagine. How on earth the man could be single was a mystery. Though, no doubt it was his choice, having a very full and somewhat complicated life already.

Therefore, this had to be just a casual vacation fling for him, and while that thought should give her peace of mind, it somehow didn't.

"Well? How goes the story?" Jaime asked. "Is the place as touristy as we thought?"

"Um…not really. It's actually really nice. The scenery is breathtaking and the people are—"

"Right, right, right, I'm sure the people are lovely, but is there a possibility that this sea serpent thing is based on anything other than a community trying to cash in? That's what you're there to evaluate. Remember?"

"I don't know yet," she said.

"You. Don't. Know," Jaime said slowly, as though not recognizing who she was speaking to.

Rachel must seem weird this morning, but something had changed in her. She wasn't sure she liked it. Jaime was right. Rachel was here to dispel the myth and she needed to stay focused. She scoffed. "I mean, of course the myth isn't real. I'm heading out today to do more research." She didn't think it was necessary to mention her research companion. "I'll keep you posted."

"Good. For a second there, you kinda freaked me out," Jaime said.

As Rachel disconnected the call, she lay back against the oversize comfy pillows and sighed. She was here to do a job and she couldn't lose sight of that. No matter how attractive Callan was.

"Who are we going to meet, Uncle Cal?"

"A new friend," he told Darcy as they walked along the pier toward the hotel early the next morning. "She's in town to write a story about Port Serenity and Sealena, so I invited her to come with us. That okay?"

"Sure!" Darcy said, skipping along next to him.

Darcy might not mind, but Callan's heart was racing at the idea of introducing her to Rachel. He hadn't dated at all since his sister's death had left the little girl in his care. In part because he was busy with work and raising the child. But mostly because he didn't want to introduce Darcy to someone until he knew there was a possibility of a serious relationship.

But he had to make an exception because he'd promised both ladies an outing this morning, and he didn't want to break his word.

When Rachel exited the hotel, the look of surprise on her face had him questioning the decision. He'd said this was a date. Would she be cool with meeting Darcy? Would she think this wasn't a date after all?

She smiled and said, "Hey, you must be Darcy," before bending to extend a hand to the little girl.

Darcy's eyes widened when she saw Rachel's silver hoop earrings. "Your earrings are so pretty." She shot Callan a look. "*He* won't let me pierce my ears."

He laughed. "Your ears are pretty just the way they are."

Darcy pouted and Rachel leaned closer. "I'll work on him." She winked at him as she and Darcy shared a conspiratorial' grin.

Wow, two seconds and they'd already joined forces against him. A warmness radiated through him that he struggled to keep in check. Rachel was just a tourist. She had no intention of staying in Port Serenity. This attraction was a temporary thing. He'd enjoy their time together, not get too close and say goodbye when she decided to leave. It was the perfect situation for him, really.

"Ready to go?" he asked.

They both nodded and Darcy stepped in between them, taking both their hands in hers. Panic filled his mind as he glanced at Rachel.

"This okay?" he asked quietly.

She nodded and his chest swelled even more as the three of them headed toward Main Street.

Five minutes later, he opened the door to the Sealena Bookstore and Museum and stood back to let the two of them enter. He hadn't been inside the store in months and it always surprised him just how much Sealena-themed merchandise and history memorabilia the store housed. Local artwork featuring the Serpent Queen was hung on the walls. Beautiful, realistic renderings and more abstract conceptual designs. Statues of all sizes cluttered the shelves and books from children's stories to coloring books to anthologies of fishermen's accounts were along the bookshelves.

Hats, T-shirts and sweaters with the Serpent Queen on them hung on racks and there was even a collection of Sealena-themed skin care products on display near the counter.

"Wow, this place is a lot bigger than it looked from the outside," Rachel said, echoing his thoughts. She scanned the items for sale and sent him a side-eye. "You know bringing me to a souvenir shop isn't helping your case, right?"

He laughed. "This is much more than it appears," he said, gesturing for Darcy to show Rachel why they were really here.

"Come this way," the little girl said, leading them to the back of the store where tables and chairs had been set up.

Sealena School was written on the whiteboard where Carly, the pretty, thirtysomething store owner, set up for the day's lesson. Darcy hurried to take her usual seat in the front and Rachel hung near the back with him.

"Teaching the new generation how to dupe people?" she whispered with a teasing grin.

"Just watch," he said, gently taking her shoulders and

turning her to face the front of the room as Carly addressed the kids.

The touch was minimal, casual and brief, yet he felt a spark between them as he quickly removed his hands from her body, then regretted breaking the contact. He wanted to touch her, hold her hand again like he had the night before, but there was definitely something between them and he had to be careful.

Rachel didn't seem the type to trust easily or fall quickly. Which should make him feel better, yet there was an unsettling feeling in the pit of his stomach.

"What are those?" Rachel asked, nodding to a long table in front of the class.

"Artifacts that divers have resurrected from this area," he said as Carly picked up the first one—a shimmering blue gemstone—and held it up.

"Anyone know what this is?" Carly asked.

The kids were silent. Several shook their heads.

"Me neither," Carly said with a wide smile, her brown eyes sparkling behind her red-rimmed glasses. The woman was obsessed with all things Sealena and loved teaching the kids. Callan hoped maybe some of her enthusiasm might spread to Rachel, opening up her mind just a little to the possibilities.

The possibility of Sealena *and* the possibility of them?

Man, he was getting ahead of himself. He turned his focus back to the class as Carly continued.

"In fact, no one can tell exactly what kind of stone this is. It was discovered near Fishermen's Peak in the early 1950s by a gold panner. Gemologists have studied it, but no one can determine the material. There are traces of limestone and aquamarine, but the binding material is foreign."

Next to him, Rachel looked slightly more intrigued as she listened, and he was captivated by the expression on her face. She was a beautiful woman and even more so when she let her guard slide, even just a little.

A child in front raised her hand. "My grandma says it's from Sealena's magical necklace."

Carly smiled. "It very well could be." She paused. "*Or* it could be something the earth has created—a new substance that scientists haven't discovered yet. Divers and panners are always looking for more. So far, this is the only one."

Rachel glanced his way quickly and caught him staring. He cleared his throat and shifted his gaze toward the front as Carly set the mysterious gemstone down on the table and reached for a slab of hardened, flat coral.

Rachel narrowed her eyes as she moved closer and then turned to him to whisper. "Is that a handprint?"

He grinned. "What do *you* think?"

She straightened her shoulders and shook her head. "Impossible to tell. Could be a starfish fossil imprint or something."

Which was exactly how Carly presented it to the kids.

The store owner continued the lesson on the artifacts, explaining their possible origins and what they could be, while allowing the children to maintain some hope in the mystery. As the class dispersed, Rachel turned to him. "Okay, so that was pretty cool," she said almost begrudgingly.

"We want kids to have an open mind about a world below the surface that we've yet to fully uncover. We want to encourage imagination, but we also want to teach critical thinking and plausibility."

She seemed to consider that as Darcy ran toward them,

her eyes wide. "Uncle Cal, did you see that beautiful gemstone?"

He laughed. "I did." He turned to Rachel. "If you couldn't tell, this one is all about the bling."

They laughed as they waved their thanks to Carly and left the store. A few blocks later, they reached the local primary school. Callan bent and hugged Darcy tight and kissed the top of her head. "Have a great day. I'll be right here to pick you up after school."

He noticed Rachel watching, a look of admiration on her face. Admiration and something else—longing?

Darcy gave her a quick hug. "Will you be here too?"

"Uh…" Rachel looked at him.

"I think Rachel may have things to do, but I'm sure you'll get a chance to see her again before she leaves town." Too much would be too much and he didn't want to put Rachel in an awkward position or let Darcy get attached to someone who wasn't staying. *He* was already getting far too attached for the both of them.

He waved as the kindergarten teacher met the kids at the door and Darcy disappeared inside.

"She's a great kid," Rachel said.

"The best."

"I can tell she feels the same way about you," Rachel said, unaware how much her compliment meant to him. He never knew if he was doing enough, so to have a stranger observe the special bond he shared with Darcy gave him hope that maybe he was doing something right.

Their gazes met and held for a long moment. The same unexpected warmness enveloping him as he stared into the most incredible dark blue eyes to ever hold him mesmerized. She was a fantastic woman. Smart, funny, easy to be around, and despite her claims of being a cynic, he'd felt the energy shift around her since the day they'd met. She seemed more open, less guarded.

"Where to next?" she asked.

"Hope you like the smell of fish," he said with a grin.

RACHEL WAS ACUTELY aware of the handsome man walking close beside her along the narrow dock. Despite her phone call with Jaime, she'd been excited to see him again that morning. More excited than she'd been in a very long time. Meeting Darcy had only elevated her admiration and respect for him. He was definitely a man with many layers, and the more she discovered, the more she liked. He was obviously devoted to the little girl and it was so heartwarming to see the two of them together. The slight tug in her chest when he'd hugged the child before leaving her at school had brought up long-repressed emotions.

How many times had Rachel wished for a relationship like that with her own father? Longed for his love and affection? Only to be disappointed time and again when his search for something bigger was more important than his family. More important than her.

They stopped at the end of the marina and Rachel read the sign on the small building perched at the foot of a steep-looking cliff. "Port Serenity Marine Life Sanctuary?"

"If you aren't buying into the emotional side of Sealena, a more scientific approach might help," Callan said, opening the door.

Rachel entered and immediately the smell of sea life and salt water filled her nostrils. Callan hadn't been kidding. But she was impressed as she scanned the high-end equipment in the small facility. Radars and instruments to perform laboratory tests filled the offices. Wildlife protection resources were stacked on a bookshelf and posters illustrating the work of the sanctuary were on the walls.

A woman dressed in a wet suit under a white lab coat greeted them as they entered. "Hey, Callan, great to see you. Heard about the bust."

"Thanks. It was definitely eventful," he said, glancing quickly at Rachel. He hugged the woman quickly, then turned to make the introduction.

"Rachel Hempshaw, meet Dr. Ann Sweeny. She's one of the marine biologists who work here, studying the various local species. Ann, Rachel is a journalist from Seattle doing a story on Sealena."

"A blogger actually," Rachel mumbled. She couldn't really call herself a journalist. She'd wanted to be a reporter at one time, but life and financial circumstances hadn't led to her fulfilling her dream of university... Blogging was the next best thing and she'd been lucky that one of her high school friends owned a magazine.

"Nice to meet you," she said, shaking Ann's hand.

"Welcome to Port Serenity," Ann said. "Let me show you around."

Ann led the way into her office, where there were dozens of aquariums full of different species of fish and other sea life. Some, Rachel couldn't even identify. She peered into the tanks and pointed to one blue-and-pink fish with big bulging eyes. It almost looked like it was glowing. "What is that?"

"That's Eddie and we're not entirely sure yet," Ann said with a laugh. "In addition to protecting this area from overfishing and pollution, one of the things we do here is study environmental DNA. Essentially, we collect samples of everything in the waters surrounding Port Serenity. Genetic material from organisms that shed into the environment tells us what species are living in the waters. Still haven't quite identified that little guy."

Rachel tore her gaze away from the tank. "Have you discovered anything that might be a sea monster?"

Ann smiled at Callan. "You were right. She is skeptical." She waved a hand and Rachel followed her into the lab. On the walls were reports from different tests performed on the environmental DNA.

Rachel scanned it.

"In each study, we were able to identify about eighty percent of the material and connect it with creatures we all know. There's fish, dolphin, seal DNA in the water, as well as eel, pigeon, all the usual suspects," Ann said. "However, the twenty percent we can't identify means it's possible that there are creatures living below the surface that we've yet to discover, to classify. Like Eddie."

Rachel nodded. "Okay, but the unknown isn't *proof* of Sealena's existence."

"True," Ann said, "but you may be interested to learn that we have discovered traces of DNA similar to human genetic material that suggest it's not completely impossible that there could be a species similar to humans in the darker depths around here."

Rachel shivered involuntarily and Callan laughed. "Slightly creepy, right?"

Ann swiped at him. "Not creepy. Fascinating."

Rachel hid a grin. Callan's hotness had obviously not escaped the doctor's notice. A slight pang of jealousy surprised her.

"Well, thank you, Dr. Sweeny," Callan said. "We won't take up any more of your time."

"Yes, thank you," Rachel said. "It's been enlightening."

As they headed outside into the crisp, cool Alaskan day, Callan's smug expression made her laugh. "You think you've proved your case, don't you?"

"I think I've introduced a fraction of a doubt in that mind." He touched the side of her head and then his hand lingered, tucking a strand of her hair behind her ear, then gently caressing her cheek.

Her heart pounded as she stared into the dark depths of his eyes, his look of attraction undeniable. She swallowed hard as he stepped closer, his hand cupping the back of her head.

She wrapped her arms around his neck and stood on tiptoes as he lowered his head toward hers. She closed her eyes as their lips met and she sank into him, into the unexpected kiss.

He wrapped his arm around her waist, pulling her closer and holding tight as he deepened the kiss with a sense of desperate urgency, as though he knew this couldn't last. She savored the taste of him, the smell of his aftershave filling her senses and the feel of his strong, muscular, powerful body pressed against hers.

It was a damn good kiss. Soft, gentle, yet demanding and passionate.

Rachel couldn't recall a kiss that had ever left her feeling breathless, but when she reluctantly pulled back, she fought for air.

"Sorry, I'm not sure where that urge came from, except that I haven't met anyone in a long time who's occupied my thoughts so much or intrigued me the way you do," he said, releasing his hold on her slowly.

"Likewise," she said, her pulse still racing. She barely knew him and yet the kiss had felt right. It had felt natural, as though they'd connected on a level that seemed impossible in such a short time.

A lot of things she'd once deemed impossible seemed possible in Port Serenity. Could the mythical Serpent Queen be one of them? And could she let her guard down enough to discover the truth?

CHAPTER FIVE

"I LIKE THE blue shirt better," Darcy said, sitting on his bed later that evening, her Sealena plush doll on her lap.

Callan eyed the green dress shirt he was buttoning and realized he did too. He removed the shirt, hung it back on the hanger and put on the blue one. "You're right. This one is better."

"It's the same color as her eyes," the little girl said.

"You're very observant." He grinned. He'd noticed Rachel's deep blue eyes earlier, as well, when he'd gotten lost in them. Eyes that always held a look of cautious curiosity. Eyes that seemed to see everything and perceive things with a rational mind.

He normally did too. But there was no explaining how these feelings had come out of nowhere so quickly. In two days of spending time with Rachel, he wanted to spend even more time getting to know her, letting her get to know him.

Since his sister's death, he hadn't opened up to anyone. He'd guarded his heart and had prioritized caring for Darcy and creating a stable, steady life for her. Falling for a tourist from Seattle didn't follow the game plan.

But an hour later, sitting across from her at a table in the pub, he had to struggle to keep from throwing the game plan out the window.

Rachel was wearing a beautiful black halter dress, her dark hair swept up in a high ponytail, revealing a long slender neck and sexy shoulders. She sipped a green serpent tail martini and cocked her head to the side pensively. "Darcy was okay with you coming out?"

He nodded. "She picked out my shirt."

"She has great taste."

"I'm definitely going to try to nurture her interest in fashion rather than her fierce protective nature. Do not want her following in my footsteps."

Rachel's smile was warm. "She's protective of you?"

"I think losing her mom so early and never knowing her real father has made her slightly fearful of losing me too," he said.

"Do you mind if I ask what happened to your sister?"

He cleared his throat and took a deep breath. He hadn't really talked about it with anyone before, but he wanted to with Rachel. "She was an incredible artist, but she had her demons. When Darcy was born and her boyfriend left them, she fell into a deep depression. Drugs were an escape... until they weren't anymore." They'd all tried to help her, but Marie had been good at hiding just how much pain she was in and how far her addiction had gone until it was too late.

"Sorry," Rachel said gently, reaching across the table to touch his hand. "Makes sense that you do what you do."

He nodded. "It's challenging, though, to figure out the bigger purpose. What does Darcy need? A father who protects the oceans and keeps harm away or someone there for her all the time. Someone at every father-daughter dance, in the stands at her baseball games..."

Rachel's expression once again held a hint of unconcealed longing as she said, "I can't imagine how hard it must be trying to make that call."

"My parents are hoping I'll take over running the tour

boat next year when they officially retire. That way I can be here full time for Darcy."

"Do you want to do that?"

"If it's what's best for her."

"Sacrificing a career you love for your daughter is very admirable," she said, glancing away and staring into her nearly empty glass. She seemed suddenly thoughtful and further away.

"So, what's your story? Why the guard rails around your heart?"

She laughed, but it held a trace of sadness. "Nothing as tragic as yours. Just repeated disappointments, I guess. My dad believed in every hoax out there. He sacrificed a lot in the pursuit of proving things to be real. The impact on our family—emotionally and financially—destroyed any possibility that fairy tales could be true. Even ones about love." She paused and took a deep breath. "Especially ones about love."

He squeezed her hand. "I'm actually starting to only *now* believe in that possibility."

She swallowed hard and he knew he'd freaked her out, but he wanted to be honest with her. Did she feel it too? This wild and unexpected connection between them? He couldn't deny the intense attraction he felt around her, but it was more than that. He couldn't describe it any other way than to call it love. Early love, maybe, but definitely love.

"I have to admit, this is terrifyingly fast, but I really like you," she said cautiously.

"But..."

She laughed softly. "Now who's digging deep?"

Her cell phone rang on the table and she frowned as

she glanced at the call display. "Sorry, I should take this. My boss."

"Of course." He released her hand and sat back in the booth as she grabbed the phone and quickly headed outside to take the call. An uneasiness washed over him. He watched through the window as she paced outside. She was here for her job and now he could understand why she did what she did. Her father's choices had left a deep impact if she'd chosen a contradictory path, dispelling myths instead of trying to prove them.

Could he dare hope that she'd found something to believe in this time?

RACHEL SHIVERED IN the cool ocean breeze as she recounted her experiences to Jaime. Leaving out the part about Callan and Darcy. "It was actually the first time I've seen a community educating kids while allowing their imaginations to go unhindered." Carly and her Sealena School had impressed her. So far, everything in Port Serenity wasn't quite what she'd been expecting. In the best way.

"We all know what happens when kids are misled," Jaime said, sounding unimpressed.

"Right," Rachel said. She knew better than anyone how disappointing it could be to learn fairy tales weren't real. She cleared her throat. "There was also a scientist at the marine sanctuary—"

"Who confirmed a Serpent Queen?" Jaime interjected sarcastically.

She swallowed hard. "Not exactly. But there are a lot of things scientists haven't discovered yet."

Jaime was silent on the other end and Rachel sighed. Her boss didn't want to hear it. Before coming to Port Serenity, Rachel's mind had already been made up too. But then things had started to change. She still didn't believe in a half woman/half serpent living in these waters, but she also couldn't claim that the search for one would be a waste of her readers' time.

Ultimately, she worked for a magazine that dispelled myths rather than proving them. And her bills were real enough to pull her out of whatever haze seemed to surround her rationality.

"You're right, Jaime. This place is a tourist trap at its finest," she said, her voice hard as she struggled with an uneasiness in the pit of her stomach. "Talk soon."

She turned and the uneasiness transformed into full-on despair, seeing Callan standing there with her jacket. "Didn't mean to eavesdrop. Just thought you might want this." His tone was slightly cold. He'd obviously heard the last part of the conversation.

"Callan, I…" What? What exactly could she say?

"Is that how you really feel?" he asked.

"It was. At least before I arrived, before I got to know the residents here and the history…"

"But that's not the article your boss wants? The one your readers are expecting."

She nodded and shivered again as a blast of wind blew her hair across her face. "Our site is focused on dispelling myths, not encouraging them."

"And none of this is real?" He took a step toward her and she swallowed hard. He was talking about more than Sealena. Unfortunately, she didn't know how to answer. She liked him. A lot. They'd connected deeply in a very short time. She was attracted to him and there was chemistry between them. But could she really trust in these emotions she'd always dismissed as just a way to get hurt?

"I don't know," she said carefully. "Things aren't always what they seem and it's complicated."

He laughed wryly. "Complicated, that's something I know well and yet here I was willing to *complicate* things even further." He handed her the jacket and she struggled to find the right words. She didn't know what to say or what to do about this connection she was feeling with him. How could she after just a few days?

His gaze searched hers, losing hope with each second of silence. His chest heaved in a deep sigh as he nodded. "Good luck with the article. Sorry I wasn't able to change your mind...or your heart," he said before turning and walking away.

Rachel's chest ached as she watched him go.

INSIDE HER HOTEL ROOM, Rachel sighed as she changed out of her dress and shoes into comfortable clothing and headed onto the deck. She leaned over the railing of her first-floor terrace and stared at the crashing waves hitting the beach.

She'd blown it with Callan...but what was really there to blow? They'd met only two days ago, and while there was a connection between them, could it lead to something more?

He claimed it was real, but in her experience, emotions blinded a lot of people to reality. How could he be so sure after only a few days? Had she ever felt so sure about her own feelings for anything? Or anyone?

What the hell was she supposed to do? She had to write the article her boss was expecting, but she didn't want to write a cynical critique of this place anymore. She wanted people to visit Port Serenity for all its wonder and possibility. She wanted them to come here for the myth and stay for the community's warmth and charm and wonderful residents.

She wanted to believe in this mythical Serpent Queen.

Staring out at the waves, which were illuminated by the lighthouse beacon, her heart stopped.

Someone was in the water. She wasn't flailing about, but she wasn't swimming against the strong current. If she was calling for help, the sound was being carried away on the breeze, overshadowed by the sound of the waves lapping against the shore.

Rachel scanned the coastline quickly but didn't see anyone else around. The beach was quiet and empty.

She had to do something. She had to help.

Her heart raced as she propelled herself over the railing and headed toward the water, twenty feet away. She removed her sweater, then took a big gulp of courage before plunging into the freezing water. Her limbs instantly felt stiff and she was gasping when she resurfaced. The water was like piercing knives digging into her skin. She plunged in again, swimming as quickly as she could toward the spot where she'd seen the woman. She caught another glimpse of her, her long hair floating on the surface of the water, her face illuminated by the lighthouse beam as it rotated past again. Expressionless, haunting, an eerie calmness…

Rachel swam faster and harder against the current and crashing waves. She stopped and scanned, but there was no one there. She turned quickly, treading water to stay afloat, feeling her limbs tiring and going numb.

Where had she gone? Had the tow taken her out farther? Or had she gone under?

She inhaled another deep breath and plunged below the

surface, eyes struggling to see in the murky depths, ignoring the fear that gripped her chest. She had no idea what was in these waters, lurking beneath her...

Feeling two strong hands wrap around her waist, her pulse raced as she was pulled toward the surface. She swung around and saw a man dragging her back toward the shoreline.

"Wait! What are you doing?" She tried to fight against him.

"It's okay. You're okay."

"I know I'm okay! There's another woman out here. I saw her."

The man stopped for a second, looked around, then continued swimming toward the shore. Rachel scanned the water frantically, but her limbs were exhausted and she was desperate to be out of the frigid waters.

On shore, she pointed to the spot where she'd seen the woman. "She was there. I s-saw her f-floating in the water from my hotel room." Her teeth chattered as she reached for her sweater, hugging it to her freezing, wet body.

The man scanned the water, then sent her an almost patronizing look. "You're staying at the Sealena Hotel?"

She nodded emphatically. "Yes, on the first floor. There was a woman out there. I'm sure of it."

"I didn't see anyone besides you. I live on that yacht over there," he said, pointing to the largest boat docked in the marina a few yards away. "I've been out on the deck all night..."

"You don't believe me?"

He ran a hand over his wet face and hair. "Look, this hotel...this entire community can make you think you saw something."

Oh my God, was he serious?

Rachel scoffed. "Believe me, I'm not prone to an overactive imagination." She shivered violently in the cold wind. "Please, just check it out."

The man sighed but nodded. "Okay, I'll radio for the coast guard to search the area."

"Thank you," she said. It was something at least. And she couldn't do any more than she had. Her case certainly wasn't helped by the fact that there was no sign of the woman. "What's your name?"

"Dex Wakefield."

Her eyes widened. "As in the Wakefields who own the town?"

"That would be my ancestors. I'm just the guy who rescues tourists from the water if they're within a mile radius of my boat," he said teasingly. "Go inside, get warm. I'll radio for a search."

She nodded as she made her way back toward her hotel room. Shivering and dripping wet, she climbed over the railing and went into the room.

As she showered, trying to fight the deep chill, she closed her eyes, seeing the woman's face. Eerily familiar... She wasn't imagining things. She'd seen someone out there.

In her bathrobe, she sat out on the deck and watched as the coast guard boat searched the area in front of the hotel. Flashing lights bounced off the waves and a diver jumped from the side of the boat and disappeared below the surface. He had to be searching for at least forty minutes.

Rachel held her breath as she waited, but his verdict was the same as Dex's.

There was no one there.

Had there been?

Going into the room, she pulled back the sheets and climbed into bed. It had been a long day and maybe Dex was right. Maybe the whole Sealena investigation had messed with her. Her argument with Callan, his disappointed look as he'd walked away and her conflicted emotions may have left her vulnerable.

As she reached to turn off the light, the statue at the base of the lamp caught her attention. The Sealena figure made her heart race. That face... That was the face of the woman in the water.

The caption inscribed along the bottom had her pulse racing.

A search for me reveals one's own self.

An eerie chill danced down her spine. Could she actually have had her own encounter with the Serpent Queen?

And had she been trying to tell Rachel something?

CHAPTER SIX

Back in her office a few days later, Rachel sat at her desk and hesitated before submitting her article. A different one than she'd originally planned on writing. One she wasn't so sure Jaime was going to like. This could be career suicide, but she hit the submit button anyway.

Since leaving Port Serenity, her mind and heart had been a mess. So much had happened in such a short time. The whirlwind trip almost felt as though it hadn't been real. Like a dream. She hadn't talked to Callan before leaving, unsure what she could say when she was still so conflicted about everything. He hadn't made an attempt to see her either.

She wasn't sure if it had been love. She didn't know whether she'd seen the mythical sea creature. But now she had enough belief in the impossible to admit that some myths might hold a grain of truth.

All those years of not believing her father seemed almost like a wasted opportunity, and a deep regret settled in her chest. She wouldn't have needed to believe in everything the way he did, but maybe she could have understood a little more, tried harder to connect with him by listening and opening her mind. They might not have been close the way she'd wanted, but maybe they could have been close in a different way. Maybe it wasn't too late...

Less than two minutes later, her boss's stilettos echoed down the hall, approaching quickly.

Here it comes...

She sat straighter and squared her shoulders, preparing to defend her article as Jaime entered.

"What the hell kind of BS is this?" Jaime asked, holding a copy of the article.

"It's the truth," she said, refusing to be intimidated. She'd made her decision and she was sticking to it.

Jaime's eyes narrowed in disbelief. "You honestly believe there's a half-woman/half-serpent creature in the waters in Port Serenity?"

The idea no longer seemed impossible. "I didn't say that anywhere in the article." She'd kept to the facts, the stories, the things she'd learned while she was in the small coastal town.

"But you also didn't dispel the myth," Jaime said.

Here was her chance...

"Maybe the magazine could have a section where we don't necessarily dispel a myth, but explain why it exists, the story behind it, the reasons people believe. Write about its origin, its history, its impact on the community." She held her breath as Jaime contemplated the idea. What would she do if her boss rejected it? She couldn't rewrite the article to reflect the point of view she'd held before traveling to Port Serenity. That point of view was different now. Rachel was different now.

"Okay, fine," Jaime said reluctantly, not looking overly pleased with the idea. "We will try it. But if it backfires..."

Her boss didn't need to finish the sentence. If it backfired, Rachel was out of a job, but she wasn't sure "new Rachel" could work at the publication much longer anyway. Her time in Port Serenity, her time with Callan had changed her and her outlook and she liked feeling optimistic, open…

Now she just needed the courage to do something about it.

RACHEL HAD BEEN gone for three days and he'd had to fight the urge to reach out to her. She'd left town without saying goodbye. They hadn't exactly ended things on a positive note. Maybe he'd overreacted to what she'd told her boss. He knew she honestly didn't think of Port Serenity that way. He'd seen the change in her over those few days.

But he'd freaked out at the intensity of his own feelings for her and the fact that he wasn't confident they were reciprocated. How could they be in such a short time? She'd been right to be cautious, hesitant…

He ran a hand through his hair as he poured coffee into a mug and sat at the kitchen table. He didn't want to read her article, but curiosity got the better of him. Curiosity and a desperate need to feel some connection to her. Anything at all.

On his cell phone, he clicked on the magazine's website and scrolled to her latest blog. His heart raced at the sight of her picture next to the headline: "Port Serenity's Sealena: A Search for Oneself."

Damn, he missed that smile and those eyes. He missed her fading cynicism and the way she'd opened up to him. The way he'd opened up to her.

He sighed and prepared himself for the worst as he started to read.

For the brave men and women who live on Alaska's rugged coastline, life is unpredictable. Rescue missions, sea pirates and navigating the open ocean pres-

ent new challenges every day for the members of the
Port Serenity Coast Guard, but it's rumored that they
often have a little help.

Port Serenity, Alaska, is a small coastal town in
the southwest region that boasts a lively tourism season due to the town's historic charm and tales of the
folklore legend Sealena. Thousands of visitors flock
to the area each year, lured by the prospect of seeing
the elusive half-woman/half-serpent creature who is
known to protect the ships at sea, unlike her Siren
counterparts. And the locals cater to the fantasy with
Sealena-themed tours, the Sealena Hotel, the Serpent
Queen Pub and a small museum and bookshop dedi-
cated to the sightings of the sea creature over many
generations. Statues have been erected in the town's
square and along the marina, and the Welcome to
Port Serenity sign features an artist rendering of the
mysterious creature. On every pier and in every pub
booth, there's a fisherman eager to tell his tall tale
of encounter to anyone who will listen.

With the breathtaking Alaskan wilderness as a
backdrop, I embarked on my mission to dispel the
myth of Sealena, but I discovered that not every mystery can be solved so easily. With eDNA suggesting
that new species have yet to be discovered and that
the ocean's depths can hold secrets long buried, and
older generations teaching newer ones that an open
mind combined with critical thinking is a much more
balanced way to live, I find it impossible to confirm
with a hundred percent certainty that this creature
doesn't exist.

As a reformed cynic, I can only suggest that you

*visit Port Serenity and decide for yourself if Sealena
is real or just a lovely story to enchant and give hope
that something out there in the vast ocean is protecting the waters and shorelines of one of the most beautiful and fascinating places on earth.*

Callan released a breath as he sat back in his chair and
stared at the article. Rachel had actually started to believe
there was more to the myth of Sealena than she'd originally thought. Dare he hope she'd also started to believe
in him? In them?

Only one way to find out.

Two days later, Callan entered a building in downtown
Seattle and scanned the directory for the office of *Dispelling the Myth* magazine. Fourth floor. Office 407.

He entered the elevator and hit the button for the fourth
floor. His palms sweat and his mouth was dry as he watched
the floor numbers light up.

He could have called or texted, but the irony was that
he'd started to fall for a woman whose phone number he
didn't even know. In a few short days, he'd developed real
feelings for her and he needed to know if they were reciprocated. He needed to know if her trip to Port Serenity had
resulted in the same connection he felt to her.

The elevator doors opened and he nearly collided with
Rachel as she stepped in, carrying a box of personal items.
Her eyes widened. "Callan?"

Damn, she was so beautiful. The sight of her, dressed in
a pretty blue blouse tucked into a tan pencil skirt, her hair
in a long braid hanging over one shoulder and a pale gloss
on her lips, made his mouth go dry. He hadn't realized just

how much he'd missed her until this tightening in his chest made it difficult to breathe.

"What are you doing here?" she asked, and it was impossible to read how she felt about seeing him. Her expression was slightly conflicted and bewildered.

He let the elevator doors close and nodded to the box. "You got fired over the article."

"It didn't go over well with our readers. Guess not every cynic can be converted," she said softly.

"Sorry…"

She shook her head. "I'm not. I like how I feel being open to the impossible." Her gaze locked with his and now there was soft affection reflecting in her beautiful big blue eyes.

"Like you and me?" he asked, setting the box down and moving closer to her.

"Like you and me," she said. She leaned toward him and he took her into his arms and kissed her gently. It felt so impossibly right holding her, kissing her, being with her. He didn't need to understand it. All he needed to know was it was real.

"So, what are you going to do now?" he asked.

"Well, I thought I should continue my search for Sealena now that I'm a believer," she said teasingly, standing on tiptoes to kiss him again.

"Need a tour guide?" he asked, his heart exploding with happiness.

"You decided to take over your family's tour boat business?"

He squeezed her tight, nodding, an idea forming in his mind. "You're currently out of a job… Maybe you'll consider applying for a position on board?"

Her face lit up as she smiled at him. "As your cocaptain?"

"Why not?" It was a long shot, but he held his breath as he waited for her answer.

"You know, I can't think of a single reason," she said as the elevator doors reopened on the lobby.

Callan's heart was full as hand in hand the two of them stepped out together, ready to embark on their next adventure—dispelling the myth that instant love was just a fairy tale.

* * * * *

*When a cheating scandal rocks Shanna Jacobs's school, she's put
under the supervision of her ex, Lynx Harrington—who wants
the same superintendent job she does. Maybe their fledgling
partnership will make the grade after all?*

Read on for a sneak peek at
Rivals at Love Creek,
the first book in the brand-new
Seven Brides for Seven Brothers miniseries
and Michelle Lindo-Rice's debut with
Harlequin Special Edition!

"Now, I know the circumstances aren't ideal, but I'm looking
forward to working with you."

She appeared to struggle, like she was thinking how to formulate
her words. "I wish I was working with you by choice and not
circumstance. Not that I would choose to," she said with a chuckle.

"I hear you. If it weren't for this situation, we would still be
throwing daggers at each other during leadership meetings."

"Put yourself in my shoes. If you were going through this,
how would you feel?" she asked, rubbing her toe into the carpet.
"Honest answer."

"I'm not as brave as you are, and I have more pride than common
sense."

She blushed and averted her eyes. "I would have resigned if I
didn't have a mother and sister to consider. Pride is secondary to
priority."

He felt ashamed and got to his feet. He went over to her. "You're right. I'm thinking like a single man. If I were married or had other responsibilities, I'd do what I'd have to and keep my job. I was hoping that Irene—" He stopped, unsure of the etiquette of bringing another woman into the conversation.

"No need to stop on my account. I know you had—have—a life."

Lynx wasn't about to talk about Irene, no matter how cool Shanna claimed she was with it. "I'm ready to fall in love, get married and install the white picket fence."

"How do you know you're ready?" she asked.

He rubbed his chin. "I'm at the brink of where I want to be professionally. I want someone to share my success with me."

"I get it," she said, doing that half-bite thing with her lip again.

Don't miss
Rivals at Love Creek
by Michelle Lindo-Rice,
available July 2022 wherever
Harlequin Special Edition books and ebooks are sold.

Harlequin.com

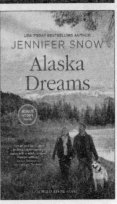

Get 4 FREE REWARDS!

We'll send you 2 FREE Books plus 2 FREE Mystery Gifts.

FREE
Value Over
$20

Both the **Romance** and **Suspense** collections feature compelling novels written by many of today's bestselling authors.

YES! Please send me 2 FREE novels from the Essential Romance or Essential Suspense Collection and my 2 FREE gifts (gifts are worth about $10 retail). After receiving them, if I don't wish to receive any more books, I can return the shipping statement marked "cancel." If I don't cancel, I will receive 4 brand-new novels every month and be billed just $7.24 each in the U.S. or $7.49 each in Canada. That's a savings of up to 28% off the cover price. It's quite a bargain! Shipping and handling is just 50¢ per book in the U.S. and $1.25 per book in Canada.* I understand that accepting the 2 free books and gifts places me under no obligation to buy anything. I can always return a shipment and cancel at any time. The free books and gifts are mine to keep no matter what I decide.

Choose one: ☐ **Essential Romance**
(194/394 MDN GQ6M)
☐ **Essential Suspense**
(191/391 MDN GQ6M)

Name (please print)

Address   Apt. #

City   State/Province   Zip/Postal Code

Email: Please check this box ☐ if you would like to receive newsletters and promotional emails from Harlequin Enterprises ULC and its affiliates. You can unsubscribe anytime.

> **Mail to the Harlequin Reader Service:**
> **IN U.S.A.:** P.O. Box 1341, Buffalo, NY 14240-8531
> **IN CANADA:** P.O. Box 603, Fort Erie, Ontario L2A 5X3

Want to try 2 free books from another series? Call 1-800-873-8635 or visit www.ReaderService.com.

---

*Terms and prices subject to change without notice. Prices do not include sales taxes, which will be charged (if applicable) based on your state or country of residence. Canadian residents will be charged applicable taxes. Offer not valid in Quebec. This offer is limited to one order per household. Books received may not be as shown. Not valid for current subscribers to the Essential Romance or Essential Suspense Collection. All orders subject to approval. Credit or debit balances in a customer's account(s) may be offset by any other outstanding balance owed by or to the customer. Please allow 4 to 6 weeks for delivery. Offer available while quantities last.

Your Privacy—Your information is being collected by Harlequin Enterprises ULC, operating as Harlequin Reader Service. For a complete summary of the information we collect, how we use this information and to whom it is disclosed, please visit our privacy notice located at corporate.harlequin.com/privacy-notice. From time to time we may also exchange your personal information with reputable third parties. If you wish to opt out of this sharing of your personal information, please visit readerservice.com/consumerchoice or call 1-800-873-8635. Notice to California Residents—Under California law, you have specific rights to control and access your data. For more information on these rights and how to exercise them, visit corporate.harlequin.com/california-privacy.

STRSMAX22